LOSING THE ~~~~~

Copyr

This is the third book of ~~~~~~~~~~~~ ica" which
follows the fortunes of ~ ~~~~~~~~~~~~ .ern Africa
from tne 1960s to the present.

You might also enjoy
Book 1 "Taking The Gap"
Book 2 "Grasping The Nettle"
(Reviews gratefully received)

All the characters and some places in this book are fictitious; any resemblance to actual persons, living or dead is purely coincidental.

Wikipedia and youtube have historical info on conflicts in Rhodesia, Mozambique, Angola, Portuguese Guinea, South Africa and Namibia.License Notes
Thank you for downloading this ebook. This book remains the copyrighted property of the author, and may not be redistributed to others for commercial or non-commercial purposes. If you enjoyed this book, please encourage your friends to download their own copy from their favourite authorized retailer. Thank you for your support.

Grateful acknowledgment to the band Savuka for superb music and inclusion of lyrics from the album "Third World Child."

10.10.2025

CHAPTER ONE
FRIDAY
Birmingham UK

"Death by a million traffic-lights" said Loretta Bustamante. James Hacking glanced at his watch and nodded. She could feel his impatience building like a tangible head of steam.
"When I was a boy they put one up in Penhalonga village but it didn't last long."
"What happened? Vandalised straight away?"
"No, As soon as it turned green the goats ate it."
She chuckled as they inched forward round spaghetti junction to re-join the M6 Motorway in Birmingham, having made an ill-advised attempt to circumnavigate road-works. He clicked the digital cab-heat control up another notch.
"English springtime and I'm freezing! Look at this weather."
Wet snowflakes billowed and swirled in the dipped headlights, and the truck tyres slid and spun on the greasy road surface.
"March comes in like a lamb here and out like a lion."
"The sooner it's out the better. God I miss African sunshine."
"It was your idea to leave" said Loretta and instantly regretted it as her partner's jaw tightened. These days he was increasingly intolerant of criticism, sympathy, help or advice. Their articulated truck finally edged up the northbound on-ramp and gathered speed. The snow became icy rain that hammered on the roof, grey spray rising in sheets from the road surface to match a leaden sky and turning the whole world dull, uniform and dangerous. Like suicidal lemmings, weekend traffic churned past Birmingham on the busy raised artery through a prematurely dark Friday evening on hissing tyres, indistinct hurtling shapes poorly lit by streaky lights refracted through greasy filthy glass. The high cab of the forty-four ton tractor-trailer combination did at least provide superior visibility.
They were both irritable due to fatigue and tight deadlines. James had been relaxed and fun in Europe, travelling under sunny skies but as usual he was becoming increasingly tense with the foul British weather and awful traffic; UK heavy-goods driving restrictions meant constantly racing against time. He was determined to get the huge vehicle and its load home on schedule so as not to jeopardise the slot-bookings in Europe reserved for their next driver; missing them would cost thousands and could create an on-going nightmare of

refused shipments with nowhere to store them, and no empty trailers to accommodate subsequent loads.

 James tried to maintain a constant velocity with sufficient space both ahead and behind but car drivers kept overtaking, then pulling in front and slowing down, forcing him to reduce speed. In frustration he indicated right and watched the mirror but hurtling cars bunched even more to box him in. Eventually another truck flashed him and he eased into the centre lane. In the fast lane cars were tearing by at an insane speed for the conditions, in excess of eighty miles an hour, and driving so close that there was no margin for error. A Mercedes coupe sped by, tailgated by a big Peugeot flashing its headlights aggressively to overtake. When the Mercedes braked unexpectedly the car behind rammed it hard and in an instant several cars were climbing onto the backs of others; the Peugeot reared up onto the vehicle in front and flipped over the central barrier in a cacophony of rending metal, shattering glass and blaring horns. On the opposite carriageway, southbound vehicles swerved and collided. Engine bonnets and boot lids burst open strewing debris just ahead of James and Loretta. There was a thud as the wheel rode over something with a jolt. A truck travelling in the opposite direction hit the cart-wheeling shattered Peugeot and batted it back over the central reservation, just behind them as they were swept on in the centre lane like a stick insect carried by a swarm of ants. The wrecked Peugeot compounded the massive accident still developing around them on the north-bound carriageway. Flicking a glance in the mirror James saw headlights swerving madly and they heard the muted din of multiple impacts. A few other vehicles made it through; one or two stopped on the hard shoulder with orange hazard lights flashing but most pulled ahead quickly, and soon when they looked in the mirrors there was nothing but blackness behind.

-xxx-
Johannesburg, South Africa

 North of Johannesburg Jemima Visser was preoccupied and it was potentially fatal; instead of thinking about the field she was spraying herself, she was thinking about which fields to send her other three pilots to next. As the owner of ZU-KAT Agricultural Aviation, running the business was a much bigger job than just dusting crops. As well as flying full-time she had to map, plan, despatch other pilots, meet customers, supervise chemical loaders, organise supplies, carry-out financial planning and do all the administration of a business under increasing pressure from competition. The Company was in financial trouble and just to cap it all she'd been dumped the night before by the man with whom she'd had the longest relationship in her life. All in all there were enough distractions in the cockpit with her to for it to be a major safety issue.

She was flying a venerable Grumman Ag-Cat G-164A/450 bi-plane powered by a nine-cylinder four-hundred and fifty horsepower Pratt and Whitney R-1340 radial engine, spraying at eighty-five knots and close to zero feet. Her eyes flickered across the instruments in a routine scan, paying particular attention to oil pressure, manifold pressure, cylinder head temperature, mixture setting, RPM and fuel flow. The engine was running on a prototype aviation-grade Ethanol-fuel being developed by the South African government rather than 100LL Aviation gasoline, and while approved after exhaustive ground-test runs it was still behaving temperamentally in the air, causing unpredictable rich-mixture misfires in the top cylinders while starving the lower. She was using it because the government paid her to test it; any revenue was welcome to keep her planes flying and her staff employed. She was also determinedly "green" by nature anyway, convinced that fossil-fuels, a major cause of global warming, were largely unnecessary and replaceable by vegetable based products such as bio-diesel and ethanol.

A sudden image of the row that morning with Francois Steenkamp flashed into her mind. They'd both been naked and shouting. She'd got up at five am to drive to the spraying site at a farm outside Hartebeestport, near Pretoria. Francois had woken too and wanted to make love but Jemima was distracted and wanted to get going. The fight had gone from zero to incandescent in an instant; Francois's wounded male ego had made him lash out in verbal frustration and a lot of concealed attitudes had poured out along with the venom. Frigid Bitch hey? Jemima snorted indignantly through her nose. He wanted children, and marriage, not sometime but right now; she was thirty-five but just not ready for childbirth. So he'd given her his ultimatum and she'd rejected it. She'd walked out unable to concentrate on his needs, her mind roiling with business and operational complications but crying inside.

She was flying up a wide, planted agricultural land of gently rising ground towards the brow of a low hill, beyond which the terrain dropped away again. The faintest vibration in the airframe, which could have been engine roughness, transmitted itself through her body and she instantly applied carburettor heat, eyes back inside the cockpit and scanning the instruments.

-xxx-

Sandro Marais had left the gaming tables of Sun City at six am having gambled all night, and was heading back to Johannesburg. Once away from the plush hotels and landscaped golf-courses, the road wound briefly through dry bush in the Pilanesberg game reserve before debouching onto the over-grazed drab plains between Sun City and the farming town of Rustenburg. As his car roared through shanty-villages peopled by desperately poor black South Africans it kicked up dust which settled as yet another layer upon them. Abandoned at birth in the notoriously crime-ridden ghetto called Hillbrow in downtown Johannesburg, he'd become a feral white teenager in the same area, carving himself a tough reputation among the predominantly white criminal gangs of the apartheid era. He enlisted under-age and after doing National Service in Namibia with 44 Parachute Brigade, the South African Parabats, had been a mercenary in Angola before returning to Hillbrow and becoming a main man in the twilight economy. Post-apartheid, when Nelson Mandela was released from prison, he'd formed an uneasy alliance with a major-league black gangster moving into the Hillbrow area. It was an uncomfortable relationship but afforded him access to influential criminal bosses and corrupt politicians.

Sandro prided himself on being above racism. He was Caucasian, his olive-skinned good looks hinting at Mediterranean parents, and he spoke English, Afrikaans, several African dialects and Portuguese. He was addicted to the invigorating rhythms of Zulu street-music bands and he'd hung out in dives and roof-top shebeens all over Johannesburg to hear them. Before the abolition of apartheid he was frequently arrested for contravening the Group Areas Act, a law designed to force different races to keep to their own areas but Sandro acknowledged no laws but the ones he made himself. He was an instinctive anarchist, determined to pursue nothing but his own agenda, and was usually cunning enough to do so without butting right up against authority.

Feeling drowsy after an all-night casino session which had netted one-hundred thousand rand, Sandro selected a 1987 Savuka album "Third World Child" on the CD auto-changer to keep him awake. Deafening music belted loudly out of the 260 watt Linn sound system.

When he hit the N4 highway the soaring lyrics of the track "Great Heart" rang out and his foot went down on the accelerator in an involuntary reaction. The six litre, four hundred and fifty horsepower aluminium V12 engine accelerated the car rocket-like down an empty carriageway, up to one-hundred and forty miles an hour in under ten seconds but still well short of the one hundred and eighty six mph capability. The lyrics spoke directly to Sandro and he threw back his head and joined in;

> The world is full of strange behaviour
> Every man has to be his own saviour
> I know I can make it on my own if I try
> But I'm searching for a Great Heart to stand me by
> Underneath the African sky.

He felt happy and invincible, confident that the Great Hearts were on his side. Not many miles away a young pilot called Julius Jongintaba was feeling vulnerable and edgy. As a commercial pilot with fourteen hundred hours, mostly as a junior instructor still learning the trade, he was finding his new job as a crop-sprayer distinctly overwhelming. Julius had flown most of his hours from long concrete or asphalt runways, instructing pupils or co-piloting mid-range airliners. He was finding the bush-pilot flying off small dirt strips with heavy loads demanding, in a noisy, dusty atmosphere polluted by the tang of chemicals, plagued by the sun's glare and the piss-taking of the roughneck loading crew that followed the pilots in trucks towing mobile mixing tanks. The team stepped down off his ship, a Piper PA 25 Pawnee, having filled the hopper. They coiled their hoses ready for the next aircraft in, one of the two turbo-prop AT-502 Air Tractors.

"Maak Gou JJ!" called a villainous looking Cape-coloured labourer.

"Perhaps if you finish quick like a good boy Meisie Jemima will give you a gobble!" He accompanied the jibe with an obscene demonstration on his thumb and the other loaders laughed roughly. Julius flushed and tried to ignore them, concentrating on fuel calculations and programming the data for the next spraying runs from Jemima's data sheet into the aviation GPS. He'd allowed the crew to goad him into drinking with them at their hotel the previous night, and although he'd had the sense to quit before he got totally paralytic his performance was definitely impaired. Not that he was drunk but a hangover was making his thinking woolly and slow. A strapping youthful black man of twenty two with a round babyish face, Julius was alluringly unsure of himself in everything but the air; it lent him an open innocence and eagerness to please that had appealed to Jemima when she interviewed him. Her top pilot Jack Dowding had checked Julius out in the air and praised his performance. In post-apartheid South Africa white men tended to be at the bottom of the "employability pile", a phenomenon known as "pale-male syndrome", but white males were still in the majority amongst pilots, so Jemima was pleased to give one young black aviator a leg-up in the industry. There was an element of political correctness in her choice; as time went on and more contracts were awarded by blacks, the more work her company was likely to be offered if it employed blacks. Julius had a dose of hero-worship when it came to Jemima and it made him fair game for the constant gossiping, prank-playing, joking and jibing of the ground team. In action they were crisply efficient but socially they were more like annoying juveniles, exploiting any personal weakness ruthlessly. With a sense of relief he climbed into the Pawnee, cranked her up and ran through the pre-flight checks before taxiing gingerly out to the threshold, the loaded aircraft rocking ponderously over the uneven rutted ground. With a last glance at the engine instruments and a look round to ensure the sky was clear Julius advanced the throttle, rolled forward trailing a dust cloud and climbed away.

-xxx-

Loretta's hands cupped her face in horror, looking at James with shocked eyes.

"Oh my God, how did we survive that? Shouldn't we stop?"

He shook his head soberly, reluctantly, knowing well the effect that hurtling metal, fire and impact would have on soft pink bodies: and on their wider families.

"No. We can't do anything except notify the emergency services."

"There's a first aid kit on board, let's go back and help!"

"How? It isn't feasible in near-darkness to reverse an artic back down the hard-shoulder for over a mile and it needs to be clear for ambulances, police and firemen."

"I want to do something!"

"That's understandable but sticky-plaster and a triangular bandage won't help those people. In reality we could make things worse and put ourselves in danger."

"Sometimes you're not the man I fell in love with at all! He would have gone to help at any cost!"

"Fine. Just call 999 and give our details as witnesses; that piece of stupidity is going to close the motorway for hours. Then check the howgowzit chart and see how long we've both got left on the tacho."

With a set mouth Loretta tried calling emergency services on the hands-free repeatedly but couldn't get through and gave up, sitting in stiff silence, working out their tachograph hours. The sensitive electronic instrument or "spy in the cab" monitored vehicle systems and driver actions with uncanny accuracy. Designed to protect the public from tired truck drivers and tired truck drivers from unscrupulous employer exploitation, the scheme often fell short of both ideals. UK driving regulations allowed each commercial driver nine hours at the wheel per day, increased to ten twice a week. Complicated "double-manning" regulations maximised the hours the vehicle could productively operate, and they were anxious to get the rig home so they could turn it over to Arthur and Haley, James' daughter and his potential son-in-law. When the younger pair departed back south to Europe they could sleep in their own bed for the first time in a week.

Infringing drivers' hours by even a few minutes could mean hefty fines and banns, and they had already been rolling continuously for eighteen hours from Southern France, having crossed into England through the Channel tunnel.

There was more congestion ahead on the M6 which seemed to be crammed with vehicles whatever the time of day or night. They caught up with the slowing traffic and were soon amongst the lemmings again. Narrow lanes with tarmac rutted like tramlines caused the truck to lurch and sway with a mind of its own, making it difficult to control accurately. A cautious car driver cruising at fifty in the bad conditions flashed James in to the left lane as he went past but he blinked right once, in thanks, and to indicate he was staying out because an Eddie Stobart Artic was joining the motorway from Hilton Park Services and he could already see cars changing lanes wildly to avoid it, and braking hard. Loretta looked up from her calculations.

"You've got an hour and a half left, me just half an hour."

James cursed under his breath because there were eighty miles to go and the traffic was proceeding in fits and starts, stretching out and closing up like a python on the move. There was no release from the tension of driving and deadlines; cruise-control was off and the GPS-readouts steadily slipped behind his constant mental updates of time and distance. The rigidity of heavy goods driving regulations meant that after a six-day journey through Europe to Malaga and back they might have to halt even if they were only ten miles from home, and take a statutory weekly rest-break. Daily rest had to be eleven hours but was reducible to nine three times a week. Weekly rest had to be forty-five hours but could be reduced to twenty-four on occasion. Having to stop ten miles from home was usually just a nuisance and meant the inconvenience of ferrying new drivers; over fifty miles was a logistical nightmare with possible missed deliveries leading to contract cancellations. Loretta gave James a worried glance. His jaw was set in familiar uncompromising rigidity and the watchful eyes were hard.

    They had left Africa to escape sad memories and dangerous enemies, to settle in Britain while young enough to get established but since arriving his frustration at the overcrowding and petty bureaucracy seemed to make him permanently angry. Having worked hard and spent heavily to convert his Commercial American ATPL and South African flying licences to European equivalents, they hadn't been able to see a future in aviation and their new life was built instead around a small family transport firm competing with giants like Eddie Stobart Trucking. They operated at a frantic pace in an industry made ever more difficult by restrictive legislation; Health and Safety, Minimum wage, Working Time Directives, European Directives, ever more demanding qualification requirements; permits and forms, licences, certificates and authorisations, a blizzard of hated paperwork. Their European and domestic trucking operation was a typical attempt by James to get an edge and maximise the revenue from any business enterprise.

    Twenty minutes of erratic progress followed before Radio Two Travel reported stationary traffic between junctions sixteen and twenty with two hour delays, exacerbated by fans going to a football re-match at Stoke City's Britannia stadium.

    "I could do with a wee" said Loretta.

    "Can't stop on the hard shoulder, might attract a nosy vehicle-inspection Nazi from Vosa, and that's all I need!"

    James checked the time and swung off at Junction sixteen, just as cars on the motorway ahead slowed and halted in a blaze of brake-lights. The slip-road was already crowded with other drivers trying to escape the congestion.

    "Think the A50 will be clear?" asked Loretta.

    "It better be or we won't make it; I've only had 15 minutes of my forty-five rest break; I need another thirty before we get home. You'll have to take over while I'm on break; I can navigate a diversion on the "A" roads."

"Can't we stop for a proper rest? I'd like something to eat and I'm really bursting for a wee."

"Not really; this jam will get progressively worse and slow us more the longer we delay. The other tractor unit won't be down from Scotland 'till tomorrow so Art and Haley can't use it, and they need to get off on time tonight. Perhaps more importantly I need a hot shower followed by a damn good swallow of beer!"

"But I'm really desperate for the loo!"

"I know and I'm looking for somewhere" said James testily.

"I need a wee right now! Stop the damned truck!"

"Oh all right!"

Traffic was moving slowly on the roundabout beneath the junction so he cut across and pulled into a zone on the central island marked "Abnormal Loads Only: Park Here and ring for Escort."

"What are you doing? It's illegal to stop here."

"Well are you desperate or not? Won't be for long; I'll put my tacho on break and yours on 'work.' We'll have a quick leak and get back on the road."

"I can't go here; we're on a traffic island surrounded by cars!"

"There are some trees and scrub-bush over by the flyover, go in there."

"Absolutely not, everyone will know what's going on!"

"Godammit! Just duck under the trailer and let go, it's nearly dark; nobody will see in this weather. You've done it before."

"Yes but not in front of a circus audience! Pull round to one of the laybys just up the A500; we're going that way to the A50."

"They'll be full of trucks already and there might not be another pull-off for miles; I thought you were desperate."

"I am! I'm going!" The evening was murky as Loretta grabbed some loo-roll and a plastic shopping bag to put the used sheets in, then climbed sulkily down into heavy drizzle and ducked between the raised trailer undercarriage legs. She glanced round uneasily, squatted and relieved herself gratefully. James followed and began peeing down a grating under the rear axle. A Highway patrol vehicle approached as he zipped up.

"Fuck!" said Loretta as it pulled up beside their truck, headlights playing on her white bottom before she was finished. She shuffled further into gloom beneath the trailer and banged her head, swearing again under her breath.

"Got a problem Drive?" asked the Traffic Officer.

"No, just stopped to take a break."

"Can't do that here, this is a restricted zone; you'll have to move."

"Well it isn't being used so what's the problem? I'll be gone soon."

"Law's the law mate. Sorry. Go on, shift it."

"Then I'd be breaking the law and could get an infringement. If you want me to move while on break I'll have to take the tacho card out and you'll have to sign the back to say you ordered me to proceed illegally."

Loretta's thighs were burning from the prolonged squat and her anger was growing. "Shut the fuck up Hacking, just agree and get rid of him" she muttered inaudibly through clenched teeth. She couldn't get her knickers and trousers up without standing and felt ridiculous. The patrol vehicle's engine switched off.

"If you're trying to annoy me you're doing a pretty good job: last chance to go quietly before I chuck the book at you."

"Okay, just give us a minute, my co-driver will take over. We only stopped to change places."

"Right, in that case I'll overlook your illegal parking."

"Very generous, wouldn't want you to panic at the thought of work, filling in all those forms" said James sarcastically.

The patrol vehicle door slammed as the officer alighted.

"Don't get smart with me pal; where is the other driver? What's he doing? Are the two of you up to something dodgy?" He noticed movement underneath the trailer.

"What's he doing under there?"

"He's a she. Squeezing the lettuce. Big emergency."

Loretta duck-waddled furiously sideways and popped up, bottom flashing in the glare of headlights before she hurriedly yanked her trousers up.

"Nice arse girl!" yelled a voice and cars with football scarves hanging from their windows hooted enthusiastically. She ignored them, trying to contain her anger. The young policeman noticed the toilet-roll and raised a disdainful eyebrow, lips parting to speak. Loretta's fuse blew.

"No I bloody-well was not! Just liquid and only because of the circumstances! Why aren't you helping the casualties from that huge accident?"

"Because I do what I'm told and you would be advised to do the same. Get moving or I will be obliged to report you under the Road Traffic Act."

"What for, being so bloody busy delivering your groceries to Tesco that I haven't even got time for a piss? Jesus!"

The Officers lips twitched.

"Language please Miss; we all lead busy lives...."

"Thank you for so much for the 'Miss,' Officer. Have a nice day! James, get in!"

Her significant other clicked his heels with a little jump and bowed.

"Yes Mein Fuhrer!"

"Twat!"

"Don't be rude to the Constable!"

"Not him, you."

Trying to hide a smile, Loretta climbed into the cab, taking off muddy steel capped-trainers and slipping on clogs. She slid into the driver's seat, clicked the tachograph 'driver two' switch from 'work' to 'drive' and pulled away in third as James slammed the passenger door shut, shaking with suppressed laughter.

"You fucking idiot, why did you provoke him to begin with? A simple 'Yes Sir' and he would have left!"

"I was buying you time to finish your business and as you pointed out, he should be helping with the accident or catching burglars, not hassling truck drivers. That football fan was right though, you've got a really nice arse!"

She glowered across, then cracked a reluctant smile.

"Yes and if I've got grease in my hair from that trailer you're dead! Pass me a sandwich."

-xxx-
Libya

Denzil Harcourt approached low over the sea and lined up for a straight-in approach to runway 13 at Ras Mohdir Airfield. He planned to turn the Twin Otter round near the control tower, load up the fugitives and depart back out over the Mediterranean on the reciprocal 31, before the Libyan rebels figured out what was going on. Right on time as arranged, the runway lights came on dimly, strength two, to be seen from the air but not the ground. He made it flat and flapless, going in hot; there was plenty of tarmac and he planned to keep rolling fast right up to the terminal buildings which were at the far end. The Sirtic desert all around was dark, other than the glowing runway markers.

Denzil reached up to set the propellers fully fine, then kept his hand on the twin over-head throttle levers, kneading them gently for synch. Pale dunes flashed beneath the plane's belly and then they were over the threshold, power off and flaring to a squeak-wheeled touchdown. Tracer from the desert suddenly curved towards the terminal and the runway immediately ahead erupted in flames as the Otter rolled into the shockwaves of a mortar blast. Shrapnel rained against the fuselage. The starboard tyre blew out and the aircraft tipped right with such violence that the wingtip bounced against the ground though the engine and prop remained undamaged. Still travelling at speed the Otter veered towards the damaged undercarriage in a cacophony of shrieking metal and sparks. Denzil kicked full opposite rudder, cut the port engine and powered up the starboard in an attempt to stay on the tarmac, finally coming to rest right in the middle of the runway, effectively blocking it. The runway lights went off.

"Jesus! You Okay?" Denzil asked his co-pilot.

"I think so. No sign of fire. Better do 'abrupt-arrival shutdown sequence' pronto."

"Indeed; fuel off, master off, battery off, fuck off!"

They opened their doors, watching and listening but there were no more blasts or gunfire so they swung down onto the asphalt.

"What the hell are we going to do now Denzil? You seem a bit laconic for someone up shit creek."

"Appearances must be deceptive. I am going to empty my trousers and try to think of a plan. Let's hope the Gaddafi relatives waiting to go shopping in Knightsbridge don't blame this hiccup on us."

The short fire-fight had died down and they could hear crickets chirping. A vehicle started near the terminal and came towards them with the headlights off.

-xxx-

As Loretta ate her sandwich, James quickly checked the Truckers Roadmap book for bridges lower than their trailer on the new route. There was one and he directed Loretta on a slight detour to avoid it. The A50 was relatively tranquil. Despite lower speed limits there were few traffic-lights or junctions and she made good progress. Knutsford village slowed them only slightly. As they passed Lymm services and crossed the motorway it was rammed with stationary vehicles in both

directions. She darted a glance at James who was consulting Traffic-Master on his smart-phone.
"What next?"
"Keep off the M6 for now. Report gives it clear north of the M62 if we go through Warrington."
"I've only got a few minutes left."
"I've got fifty, we can do it!"
"Wouldn't you rather pull into Lymm truck-stop and get Art and Haley to meet us there?"
"Negative. They'd have to go back for the other trailer and waste a couple of driving hours."

They changed places again at a red light, bypassed Warrington town centre catching all greens and re-joined the quiet M6 North at Junction twenty-two. James cranked the Scania to max, set the cruise control and relaxed for the first time in hours but the GPS still showed minutes slipping by faster than the miles to their destination. Loretta slid a Marie Erasmus 'Boere-Musiek' CD into the player and cheerful Afrikaans accordion music filled the cab. She slumped in her seat.

"We'll probably make it now but what a day, I feel exhausted! Maybe we should try something else to make a living, these roads are lethal."

She unbuckled, stood up and massaged his neck and shoulders. He wriggled and sighed, pushing up against her strong elegant fingers. Loretta was almost fifty but had lost little of her fiery beauty: exercise and careful moisturizing had kept her olive skin supple and her muscles, breasts and buttocks firm. Working in the tough world of transport had made her more determinedly feminine; hair nails and clothes were always perfectly presented and like most female drivers she attracted attention wherever she went and enjoyed it. The hands-free phone on the dash rang, showing 'Arthur' on the display. Loretta pushed to answer but James said "Speak, oh Idle one!"

"Piss off. Where the hell are you?"
"Junction twenty-seven, be with you in about twenty minutes. Do press-ups 'till we get there."
"Funny!"
Loretta shook her head.
"It must be your mission to annoy everybody today."
James was very tired and took it too fast down Parbold Hill, swinging wide round the sharp final curve before the village. The tarmac road surface was worn-out, slippery and pot-holed.
"Watch out for that thirty mph speed camera James!"

Loretta had received a fine and three points on her licence for doing thirty-four miles an hour through the speed trap only a month before.

"Shit, I forgot!"

He braked on the bend and tapped the transmission selector down a gear. The trailer-brakes snatched and it skidded out, losing traction on the slick crumbling macadam, jack-knifing into the path of an oncoming car. James had no alternative but to accelerate and pull it straight before the jack-knife took over and killed everybody. There was a glaring flash of light as the speed camera went off. When the trailer was behaving again James slowed down and banged the steering wheel in frustration.

"What do we pay taxes for? There are better bloody roads than this in Mozambique but instead of fixing them they put fucking cameras everywhere, and not for safety either but to gouge money out of the public!" He was working himself into a real rant, hating the loss of control even as he was doing it. More than anything in life he detested his own mistakes and somehow his anger always seemed to be more molten when there was a witness. Loretta eyed him warily. He was used to clear skies and space; the crowded British Isles, restrictive practices and bureaucracy of their self-imposed exile pressed in on him like virtual prison walls. She worried that James would completely flip one day and end up behind some real ones. Since he had only left Africa to protect her from possible reprisals by ex-President Katsiru, perhaps there was concealed resentment. Left to himself he would probably have gone after the renegade politician, finished that awful business between them and stayed in Africa.

"Don't go crazy, it might have run out of film."

James curtailed his tirade with difficulty and a few minutes later pulled onto their muddy transport yard on the outskirts of Newburgh Village with just four minutes of driving time to spare. It consisted of the farmhouse and an acre of land from sub-divided Bridge Farm, which had been in his possession for upwards of twenty years; his emergency bolt-hole from Africa.

"Well done James; made it again by the skin of our teeth."

"Yes, but the stress has probably knocked years off our lives. Get the cards out quick will you Sexy?"

Loretta set both drivers to 'break', clicking their two cardboard tacho-discs out from the recorder unit before he backed in beside another rig. When the trailer legs were over concrete slabs, he turned on a rear-facing lamp to illuminate the services cat-walk. Arthur darted from his car through the streaming rain clad in yellow waterproofs and retrieved the rear number-plate. They heard compressed air hiss as he applied the trailer hand-brake followed by the gear-leg cogs grinding as he wound them down. Leaping onto the catwalk he disconnected the five service leads, then ran round and pulled the coupling disconnect-lever, giving a thumbs-up to James who edged the tractor unit out from under the semi-fridge and backed under the one adjacent. The fridge engine was humming to keep its cargo of Scottish beef for France frozen. Arthur reversed the uncoupling procedure and appeared beside James hanging off the big mirror, grinning and panting, expecting praise and thanks. The electric window eased down slightly.

"Nice one Bozo" said his boss and potential father in law.

"No point in everybody getting soaked, hurry up and get your crap out so we can get going! How many cards did you use?"

"Hi Arthur, six each" said Loretta as she stored them tidily in her folder with the others from their recent trip. They had deliberately leased vehicles with the older manual recorders as the new all-electronic ones recorded on digital 'driver cards' and left no leeway for what James called 'slight modifications to the truth' by 'losing' a tacho card and wiping out some hours.

"Come on Haley, what the hell are you doing?" shouted Arthur and James's daughter minced through the mud towards the truck like a fastidious cat.

James waved to her and continued briefing Art.

"You two need to be at the Carrefour Supermarket Main Distribution Centre in Paris to tip by noon hey? Then you load cheese for Madrid. I'm still working on a load for Madrid down to Malaga, where you get sherry and wine to haul back here."

"Yeah I know, had a good look at the consignment notes while I was waiting. No sweat, we'll roll all the way through to Paris tonight, be well ready to tip by midday."

"Good; you'll have to take the A50 from Stoke to the M1; there was a mega-crash just North of Birmingham."

"I know it's been on the news, many already declared dead, dozens of severely injured. Terrible; the M6 is closed both directions until at least six in the morning. How's the diesel?"

"Three quarter tanks, filled them both recently in Calais. Make sure you do the same, it's way cheaper."

Loretta had already collected together their rucksacks, sleeping bags and everything that made travelling comfortable. She passed it out and Art carried it all to the open garage beside the cottage as the teams switched smoothly.

"There's milk, butter, chorizo sausage and some beers in the fridge, bread in the top locker. The TV remote is where it always is, make sure it stays there. Drive carefully and don't show off" scolded Loretta playfully, giving Arthur a brief hug.

"As if!"

"Read the Road Atlas with the bridge-height information and don't just follow your damned GPS or you'll end up on a canal tow-path, knowing you!" added James.

"Yeah yeah; any more wonderful advice?"

"More of an order; don't break anything, and look after Haley!"

There was just time for a quick exchange of hugs and kisses before he and Loretta ran through the downpour to shelter. Illuminated by the interior cabin lights Art stuck two fingers up at him, grinning, then selected forward and the faithful Scania hauled its load away, off on another multi-thousand-mile continental trip without the big diesel engine even stopping. Haley waved energetically, blowing kisses, and they waved back from the garage, watching as the tail-lights faded.

"They're so young, I hope they'll be allright" said Loretta worriedly.

"They're in love, it's an adventure and they always have been before" said James gruffly.

"I know, but that accident has unsettled me...."

James looked in disgust at the mud coating their boots from the yard, which under floodlights looked like the First World War trenches of Flanders Field from the continuous precipitation and churning wheels. He shivered. British cold invaded your very bones. Loretta wiped a drip from her cold nose.

"This is a horrible job; there must be an easier way to make some money!" She picked up some of their stuff wearily and headed into the house through a connecting door.

"You're just tired. It won't be for ever and at least we're working and spending time together."

"Well it's a challenge, for me anyway! You've always loved operating machinery so it's different; you're always in your comfort zone."

"Not at all times by a long shot."

"Well we survived another one and since the children have gone we might as well reward ourselves for a job well done."

He slapped her trim bottom.

"Good idea, go run a bath and I'll bring you a gin; we deserve some fun."

He started the heating, opened a beer and got a roaring fire going in the hearth, then took the gin up and joined her in the big corner bath where one thing led to another despite their tiredness. Afterwards she defrosted a home-made Lasagne, tossed a quick salad and they ate in front of the television with big glasses of the delicious thick Rioja hauled from Spain. Within minutes after eating they both dropped into an exhausted sleep.

-xxx-

Johannesburg

Ahead of Jemima on a brow of rising ground was a narrow strip of trees that divided two long fields. She and Jack Dowding when planning the job had decided to view the two fields as one. Given the position of the makeshift airstrip and their payloads, it was most economical to live with the inconvenience of pulling up over the trees and dropping down again on each pass. She shut off the spray and applied gentle back-pressure on the stick, keeping an eye on airspeed as the aircraft climbed to clear the obstacle. The pitched-up attitude of the nose obscured her forward vision and she moved her head to the right to see past it. Julius's Pawnee popped up over the trees directly ahead, their combined closing speeds in the region of one-hundred and fifty knots. Jemima's heart-rate leapt and her hand moved instantly to punch in extra power, almost bending the lever over the quadrant as she whipped the Ag-Cat into a violent climbing break-right manoeuvre, praying silently that Julius followed the training drummed into them and did the same, turning away from her to his right also. The extreme banking-angle loaded up the wing, increasing the stall speed dangerously. When she wasn't dead in two seconds Jemima knew she wasn't going to expire in an airborne collision but a similar outcome from an abrupt meeting with the ground was still firmly on the cards. Time seemed to stand still as she fought to keep the aircraft, cumbersome and slow with a half-full hopper of sloshing chemicals, from piling into the deck. She cleared the tree line, reduced the bank angle and pushed the nose down gingerly, flying obliquely to her previous course but solely intent on keeping flying speed, and control of the staggering aircraft. Just when she thought she was out of the woods the increased RPM caused a rich misfire condition in top cylinder nine and a lean condition in the bottom cylinders. The power output instantly decayed.

"Oh fuck no!" breathed Jemima, simultaneously spotting a high voltage line ahead, knowing instinctively that the Ag-Cat in its present condition had no chance of climbing over it. The ship had been her step-father's baby, his first crop-sprayer, and it was pristine. The registration on the gleaming yellow paint in black letters was ZU-KAT from which the company took its name, and Jemima was loathe to be the one who pranged it.

-xxx-

On the N4 highway Sandro Marais was loping along at a hundred and forty mph in the Aston, minding his own business, lulled by comfort and tiredness into a hazy dwaal almost approaching sleep, relying on a radar-detector to warn of traffic cops. The road ahead went into a long, tightly curving bend between the steep banks of a cutting through a kopje. Suddenly there was a hellish roaring and Sandro sat up shocked, unable to comprehend what was happening, gripping the steering wheel tightly, trying to figure out if his engine was going to disintegrate or the transmission explode. His instinct was to touch the brakes tentatively. Suddenly a huge shadow blocked the light from the wide windscreen and Sandro yelled in fright, his imagination running riot.

In the sky Julius's mouth was dry and his hands were shaking as he climbed the Pawnee to a safe height, banking to see what had happened to the Ag-Cat after their narrow miss; someone had screwed up badly and he had a nasty feeling it was him, that he'd programmed the same field as Jemima into his GPS. Movement caught his eye and far off he saw a flash of the Ag-Cat's yellow paint, impossibly low to the horizon; then it was gone and shortly afterwards a faint stain of yellow dust flew up, silhouetted against the blue sky. With his heart in his mouth and a blanket of impending doom falling on his already low spirits he turned towards the place it had disappeared, dreading what he would find.

Jemima's mind was in overdrive, juggling engine and flight controls, trying to get full power back and doing everything possible to keep the aircraft flying and avoid obstacles, utilising every dip in the ground to keep the nose down and grab a knot of airspeed. She flew under the power line and making an instant decision, dropped the left wing towards a ninety-foot deep road cutting which opened suddenly beneath her. She dived into the unexpected space gratefully and steeply, trading height for desperately-needed airspeed. With her wheels almost on the deck and wings seeming to brush the embankments she levelled out. The power seemed to stabilise as she held the aircraft steady and airspeed built rapidly in the ground effect while Jemima followed the bend in the road, buttocks tense on the seat. She was trying to decide whether to put the ship down on the highway or trust the engine and climb again when the decision was taken abruptly out of her hands. A blue sports car hurtled round the corner towards her, the driver's shocked face briefly visible before Jemima tightened her fist on the stick and lifted the aircraft into a gentle climb.

 When a speeding biplane appear round the corner dead ahead of him like an eagle pursing prey, Sandro jerked his steering wheel abruptly left. The Aston Martin left the tarmac, dropped into the shallow ditch full of weeds alongside and then mounted the cutting embankment like a wall-of-death motorcycle rider, bucketing, bouncing and banging over the rough surface of the soft conglomerate rock, sending up a boiling plume of yellow dust, seen from far-off by Julius. Sandro's harness saved him but nonetheless he was shaken and pummelled until he thought his teeth would fall out. Aware that the car was in danger of flying over the lip of the cutting he managed to guide it parallel and as the speed bled away, to aim it back down at the road. The car came banging, screeching and bouncing down the cutting side, watched by a male tourist at a picnic lay-by who had been videoing his wife but moved the camera to record this more interesting spectacle instead. The blue car swooped back into the ditch, rose up the other side, became briefly airborne and then crashed back onto the road, making a tyre-shrieking 180 skid before it came to rest. Of all the emotions coursing through Sandro rage was uppermost. The car was facing back the way he'd come and he could see the offending yellow aircraft against the blue sky. He saw the tourist pointing his video at the Aston.

 "Hey Meneer, you got that on video right?"

 "Damn right I did, fantastic footage!"

 Sandro memorized the man's car registration number, then drove over and leant out to give him a business card.

 "Call me, I might need you as a witness and I'll make it worth your while!"

He jumped the clutch, wheel-spinning until the tyres smoked as he set off to pursue the Ag-Cat.
"Do you think someone's making a film?" asked the tourist's placid wife. "That man looked like James Bond."
-xxx-

Harare, Zimbabwe

Zimbabwean President Primrose Mpofu finished re-reading a briefing paper about Chinese involvement in Africa. The Chinese were popular with many African leaders because their investment came without the western block's moral clauses specifying human rights compliance as a condition. There was a discrete knock and the splendidly uniformed Zimbabwean Supreme Commander Nigel Mabvudza entered her office followed by Chief Superintendent Simon Ndhlovu in civvies. Primrose took off her stylish reading glasses, smiled, and stood to receive them. At fifty-one she was as buxom and wholesome as ever, kept fit by tennis to which she was still addicted. She moved towards them with the innate grace of many African women and gestured them to a lounge suite, sitting down herself. Originally elected in 2003, Primrose was one year into her third presidential term, having volunteered to retire after the second. However public demand had resulted in her standing again and she had cruised effortlessly back into power on a wave of continuing popularity. After several minutes of traditional African politeness she got down to business.
"Now then Nigel, these Militias in Manicaland; how worried should I be about them?"
He cleared his throat and looked at Simon.
"Very worried. Despite good employment the province has many ex-veterans not interested in honest work, especially since they began pushing into the Chiadzwa diamond fields where there are easy pickings and great wealth to be had. Unfortunately the Chief Superintendent's intelligence suggests that an increasing number of forcibly-retired high-ranking army officers are also joining their number, resulting in greater cohesion and discipline than was originally the case. Previously there were perhaps a dozen gangs, I would almost call them rabbles, which caused trouble and lived mainly from crime. Now I fear they are banding together into a quite

formidable force that would give our regular troops a hard time if it came to a confrontation."

"Shouldn't we attack now then, before they get any stronger?"

"We believe not, for two reasons. Firstly, they were originally equipped with the usual old eastern bloc weapons and limited ammunition, but now someone is arming them with newer stuff and greater quantities of ordinance; in short they have a sponsor. Secondly, the increased budget and recruitment campaign you authorized for our regular forces at the beginning of your third term is paying off. Numbers increase monthly, training is vastly improved and morale is surging. It will be far less costly in terms of both life and equipment if we can neutralize the sponsor and take out the leadership. In a few months our Armed forces will be approaching full strength again."

"Any idea who their new backer and main leaders are Simon?"

"We know many of the senior ranks who have gone over to them and I have been contacted by a new informer who says he will give me the sponsor, in exchange for a large sum of money."

Air Vice-Marshall Mabvudza coughed discreetly.

"We are short of air-cover for our troops. Unfortunately most of the fighters, bombers and helicopter gunships were stood down a few years ago at Grand Reef where the Militia is based. The best we could manage would be a few obsolete jets, some Lynx ground-attack Cessnas and a few machine-gun equipped helicopters."

"Yes I know. I shall be reviewing the budget and will recommend procurement of up-to-date military machinery." She made some notes and then looked up again.

"Okay. Now to Chiadzwa Diamond Field; I have nationalised it for a reason. The output has been estimated at potentially 185 million US dollars a week, valuable foreign currency with which to rebuild the country and I am determined that the people as a whole should benefit. However the wealth is haemorrhaging as stones make their way to nearby Mozambique and are snapped up cheaply by Lebanese, Russian and European buyers. I want a cordon along the Eastern border to block that illegal trade, and any foreign buyers in Mutare closed down. Can you do that?"

"We can" said Ndhlovu, "but it will be heavy on manpower, of which the Vice-Marshall is short. There was a fence and clear-cut during the Chimurenga. I can get that repaired but it will always be porous."

"Repair it anyway; choke the flow of stones out of the country as much as possible."

"The CIA have offered to get involved. Al Qaeda and other terrorist groups frequently use diamonds as currency since they are easy to transport and difficult to detect."

"Pass them what you feel is justified without allowing expansion of their personnel already at the embassy in Harare. The Americans probably mean well but their military and intelligence arms have a tendency towards mission-creep and I want everything going on here to be firmly under Zimbabwean control."

The two men nodded.

"I understand that the Militias control about one third of the diamond-bearing territory and are running virtual slave-labour camps there reminiscent of the Congo. I don't want them to encroach any more. How are the new barracks and road system coming on?"

"The Barrack work is well advanced, roads less so. The rains began early and the heavy plant was trying to operate in a virtual quagmire for weeks. Things are dryer now and construction can accelerate."

"Good. Nigel, stay in touch. I needn't keep you from duty any longer."

"Keep him from the golf-course more likely" growled Ndhlovu and they all laughed. The Air Force Commander's love of the game was legendary.

Primrose waited until the door closed.

"This sponsor, Simon; could it be Katsiru? He has much money, looted from Zimbabwe's coffers; more than enough to buy people."

She'd known Ndhlovu and trusted him for years, before her husband Elias had been murdered by Katsiru henchmen.

"Primrose, I don't know, but it is possible. Since he escaped custody his tracks have been well covered. I am always alert but there is never anything really concrete; just a rumour here, a whisper there. I am more concerned about the Militias being involved with organized crime. There is a criminal syndicate known as the Black Mambas based in South Africa that is beginning to spread into Zimbabwe. I am in regular contact with Brigadier Thandiwe of the South African Police about it. I almost wish the Chiadzwa diamond fields had never been discovered, they are luring every crook and corrupt hyena in the region to our country; it is the very kind of thing that would attract Katsiru, for if he controlled that wealth coupled with what was already stolen, he could easily launch an attack one day."

Primrose sighed.

"I was premature in cutting back our defences Simon; naïve in the belief that we no longer had enemies. Find out what the new informer knows as soon as possible. This smells of Katsiru to me. Go back through the records and his history for anything that could be used to defuse, control or eliminate him."

"Your concern is justified, everything you have achieved would be undone if a man like that forced his way into power again. I will keep you closely informed."

He hesitated.

"This sponsor may be trying to get into the pocket of the Chinese, Primrose, by promising natural resources in return for military aid."

She sighed. "Yes, our neighbour Zambia serves as an example. Even without military intervention Beijing is turning the country upside-down."

She opened a classified folder, reading paragraphs at random while the policeman stroked his nose thoughtfully and listened.

'Chinese interest in Africa amounts to little more than another round of foreign plunder, as Beijing extracts minerals and other natural resources at knock-down prices while battering the continent's economies with a flood of subsidised goods and surplus labour. No one can say how many Chinese are in Zambia. The government says 2,300, but economists say the real figure runs into the tens of thousands. Many are pushing wheelbarrows and selling vegetables in the market; they are not needed: Zambians can do that.'

'Many of Zambia's mining companies are foreign-owned, and China has invested more than $400m (£250m) in Zambia, but a 2011 report by Human Rights Watch (HRW) said that, despite general improvements in recent years, safety and labour conditions at Chinese mines were worse than at other foreign-owned mines. Chinese managers have even fired on Zambian miners protesting against low pay.'

She slapped the report and looked up.

"And perhaps most telling, this comment from one of their senior diplomats:

'Chinese people can stand very hard work. This is a cultural difference. Chinese people work until they finish and then rest. Here the local population are like the British, they work according to a loose plan, have many tea breaks and a lot of days off.'

She snorted.

"In other words, black people are lazy! Life is for living Simon; our people should be carefree, with time for leisure, not wage-slaves as Muammar Gadhafi was fond of saying. The Chinese always remind me of ants somehow, always running running running, while somewhere a queen ant sits getting fat and does nothing but cause mischief!"

"I agree. We are better off allowing foreign trading partners to invest, but keeping control and management of our own assets. The Chinese are ruthless, cunning and patient. If Katsiru or some other antagonist with sufficient wealth wants to mount a coup in Zimbabwe they will need vast access to military hardware. The Chinese want to get in here and grab our minerals and agricultural products at rock-bottom prices; if you won't play ball they might go round you, by supplying someone like Katsiru with arms in return for access to natural resources. They could ship heavy weapons to Mozambique and fly them in; say to Grand Reef in Manicaland. Perhaps they have already started."

"Well what am I to do? Beg the West for help to keep the Chinese out? Europe and Britain have few reserves, tied up as they are with the Muslim question. The Americans seem to have lost their stomach for intervention in Africa after Somalia."

Ndhlovu smiled.

"Be cunning, like the Chinese themselves; smile and smile and be a villain."

"Very apt Simon; I had forgotten you acted at school."

"Acted the fool mostly; we staged Shakespeare productions most years, in the open air-theatre at Bernard Mizeki. My biggest roll was Falstaff. I got drunk on some disgusting wine we made illegally in the dormitory, fell off the stage and puked on the headmaster's shoes."

Primrose smiled.

"I should be pernicious though, like Hamlet's mother."

"Exactly; give vague undertakings but promise nothing. Keep their representatives languishing for months like ours do in Beijing. If they believe you will eventually co-operate, the Chinese government is unlikely to waste time and resources backing anyone else, or risk the opprobrium of our traditional allies in the west. It may buy us time at least."

"Yes. Have a quick drink with me Simon."

He looked at his watch.

"That would be nice; then I must go to Manicaland to debrief this new asset personally."

"Let's hope he does prove to be an asset. Beer, isn't it?"

She pressed an intercom and asked for drinks. Primrose's personal aide was a slim, handsome black woman in her late forties who curtsied as she set the drinks down.

"Good afternoon Superintendent, I hope you are well. Did you catch that devil Katsiru who killed my husband yet?"

She asked the same question every time they met.

"I am afraid not Fanny. Think back in case there is anything which might help me pick up his trail."

He had known her since she was a young woman, whose husband was killed by the ex-president as revenge for informing about him to James Hacking and Simon, then in the Selous Scouts. Ndhlovu, impressed with Fanny's courage integrity and determination, had recommended her to Primrose as an aide when she won her first election.

"I doubt it, having thought of little else for many years. I shall rack my brains again though."

She went out closing the door. He finished his beer quickly and stood up.

"That was most welcome Primrose. Please excuse me, I am anxious to get started."

"In Manicaland you must be very careful. Beware of traps."

"So must you Primrose; listen to your security advisors. I applaud your policy of accessibility to the people but you are a unique symbol that has united Zimbabwe. If anything untoward happens to you we will be cast into darkness again."

-xxx-

Johannesburg

Julius had tucked into formation beside Jemima at fifteen hundred feet above ground level feeling relieved, though he was dreading seeing her on the ground; he was sure he'd just blown his new job. She jabbed her finger grimly towards the farm airstrip in a peremptory gesture and he slipped behind to follow.

Sandro hurtled along gravel farm roads like a man possessed, neck craned out of the Aston's window to follow the two airplanes. He saw the monoplane begin to orbit while the biplane made its approach to an airstrip he couldn't see but which could only be ahead on the track he was following. He put his foot down and stones rattled and bumped under the chassis as the sleek car wheel-spun, fishtailed and slid recklessly along the narrow road. He arrived at the strip to find a cluster of trucks, cars, trailers and equipment near a big dilapidated farm shed. The Biplane had landed and its propeller jerked to a halt, canopy sliding open. Scrambling from his car Sandro sprinted forward. As the pilot stepped backwards off the lower wing Sandro grabbed one shoulder, spun him round and punched for the heart. The slightly-built figure crouched and Sandro's fist connected with the helmet as a rapid defensive kick landed with precision in his balls. He shouted in shocked surprise, realising that the pilot was female, very fast and probably tough. Jemima's crew dropped everything, ran over and tried to grab him but he brushed their arms aside contemptuously, blocking blows effortlessly despite the pain in his lower belly.

"Jammer Meisie, I don't usually hit girls" he called "but look what you did to my bleddy car! You can tell these people to stop, I won't hurt them."

Jemima relaxed her alert stance and stood upright.

"Okay leave it guys, just keep an eye on him."

She was in a strange mood, half euphoria from a narrow escape by her own flying skill and half depression because of the air-proximity incident between her and Julius. Removing the helmet she shook out sweaty raven-coloured hair, enjoying the cool breeze on a scalp itchy from confinement.

"You must be that guy in the car back there?"

Sandro was transfixed. It was quite literally love at first sight. The woman's clear cobalt blue eyes looked calmly into his and seemed to know him entirely; she had a gaze like a laser, confident, almost teasing.

"Well ja!" he stammered. "Man, I nearly kukked myself; must have been your engine I heard but I thought at first it was my own, about to explode or something. Then there's this bleddy airplane flying down the road, right towards me. A man doesn't expect that at seven in the morning! So I swerved and the car took off up the wall riding sideways like I'm Evel bleddy Knievel or someone; I tell you I was this close to dying. And the poor car, it was like it's in a concrete mixer, going to be some damage, I can tell you, especially underneath."

"Let's go take a look."

As she brushed past him Sandro swivelled to follow and his eyes drank her in. The overalls fitted like a tailored suit, accentuating wide shoulders, a slim waist, feminine buttocks and long elastically striding legs. She moved in a graceful balanced way like an antelope. Jemima circled round the beautiful vehicle followed by a procession of admiring loaders who made grubby smears on the glass as they peered inside.

"You're lucky to own this, they retail at over one hundred thousand pounds sterling. Look Mr... what's your name? OK Mr Marais, I accept that you've had a bad scare but the car doesn't look too bad, a few scratches on the moulded bumpers at front and rear, otherwise no dings like you might expect from flying stones."

She dropped lithely into the press-up position, lowering her body to within an inch of the ground to avoid getting dust on the fitted overall as she peered underneath, then sprang effortlessly upright again.

"Nothing hanging down either, silencer and exhaust look okay but you'll need to get it checked, specially the brake-pipes."

She had a captivatingly clear accent that made Sandro think of cut-glass ornamental chimes he'd seen and heard in jewellery shops, a few of which he'd robbed in his chequered career.

"A Rhodesian" he thought; "English accent with just a hint of Afrikaans inflexion." His rage had dissipated, replaced by raw masculine interest. He walked round the car too and had a quick look underneath.

"The damage isn't as bad as I first thought but some work needs doing and it was your fault!"

Her eyes crinkled.

"If it was, and I'm not admitting anything, what do you propose we do? I loathe filling in forms."

"No 'if' about it, there was a guy in a lay-by got it all on video and I have his number." His eyes flicked across to the Yellow AgCat.

"Tell you what; if you give me a ride in your aeroplane we can forget all about it, I'll get the repairs done myself."

"What, right now? Okay Mister, done! Jaapie, get the gentleman a helmet!"

In the sky Jemima gave Sandro his money's worth, making several fast low spray-simulation passes with stall turns, then climbing to ten thousand feet and carrying out fifteen minutes of aerobatics before terminating with fifteen minutes of basic instruction on the controls.

He was buzzing when she landed.

"Man, that's it, I'm hooked. I'm getting flying lessons!" yelled Sandro, taking off his helmet as she parked, "But I've got one more condition before I forget the damage to my car!"

Jemima cocked a cynical eyebrow at him.

"Oh yes?"

"You must let me buy you dinner, to apologise for hitting you."

Jemima laughed at his psychology; he'd conveniently blotted out the fact that she'd landed the most telling blow. However she'd learnt from her weird surrogate father that it was wise to let people keep their dignity. Marais was obviously a rough diamond but the whole day, from the argument with Francois to the recent airprox occurrence had put her in a reckless mood. Also there was something dead sexy about him.

"OK, it's a deal Mr Marais. My name is Jemima Visser." She held out her hand.

"Sandro." They shook and he flipped open an expensive-looking phone, putting her number in as she rattled it off.

"How about tomorrow night? I know a really lekker Italian place."

"It needs to be somewhere I know; how about Redwoods in Sandton on Sunday?"

"Sound, where shall I pick you up?"

"I'll meet you there at seven pm."

Jemima held the Aston door for him, scrutinising surreptitiously. His body looked firm and compact with a muscular chest under an extremely expensive suit-jacket, rumpled from the brief fight. No tie, cream silk shirt casually open at the neck, thick dark hair slicked back from a narrow forehead above a pronounced beaky nose and firm full lips. His facial skin was tanned and healthy and he smelled of powerful aftershave and smoke, though she hadn't seen him light up. He looked like he'd been on the town and not got home. He swung easily in, slammed the door, thumbed the glass start button and waved as the V12 rumbled to life, departing in a flurry of spinning wheels on gravel. She watched him go and then turned to amble towards the shed thoughtfully.

"Who's your new boyfriend Miss Jemima?" called the irrepressible Cape-Coloured named Jaapie.

"Go shit in the mealies Jaapie" she replied in a distracted uninterested tone.

"See if you can actually get some work done instead of bullshitting all day."

He chuckled, lowering his voice.

"That chick knows how to live hey kerels? And how to fight; she kicked that guy sweet in the nuts, couldn't have done better myself."

"What do you expect from Dougie McIntyre's daughter?" said another worker. "He was always fighting and she was often around when he did, even when she was a picannin."

They moved off back to their equipment as Jack Dowding's Air-Tractor landed and taxied in for hopper replenishment, turbine whistling and quiet, slow-turning, five-bladed prop thrumming.

Julius was hovering nearby, envying the easy way she handled the rough men in her crew. She jabbed a finger at him.

"Right JJ, get me your GPS, let's see what went wrong."

-xxx-

Zimbabwe

"My extraction process is satisfactory for now and at last the workers are performing adequately" remarked Spencer Katsiru, ex-President of Zimbabwe and a wanted criminal. He was standing on the edge of a deep muddy pit in which filthy Africans clad in tattered clothes were working with pics, shovels and reed baskets. Many were old women and adolescent children. Beyond the series of pits stood a shanty town of huts with ragged, rain-rotted thatch roofs and makeshift dwellings of hessian, plastic sheeting, Styrofoam, plywood boxes and reeds.

"Yes Comrade General Katsiru" agreed Sharpness Malinga dryly, "if not exactly enthusiastically."

The unwilling miners were given food but no wages and were guarded by armed Militia soldiers.

"I have said before not to call me that you fool!" Katsiru admonished his aide. "Until I retake Zimbabwe refer to me only as Silas Lembede."

Malinga gave a tight smile.

"Excuse my slip. The stones seem to be selling well over the border for good prices too."

"Yes but depressed because they are so-called illegal 'blood diamonds' and the scavenging buyers exploit that to drive prices down. Once the next part of my plan falls into place they will reach world markets with a clean pedigree and be worth at least double. Now listen, I want to know more about that new barracks the Mpofu bitch is having built over on her side of the diamond field. I don't want a direct clash with regular Zimbabwean forces yet but I must know what we will be up against when we take over the whole Chiadzwa field."

"Very well, I will get you a report" replied Malinga.

"I don't want a report; I want to see it for myself! There is construction going on all the time, we can get in as workers."

"We could try driving in as contractors but they might get suspicious and arrest us. Is it worth the risk?"

Katsiru fixed him with a disconcerting gaze, his artificial eye unblinking.

"That's a good idea Colonel. The trick will be to go in as something they are expecting, it will make us invisible."

Later they drove south from Mutare on the A9 and Malinga concealed the Toyota Land-cruiser. He and Katsiru then walked along paths for some way, and finally came out on a gravel road leading from Hot-Springs into the Marange district. They crossed the low-level narrow bridge over a river swollen by recent rains and changed into workers clothes from the rucksack on Malinga's back, stuffing it into an ant-bear hole for concealment and sitting down to wait. A few battered pickups rattled past and each time Katsiru shook his head. Finally they heard the growl of a heavier engine.

A six by four semi-truck came into sight hauling a flat-bed trailer stacked with bags of cement. It ground cautiously down the steep bridge approach, air-brakes hissing and compression-release engine-brake growling.

"This will do."

"What? Are you sure you can drive that thing boss? It's huge."

"Of course, it is like riding an injinga and I was practically born in the seat of a truck! My father was a haulage contractor as you well know."

"Well if you say so."

Katsiru and Malinga pulled on balaclavas and each stepped up onto a running board as the truck cleared the bridge. Seeing their guns, the elderly driver and his mate stepped down with alacrity when instructed. They stared with big uncomprehending eyes as Malinga explained that the load would be delivered, after which the vehicle would be abandoned by the bridge again. After a few false starts and much hissing of brakes, Spencer got the heavy combination moving only to stall it near the top of the steep climb out. He had not selected a low-enough gear. Snubbing on the dead-man handbrake he put in the clutch and restarted the engine. Malinga looked worriedly back at the bridge which seemed a long way below.

"Do you mind if I get out?"

"Stay right there Colonel! Are you a man or a mouse?"

Malinga looked at him in astonishment. Ex-President Katsiru didn't do jokes! Suddenly he realised that for the first time in the almost thirty years he'd known him, Spencer Katsiru was actually enjoying himself.

"Squeak!" he replied.

"Very well, get out. And make sure you run to catch up, don't keep me waiting! Damn coward."

Walking forward to get out of the line of fire, Malinga turned to watch. The dead-man handbrake went off and for a split-second the rig rolled backwards but Katsiru responded with power and clutch before it ran away. With much scrabbling and spinning of the twin-axle drive-wheels the combination began to grind upwards again. The ex-general bared his teeth at Malinga as he went past in a boiling cloud of dust and deliberately didn't stop 'till he was half a mile down the road. His aide was panting hard when he climbed back aboard. There was an office portacabin at the site of the new barracks. A Sergeant and a site engineer came out with a map.

"You're late, where the hell have you been? These are the guard-posts round the outer perimeter road" said the engineer, pointing. "There are ten in all. Drop two pallets of cement at each and then bring the other six back here. Take two labourers to help you."

Spencer pretended to be a bit dumb and took the map, turning it various ways up but in reality using the extra time to memorize as many pertinent facts as possible such as drainage, power, manholes, sleeping quarters and armouries. Finally the Sergeant snatched it back, motioning to a couple of manual workers squatting nearby.

"Get on with it you fool! You two, show these idiots where to go!"

The ex-President worked as hard as the others, unloading heavy awkward paper cement sacks by hand from pallets, two men on the trailer and two on the ground stacking. They took it in turns and during infrequent breaks when the labourers stopped to smoke, Spencer and Malinga listened more than they talked and picked up much useful information from the gossip.

As he showered back at Grand Reef Aerodrome the ex-president hummed a few bars from a long-forgotten school hymn. He had enjoyed driving again and the simple physical task of unloading. He felt fit and strong after the exercise; it had been good to feel honest sweat running and perform a man's work. Whilst soaping, his hand touched the knotted cicatrices of scar tissue between his legs where testicles would normally be and as always, with a sense of shock that never diminished, he realised he would never be a man in the full sense again. Well balls weren't everything! Power could be more satisfying than sex.

While dressing he could see troops mustered on a runway of the former Rhodesian stronghold outside Mutare in the Eastern Highlands. Through them he now had control over more than a third of the phenomenally rich Chiadzwa diamond fields. Several years previously when Primrose Mpofu had withdrawn all Zimbabwean troops from the Congo, where they had been propping up a corrupt regime in return for riches from diamonds and timber for the Commanders, she had also systematically retired the entire old hierarchy from Military, Police and Intelligence services. It had played into Katsiru's hands because they were flocking instead to his own growing army. Zimbabwe had no real apparent enemies so Primrose had opted for a small professional Civil and Military force of new blood which was cheaper to maintain and more popular with the people, but relatively inexperienced. The force of seasoned veterans Katsiru was assembling greatly outweighed the newcomers in terms of battlefield knowledge and if all went well would soon do so in numbers too.

Most of the Air force of Zimbabwe's attack aircraft, both fixed and rotary wing, which had fought in the Second Congo War of 1998-2003, had been mothballed at Grand Reef after Primrose's Libyan-backed coup in 2003. Consequently Katsiru had few worries about reprisals against his burgeoning Army from the air; what he really needed was enough money to buy the loyalty of their former pilots and technicians, to get them back in the air again on his side. The forced-labour mines under his control a few miles away in the Marange area were bringing in a landslide of high quality diamonds but because of the harsh conditions and disputed ownership of the field they had been blocked from International markets and classed as 'Blood Diamonds.'

In his other identity as Silas Lembede, respected South African Business Tycoon, the next part of his plan involved setting up a legitimate route-to-market for the vast wealth represented by the Chiadzwa gems. Coupled with the millions already under his control from his time as President, he would soon have enough money and power to resume control of his homeland and restore the dignity which had been sorely missing through the latter part of his life.

A black twin-turboprop King Air was waiting with a consignment already aboard and as he walked towards it an Immigration Officer handed their travel documents back to Sharpness Malinga. As Lembede he liked to travel transparently rather than clandestinely so the Mutare Customs house was always notified if he flew in from an external country and sent an Officer to complete the formalities. The officials rotated and this man, who had performed the duty before, suddenly looked at him directly and glanced down again quickly. Katsiru's hackles pricked. There had been a brief expression of gloating dislike in those eyes that was sufficient alert.

The Immigration official, who had been abducted from his school aged fourteen and taken for guerrilla training in Mozambique, had recognized Spencer Katsiru despite subtle and expensive plastic surgery. The ex-President, at that time a training Captain, had beaten him and deprived him of food on many occasions for failing to keep up on cross-country forced marches. He knew Silas Lembede was Spencer Katsiru and the knowledge was going to make him some money and extract revenge.

Katsiru muttered some instructions to Malinga who glanced back at the Immigration Officer and peeled away to give the necessary surveillance orders. When he joined his boss, the aircraft took off and set course for South Africa via Chimoio Airport in Mozambique. The flight had requested transit permission only, for refuelling and remained on the apron in Chimoio. A car pulled up and the lone passenger, a stocky stern-faced North Korean walked to the King Air and went up the steps. He bowed and sat opposite Spencer Katsiru, pinching the creases of his immaculate trousers.

"The Democratic People's Republic is sympathetic to your quest to be reinstated as President of Zimbabwe, having been unlawfully overthrown by the coup of Primrose Mpofu. In order to limit bloodshed the Republic accedes to the requested air-cover for your troops. Four Sukhoi Su-25 ground-strike aircraft from our Military Advice mission to Mozambique have been moved here to Chimoio. In addition, two Ilyushin Il-76 heavy transport aircraft are here and will assist in airlifting infantry equipment and supplies. All is subject to you successfully taking the town of Mutare, the airport there and the Military barracks. Once the only two large Airfields in eastern Zimbabwe are secure and you dispatch columns to Harare and Bulawayo, the airlift will begin and the strike aircraft will cover the advance."

He accepted a cup of black coffee and left after discussing communications. The King Air closed up and took off.

Malinga grunted. "So the Chinese People's Republic gets the North Koreans who the whole world hates anyway to front their support mission, so if we fail they can hold their hands up and be squeaky clean. If however we succeed, the chinks will come piling in like they have in Zambia, demanding access to all our raw materials."

Katsiru pulled a face.

"Pretty measly assistance too, although it will be better than nothing. And they don't want to get involved until it looks like we are going to win anyway."

"Will we win?"

"I believe so. The hard-core of ZANU-PF are adept at making the people see the correct path. Once we take Mutare and secure Manicaland we will be in a much stronger position. Without air-cover Mpofu's untried forces may not be very keen to fight."

"And if they do?"

"The Sukhois will obliterate them in large numbers and word will spread."

-xxx-

October: Johannesburg: Friday

Jemima and JJ leant against her dusty sports car checking the coordinates and he'd programmed the wrong ones. She exploded.

"You fucking idiot, what the hell's wrong with you? You arrived late, unshaven and looking like something the cat dragged in; your head's been up your backside all morning!"

He hung his head and began to stammer.

"I'm sorry Jemima, really. I was stupid, I had a few drinks with the crew last night, probably too many I admit; you know how it is, they kind of get at you, belittle you and before you know it you're trying to prove something to them…."

Jack shut down his Air Tractor and in the abrupt silence Jemima's furious voice was whiplash clear, like someone who keeps singing in church when the organ music stops.

"Prove something to that shower of shit?" she yelled. "You must be bloody joking! They've got some excuse, being semi-educated bloody roughnecks but we're all supposed to be professionals. If any one of us screws up somebody could die and you just did screw up, big-style! At least they all arrived on time and can do their jobs, after a fashion. If you're not mature enough to deal with them then say so and ship out. Take this as a final warning; pull yourself together or you're fired! Understand?"

"Yes Jemima."

The crew were milling uneasily and pretending to be busy, ears pricked, like a pack of hounds fearful of an angry master.

"That goes for you lot too. Start behaving like adult men instead of pubescent half-witted teenagers. For two pins I'd fold this circus and fire the lot of you, I don't need this shit but you do and you'd be well advised not to forget it. Get on with your work!"

"Jussus!" whispered Jaapie. "Watch it boys, she's on the rags and the warpath!"

"And you Jaapie; if you ever repeat anything like that again you'll be the first one down the road. Klaar?"

"Klaar Miss Jemima!"

She spun on her heel and climbed into the car, shaking slightly with emotion and the delayed effects of her narrow escape. She examined her sweat-shiny face and dishevelled hair in the rear-view mirror, grimaced and slumped back into the seat with a sigh. Jack Dowding wandered over and raised an eyebrow at the crestfallen young pilot. Julius dejectedly described his error and the subsequent aircraft proximity incident while Jemima rested for a couple of minutes with her eyes closed, getting her thoughts in order.

"Don't beat yourself up too badly laddie" said Jack. "You made a serious mistake but to some extent it's my fault and Jemima's too, one of our jobs is to brief the pilots and you're still inexperienced."

"That's right" agreed Jemima, joining them. "I meant every word I said but you're a good pilot, just concentrate and don't let yourself be distracted by that rabble."

"Thanks Jemima but I do take it badly. I was unprofessional and it nearly killed you."

"Well nobody died, OK? The responsibility is as much mine as yours. Let's all learn from it. Never skimp on safety checks, double-check everything and if you're in doubt, ask. Hell, if I was being really professional I'd contact the CAA, make a clean breast of things, report the air-proximity and so on but I don't need the hassle right now. Nobody else knows so let's keep it that way huh? Anybody asks, I had an engine problem and you rushed over to ride shotgun. Now let's get on with the job."

Julius nodded.

"Thanks Jemima."

"Looks like your ship's ready so go check your damn GPS before take-off!"

"Yes boss!" Julius managed a wry smile and strode towards the Pawnee.

"Hey Julius!" called Jaapie softly as he went by, sucking his thumb obscenely and slanting his eyes towards Jemima. The youngster swerved towards him.

"Jou Moere's gat Jaapie, you toothless wanker! I bet with those bare gums you give a good gobble yourself hey?"

The loaders guffawed with lewd laughter and the tough coloured man shook his fist in mock anger. The puppy was developing some bite but there was plenty of sport still to be had at his expense. Jemima's mind had already moved on. So many items ticked off her list, so many more to do. She remembered the intermittent vibrating of her phone during the flight and pulled it out. There were several missed calls, five from Francois. Well he could gaan kak in the mealies, she was still smarting and pissed off with him, not sure what her decision would ultimately be if he wanted to make up. Two missed calls from the bank; well they could definitely gaan kak. One missed call from Theo Bustamante. Jemima was paid a retainer by Bustamante Enterprises to fly their Beechjet when required which brought in much needed cash and kept her type-rating on the jet current. It wasn't always convenient though. Her thumb rubbed the phone thoughtfully, then hit the call button.

"Theo Bustamante."

"Bunter, got your message, what can I do you for?"

"Jemima, thanks for getting back. Need a favour; can you work for us on Sunday? Know its short notice but I need to take someone up to Botswana in the jet."

His voice was stand-offish, he didn't particularly like her pet name for him but they went back a long way.

"Yes but look, I'm really busy right now. I'll be in town tomorrow; shall I pop over to your office for the details?"

"Please do, we're here 'till noon most Saturdays. Bye now."

Jemima discussed the rough-running of the Ag-Cat's radial engine with Jack Dowding. He was the most experienced pilot she knew and had flown just about everything. He was sixty-seven but still going strong; Dougie had trusted him implicitly and so did Jemima. He promised to ground-run the Ag-Cat's engine to test it again and they discussed wrapping up the job. They were due to move on to another nearby client's farm the following week and were ahead of time on the current task, with not many more sorties to fly.

"Jack, there's a moere of a lot of planning to do for next week's job and I'm flying for Theo Bustamante on Sunday so I need to prepare for that. I'll do it at home where I can get some peace. You can finish off without me yeah? When the guys have tidied up let them do an early dart for the weekend, not that they deserve it after getting Julius pissed last night. Tell them to be back here bright-eyed and bushy-tailed Monday 0600. No hangovers or excuses."

Jack was a tall, laconic man with bushy eyebrows and a lean face like a worn leather saddle.

"Roger-that Jemima, leave it to me."

He put his arm round her shoulder as they walked to the car.

"You've been working hard; try not to burn out hey? Jaapie's worried about that bloke Marais, says he looks like a skellum. Make sure there are people around if you meet him again, know what I mean?"

"I will Jack; see you Monday." She kissed his cheek and gunned the Porsche Carrera away with a feeling of relief at the sudden freedom. Jack watched her go worriedly. He had kids and grandkids of his own. Jemima was a toughie and soldiered on but he wondered how long it could continue before she cracked up. The business environment was tough. He wished something good would happen, some lucky breaks for a change, or maybe a really nice man to help and support her. Jack didn't rate her current one, the supercilious policeman Steenkamp, and hoped like hell she didn't marry him; Dougie would have a heart-attack, even in his grave.

In the car Jemima's cell phone rang and seeing Francois Steenkamp's number on the screen she rejected the call. She wasn't being otherwise, just really didn't feel like talking to him; she was beginning to realise that his 'take it or leave it' ultimatum was probably the very get-out clause she'd been unconsciously looking for. She pictured herself at home, bored, with a stomach blown up like a baby elephant, piles, cravings, breasts like melons. It made her shudder, as did the image of Francois arriving through the door and calling "darling I'm home, what's for supper? I had the most interesting case today." He would find someone to fit the role of dutiful Afrikaans wifie but she also knew he genuinely loved her and would be regretting his outburst. There wasn't much of her stuff at his place so she went to her own townhouse in the up-market Johannesburg suburb of Bryanston. On a table by the door was a picture of Dougie McIntyre, her step-Dad and first flight instructor, standing in front of his favourite aircraft, a Piper Malibu. The eight-seater was a muscular, elegant looking airplane with a vast turbine in the nose and a four-blade paddle prop; Dougie had never trusted small twin-engined aircraft. His wife Moira was standing beside him dressed as if for a garden party at Buckingham palace, but he was clad like an itinerant native in ragged shorts, tee-shirt and bare feet. Jemima picked the photo up and kissed their images, thinking about the couple who'd become her legal guardians when Ouma and Oupa Visser died.

    She was orphaned while young, her father Gert Visser dead in a farming accident in Rhodesia, her mother Dawn soon after in a firearms accident during the bush war, or so she believed. Her Grandparents had subsequently fled the violence of land-reform in Zimbabwe when their farm was invaded by black war-veterans after Dawn died. Taking Jemima with them they settled by the sea in Knysna, an idyllic town in the Cape region of South Africa. Dougie had taught her to fly there when she was sixteen, and volunteered to become her legal guardian when her elderly Grandparents passed away together in a boating accident, sunk running the Knysna Heads in a storm. He had been a dubious role-model. Raised on a Rhodesian farm, he seldom wore shoes and went on long drinking binges in the bush with just a rifle, some salt and whisky. He drove an old 4x4 bakkie, travelling always with two faithful black employees and a lump of smouldering lead-wood in the back to provide the campfires to cook meat and sadza which were his main diet. He drank and fought in bleak South African bars from which women were excluded, perpetually bare feet like leather and fists scarred. His wife Moira had loved him desperately and stuck it out through humiliation and heartbreak, until one day an air crash had claimed them too. Jemima inherited their entire estate and became the owner of ZU-KAT Agricultural Aviation. So in the space of thirty-five short years, Jemima's parents had died, her grandparents had died, and then her surrogate parents had died. Sometimes she seriously wondered if white Rhodesians were jinxed.

    Banishing morbid thoughts with a conscious effort she stripped off her sweaty flying clothes and threw them straight in the washing machine, then popped the cap off an Amstel beer-bottle and walked around naked doing a few house jobs, enjoying the cool tiles beneath her soles. Passing the full-length mirror in the hall she did a pirouette. The sight of her own naked body was horny and quickly applying suntan oil, she slipped into a bikini and took another beer to the communal pool which was deserted. Jemima sunbathed, excited by the thought of possible new romance with Sandro Marais. An hour of increasingly erotic imaginings followed while lying in sun-stunned torpor and the blue bikini bottom grew dark with moisture where her vaginal lips pushed at the material. Plunging into the pool was heaven, the cool water like a lovers caress, her sexual tension suddenly almost unbearable and she vaulted out, grabbed her stuff and ran back to the house.

Wet bikini was hastily shed in front of mirror; swollen slippery clitoris was stroked causing orgasm almost immediately, body doubling up with intense racking thrills. The sexy images fuelling her excitement were all of her and Sandro making love; Francois Steenkamp was forgotten. She staggered to the big low couch and collapsed onto it, fingers strumming, climaxing three more times in quick succession, low cries of ecstasy ringing round the room. With a slightly embarrassed smile on her lips, Jemima pulled a light throw over herself and sank into a dreamless sleep. She awoke at dusk feeling deeply rested and happy in her solitude. She ordered pizza and drank gin, polishing off the planning work in record time while waiting for delivery, then watched a film and devoured pasta and salad in front of the television. After a hot bath and re-coating of finger and toenails with a pretty colour she went to bed feeling renewed, ready for anything the morning could throw at her.

-xxx-

When Loretta woke up and stumbled wearily off to bed James took their plates into the kitchen. The sink was full of crusty dishes and cold greasy water, left by Haley and Art. He sighed and sent them an irritable text.

"What did your last servants die of? There's a week's worth of dishes in the sink! Who do you think's going to do them?"

A reply plinked onto his phone immediately.

"The washing up fairy, what else are Dad's for? I'll make it up to you when I get back. Love you! Hales. X"

He smiled and began cleaning up, hating to come down to a mess in the morning, then joined Loretta who was snoring gently. The comfort of a king-size mattress with crisp sheets was luxury after the bunks in a truck.

CHAPTER TWO
SATURDAY
Lancashire

The alarm rang at 0400 and James rose again after a brief sleep, feeling sick with tiredness. Peering blearily through a downstairs curtain it was apparent that the night-man had arrived safely from Scotland and parked the Volvo up. The truck was there, but no sign of the Agency driver who was supposed to take it and the Scottish load on to Manchester. He phoned the sleepy female Agency despatcher who apologised profusely and promised to get another driver. James made a cup of tea and drank it, looking at his watch impatiently, toying with the idea of doing the job himself. It would be very risky; having driven for six days he needed a weekly break of at least forty-five hours, having already used a twenty-four hour reduction. If VOSA stopped him and checked their tacho records he faced a huge fine and driving ban which could put them out of business. Loretta could do it, her last weekly break had been a forty-five but she was exhausted.

Disgustedly he tossed dregs in the sink, banged the cup down and phoned again. The despatcher had found a driver but he would take an hour to arrive. James spent it trying to get through to a manager at the receiving depot in Trafford Park to advise late arrival and rebook a tipping slot. It was eventually agreed by a surly unhelpful clerk as James suppressed an urge to tear him off a strip. Making sure the replacement driver knew where he was going James went back to bed. An hour and a half later the phone ringing gradually penetrated his deep sleep and he sat up groggily, peering at the alarm-clock. The driver reported that while reversing onto a sloped docking bay with rear doors open, two double-stacked pallets of oat cereal boxes had fallen out under the rear wheels. The Manager was refusing the whole load.

"Well sort it out; get him to drop some pallets and a skip at your bay. Start restacking the good packages, bin the ruined ones and I'll be there in forty minutes to help" said James, putting down the phone on the driver's protests. He made it in thirty-five on empty roads. It was drizzling but at least a more co-operative day-Manager had taken over and after an hour's furious work by James and the driver, he accepted the whole load. James bought the youngster a bacon and egg butty from a van outside the yard.

"You've chosen a tough profession so try to make things easier on yourself and me. Next time check the straps on a load like that before you reverse and if there aren't any, put some on and save everyone a lot of hassle!"

The rest of Saturday was taken up with paperwork and maintenance. A truck failed to start on a customer site and another needed a tyre change. His weekly rest-break continued as usual with work but none that VOSA could prove under the EU working-time directive. On Sunday they woke to a crisp cool summer morning and James went for a pounding run up Parbold hill, like a hound released from a long spell of captivity. His intention had been for them both to have a full forty-five hour weekly break from driving to set the slate clean but another Agency driver failed to turn in. James cursed and asked Loretta to do the short job which was to trunk one trailer into Manchester, drop it and pick up another. As he stepped out of the shower a phone rang.

"It's for you" called Loretta.
"Who is it?"
"Dennis."
"Who?"
"Dennis Mallard!"
"What's he want?"
"He didn't say! Here, ask him yourself." She leant into the bathroom and thrust the handset forward. His hackles rose as usual on hearing Mallard's slightly plummy voice.

"James, any chance you could do a lesson for me in the Tiger Moth at Barton aerodrome this afternoon? The student wants to practice some aerobatics."

James glanced out of the window at sunbeams and clear blue sky, rubbing his hair with a towel.

"Could do I suppose, we've got to drop off a trailer of chilled salad stuff from Spain at the International Freight Terminal in Trafford Park nearby. What's the cabbage patch like after all this rain?"

Barton was an old wartime airfield fringing the western suburbs of Manchester a mile from the Trafford Centre and notorious for the bogginess of its short grass airstrips.

"Not too bad surprisingly; I phoned the tower to check. I've asked the flying school to pull the Tiger out ready for you."

"Okay Dennis, I'll be there."

Loretta was doing her hair in a dressing-table mirror and turned off the dryer.

"Dennis mentioned a joint aviation venture you might be interested in."

James grunted.

"Doubt it, I don't really like the bugger much, or trust him."

"Why the hell not?"

James grinned.

"Gut feeling: he's an oily poof. We should concentrate on building our own business, sell it and head over to Canada where the sun shines occasionally."

"He's not gay and it might give you a chance to get back into aviation commercially! We've hardly got established here and you want to be off already! God you're a rolling stone."

"Not true. I was perfectly happy where I was born until a bunch of arseholes screwed it up, but I do miss the space, the sunshine and the freedom of Africa. You know, in Britain during the war-shortages you could go down to the railway line for a piece of coal to keep warm, and maybe even bag a rabbit to eat, but there's no coal or rabbits left here, just millions too many people. If trucks like ours stop rolling for six or seven days bringing the proles their food and opiates, there will be anarchy; pitched battles in the streets for a crust of bread."

"Oh you do exaggerate!"

"No. In Canada there is space, clean air, sunshine and resources. In a similar situation you could shoot an Elk, or catch a fish or grow some corn to survive, cut down a tree to keep warm and cook. The Britain we live in has just fourteen days gas supply stored, and it comes in a pipeline controlled by the Soviets and which crosses Iraq where we are at war."

"I don't know that I want to go to Canada; it's even further away from my relatives."

"Yes but the Rockies mountains have space, blue skies and there are no war veterans trying to shove an assegai up your zoom-pipe for sixpence."

"I know that you're really beginning to hate the trucking job and would be happier back in aviation. The UK might not be so bad if you were flying regularly."

"I don't mind the trucking job, I just hate the fact that in this country I can't get anywhere because the roads are all clogged solid with traffic and business is clogged solid with bullshit legislation that completely stifles initiative."

"It amounts to the same thing; you hate what you do, here, at the moment. Listen to Dennis, if only for my sake, because I am starting to hate the trucking job too; getting up at stupid hours in the dark, the physical danger, road danger, crime danger, ridiculously long hours, dirt and grease up my nose and in my hair."

At eleven am a tractor unit was free and Loretta hauled the Spanish trailer loaded with salad to Trafford Park. The yard was tight for manoeuvring and very busy, their allocated bay an end one with a blind side reverse.

"Hop out, sexy, I'll do it" said James.

"What? Why?"

"Because I'm much better at it than you, we don't have time to waste and I don't want any damage and forms to fill in."

"You patronising baboon! How am I meant to improve when you never give me a chance?"

"You're getting better but this is really difficult and there are dozens of drivers watching; you always go to pieces under pressure."

"I bloody-well do not!"

"Sorry, that came out wrong. I just know you get nervous in front of an audience, even at the climbing wall."

She relinquished the driving seat reluctantly, even though she found reversing the big articulated trucks unnerving; what he had said was true but she hated backing down from a challenge. James opened the rear doors and reversed the artic onto the bay with one deft alignment shunt, then uncoupled it. Loretta took over again and proceeded bob-tailed the few miles to Barton aerodrome.

-xxx-

Johannesburg: Saturday

On Saturday morning Jemima went for a run, had a swim and breakfasted on Special K and scrambled eggs before heading for downtown Johannesburg where she parked with difficulty, then listened to the company accountant whine for an hour, got a parking ticket which she hurled onto the back seat along with half a dozen others and headed over to Bustamante Enterprises' ostentatious skyscraper. Once through security a receptionist rang Theo's secretary upstairs.

"Sure, ask Miss Visser to come straight up Elaine" said Theo Bustamante. He waited eagerly, staring round his large corner office with views of the yellow Johannesburg mine-dumps south of the M2 highway. Light Saturday traffic roared busily along the southern section of the ring road under a cloudless sky. His gaze settled on a portrait of his grandfather Emilio Bustamante, a Rhodesian of Italian descent who had flown fighters for the Royal Rhodesian Air Force with Prime Minister Ian Smith in North Africa during the second world-war. Afterwards he had started a civil engineering construction company which flourished and expanded, into Zambia, Botswana and South Africa, into mining and farming and industry until the conglomerate was the fifteenth largest in Southern Africa. His son George, Theo's father, had been schooled at Peterhouse with Jemima's Dad Gert Visser, James Hacking and Spencer Katsiru, the deposed Zimbabwean dictator. There was a photograph of Emilio and George standing by an aeroplane with Dougie McIntyre, Jemima's flying instructor, guardian and surrogate father. Dougie had owned a crop-spraying Company in the Transvaal and had inexplicably crashed whilst flying his Malibu between Knysna and Johannesburg, killing himself and his wife. They left everything to Jemima. Theo sensed loneliness behind her air of reckless fatalism and felt protective, though she had aggressively expanded the crop-spraying business and continued to live lavishly in a townhouse in Bryanston, with swimming pool, gym and tennis courts. Too comfortably, Theo suspected, because the retail-therapy floodgates had obviously opened; Jemima was a generous and ostentatious spender. He didn't know it but the freehold townhouse which had been inherited debt-free now had a growing mortgage on it to subsidise prolific expenditure on lifestyle, clothes and fast expensive cars and she'd drawn money out of the crop-spraying company too.

In the elevator Jemima was cogitating pensively on the financial troubles facing ZU-KAT Agricultural Aviation and her accountant's pessimism when the lift doors opened. She squared her shoulders and strode towards Theo's office.

-xxx-

James's student was a wealthy high-hour PPL, already well into an aerobatics course with Dennis. Loretta went to the club-house for a coffee and then sat in the sun watching airplanes come and go, thinking about the possibility of James and Dennis in business together. She'd had a brief affair with the airline Captain on a skiing trip when he was a 'hooray henry' studying aeronautics at University. He was still full of himself but Loretta sensed that the bluster covered an underlying vulnerability that made her want to mother him. He'd done well and earned a lot of money and as a team they had the possibility of earning a lot more without being tied so totally into work that they couldn't enjoy life. And she wouldn't get grease in her hair quite so often.

In the exercise area James and the student climbed and plunged for over an hour, practicing spins, chandelles, stall-turns, falling-leafs and loops. Runway 27 had a curious bump in the middle. On return the tired student landed long. Blinded unexpectedly by the afternoon sun emerging from behind a cloud he dropped hard onto the grass runway. As the Tiger Moth lost speed the bump bounced it back into the air on the edge of stalling. The student hesitated between going round and trying to land again, then applied power tentatively. The Tiger was wallowing, almost behind the power curve without enough energy to climb away. Ahead was a power-line with a hedge of trees in front. The young pilot pulled back on the stick, desperate to clear the obstacles and the Tiger staggered, stall warning screeching. Onlookers in the club garden gasped and jumped to their feet as the vintage aircraft mushed straight for the trees.

"Push!" said James, putting his hand on the stick in the rear cockpit and applying full power. Just before they crashed he weaved left through the lowest point in the reaching branches and flew under the power-line. Loretta was waiting agitatedly as they touched down a second time and helped re-hanger the Tiger.

"God that looked close, my heart was in my mouth! What happened?"

"I made a nearly fatal error close to stalling Mrs Hacking. Sorry James. If he hadn't taken control we could both have been killed" said the sheepish student.

"Thank heavens you're both safe. Dennis phoned. He's on his way over to have a drink with us in the bar James, and discuss his proposition."

"Hooray! You can only drink with a rich man once and even then you have to buy it."

"What the hell is it with you recently? Why?"

"Because rich men always try and take your life over."

"Rubbish, he's not that well off and we're not exactly paupers."

"You might not be but I will if I don't do something about it; and I am, alone. I don't really like fat pampered poofs with inherited money who don't get their hands dirty."

"Shut up about him being a poof, it's really offensive. And as for inherited money, that's hypocrisy; we were both born with a silver spoon in our mouths!"

"Yes, but I've lost mine; or rather had it stolen!"

The student left, embarrassed by the bickering and Loretta stepped in front of James.

"What is it really? Do you want to go back to Zimbabwe? Or South Africa? Do you resent me because we're here and not there?"

"No. We did right to leave and I don't mind hard work but here the odds are stacked against us. Too many people; too much competition from big, greedy voracious companies; too many government-sanctioned thieves getting rich and way too many rules."

"Everywhere has rules!"

"Yes, but for the guidance of the wise, not the slavish following of by corrupt British bureaucrats who implement every petty European pronouncement to our detriment and get their own snouts ever deeper into the trough."

"Well then, at least listen to Dennis, maybe you'll learn something. What he's proposing makes a lot of sense."

"So you already know what he's going to say?"

"Yes. No. Well some of it, he ran it by me on the phone a few times."

James gave her a piercing look and rather wintery smile.

"Okay, then let's go and see what Mr Mallard has to say, I quite fancy a pint."

They found him already in the Flying Club bar. Dennis had allegedly once been a rugger man but was spreading rapidly due to insufficient exercise.

"I hear you nearly crashed and burnt my precious Tiger James!"

He just received a withering glance but Loretta was quick to answer.

"Well actually he prevented an accident rather than nearly causing one!"

"Look at this" said the burly airline captain once James had bought drinks, brandishing a local newspaper called 'The Advertiser,' folded open. James flipped it from side to side, puzzled. Dennis tapped a notice irritably and James read it aloud.

"Tenders are invited for Leasehold possession of the former Naval Air-Station 'Ringtail' also known as Burscough Disused Aerodrome; so what?"

"Not so loud! I have a good friend on Lancashire County Council who tipped me the wink. It was recently reinstated as an active airfield without disturbing the existing businesses which had taken over the facilities in recent years and whose rent brings in a handsome income. It would be an ideal place to run your trucks from too, and we could run the flight school between us. The chap who reinstated it died recently, and his squabbling heirs want to get shut quickly. He reckons we can get it at a premium, way less than it cost to set up."

James finally looked thoughtful. The money spent to convert his commercial flying licences to a European Joint Aviation Rules equivalent that included the UK hadn't left enough to start an aviation enterprise and his age had prevented him securing any decent paying work in the mainstream British commercial industry. The best he had been offered was as First Officer flying graveyard shifts on a Hawker-Siddley 748 without auto-pilot, for a lot less than he could potentially earn operating their transport company. Mental cogs began to whirr. Flight students in Manchester, Liverpool and Blackpool wasted valuable air-time and fuel on the way to training areas in order to complete exercises. Burscough disused Aerodrome was slap in the middle of a training area, with easy access to three major twenty-four seven Airports complete with Instrument Landing Systems for advanced night and precision-approach training. It had plenty of hanger space for aircraft and hard-standings to operate trucks from, instead of a mud-bath yard.

"I dunno Dennis, there's a lot of opposition to existing aerodromes from Nimbys and the paperwork involved would be horrendous. I've got my hands full already with the trucking business."

"Yes, but wouldn't you like to be an eagle again rather than a grease-monkey?"

James glanced pointedly at Mallard's burgeoning belly.

"I'd hardly call you an eagle Dennis; if you'd been in the Tiger just now it would have crashed for sure, and the insurance wouldn't have paid because you'd have been over the maximum landing weight." A further amusing comment about pigs flying sprang into his mind but he managed to stifle it.

The other man flushed.

"No need to be offensive."

"Exactly. Trucking is hard physical graft. You should try some. Anyway, we'll think about your proposition and let you know."
"I'd take care of the bumph; know you don't like red-tape."
"What do you need us for at all? Why not just do it yourself?"
"Don't have enough time or cash and it's too big for one person; I want to keep my full-time airline job as long as possible for the pension, and in case this scheme doesn't work out."
"That's positive thinking. Okay, Loretta and I'll discuss it."
As they left Dennis was having another pint and shovelling free peanuts into his mouth like an efficient conveyor.
"We should do it you know" said Loretta as she guided the Scania unit out of the car park, en-route to collect the trailer.
"I don't think so, I've got enough debt, hassle and paperwork as it is."
"James, you're a pretty good truck driver but an exceptional pilot; the transport industry is turning you into a cynical whinge-bag."
"Thanks."
"Don't get the hump; you know far more about flying than trucking and enjoy it more too. Most importantly you're a doer with good manual skills. Dennis is very smart financially but pretty hopeless practically. Don't forget I was the finance Officer at Bustamante Enterprises for years. Between us we'd be a great management team; if the three of us each find a hundred grand each, the rest can be raised from capital investment banks and grants. And I grew up as a tomboy driving tractors, just like you and there will be lots of jobs I can help with on the airfield. I'm not just a pretty face Hacking! "
"Not even a pretty face."
She swatted him, smiling.
"It's a great opportunity and if we don't do it someone else will and you'll end up kicking yourself."
"There's no way I can get hold of that sort of money right now."
"You could sell the farmhouse, or take a loan out against it and rent it out to pay the loan. The buildings available on the airfield can be made more liveable really easily; we'd actually be more comfortable there, and the trucks could have some garage space in hangers and operate on a well-lit hard standing instead of glutinous mud. The aerodrome is licensed and the old boy ran the flying school for a few months with casual instructors before he died. There are so many possibilities, maybe even a caravan-park or B&B for visiting pilots; there's plenty of land."

"How do you know all this?"

"I've seen it. Dennis and I visited the airfield incognito after that friend on the council got us maps and a prospectus from the original tender."

"The plot thickens. When did you get so pally with old Den again?"

"I've always liked him, as you well know; we met when daddy sent me to finishing school in Lausanne. He was skiing there with a bunch of aeronautics undergraduates and we had a brief fling."

"Hmmm."

"What does Hmmm mean? Oh don't be stupid, it was decades ago and he's been very good putting flight students your way."

"Very noble of him."

"You're not really jealous are you? You said he's gay!"

"Hmmm!"

"You are! How sweet!""Where will you get your stake?"

"I could sell some of the shares I have left and ask brother George for the rest; he's the Bustamante Trust administrator and probably keen to get capital out of South Africa right now in case things take a turn for the worse. The black miners rioting and getting shot have made him jumpy and he will recognise a good prospect when he sees one."

"Ah; another great omniscient businessman."

"You know what James? You're starting to really piss me off a bit with this negative chippy attitude. It's as if the whole world is against you."

"It is, but I feel up to the job on my own. Partners just mean meetings and endless time-wasting discussions."

"You're a stubborn fool; we could make a real killing out of this."

"I said I'd think about it and I will."

-xxx-
October: Johannesburg: Saturday

With a peremptory knock Jemima thrust Theo Bustamante's door open and breezed in, landing a friendly kiss on his cheek before plumping herself down on a chair.

"Lovely to see you Bunter, how may I assist?" she enquired.

Theo flushed at Jemima's casual reference to his girth.

"I wish you wouldn't call me that" he hissed in a low voice, heaving himself up and hurrying to close the door.

"I'm Managing Director; it doesn't do for the staff to hear that sort of thing."

In spite of his pique Theo's eyes drank Jemima in. As usual she radiated exuberant good health. Fit, elastic muscle filled out skin tanned a golden brown and her limbs were long and powerful with sleek wrists and ankles. Short well-groomed black hair hugged a rather square face from which gazed eyes of cobalt blue that tilted slightly towards the bridge of a short straight nose. They gave her face a foxy air of permanent, wry amusement. Theo settled his bulk back into an opulent black leather directors' chair behind the expensive desk, puffing slightly.

"You need more exercise, Bunter."

"It's not easy to stay fit running this damn company but I'm dieting. Can you do a flight plan for the farm strip at Thune Mine tomorrow? I've found a possible buyer, and since the yield has dropped we're anxious to get shut."

"If the yield has dropped, why does he want to buy it?"

"Not my problem; maybe he thinks the price of gold is going to rise, or his geologist knows something we don't. Whatever; I need the Capital for my new Motor Parts Business. At the rate South Africans break motor cars it's a licence to print money."

"It is Sunday tomorrow you know, I had stuff planned."

"I'll make it worth your while. The buyer is a black businessman with heavy political clout; he wants to inspect the operation and be back in Johannesburg no later than four pm to catch a scheduled KLM flight to Amsterdam at six."

"Perfectly possible if we depart at 0900 sharp Theo. Sorry for teasing you."

"Well I am too fat; how about some lunch?" She laughed and used his phone to call National Air-Carriers at Lanseria airport north of Johannesburg. Piet Schuman answered.

"Jemima here Piet, how much fuel is in the Bustamante jet?"

"I'll check the log, standby. Only a thousand pounds Jemima."

"OK, be a china and put another two thousand pounds in, I'll sign for it tomorrow."

"Sure, sexy-legs. Where you going? D'you need a First officer?"

Jemima shook her head.

"Not this trip Piet, we're just going to the Mine at Selibe-Phikwe with some buyers. Theo can help me out as co-pilot."

The Afrikaaner's guffaw echoed down the line.

"Theo's flying isn't going to impress them! See you tomorrow Biggles. And listen, ask those tight bastards at Bustamante when they're going to pay my account. Totsiens!"

"Be nice Pete. Totsiens" said Jemima protectively and replaced the receiver.

"What was Schuman saying?"

"Nothing, he was being a jerk. I'll see you at Lanseria Airport tomorrow Theo; don't be late."

She stood, kissed his cheek and walked to the door but he remained seated. The instant erection which her touch caused him would have been glaringly obvious. He'd been in love with her since boyhood. In his desk drawer was a beautiful gold engagement ring rimmed with diamonds and dark sapphires which exactly matched the deep blue of Jemima's eyes. He opened the box and poked the ring moodily with a sausage-like finger, then wandered over to the window to watch her emerge from the building. He vowed to get fit again; if he looked his best she might come to regard him as more than a friend. On the street she unlocked her car, snatched the parking ticket out from under the wiper, screwed it up and tossed it into the gutter with an oath. Then she started the engine and threw her briefcase into the baking interior, putting the air-conditioning on max before grabbing a mail-bundle she had collected from her Bryanston post-office box but not had time to read in the morning. She perused it while the aircon flushed heat from the cabin.

"Shit" she said, re-reading one from the Bank Manager, cupping a hand over her eyes as if shielding them from the sun, in a characteristic gesture of dismay. "This sounds bad."

Certain phrases struck chords of unease in her.

"Essential we consult most urgently"; "overdraught"; "threshold exceeded without authority"; "withdrawal of credit facilities."

Theo sighed despondently as Jemima leapt into the car and gunned it through the glittering skyscrapers of Johannesburg's commercial centre, impatiently dodging round the people thronging the streets and intersections. Still at least he would be spending the whole day with her tomorrow, even if it wasn't exactly a date. She roared up the ramp of the old De Villiers-Graaff Highway and headed north fast with the aircon blasting cold air into the cabin, towards Sandton City and the Bank. There was never a good time to see a Bank Manager, Jemima reckoned, so she might as well get it over as soon as possible. With luck she might get an hour by the pool afterwards, before the afternoon thunderheads building from the south-east dumped their load on the parched, dusty City. She parked the Porsche on the roof of Sandton's elaborate shopping centre, was frisked by a security guard, descended three floors by escalator to the Banking Mall, and pushed through glass doors into the Trust Bank.

"I would like to see the manager" she told the girl at enquiries.

"What is it in connection with? He is rather busy at the moment."

A note of testiness entered Jemima's voice and she scrabbled in her handbag.

"I have here a letter asking me to come in, which I have taken the trouble to do. I would be glad therefore if the person who sent the letter would extend me the same courtesy."

"Very well Madam" said the girl with what Jemima could swear was a sympathetic expression. "If you wait in the reception area I will tell him you are here."

Jemima sat in an armchair under a large green plant and her mind wandered. She had always got on well enough with old Groenewald the Manager and she was confident any difficulties could be ironed out quickly with him.

She had a habit when initially meeting people of instantly labelling them with her mental first impression. Thus when a clipped voice said "Miss Visser?" at her elbow and she looked up, she immediately thought 'Prissy nerd.'

A skinny fellow in his thirties wearing a pond-green tie and yellow shirt beneath a brown tweed jacket stood looking down his sharp nose at her through round glasses. Pale grey eyes gleamed zealously through thick lenses. He wore a sharp-pointed, russet-coloured Vandyke beard and a moustache several shades lighter. He stood with heels firmly together and arms behind his back, upper body inclined slightly forward. It was apparent that he had recently visited the bathroom, for his fly was partially undone with a corner of the yellow shirt protruding.

"That's right, who are you?" asked Jemima unfolding lithely from the low seat until her eyes were on a level with his.

"I am the Manager. Shall we go to my office?" He flung his port arm out suddenly with almost robotic precision and Jemima's confidence took a sharp dip.

"What a dreadful Rock-spider" she thought, preceding him into the room and talking over her shoulder.

"I usually deal with Mr Groenewald, Is he on holiday?"

The man left the door ajar and marched behind a neat desk.
"On holiday, no. He is suffering bad health from stress of work. Now you will deal with me instead."

It sounded almost like a threat but Jemima was aware that in multi-lingual South Africa, many Afrikaans people seldom used English and therefore sometimes employed abrupt, even rude sentence constructions, without being aware of them.

"Your English is very good Mr Klaasens" lied Jemima, taking the name from the sign on the desk. "Where did you learn it?"

"I learned it at the Afrikaans university at Stellenbosch but until I come to the Transvaal I speak it not often."

"Ah yes," thought Jemima, paraphrasing in her own mind Klaasens probable mental postscript; "and my great grandfather Oom Koos Van Deventer was shot by the English in his buttocks at Paardekraal in the Boer war which we would have won but for the traitors and I don't like the English or their language."

Klaasens was leafing through a buff folder.

"You have more than one account with us Miss Visser. You have a current account with a ten thousand rand overdraft facility, on which you are at present sixteen thousand overdrawn. Then you have a savings account which has a credit balance of..?" he consulted the papers.

"Three cents. Then there is a business account with a credit balance of...?" He peered again, "Eleven cents. However....." he withdrew a bundle of cheques from the folder, "There are cheques against the accounts totalling more than two-hundred thousand rand with no funds available to honour them. Elastic cheques."

"Rubber actually" corrected Jemima. "I wish they were elastic, they might stretch a bit further."

"Exactly, rubber. It is a criminal offence to issue cheques for which no funds are available. Altogether your financial affairs are not satisfactory."

Klaasens sat back, gimlet eyes triumphant. Jemima remained composed with an effort.

"Look Mr Klaasens, I've banked with the Trust for ten years and Mr Groenewald never had a problem with our financial arrangements. Just honour the cheques and I'll settle the overdrafts on both my own accounts. Hell, charge me interest. Isn't that what banks do to make money?"

Klaasens lunged forward in his seat.

"There now is the trouble. How precise will you settle the overdraft?" Jemima waved her hand in a vague dismissive gesture.

"Oh I don't know, my salary will be paid in soon. Or you could add it to the revolving credit and I'll pay it off bit by bit, sign a stop order for a hundred a month or something. And as for the business account, well that's just a matter of cash flow. We're owed far more than we owe. Mr Groenewald never had any difficulty sorting it out with my accountant."

Klaasens flushed at the implied slur on his ability.

"I am not Mr Groenewald! The facts in this matter are that the figures do not add up. You owe the bank two hundred and seventeen thousand rand. Your monthly salary is only thirty thousand. There remains a huge difference and the Bank has concern for this. You cannot just keep spending money you haven't got."

Jemima looked puzzled.

"Why not? Everybody else does, even the Government does; in fact especially the Government. I don't know what's wrong with you, are you really the new Manager? You don't seem to know much about money."

Klaasens sallow face flushed a dark brick red and he banged his small fist on the desk.

"You are not the Government! "

He banged it again.

"I am the Manager!"

He banged it again.

"I am not Mr Groenewald! You may have been able to pull the sheep over his eyes with your clever English talk but not me! You are living outside your money!"

Jemima burst out laughing but her eyes were blazing. She leant over and jabbed her finger repeatedly on Klaasens blotter.

"Don't you bang your puny little fists at me Mr Klaasens, or tell me how to damn well live my life. I know you bloody Afrikaaners; you all have an inferiority complex so you try and take the grudge out on other people. Well, we're in the real world now whether you like it or not so don't try and browbeat me to bolster your own inadequacy. Apartheid is gone and there are plenty of educated eligible black people who could do this job better than you, so watch out! Now I want to see someone with more authority and quickly; I will wait in the reception area."

She stalked from his office.

Klaasens scurried after her, his voice high, icy and trembling. "Your cards first before you leave, all your bank cards and your cheque books. Your credit is suspended and all your accounts frozen, especially those of your company ZU-KAT. Your file goes now to our collection agency. A court order will be made to recover all debts. They will seize your car, Miss Visser, and your goods, and if still you owe us then you will go to jail! Ja, to jail you will go with the other damned verneukers who scorn us and think they can live forever like Roosters on a dunghill. Well your dunghill was too hot and has collapsed!"

The last word emerged as a startled yelp, for Jemima had turned, grabbed his tie and jerked it.

"You're an anachronism Klaasens, just like your verkrampt leader Eugene Terblanche in the AWB was: Dinosaurs, doomed to disappear from the New South Africa. You can't even dress properly!"

Jemima pointed and Klaasen's hands fumbled hurriedly to zip his fly like an embarrassed schoolboy.

"I've wasted my time and achieved nothing thanks to you. I shall make an appointment to see one of your superiors and they will not remain unaware of my displeasure."

A smirking security guard held the door open and she strode out of the bank with her head held high. She did not take Klaasens threat to foreclose seriously. Things would get settled when Groenewald returned. Neither did the twenty thousand rand outstanding on her American Express and the ten thousand on her Access worry her unduly. They were far more sensible institutions who never bothered about her balance so long as she paid the interest, and they kept increasing her credit limit too.

-xxx-
Merseyside

That evening James had another lesson scheduled, for a newly qualified PPL pilot working on a night-rating at Liverpool airport. The plane was a Cessna on the General-Aviation apron run by the main Base Operator which ran a flying school and charter company. A gate-code admitted them to the secure vehicle park. The GA apron was a bleak place at the best of times but after-hours there wasn't even the possibility of a machine coffee or toilet facilities. The aircraft was a long walk away in a chilly breeze through line upon line of parked aeroplanes, and they had to remove chocks and heavy unwieldy restraints from wings and tail, then carry them back to the apron edge. Once airborne they flew north towards the practice area and Burscough disused airfield, to carry out side-slipping exercises and 'Practice Forced Landings" without power, almost down to the threshold of the unused runway. It also afforded James a good look round at the Burscough facilities. As dusk fell the student began a night cross-country flight. The few clouds about were easily visible and there was a surprising amount of darkness on the ground for a country as crowded as Britain.

"If the engine fails at night, is it better to select the landing light on or off?" asked the student uneasily.

"On, but if you don't like what you see, turn it off again."

Liverpool ATC directed him to re-join at Seaforth docks along the Mersey River past famous buildings on the refurbished waterfront. It was a flight James had made dozens of times and always enjoyed, though there were not many places to put an aircraft down if the engine failed, other than the river. His entrepreneurial instincts were seldom dormant and it occurred to him that a seaplane service from Liverpool to Dublin bay would be much more convenient for regular commuters than travelling to the Irish city's traffic-bound airport on the awful M50, and then fighting more traffic to get to Liverpool city centre. The journey could probably be done in an hour including boarding and debarking; so many good ideas but all requiring pots of money. The student's final approach was too high, a frequent mistake on wide runways at night.

"Look at the Visual Approach Slope Indicator Lights" said James. "White and white you're high as a kite, red and red you're dead, but red and white you're alright."

The student reduced power and re-trimmed.

"Good" said James and left him to it, not speaking or twitching again until the tyres kissed the tarmac with the gentle yelp of a perfect landing.

"Good note to end on, well done."

They taxied back to the GA Apron and shut down, followed by the irritating business of fetching the heavy weights to restrain the Cessna adequately. A sudden sharp summer rain shower caught them and after huddling under the wings for a couple of minutes they ran for the distant car park, getting moderately soaked on the way. The exit gate which could normally be opened by code was padlocked. It took several phone calls to reach the duty manager and a tedious wait ensued. When the burley executive arrived he was surly and aggressive and James could barely contain his rage.

"What is the point of padlocking a coded gate?"

"To stop people who don't use our facilities from getting free parking. Their friends give them our code."

"That's stupid, it penalises everybody and we're regular paying customers; just open the bloody gate!"

One glance at James's face convinced the bigger man. With disgruntled muttering the padlock was removed. Once through the security fence James went to the manager's BMW and seeing keys in the ignition, hurled them far into some scrubby bushes beyond the fence. The student looked impressed and uneasy.

"What if he complains?"

James' heart was still hammering with anger but he fought it down and chuckled.

"Who can he complain to about mislaying his car-keys?"

On the journey home his mind was busy with plans and possibilities and he went straight to the fridge for a beer. Loretta put out a late supper of pate, garlic-bread and salad on the kitchen table. He told her about his recent experiences as they ate.

"There you are James, another perfect example of how much better we could do things with a flying school at Burscough."

He wiped his mouth and finished chewing.

"You're right. Learning to fly should be fun and that tedious experience at John Lennon airport tonight wasn't. Flying students and local private pilots operating small GA aircraft deserve a civilized friendly base to operate from with a supportive club atmosphere. So let's look into the Burscough deal a bit further."

Loretta put her wine glass down, eyes shining.

"I think that's a really good decision James and I'm sure Dennis will be pleased."

"Who said anything about Dennis? The whole idea is to be free of idiots like him and that stuck-up base manager at Liverpool."

Loretta shook her head in disbelief.

"Just joking; we probably will need his financial input unfortunately and someone will have to be Chief Flying Officer. I hate all that stuff but Dennis will probably revel in the role."

"But we're going to do it?"

"Oh yes madam, we're going to do it!"

Loretta whooped and got up to hug him.

"What about the money, how are we going to finance it?"

"God will send us some."

Buzzing with excitement Loretta went upstairs to shower and the phone rang. He picked it up.

"James Hacking, good evening."

"Rodriguez Da Silva here James. I was in the Support Unit with you back in Rhodesia and we met up once or twice in Angola."

"I remember Rod. What's up?"

"This phone encrypts so we're secure. Denzil Harcourt went into Ras Mohdir Field to extract some Gaddafi relatives and his wings got zapped by a mortar on arrival. He needs help."

A silence followed.

"Jesus. I thought there was a no-fly zone in place."

"There is: Security Council Resolution 1973. But Denzil's mercy-flight had Allied sanction with a discrete squawk and you'd get the same no-shoot-down status. The Resolution is specifically to protect civilians and though Denzil is being paid by the regime it is a humanitarian flight; one that most humans weren't stupid enough to try, I may add. Anyway, you'd just have to worry about the local nasties that bagged Den's aircraft, not the NATO forces."

"How nasty are they? What's the situation on the ground?"

James was seated at his computer and began to bring up internet explorer windows as he listened.

"Denzil's OK. No wounded but the runway is blocked. Seems the show is nearly over for Gaddafi loyalist troops. Tripoli fell in early August and Big G regrouped on his home town Sirte, declaring it the new Libyan capital but they've already been pushed out and are falling back on small towns in the Gulf of Sirte. There's a pocket of loyalists holed up at Ras Mohdir port, protecting regime relatives who might be vulnerable to reprisals, mostly old men, women and kids. Money to get them out was apparently no object. One of Denzil's CIA pals from Angolan days tipped Den off and he bit. I gather you were based at Ras in another life?"

"I was, but I've got nothing to get in there with, especially at short notice. Doubt if I could rent anything suitable either! If the runway is out, they're buggered for airborne extraction anyway."

"Not necessarily; you've got time on Otter seaplanes right? Well Denzil was paid really large for this by Big G's family so funds aren't a problem. I've managed to rent a float-equipped Twin Otter in Malta with a long-range tank; virtually had to purchase it actually, the owner was very twitchy. Two million US deposit he stung us but I didn't have time to shop around. Anyway, I took the liberty of booking you on a Manchester to Valletta flight at 0700 hours tomorrow morning; check-in just needs your passport. Does 'lining up on Berth 5 for a straight in to the lee of the marina at slack water' make any sense?"

"Well I logged about a thousand hours on twin Otters many years ago, for a float operation in the Seychelles and I've kept my rating. Berth 5 is the closest inshore Single-Point Mooring Buoy for tankers at Ras Mohdir Marine terminal; it'll make a good VRP for sure. The marine basin would also make a good defensive perimeter if the rebels are pressing hard. What series is this Otter?"

"1978 DHC-6-300S, the most powerful one before the 400 series came out recently, with enhanced STOL performance kits apparently."

James clicked his mouse on Navbox proplan.

"Good, they only ever built six of those but I know the type. With a 2500 pound payload and the extra tank it'll give me 1300 kilometres, and the round trip is about 1350 according to my flight-plan software with no viable alternative, friendly or otherwise. Tell the guy you rented it from to chuck the passenger seats out if it has any."

"Can't you land on the Med if necessary?"

"Well possibly but not just anywhere. The Med has big swells, as I know to my cost; not really suitable as a fuel planning option!"

"So you'll do it?"

"Roger. From memory the cruise is about 170 knots, so flight-time will be just over two hours each way. They need to work that back from slack water and hope it's in daylight. About how many packs does Denzil envisage?"

"Near capacity. He has a co-pilot and there are two Merc contractors riding shotgun on the Gadaffi relatives, so eighteen or nineteen in all but several are kids."

"Hmmm. You got comms with Denzil?"

"Yes. He has a sat phone but only listens out for five minutes on the hour every hour to conserve batteries; he wasn't expecting to be there long!"

"OK, I'll need to speak to him when I get to Malta. Where are you?"

"Djerba Island in Tunisia, ostensibly on holiday but I'm back-up for Denzil. There's a Tuninter flight to Malta I can catch if you want me along."

"Might as well be there; we can decide after a full weight, balance and endurance calc."

"OK, I'm on it. Denzil will see you right for this James, he told me to say that."

"I'm not doing it for money Rod, somebody's got to save the old fool from himself and at least I'm used to it. Text your cell-phone number and I'll see you there."

"Okay. Tot siens"

James put down the receiver muttering softly and his heart was hammering. This was a challenge and though he was genuinely doing it out of friendship, there was a good chance of a considerable bung if they all made it out alive.

"What was that about James?" asked Loretta, padding through from the kitchen in her dressing-gown with a carafe of coffee.

"I just accepted an unexpected flying charter."

He didn't enlarge, knowing she'd go ballistic if told the truth. She put down the coffee with an ominous thump.

"It's very inopportune and actually downright selfish. Just when we decide to turn life around by purchasing Burscough Airfield, you decide to swan off into the blue. We'll need to act fast and Dennis needs to be told. And you promised we'd have a couple of days off together in the Lake District! How long is the charter for?"

"Just a few days."

"What kind of aircraft and where's it based?"

"An Otter floatplane in Malta; they've arranged a ticket for me from Manchester and I need to check in by 0600 at the latest for an 0700 departure, which means we'll have to get up at the ungodly hour of 0500. Good thing we're truck drivers and used to it. Better get my backside in gear!"

"Sounds nice apart from the disgustingly early start! I haven't been to Malta, can't I come?"

"Not this time. You need to tell Dennis and arrange a couple of Agency drivers to keep things ticking over while you two concentrate on the airfield. Offer Paul at DPS a bung to look after things for us; he's done it before when we went on holiday. You've got my power of attorney so you can sign anything necessary until I get back."

"This isn't fair!"

"Life seldom is but we need money. Change is always stressful and you instigated the change. We can have a jolly to Malta when the new venture is up and running."

"I'm getting really sick of broken promises!"

"I told you God would send us some money, he's just been quicker than expected. I didn't arrange this just to piss you off."

"Perhaps not but you're doing a very good job anyway!"

"Why turn a job down when we're scraping for money to make this work? I'm sorry things are so hectic but God helps those who help themselves." His fingers were rattling on the computer keyboard.

"Shut up about God you idiot, blasphemy isn't funny and it's tempting fate."

With difficulty he tore his eyes away from the computer screen, got up and tried to give her a hug. She avoided it, slopped coffee into a mug for him and stalked out.

-xxx-

CHAPTER THREE
SUNDAY
Johannesburg

On Sunday morning Jemima was at Lanseria airport bright and early to do pre-flight checks on the Beechjet, dressed in her crisp captain's uniform; Theo's usual late arrival irritated her. The jet was standing on the apron; she hurried through the external "A" checks, redid her calculations and requested additional fuel. She was supervising the fuel loader when an expensive limousine glided to a halt alongside. Distracted and assuming them to be Theo's party of buyers she swore under her breath and went to welcome them on his behalf which she didn't consider to be part of her duties. She left the fuel loader to it and so didn't notice that the "Prist" anti-fuel-icing additive pump wasn't running. The Beechjet had no fuel heater so the additive was vital to prevent fuel-icing in the very low temperatures at high altitudes.

The uniformed chauffer opened a rear door and a handsome middle-aged black man in an expensive suit alighted, accompanied by what looked like two bodyguards. The arrogant middle-aged black man had a discomfortingly direct, insolent gaze which she suddenly realised was partly caused by having one false eye. It was very difficult to detect because it moved naturally in the socket but lacked the glitter and sheen of its genuine companion. She began making excuses for Theo but he cut her off brusquely.

"Where is Bustamante?"

"I was just explaining...."

"I don't care about that, he knows I am on a tight schedule. Get him here immediately! You can use a telephone I assume?"

"I'm the pilot, not his secretary. Get him yourself. You can use a telephone I assume?"

A look of pure fury contorted the man's features and despite her anger Jemima felt an internal shiver of apprehension. She had never known anyone capable of such an air of menace; it was as though he were surrounded by a dark cloud. As they faced off a gleaming Aston Martin swept onto the apron and parked by the hanger. Sandro Marais stepped lithely out.

"Morning all" he said cheerfully. "Howzit Jemima, we meet again! I see you've met Silas Lembede my business partner. Just had a call from Theo Bustamante Silas, he's running a few minutes late but says we'll make it up in the air. Theo just told me you'd be our pilot Jemima. Cool!"

He was very handsome, neat and dapper as a new pin and was perusing Jemima with undisguised admiration. Her cell rang. It was Piet Schuman of National Air-Carriers.

"Hi Sexy legs, Listen, we're a pilot down. Can you do a gold run from Welkom in the Twin Otter for us tomorrow? It's not until the afternoon and we'll pay top dollar."

Jemima havered. The state her finances were in, every rand was useful.

"Sorry Piet, we're starting a big job for a new client and I need to be there."

"No probs, I always call the best first Jem and I won't hold it against you, talk soon."

"Not more work?" asked Sandro.

"Yeah, Piet Schuman wanted me to fly a shipment of gold bullion from Welkom tomorrow but I can't…" Silas Lembede stood nearby with hooded eyes, plainly listening, and she was being indiscreet. Blushing slightly at Marais' overt ogling and disquieted by Lembede's glowering presence she used Theo's arrival to make a withdrawal, retreating to the cockpit. Lanseria was if anything even busier at weekends and once on the taxiway there were several small aircraft queuing at the threshold for take-off so she pulled rank to avoid antagonising Lembede further.

"Tower this is November two one eight four Romeo, Beechjet outward bound for Botswana. I'm burning fuel I can't afford to lose in this queue, Can you help?"

"Roger eight four Romeo, taxi up front."

Jemima rolled the jet past the smaller aircraft and halted. A Cessna 206 accelerated away and became airborne.

"Eight four Romeo, clear take-off" said the tower and Jemima turned onto the runway and advanced the throttles fully. Once airborne she cleaned the jet up and was given frequency change to Oliver Tambo International Approach, Johannesburg's largest airport, formerly known as Jan Smuts International. She requested permission to fly low on visual flight rules until past Hartebeestport Dam.

"Might as well give your businessmen something to look at Theo, they won't see much when we climb to altitude."

She relinquished control formally but kept an eye on both him and the instruments. Theo held a private licence but was a nervous, jerky pilot in spite of a respectable number of hours in his log-book. The jet was restricted to 260 knots at low altitude and Theo's lack of sensitivity frequently caused him to go ever speed. They flew across the bright blue waters of the dam, already dotted with the sails and powerboat wakes of weekenders, and climbed out north over a ridge of the Magaliesberg hills which fringe the lake. A hang-glider recently airborne was cruising thermals near the cable-car station. The lake and hills were calm and peaceful in the early sun. Theo went aft to the main cabin and handed round coffee, giving Sandro an opportunity to slip into the co-pilot's seat.

"Well, what do you think of my business partner Jemima?"

She pulled a face.

"Triple-A creep! An Arrogant African Arsehole; apart from that I quite like him."

He laughed.

"Yeah, right, he definitely failed charm-school and this is actually one of his better days. So this is your office hey?"

He cast a glance at the tanned bare legs below her rucked-up blue skirt.

"Yup. On days like this I have the best job in the world."

He asked a barrage of flying questions, interspersed with personal ones and Jemima replied animatedly, happy to show off her expertise and let him try the controls.

"So what are you guys coming up to Botswana for?"

"Bustamante Enterprises are selling this Thune farm with a gold mine on it and we're interested, if the price is right."

"What in mainly, the farm or the mine?"

"Both. For different reasons."

He didn't elaborate.

"And do you know about farming and gold mining?" she persisted in a teasing voice.

"Let's just say I know about opportunities and Lembede values my judgement. He also likes my financial input; it limits his own liability and I don't ask questions like Banks. We buy in any expertise we need."

Sandro changed the subject back to aviation again, leaving her curiosity about the means to his apparent wealth unsatisfied. Selibe-Phikwe was only forty minutes flying time in the jet. The rich green Afrikaans farms at Rustenburg west of Pretoria dropped behind, the ground becoming browner and more featureless as they climbed to 36000 feet over Botswana. Scattered clouds dappled the earth with their shadows. Let-down began almost immediately above the confluence of the Limpopo and Mokolo rivers. The flight passed quickly as they chatted, both flirting modestly until Theo reclaimed his cockpit seat. Jemima found she was increasingly drawn to Sandro; there was definitely the prospect of new romance and the thought buoyed her up. Visibility was almost infinite in the dry air and after landing they all walked across the hot apron past the control tower and entered a large room with a customs and immigration counter. There was a very African air of nothing much happening and it was warm and silent except for the peeved buzz of a fly's wing against a window. A poster advising tariffs on Rhodesia Railways adorned the wall though that country had become Zimbabwe and Independent over twenty-five years previously.

Theo was making stilted conversation and glancing testily at his watch. He slapped his briefcase down on the counter with an exasperated sigh and there was a loud answering "CLONK" as the chief immigration officer lurched convulsively awake from his slumbers on the shelf below, banging his head with enough force to disturb dust on the desk-blotter. The passengers stifled smiles as Mr Madzimbamuto climbed out and became erect, massaging the wounded portion. He was a short man smelling strongly of sour African maize beer, with an oblate head the shape of a rugby ball lying on its side and muddy-coloured bloodshot eyes. Attired in a grubby check shirt, corduroy trousers and sandals made of car tyre, he stood with his hands on the counter blinking slowly at them like a sleepy but not unfriendly toad, lips open in a slight smile.

"Ah, Gift!" said Theo heartily, "Nice to see you again. These ladies and gentlemen have come to visit the Mine at Thune. They're very excited to be in Botswana."

Gift continued to blink and gaze wordlessly, in the manner of an acute headache sufferer. A thin bony woman appeared through a door and stood at Gift's side. She was clad in a plain brown dress of material so thin that it looked like a flour sack. She held out her hand silently for the passports and Theo continued to make jollying-along chatter, apparently unconcerned with the total lack of response. The woman took her time leafing through the documents, giving away her function as assistant immigration Officer. Theo pulled a roll of small-denomination Pula bank-notes from his pocket. He divided it roughly and placed it in two piles on the counter midway between the blinker and the his 2 i/c who both appeared at first not to have noticed, but after about thirty seconds two black hands crept like apprehensive lizards across the counter, folded gently over the notes and withdrew again. There was a dreamlike feeling to the whole affair, as if the officials were moving not in air but a movement-impeding liquid. Theo produced some already-completed customs and immigration forms and laid them before the blinker, who slowly dropped his eyes to them, being careful of the ache in his head.

"Nothing to declare Gift, just a quick trip in and out." said Theo. "All we need is a stamp."

He pointed to the box on the forms requiring stamping and the stamp standing a few inches from Mr Madzimbamuto's hand. He began to move his own fist back and forth with a light thumping noise, from near the stamp to the forms, in a pantomime of the action which he wished to take place. She'd seen it before but Jemima watched fascinated as Gift's hand twitched, then seized the stamp, banged it in the ink, banged it on a form, and again, and then again as Theo deftly manoeuvred the customs forms to facilitate the process. Getting the Black officialdom of Third World African countries to do what he required was something Theo really excelled at; his civil engineering and business degrees weighed lightly against that skill in achieving corporate aims. Bustamante Enterprises had to obtain grants, secure tenders and gain licences to operate in Botswana and it was Theo who oiled the wheels, always polite, calm and outwardly patient but knowing just when to coax and when to kick. He deftly separated the carbon copies from the originals, folded them and pocketed them, leaving the originals neatly on the counter. The woman held all six passports limply in one hand whilst the forefinger of the other dealt with an irritation of the nose.

"Thank you Cassandra" said Theo and slid them gently from her grasp. He picked Gift's limp hand up off the counter and gave it a friendly shake.

"We'll be back later on our way to Johannesburg."

Walking out, Jemima felt as if she had been through a time-warp but in reality the whole process had only taken twenty minutes. She squinted against the strong rays bouncing off whitewashed walls, against which several struggling bougainvillea plants with scarlet flowers made a brave show of colour.

"You're very good with them Theo, how come they don't infuriate you?"

"They're just nice, ordinary Motswana people who do things at a different pace to us. We're here to build roads, bridges and dig mines.

Working with officialdom is just one of the problems of production which have to be overcome. Old Madzimbamuto is OK but it's the weekend so he's been at the beer."

Jemima snorted. "You can stare into his eyes and see straight out his bum."

She held the jet low on a reduced power setting of seventy percent for the fifteen minute south-east flight from Selibe-Phikwe to Thune Mine, situated just a few hundred yards from the Limpopo River which marked Botswana's eastern border with South Africa. The pitted three thousand foot bitumen runway at the mine was short for the jet, even with a reduced fuel load, but she greased the heavy aircraft onto the threshold yards from the end and the landing gear began to rumble with scarcely a bump.

"Dump the lift" she said tersely to Theo who leaned forward and pulled a lever on the console. Spoilers appeared on the leading edges of the wings and the aircraft settled more heavily onto its landing gear and as reverse thrust was deployed it slowed rapidly. When the jet was completely stationary Jemima began to taxi, keeping well away from the crumbling edges of the bitumen. She opened the hatch and a plump man in khakis standing beside a white Toyota minibus waved.

D'you want to come along Jemima?" asked Theo hopefully.

"No thanks. I've brought a pile of business paperwork to plough through; balance sheets, cash-flow forecasts and other scintillating reading. Try not to be late getting back: sitting about on hot runways isn't my favorite pastime."

Lembede descended from the plane and looked around curiously. This was the place to which his forces had followed Elias Mpofu so many years ago, to eliminate him as an election rival. The property was very close to the Zimbabwe border and would be ideal if everything else matched his requirements. The minibus left on an inspection tour and Jemima spent the time working except for a walk into thorn scrub skirting the strip to urinate. She had a wander about, poking at termite nests with a stick and listening to the banshee yelling of the cicadas in the bush. It was very hot and she sweated, leaving traces of dry salt on her bronze skin. Returning to the jet she went over the fuel figures again. She had only been able to use 3000 pounds of the Beech's 4800 capacity because of the short Thune Mine airstrip. At 30 degrees centigrade and three thousand feet altitude, and with six aboard, the Beech would need every foot of runway available.

Sunday 0600 Manchester Airport, UK

At the Manchester airport drop-off point Loretta pulled her Jaguar coupe over and accepted James's farewell kiss grudgingly, still miffed, then roared away with her nose in the air and stopped at the airport BP garage to fill up. With fuel hissing into the tank she typed a text message. A booming loudspeaker-voice objected to her using her phone near the pumps. She glared at the watching attendant in the kiosk and gave him two fingers before turning her back. Her phone rang almost immediately.

"Loretta you gorgeous woman, what are you doing up at this time of day? I'm pining for you. Let's get together without your tame guerrilla."

"That's why I texted. I didn't really expect a reply so early on a Sunday morning Dennis but I've just dropped James at Manchester Airport. He'll be away for a few days on a flying job, but we're definitely interested in the Burscough Airfield project. That's if you still are."

"Hallelujah, of course I am, that's terrific news! I'll be back home from Heathrow by ten, I flew the red-eye shuttle down and that's me done for the day. Let's meet at my place in Wilmslow and get the planning started, I'll text the postcode and your GPS will find it easy enough."

"OK, I'll get an early breakfast somewhere and go to the Trafford centre for an hour."

"Fine; see you soon, this is very exciting!"

The traffic at that hour was light and Loretta cruised round the M60 in her Jag and had a relaxed breakfast at the Brewers Fayre Pub attached to the Premier Inn at Trafford Park. Stores in the huge shopping centre were just beginning to open and she bought some tight white pedal-pushers, a very sexy blouse and expensive designer sandals that all showed off her figure and tan, putting them on in the store changing room. On an impulse she popped into a manicurist and had her finger and toe-nails freshly lacquered too.

"Wow!" said Dennis at his bachelor pad an hour later, giving her a big hug, inhaling her perfume deeply. "You look and smell so sexy and fresh!" Turning her to examine every angle he managed to brush her boobs and bottom intimately.

"Those feet! I could eat those feet!" He knelt and slipped off her sandals to caress them, running his fingers over the lacquered toe-nails, pretending to bite them. Loretta shivered in delight and laughed.

"Don't be so silly Dennis!"

-xxx-

In Malta the sun beat down out of a clear sky and the sea sparkled. James revelled in the heat and fine weather. Rod and Captain Christopher Fiorentino who owned the Twin Otter met him off the flight and they immediately flew some circuits, to get James used to the Twin Otter and floats again. Rod sat in the back. All went well until a sail-boat strayed into their touch-down area. When James applied power nothing appeared to happen at first and they were uncomfortably close when the engines finally delivered enough for a go-round, nearly blowing the yacht flat as a result.

"Hope they were too busy to see the registration, you can expect that skipper to lodge a complaint" chuckled Christopher. "It was a good practical lesson though; these Pratt & Whitney engines have a tendency to spool down to idle during descent so power isn't quickly available to the propeller. If you need some for reverse thrust after landing or to go around on a missed approach, there will be lag, and you will shit yourself when nothing happens! For STOL approach procedures I recommend coming in low with large flap extensions so you can carry more power and keep them spooled up for instant thrust."

"Gotcha, thanks Chris. I guess the large flap extensions will make control harder in windy conditions though."

"Certainly, but ideally you will be landing into the wind anyway."

Afterwards the Maltese helped James with a flight-plan using all 1000 pounds available in the right-central mounted auxiliary tank; the figures ruled out Rod going along and after topping off the tanks they went for a meal. The other two had a few beers but James stuck to 'water with gas.'

"Unhealthy! You've got way too much gas already" remarked Rod as his cell rang and he looked at the screen.

"Tis himself." He passed it to James.

"Greetings, oh fucking idiot. How is it in the frying pan?"

Denzil laughed.

"Warm and dry; had a glass or two of flash last night that tasted like petrol but went down smooth enough. How's it looking there?"

"All set to go. Got a time for slack water?"

"1700 hours. The tides don't seem to move that much here anyway."

"I remember the swell on the bar getting pretty big at times. Better to aim for slack. What about hostiles?"

"Just a small outfit that seems content with passive containment, probably waiting for reinforcements when they get less busy; the protection force we're with seem to know their stuff. The man in charge is an American defence contractor you might know, Lance McDonald, works for Conflict Logistic Solutions."

"I've heard of the Company but not him. How are the rest of the packs shaping up?"

"Well CLS are big in Afghanistan and Iraq as well as Libya and McDonald seems competent. The packs are worried but calm."

"Okay. Well shout if anything kicks off. I'll plan to lift off at 1500 hours to be with you at 1700."

"Roger, thanks. Let's hope that discreet squawk of yours works or we won't be seeing you at all; there are Allied fast-movers rumbling up above all the time. It's still a pretty vicious war on the ground here."

"Thanks for the reminder. Anything else?"

"What about weather?"

"They're giving it CAVOK for the whole region at present."

"Hooray. I can get QFE from the Oilfield control room on a radio so you'll have a reasonably accurate altimeter setting on approach; these seas are beautifully clear but difficult to judge height over."

"Good, copied. Okay then; hasta later."

"Buy you a beer in Valletta."

"Already there and I've got one."

"Fuck off then."

"You too."

Rod and Chris had another Hopleaf each and then drove James to the Marina.

-xxx-

Botswana

By the time Theo returned an hour later than promised Jemima had drunk every available drop of liquid and was still thirsty. As her passengers trudged across from the bus a huge Kudu bull walked out of the bush behind them. She snapped a picture on her camera phone of the jet, the passengers, the antelope and the empty African bush. Theo was ahead looking large rumpled uncomfortable and grumpy, with dark sweat-stains at armpit and crotch. She called out, pointing at the Kudu. Everyone turned and Theo took a digital camera from his pocket, firing some shots. When Lembede noticed, he said something to his bodyguards who approached Theo and snatched the camera. He remonstrated and an almost comical struggle began for all three were big men. Sandro walked over to the melee, removed his dark glasses and took the camera from Malinga, then motioned the bodyguards away.

"Sorry about that Theo, Mr. Lembede is a bit sensitive about publicity. I'll just erase the most recent shots when we're on board and give you the camera back."

Furious, Theo stalked over to the jet and boarded. Jemima followed the passengers into the aircraft, pulling up the stairs and securing the hatch. He was sitting in the co-pilots seat.

"Fucking pricks, if I wasn't trying to do business I'd beat the shit out of the whole damn lot of them!"

"Absolutely, that was bang out of order. Listen Theo" she said while the engines spooled up and the hot sun beat through the windscreen on them. "I'd planned to take on fuel in Selibe, but we're late now. If we do Lembede will definitely miss the Amsterdam flight."

Theo massaged his temples.

"Well we have to clear customs and immigration somewhere in Botswana. Leave the engines running to speed things up."

"That's an option but it will cut our fuel reserve to fifteen minutes. You'd have to work magic to get us in and out of border-control that quick."

Theo grunted and stared at his watch.

"This arsehole is really unpredictable. He signed the deal, but any glitch could make him rescind it. Let's take a chance, I can't wait to see the back of him."

Jemima nodded and slowly applied power to get the aircraft rolling. Seventeen minutes later they were on the ground again at Selibe-Phikwe. The high-pitched shriek of the idling engines entered the cabin with piercing effect when Theo unlocked the hatch and lowered the steps. What with the sun-glare beating through the Perspex into her eyes, the noise and the sickening paraffin smell of jet-fuel, Jemima could feel a headache beginning and massaged her eyes with the heels of her hands. She badly needed some liquid. Theo had her passport and Jemima crossed fingers that all would go well as he followed the passengers into the airport buildings. Her back ached and she looked at her watch frequently; after ten minutes a knot of tension began to build in her stomach.

"Come on, Come ON" she breathed and banged the dashboard with the heel of her fist. She suddenly couldn't bear the thought of sitting on the ground any longer in the baking afternoon sun while Theo made inane small-talk with Gift Madzimbamuto. She walked back along the cabin to stretch her legs and noticed a bulge in one of the seat pockets where the sick bags were stored. Inside was a fairly large grubby cloth bag and when Jemima opened the drawstring she saw that it was full of rather muddy little rocks. She shrugged and put it back, assuming one of the passengers had taken samples from the mine to analyse.

Inside the building Gift was being disdainfully observed by his boss Mr. Jesus Phutimaluti. He was a sharp-faced querulous individual, scrutinizing everything in a very irritating way. Gift quickly dealt with all the clearance papers while Cassandra stamped the passports. She handed them back to Theo but Mr. Jesus elbowed his underlings rudely aside.

"Why have the airplane's engines not stopped?" he demanded and listened to Theo's necessarily complicated explanation, giving no indication whether he understood a word or not. He re-examined the passports, flicking through them comparing photographs to faces.

"Six passports, only five people; where is this other woman?'

"Miss Visser is the pilot. She is looking after the airplane." explained Theo.

"This is suspicious; I must see all persons on the manifest. Also I will search the jet."

"We know these people very well boss" said Gift anxiously. "They always coming through here, good business people for Botswana, never make any mischief."

Mr. Jesus sniffed disdainfully.

"Exactly, and I have observed that you are too friendly with them. Maybe they are smuggling something under your very nose. There is a gold mine at Thune."

Theo's heart sank but he answered with a smile.

"Of course we're not smuggling anything my dear fellow but you're welcome to check. Follow me."

Jemima glanced at her watch again; twelve minutes. She cursed and looked up, sighing with relief as Theo appeared but the relief was short-lived; behind him were Gift, Cassandra and an officious looking man in a crisp uniform. Jemima stayed seated and listened to the clumping noises of ascent from the hatch behind.

"These gentlemen need to search the jet Jemima" announced Theo, rolling his eyes at her. "Might as well cut the engines, this might take a while."

"It won't" said Lembede, "Leave the engines running, I must make that connection."

Phutimaluti looked into the cockpit then strutted aft, clearly without much idea where to begin searching. Lembede's cold eyes followed his every move. The official opened and rummaged in lockers and the pockets behind seats, poking and prodding ineffectually until he found what looked like a child's toy-box in an overhead locker above the seat with the bag of rocks. Lembede tensed. Phutimaluti took down the battered yellow box and examined the contents. Inside were a few playthings; a metal pistol and a hand-grenade made of chocolate, covered in metallic-looking foil; a spark of triumph flared in his eyes.

"What are these?" he asked. "You didn't declare any arms on the Customs form."

Theo cast his eyes heavenward but answered calmly.

"They're not real weapons, just some toys left up there by mistake."

Phutimaluti stood looking at them sternly.

"So you say but I will need to investigate further; tell the pilot to turn off the engines!"

"Malinga!" grunted Lembede and his Lieutenant strode up the aisle drawing a very large semi-automatic handgun which he shoved roughly into Phutimaluti's mouth.

"This is so you will know the difference between a real gun and a toy one" he snarled.

"Silas, let me handle it!" shouted Sandro Marais but Lembede followed and picked up the chocolate hand-grenade. Malinga shook the immigration official by the neck like a small dog, grinding the gun-muzzle into his ear while his boss stuffed the egg, silver foil and all, brutally into Phutimaluti's mouth.

"Can you eat hand grenades you bloody fool? Never delay me in this manner again or you will be sorry!"

He leant closer to the official and whispered briefly in his ear. Phutimaluti went as ashen as an African is able and nodded frantically, then scurried down the aisle.

"You are free to go" he called as he shot out of the door, spitting bloody phlegm from his damaged gums. Jemima noticed Lembede casually slip his hand into the seat pouch and pocket the bag of rocks before sitting down. She moved up the aisle slightly.

"I intend to make a report about that unjustified assault!" His insolent eyes looked directly into hers.

"You heard the man, we are free to go. Do your job, I've got a connection to catch!"

Sandro squeezed her arm warningly and pushed past, speaking in a low intense voice to Lembede. They were obviously arguing as she went back onto the flight deck.

"We've wasted enough time and fuel Jem" said Theo. "Let's just get the hell out of here while we still can."

Her hands flew over the controls, taxiing out fast, feeling shaken by the swiftness and viciousness of the incident as Theo obviously was too. Dehydration was making her headache worse and she felt shaky from low blood-sugar. She stuffed a Mars bar from the flight bag into her mouth and felt better but it made her thirstier too. She ran a hand through her sweaty hair.

"Jesus I'm parched, I badly need something to drink Theo."

"Yeah, sorry; there's nothing but beer, spirits and cold coffee left in the galley so I got you a tin of coke from a machine in the terminal."

He fished it from his coat pocket, snapped the pull-ring and passed it over. She gulped at the cold liquid desperately, panted and sighed.

"God thank you so much Theo" she smiled. "Here, you have some."

"No, you need it more than me."

The rain radar showed green patches of thunder clouds ahead and soon Jemima could see them rising up from the horizon like a dark grey and black wall. She went to full power intending to climb over them but at forty thousand feet and top of descent had to make a decision since they couldn't clear the front in time and descend. As they flew closer to Johannesburg on the letdown to Lanseria, fissures between the lightning-riven cliffs of dark cloud became apparent. Making a terse turbulence announcement she guided the jet on, deviating left and right of her heading as they cruised downward through great canyons between the clouds. Splatters of rain and hail drummed periodically on the aircraft skin like flung gravel, and they flew every now and then through a cathedral of fan-like sunrays making moving rainbows of the water droplets. Gusts made the airframe shudder and ice developed on the flexing wings. She flicked on the external de-icers, unaware of another danger that was waiting to pounce due to the low temperatures. The "Prist" anti-icing concentration in the fuel was too low and consequently water in the fuel lines was not all being held in suspension. Small accretions of ice began to build in filters and at pipe bends.

Twenty minutes out Jemima contacted Oliver Tambo International approach and was allocated a slot in the stack of aircraft flying holding patterns over the beacon at Hartebeestport dam. OTI controlled all aircraft above eight thousand feet in Johannesburg's airspace; they advised that due to an earlier runway-closing incident at Lanseria there were dozens of aircraft holding for that destination. There was no instrument landing system at Lanseria either and Jemima realized the laborious process of them all letting down a thousand feet at a time was going to be complicated by poor visibility in the rain and cloud. Her headache felt worse and her concentration was slipping. She scribbled calculations on her kneepad, trying to work out exactly how much fuel remained and translate it into flying time available before the engines sucked air. She contacted Approach again.

"This is Beechjet November eight four Romeo. Any indication what sort of delay we're looking at for Lanseria?"

"Eight four Romeo, roger, I estimate thirty minutes but it could be longer."

Jemima's heart sank; she had been hustled into a serious situation.

"We're in a stack Theo without much fuel. Go tell Lembede he will definitely miss his connection if I hold for Lanseria because of the road transfer time. If I divert to Oliver Tambo it will depend how busy they are and where they slot me in the sequence." "OK but I might come back minus a few teeth; he doesn't seem partial to bad news."

"The news will be even worse if we run out of fuel; it's not my fault you took so long on your damned inspection!"

She took a deep breath. Oliver Tambo got busier in the evening as big long-haul aircraft timed arrivals and departures for the denser cooler air. There was the sound of a scuffle as Lembede shouldered roughly past Theo and pointed at her.

"It is bad enough that I will have to travel without my baggage and business computer which is at Lanseria, but if your incompetence makes me miss that International flight from Oliver Tambo there will be hell to pay. Do whatever it takes; declare an emergency if necessary to get priority landing!" He glared at Jemima and went back into the cabin.

"Can you do that Jem?" asked Theo worriedly.

"No! Professionally it would make me look terrible, I would have to explain our low-fuel state and the Civil Aviation Authority might get involved." She thumbed her mike.

"Approach this is November eight four Romeo requesting diversion to Oliver Tambo for an ILS." They moved one place down the stack and sank into blanket cloud. Jemima switched over to a full instrument scan and redid her calculations yet again, waiting impatiently for the diversion to be approved.

"Eight four Romeo this is Oliver Tambo International Approach. Diversion approved. Squawk 4161, ident, and steer one three zero for vectors onto ILS. Descend flight level 145 on QNH 1013."

"Jesus, at last" muttered Jemima through gritted teeth.

-xxx-

The afternoon was calm and beautiful. At the seaplane marina in Malta, James tapped a quick text message to Loretta and after a rapid pre-flight, lifted off. His spirits rose with the airplane and the warm sun beating into the cockpit. He set a course of 140 degrees and quickly worked out that a south-westerly breeze was pushing him off. He adjusted to 145, glancing at the GPS, compass and DI regularly. As the Otter crossed into Libyan territorial waters he spotted two dots far above. One stayed up but the other fell down the sky like a falcon, growing large with unbelievable rapidity. The French jet didn't attack which presumably meant his Allied squawk code was good. The fighter pulled a few sexy manoeuvres to show off and check him out before the frog pilot drew abreast, circled a finger near his forehead to indicate insanity and launched himself into the heavens again on afterburners.

"Smart-arse" said James enviously.

He kept the Otter out of sight from land until he was east-abeam Ras Mohdir then turned toward the Libyan coast. The camp mosque minaret rose above the horizon. By squinting against glare off the sea he could also make out dark specks which were the single-point mooring buoys; there were no ships loading. Shortly afterwards the port harbour buildings became visible. James checked the VHF frequency Rod had given him and thumbed the mike.

"Inbound. Estimate berth 5 in two minutes. Go with information."

"Roger, QFE 1013, wind 300 at 12 knots, slight swell from same bearing."

That was Denzil all-right, the Manc accent still detectable after forty years in Africa. James rubbed his chin with the mike, looking ahead.

He could see the airfield inland with Denzil's damaged Otter still blocking it. There was a column of military and civilian vehicles crawling slowly down the road from the main camp towards the sea, including a pickup with a recoilless rifle mounted in the back. A long curved mole stretched east into the sea protecting the marine-basin from the prevalent north-west wind and sea. James banked left over the big mooring buoy, setting the altimeter to 1013 which then showed steady at 1000 feet. He set the aircraft up for landing as Chris had advised.

"Joining right-base over Berth five; heading 210 to land final 300."

"Roger we have you visual; Seaman's launch dispersing fuel-oil on surface now."

The oil probably wasn't necessary given the calm conditions but he was rusty on floats; the fuel would smooth the water slightly and reduce any chop. The downside was that it could potentially be ignited.

"Greenpeace won't like that!" he transmitted. "Be advised, vehicles approaching along shore road, distance approx one mile."

"Copied the visitors. We've been getting sporadic probing fire. You look high and hot from here."

"Any fuel available?"

"Negative our kid, so don't waste any on a go-round, you'd be a sitting duck too."

James turned final. Leaving power on as Chris had suggested was making it difficult to slow the Otter down. He chose his aiming point for touchdown, just seaward of the swimming-raft moored offshore of the expats-club. Memories flooded back of swimming to it and sunbathing years previously. Things began to happen fast. Tracer suddenly flew above the cockpit and he realised Denzil was right, both speed and height had to be scrubbed off quickly. He left some power on but raised the nose, banged in more flap and initiated a sideslip all at once. Increased drag caused sink just as a rocket whooshed overhead. The floats acted like a pendulum, exaggerating control inputs and his landing degenerated into a pitching, oscillating nightmare that was quickly getting away from him. It was way too late for a missed approach and James realised with certainty that there was going to be an ugly arrival.

-xxx-
Johannesburg

An orange lamp flickered on the console and went out. Theo glanced at it and fear flowed into his eyes; the legend underneath the lamp said 'Fuel Low Warning.' They were in grey blanket cloud, visibility zero and he was completely disorientated; he would be no help to Jemima if she needed it. Her legs were shaking with tiredness on the rudders as she made a ragged turn onto the new heading, adjusting the transponder squawk as she did so and confirming "Squawking 4161 and heading one three zero. QNH 1013 descending flight level 145."

She trimmed and checked the descent speed was right. The controller periodically gave her heading, level and speed instructions to slot her into the circuit east of Johannesburg. Suddenly there was a muted bang from outside; they felt a jot and looked at each other in consternation. A warning began to warble. Theo's voice was nervous.

"What was that?"

"Don't know yet….Oh shit, look at the RPM needles! The starboard engine has flamed out. That idiot Lembede has got his Emergency now!""Oh my God no; surely we haven't run out of fuel? The other could shut down any second!"

"Shuddup please; could be fuel icing: I'm trimming for relight speed; Jesus let me get this right!"

Dropping the nose she let her speed rise. At lower warmer altitudes the ice should melt to water and be re-suspended in the fuel so it could be burnt through. She was still loathe to call an Emergency since any investigation would reveal their low-fuel state. Jemima muttered procedures to herself as they flew on, heavy raindrops bursting on the windscreen, wipers going and her eyes kept up their metronomic scan of the instruments, which had become her senses. The controller's calm voice floated over the ether onto the quiet flight-deck with brief instructions on heading and height.

"Steer zero nine zero and watch your speed please."

"Aren't you going to try and relight starboard?"

"Not yet, we're trimmed out and gliding OK on port. I want to get lower and warmer before I try."

"Steer zero six zero and report passing eight thousand feet. Reduce speed now to two hundred knots as instructed."

"November eight four Romeo, wilco."

She ignored the speed instruction again. Tension in the cockpit was extreme and Theo farted thunderously, apologizing hastily. Jemima screwed up her nose but chuckled.

"That might be a good omen for ignition. Okay, come on baby, light my fire!"

Dropping the nose yet further for speed she began the relight sequence. The starboard engine RPM began to rise just as the controller instructed her to slow down yet again and maintain separation. Their hearts were in their mouths. The starboard RPM needle jerked, rose, fell back, then rose again quickly, engine-noise becoming audible above the other which was idling in descent revs. She put in some flap and raised both engine RPM's and the nose to reduce forward speed and maintain descent rate but keep the engines warm.

"Looking good; steer zero three zero for runway zero three left and contact the Tower. Goodbye."

Jemima had the tower frequency already set up. She said goodbye, prodded the toggle switch to tower and called them.

"Good afternoon eight four Romeo: Continue" said the new controller in a thick accent.

"How far out are we?" asked Theo.

"You tell me, look at the DME!"

"Oh, right. Four miles DME."

He stared forward fearfully into the rain and whipping rags of cloud, flicking his eyes at the fuel low warning which was now glowing continuously. The controller's voice blurted into their earphones with a new urgency and Theo jerked spasmodically.

"Closing the localizer from left to right; cleared for the approach."

At the same time the veils of fleeting cloud were torn away from the nose, enveloped it again, and then they were below the cloud ceiling, the runway dead ahead. With ILS needles centred the Beechjet crossed highway R22 and sank firmly to earth, its roll-out completed before passing the terminal buildings.

"Thank God! You look exhausted Jem, will you be able to take the Beech back to Lanseria tonight?" Theo asked with concern in his voice. They were on the wrong side of town away from their cars and multiple other inconveniences but they were alive.

"Negative, I'm pretty much maxed out. Flying this thing single-operator is no damn picnic. Besides, there's no ILS at Lanseria, the weather is IMC, it's nearly dark and I need a bloody stiff drink!"

"And I'm going to buy it, you were marvellous!"

She patted his hand.

"Thanks co-pilot, you helped just being there."

Jemima felt washed out as she taxied in and shut down. In the cabin behind them Lembede passed the bag of stones to one of his bodyguards.

"Carry this for me and return it in Holland."

The minder took it without comment, his boss was not someone worth arguing with, whatever the security notices said about not accepting things to be carried on aircraft from third parties. Lembede had meant to drop them off before departure with a high-level contact to be put in the diplomatic pouch to the South African embassy in The Hague. Theo opened the cargo hatch and said a stiff farewell to Lembede, who then walked past Jemima without a word as she stood on the steps.

"Oi, you, I will be making an official report on your conduct aboard my aircraft" she called. He paused to fix her with a stare of absolute malevolence then walked on quickly towards the terminal. Sandro was still in the cabin behind her. Theo came round the wing with his briefcase and laptop, waving his phone.

"Got a cab booked Jem but I'll have to call at the office before we get that drink to fax these contracts to my lawyers."

"You know, I'm really pretty tired...."

Sandro spoke over her shoulder.

"I'll drop Jemima home Theo, I have to collect my wheels from Lanseria. We can share a taxi."

Theo's mouth dropped open comically as he looked from one to the other. He cleared his throat.

"Fine, you OK with that Jemima?"

She just wanted to get home as quickly as possible for a shower and a whisky.

"Yes, you get off Theo; I'll wrap things up here."

He hesitated.

"Okay, well I'll talk to you tomorrow then. Well done, and have a good evening."

He walked away dejectedly, slump-shouldered. She phoned for a fuel bowser and requested fifteen-hundred pounds each side from the operator rather than full tanks; she didn't want him to realise she'd almost run dry. When he'd gone she hurried to complete the tech-log and secure the Beechjet. She fell instantly asleep in the taxi and when it reached Bryanston Sandro woke her gently. "Hey dormouse, you forgot our date. If you aren't too tired there's a hot band playing at a shebeen in Hillbrow......."

She blinked sleepily and stretched.
"Isn't that area a bit dangerous?"
"You're funny; what, after all the excitement today? Don't worry, I know my way round."
"And I feel way better after that nap. What the hell, let's go. You're right, a bit more excitement won't make much difference."
"Good, I'll collect the car and be back soon."
-xxx-

Ras Mohdir

James got everything sorted out in the final instant and the Otter dropped onto the sea with a tremendous splash, partially inundating the floats. Sharp deceleration threw him against his harness but the empty aircraft bobbed up on a swell surging over the bar and carried her forward, surfing lightly.

"Whoa!" breathed James, fumbling to get reverse thrust sorted out as he raced towards the harbour wall. He managed and walled the props, kicking rudder simultaneously. The Otter's engines responded instantly. She tipped forward and slowed rapidly, great plumes of spray curling into the air. The nose swung through ninety degrees, missing moored vessels by a few feet. James cut power, then nudged the throttles back up and tested the rudders gingerly; he was a boatman now and he turned the nose left towards the slipway at the back of the basin, searching for Denzil as the Otter wallowed slightly. Thank God for Chris's training tips he thought.

"That was quite an entrance" crackled Denzil's voice over the radio. "Nice ship but I don't much care for the two-tone colour. Bright red! Very ostentatious."

Two plumes of white water rose suddenly from the basin; the visitors had started mortaring.

"You know about beggars. Where do you want me?"

"I'm on a pontoon near the east harbour wall between two launches; it's in the lee of any small-arms fire. The packs are all with me."

"Okay, got you visual."

James hadn't seen Denzil for several years but he didn't seem to have changed much, though he must be in his late sixties. He wore blue slacks and a white shirt with Captain's epaulets and his stocky frame looked strong and spry.

"How many passengers are we looking at?"

"Fifteen, plus me, Andreas my co-pilot, Lance the defence contractor and his sidekick. Nineteen in all but eight are kids, not very heavy."

"Full load though. Any sign of the protection force wanting to claim priority boarding?"

"Not really, except the interpreter who seems pretty jumpy since those first mortars landed in the harbour. I'll keep an eye on him. The other infantry are cool, pretty hard-core. They have plenty of boats to fuck off out to sea with if necessary, they're all geared up to leave after us. I dined with them last night and liked their style."

"Okay, I'll put my starboard float against you for an immediate departure."

James made a good job of the mooring approach, using a bit of port reverse thrust at the last minute to nudge up to the pontoon. Denzil grabbed the rear ladder which formed part of the float strut and held the airplane steady while James cut the turbines. He went aft and opened the door above Denzil's head, looking down at the frightened Libyans sitting in three lines on the pontoon and dredging his memory for Arabic phrases.

"Salaam Aleikum!" he called and smiles lit their anxious faces.

"Aleikum a Salaam!"

"Kaif halak?"

"Kwaais! Kaif halak inta?"

"Alhamdulillah! Marahaba!" He beckoned them forwards. "Imshe, imshe!" Several old men stood up first, throwing the tails of white blankets across their shoulders and strolling to the aircraft. No panic with these guys, they were dignity personified. One took hold of the front ladder and the others went to the rear, standing aside and offering their hands to the women and children. James shooed them forwards into the empty fuselage, indicating where to sit on the floor against the bulkhead, facing aft. The old men followed last. When they were all in James heard hysterical shouting and looked out of the rear hatch. The youngster Denzil had been worried about and three others were waving dirty Kalashnikovs at Andreas, Denzil and the two contractors. One was yelling in good English.

"We don't want to die! There is no need for extra pilots; you four will stay here and we will go. The Rebels will not harm westerners."

"Hey listen, take it easy!" said Denzil, stretching out a hand. "Get off the pontoon, get up on the dock, we don't want you near us when we board. I'm not playing! Move"

He awkwardly flicked the safety down to fully automatic and fired a short burst into the harbour. The magazine was loaded in a ratio of four ball and one tracer, which ignited the oil on the sea. Black smoke billowed, licked by yellow flame. The well-armed and slighter-built of the two contractors stepped forward and began to talk in rapid Arabic. James hadn't taken much notice of them before but it was a female voice and when he looked more closely, realised that it was a very striking woman. An impassioned argument ensued in Arabic. Andreas looked stricken and panicky, Denzil cunning and Lance angry but they all moved slightly back, eyes riveted on the weapons. James flicked a glance at the dockside but all the other Libyans were intent on the vehicle convoy beyond the basin, and there was no way of knowing what their reaction would be anyway.

"Sadiq!" called James. "Zweya! No need for panic, there is room for all. You and the co-pilot come to me up here and I will show you where to sit, I need the other captain in front to help me."

"No! I heard them talking about too much weight. You go to the cockpit. I will sit beside you. Do it now or we will shoot your friends!"

He raised the rifle and sighted along it. The others hesitantly followed suit. They looked like unwilling conscripts and would probably not have the conviction to shoot anyone.

"OK, OK, I'm doing it" said James. He secured the rear hatch and went to the flight deck as the hijacker yelled instructions.

"Get into your place and wear the seat-belt. If you do anything stupid I will kill you and take another of the pilots!"

Muffled curses, clumping sounds and the chink of metal followed.

"Okay, I am secured" lied James.

The young nervous Libyan drew an automatic pistol from his belt holster, chambered a round and quickly slung the AK from his shoulder. Shouting instructions to his unsure companions and flicking glances at Andreas, Denzil and the European mercenaries, he began to climb the ladder: they were too far away to do anything except watch helplessly.

-xxx-
Johannesburg

Sandro returned in under an hour and she was ready, showered, fragrant and excited to be doing something different. He jerked up his hands in a stop gesture when she opened the door.

"Whoa, you can't go like that!"

"Oh! Not smart enough? Too smart? "

"Too beautiful; you will cause a riot. Let's move, I can't wait to show you off!"

He took her hand, crossing to the Aston Martin.

"Do you want to drive?"

"Wow. Yes please!"

"Give her a blast on the western bypass then go south on De Villiers Graaff freeway."

She sank into the perfect seat, got onto the ring-road and floored it, whooping as the smooth power pinned them back. Sandro thumbed the CD changer and the invigorating driving beat of David Hasselhoff's 'Hooked on a feeling' burst deafeningly from the speakers.

"The Hoff! I just love this song! " shouted Jemima.

Sandro groped in a plastic "Benny Goldberg" bag, producing two cans of cold Castle beer from a six-pack. He snapped the ring-pulls and passed her one.

"Castle! I just love this beer! You think of everything!"

"I certainly try. What are you hanging about for, put foot!"

She was still thirsty after the tense flight and glugged beer, glancing out of the corner of her eye at the glowing speedo. They were pushing one forty miles an hour. A feeling of complete recklessness swept over her and she accelerated yet more, hurtling down the highway until the other cars were just blurs.

"Yiha!" shouted Sandro, holding up his hand for fives, grinning like a crazed adrenalin junkie. She slapped his palm vigorously and laughed back. He eventually directed her to park on a steep street in Hillbrow. A wild looking gang of black youths appeared from the shadows and he laughed and joked with them in a language she couldn't understand, dropping a few banknotes.

"I grew up round here, they'll make sure the tyres stay on."

Very loud , very rhythmic African music was belting into the night as he took her hand and led her past bouncers into a tin-roofed building, through a bar and into a courtyard crammed with jiving bodies. The five piece combo was sensational; at least once in every number the lead singer stopped singing and just danced to the intoxicating music; Sandro could do the fast intricate steps too, and every time the other dancers paused to watch, applauding them both. They danced and sweated, drank out of beer-bottles from a bathtub full of ice and ate sweet potatoes and boerewors sausage grilled on coals in halved forty-gallon drums. The hoolie was still going strong when they left just before midnight.

At her townhouse she invited him in, heading straight for the small bar where she poured two humdinger drinks with 40 percent Portsmouth gin and very little tonic. Sandro looked round the expensively decorated room appreciatively as they chinked glasses. Pointing a remote control at her Bang stereo she selected Paul Simon's 'Diamonds on the soles of her shoes' and turned it up to max.

"It was one great evening Sandro. I want to learn how to do that dance."

She was clumsy at first but soon caught on. When they finally took a rest she was hot and sticky all over, with aching shoulders.

"I need another shower and you better crash here tonight." She showed him the spare en-suite ground-floor bedroom, showered and went back down in a fluffy robe, her hair up in a towel. She was on the sofa rolling her neck and kneading it when he came in with a towel round his waist and one of Francois' shirts on.

"Must be tension" he observed putting strong hands on her collar bones and kneading. Jemima leant back towards him, groaning with pleasure as his strong fingers probed the muscles and knots. He smelt clean and good. She flopped like a cat, enjoying his touch and one limp arm dropped onto his lap, feeling immediately the straining erection.

"Well why the hell not?" thought Jemima. "I've nearly bought the farm twice in two days so I may as well live a little." She swiveled so that her hot wet mouth closed over his, the robe falling open. Sandro needed little further invitation and was naked in a flash. His hands roamed over her expertly, taking his time, finding the tender places that made her twitch with pleasure and murmur softly as she felt the damp dew start between her legs. His fingers soon found the moisture; she felt him smile as they kissed and he opened her gently, beginning a practiced kneading that made her clitoris swell and her excitement rise. She glanced at his large curved penis which was leaking clear fluid like an excited stallion. Patiently Sandro worked and she felt her tension build as orgasm approached and receded twice. She felt perspiration ooze on her skin, making her scalp itch and began to thrash in frustration and close her legs. She was sick of men of who couldn't make her climax, leaving her high and dry. He pinned her and whispered "don't be so impatient bitch, you're nearly there! Let someone else take charge for a change!"

She laughed into his mouth, relaxing her thighs to unclamp his hand which resumed work and within a minute she was shuddering and crying out at the force of the orgasm that swept her. As she lay panting, his warm mouth suddenly replaced the fingers and she gasped, protesting, even as she pushed her sopping mound upwards in delight. Finally her clitoris was too sensitive to bear more and she was climaxed out.

"Your turn now Sandro; quickly please!"

He came up for air looking faintly embarrassed.

"What's wrong?" she asked in alarm.

"Uh, nothing, but I haven't got anything with me.....I never expected...."

Her brow furrowed momentarily, then cleared in understanding. "Oh shit, that! What a gentleman! Some in the downstairs bathroom cupboard. Hurry!"

-xxx-

Ras Mohdir

A cacophony of firing from the desert suddenly broke out and the loyalist soldiers returned it in spades. Big splashes from mortar rounds appeared again as they lobbed overhead and detonated on the water.

"Look to be set for contact detonation, not airburst" noted a part of James' mind as he peered over the windscreen combing, then ducked down again ready to repel his unwanted boarder, heart thudding and mouth dry.

"Oi, Mustapha!" called Denzil loudly and the startled Libyan twitched physically at the top of the angled steps, trying to swing towards his voice and keep watching the cockpit at the same time, the automatic pistol in his free hand moving towards Denzil.

"What? He shouted in a cracked voice."

"Nothing, have a pleasant flight."

James struck the Libyan's hand with one fist breaking his hold in the hatchway, then pushed him hard in the side of the face. He yelled with pain and anger, rotated outward and fell under the aircraft nose between the float, the ladder and the pontoon, banging his head hard. The pistol discharged as he hit the dirty basin water.

James saw the female defence contractor dart forward and yank the rifle from the hands of one of the three startled conscripts, covering the other two. Lance had rapidly drawn a large Ruger handgun and was set to pull but she shouted "No!" and stepped in front of the young Libyans. She barked rapid Arabic and gestured with her weapon; they dropped their rifles and backed away, then turned and ran up onto the dock. The Otter drifted slowly away from the planking. Andreas jumped on clumsily and went up the rear ladder, waving the two contractors urgently aboard as James began the starboard turbine start sequence. Denzil strode lithely onto the float and clambered up beside James.

"Have a pleasant flight! I'm a card aren't I James?"

"Fucking hilarious! Switch on Denzil, we aren't sipping cocktails in Malta yet! Luckily those mortars look to be set for impact detonation not airburst so they're fairly unlikely to get a direct hit on us but I want to get out of range pronto."

James had the propeller levers forward, power levers at flight idle and DC master switch on. His gaze flicked from inside to out; the Otter was being pushed by the wind. Denzil was shrugging into his harness running his eyes over gauges. He began to join in the start sequence, snapping on boost pumps and checking voltages.

"Hit starboard!" he called and James engaged the start switch.

"T5, Ng 20%, oil pressure good" called Denzil introducing fuel, and James heard the engine light-off and begin to spool. The secondary kicked in and the whine rose quickly to a howl, burnt kerosene wafting into the cockpit.

"T5 peak....stable, in the green! Start complete, all good."

James released the start switch and concentrated on the starboard power and prop levers.

"Roger. Taxiing, you start port."

The fuselage began to tremble as the live propeller picked up speed, batting noisily at the air. With relief James felt some feeling come into the rudders, a sense of being in control again instead of just pushed about by the wind, drifting helplessly. A recoilless cannon shell smashed into the fifty-ton slipway crane, toppling it towards the aircraft.

"Look out!" shouted Denzil.

James advanced the power-lever and pushed hard on the rudder. The Otter responded sluggishly, fluky wind acting on the fuselage and tail, working against him. The starboard wing came round and obscured his view of the falling crane, nose lining up with the exit bar. The aircraft rolled as something struck it on the right, wings rocking, but it kept moving towards the open sea.

"How bad?" shouted James above the racket, wishing they'd had time to put on headphones. Denzil flicked a searching glance to starboard. The crane gantry made a gigantic splash as it hit the water and generated waves that made the wings rock yet more.

"Can't tell, doesn't look too bad. I've got my hands full with this bloody engine though, it's hung. It's pretty hot so I'm going to attempt a generator-assisted start, try and give me eighty percent on starboard and turn that genny on!"

"Shit! I was going to depart straight down wind. By the time it starts we'll have to take off back towards this incoming ordinance."

"Can't be helped. An into-wind take-off will be safer with this high gross-weight anyway."

"Yeah. Hobson's choice."

"Who the fuck's Hobson when he's at home?"

"He doesn't have a home; he lives in a fucking cave, like you!"

They grinned at each other as the Otter surfed buoyantly across the bar and headed south-east towards Ras Lanuf where James had been incarcerated once, many years before. Although brief it was not a pleasant memory, a timely reminder of what was at stake if they screwed up.

"At fucking last! T5 on port and Ng good, introducing fuel…..Got her… Light off!"

The secondary kicked in shortly after and the noise increased so they quickly donned headphones and tested comms. The engines howled healthily and their instruments were good. Together they quickly performed all the remaining checks, did the main run-ups and the before-takeoff routine. The wind had pushed them quickly downwind, aided by the engines at half power and James kept going until the water began to get too lumpy, then swung smoothly into wind. The airplane slowed as the offshore breeze held them back. He carried out a full and free control check and they both looked landward. It was hard to tell from this distance if the fire-fight was still going on.

"We're ready for departure. All okay in the back Andreas?" called Denzil.

"We're fine Skipper."

"Shit" muttered James as rebel troops in the recoilless-rifle pickup careered onto the beach, followed by a truck. Troops spilled out onto the sand and dropped into aiming positions.

"It must have sunk in that Big G himself could be aboard and trying to get away."

"So they're going to want to stop us pretty bad."

"Affirmative, he's the number one prize so if you know anyone to phone for help, do it now."

James could see the recoilless gun muzzle swinging towards the Otter.

"We're going to get pretty close to those boys if we go from here; think we can taxi further downwind to get airborne further away from them? Or take off downwind?"

"Neither pal, we're too heavy and the water's miles too choppy further downwind from the harbour."

'What then? Shall the boys stand on the burning deck……?"

"Fucking hope not: give it death! They might just be there for a picnic."

James laughed.

"Okay. Call 'rotate' for me Denzil, I want to keep an eye on those guys; think I have a plan."

"Roger, it better be a good one!"

James fed in full power and once the Otter's floats got on the plane it accelerated, hurtling across the water, bouncing and rocking. It was very noisy with spray splattering across the windscreen intermittently. James scanned the shore for obstructions; tall poles, masts, overhead cables. Any or all would make his idea too risky, but none were apparent. Immediately after take-off he intended to bear left and fly directly at the aggressors, passing low overhead so that the turboprops churned up sand. At closing speed their range would be hard to assess making them a difficult target and once overhead the soldiers would get grit and sand blown in every orifice making their aim still less accurate. He hoped.

"Sixty knots…. seventy knots…..Rotate" called Denzil and as he glanced up from the airspeed indicator there was a streak like lightening from the heavens followed by a thunderous detonation on the beach where the rebels had been. He blinked, hardly believing his eyes. Red flame and black smoke billowed while debris was blown high, tumbling in all directions. The explosion caused a yellow storm of sand and wreckage to swirl towards them as James lifted the Otter off and began a very shallow turn away from it, not wanting to load up the wing while low, slow and near the stall. The airframe shook as the blast moved across it.

"Good move, don't want that stuff in the intakes! Did you call that friend of yours?" asked Denzil.

"Negative but someone must have been watching! Jesus have you ever seen anything like that?"

"Yes; must have been a Hellfire, probably compliments of some guy sitting in an air-conditioned trailer in California sipping coffee. The cousins told me there were some drones in this theatre."

James shook his head in bemusement. "Aren't the Yanks, the French and the British supposed to be suppressing the Gadaffi Loyalists and assisting the rebels?"

Denzil shrugged. "Well yeah, but Resolution 1973 is to protect innocent civilians, which is us and the packs in the back, so those rebels on the beach were about to violate it. Thank God for big brother. What was your plan by the way?"

"To blind them with sand."

"Fuck, was that all? Luckily the cousins did it better than you. Passing 400 feet."

"Roger, auto-feather off, flaps up. Okay smartarse, anything else to consider that might interrupt sun-downer time?"

Denzil sat back, clasped hands in his lap, thinking.

"Nope; unless that falling crane did something nasty but we'd probably know about it by now; don't fancy stopping to check; do you?"

"No, I want a nice uneventful flight, a hot shower and a cold beer."

The Otter was up to four thousand, engines droning comfortably, the sun was shining and the view of the coast spectacular. The beaches and clear sea looked peaceful and inviting, giving no sign of the upheaval taking place inland for Libya's inhabitants.

Denzil cleared his throat and looked across.

"Thanks for riding to the rescue James."

"Who could refuse an invitation to the Mad Hatter's tea party?"

"Plenty turned the invite down. We did a good thing though. It's chaotic down there; the National Transition Council couldn't have saved these people in the back. Ugly revenge is being inflicted on completely blameless regime relatives."

"And the money was good! How come you got involved?"

"A request from Gadaffi himself; we met a couple of times, after Libya helped Primrose liberate Zimbabwe from Spencer Katsiru. You did too if I remember rightly."

"And in his hour of need he thought "I require an idiot and I know exactly where to find one!"

James reached over and prodded Denzil's shoulder sharply, grinning.

"Yes but he waved wajid fellous at the idiot, who then talked to the CIA who said it should all be straightforward!"

"What do you plan to do with this aeroplane?"

"Return it and get my deposit back I hope."

"Suppose it was possible to get a licence to operate it off the Mersey River at Pier head where the ferries dock? Do you think any money could be made?"

Denzil looked out of the window.

"Interesting; where would it go to? London?"

"I was thinking Dublin but London's another possibility; straight to the city, cutting commuter-time getting there from Heathrow or Gatwick. Hell, I think we might be onto an earner Denzil, though getting a licence will be the hard part!"

"I know some people. I'll crunch numbers and make some calls when we get to the UK. I've got another job for you first though."

"Oh yeah? What new stupidity?"

"I'm going to need someone to fly me, an Aircraft Maintenance Engineer and some spares back into Ras Mohdir to repair my Otter and get it out. The pay will be good."

"It'll have to be. Don't know if I can manage it Denzil, things are always busy with the trucking but my arse is really going to be run ragged from now on."

James told Denzil about their plan to buy an Airfield and he grunted in approval.

"Going to need a lot of moolah to get an enterprise like that off the ground though, and keep it flying. I won't need you to retrieve the Otter immediately. You might as well have the money and I don't really trust anyone else, anyway."

He glanced at his watch.

"Looks like we missed lunch."

"There are many delicacies in Malta, what do you fancy eating?"

"Hot pussy."

"No shortage of that there, even for rich old farts; I'm just not sure how low their standards are."

Denzil gave him the finger.

Smirking, James levelled the Otter off at ten thousand and adjusted props and power levers for endurance cruise. There was no sight of land in any direction and only one ship, with a smudge of smoke above its toy funnel. All felt right with the world. "By the way, I presume this operation is going to be kept pretty hush-hush hey Denzil? I wouldn't want Loretta to find out and be upset."

"Tighter than a clam's backside my boy."

-xxx-

CHAPTER FOUR
MONDAY
Manchester

Loretta awoke feeling wired and sick, with a hammering erratic heartbeat and sense of foreboding. Comprehension gradually penetrated a savage hangover and her first instinct was to get dressed and run but she knew it would be pointless and undignified. Dennis sprawled alongside like a beached whale, looking at her, and she remembered achieving one rather flat orgasm the previous night that had been mostly her own doing.
"What the hell did you give me Dennis?"
"About a bath-full of Champagne."
"Not that, what else?"
"We shared a pretty big hit of Speed. I scored it in the last dance place."
"Speed! Oh my God, I've haven't taken drugs since I was a stupid teenager!"
"You didn't say no when I put it on your tongue."
Memory flooded back.
"I'd swallowed it before I even realized, what was I thinking?"
"Probably the Champagne was doing any thinking by then. I'm sorry Lorr but I don't really regret anything, you were dancing like Madonna and sensational afterwards in bed. Look at all these bites!"
"You seduced me when I was feeling a bit lonely, very drunk, and cross with James!"
"Hey, easy! You seemed pretty enthusiastic; why were you angry with James?"
"I really don't know. Because he went to Malta without me perhaps. Anyway, you're not nearly as good in bed as he is."
"Thanks very much! Not!"
"Well you're not, so don't sulk, I didn't say you were bad, just not as good."
A rumpled condom filled with semen still clung to Dennis's penis from the night before and she thought with ludicrously loyal satisfaction that it was nowhere near as large or beautiful as James's when erect, nor had Dennis tried to coax anywhere near the number or intensity of orgasms from her. His hair was thinning too.

"Look Loretta I might not be Prince Charming but I showed you a good time and I think you are absolutely wonderful. I'd marry you in a shot, unlike James."

She stared at the ceiling.

"Only to possess me like your swanky cars and houses and airplanes; something else to show off. You don't know that he hasn't asked anyway."

"Well would you, if he asked?"

"Mind your own bloody business. He mustn't find out about this. We've parted and got back together a few times over the years but I can see us getting old together."

"I'm a one-woman man, me."

Loretta laughed mockingly.

"Fibber! You've got your regular posh squeeze Alison; why don't you marry her?"

"Because I want you! I mean it."

"You just think you do. Be honest, you'd run a mile if Alison or I said yes; you're one of life's natural bachelors. A solitary bull that joins the herd to have his wicked way now and then with the cows and afterwards goes back to happy solitude. Just enjoy the bit of me you've had, most men would kill for it!"

Dennis pondered the image and laughed, deciding he liked it. With the dark cloud of her hair spread on the pillow, flashing eyes, exquisite Mediterranean skin and fit supple figure, Loretta was dynamite. She was right too; men half his age would queue up to fuck her.

"We could manage the Airfield business without James if you married me."

"Not a chance. You approached James because he makes things happen, whereas you are a spoilt lazy bastard who doesn't know one end of a hammer from the other. Don't get too greedy or ambitious."

She tucked the blade of her hand intimately behind his large sweaty balls and squeezed warningly making him wince, then swung her legs off the bed and stood lithely up, aware of sticky juices round her vagina, bottom, and down her thighs; they were all hers, she'd insisted Dennis wear the condom, and thank God.

"Hey, come back, I haven't finished with you yet."

She headed for the shower, feeling unclean.

"I'm not an airline captain, I can't lie around in bed all day; do you ever watch Friends?"

"I am an airline captain and lie around in foreign hotel beds for weeks every year. The only thing that's ever on TV is 'Friends' so of course I watch; could probably win bloody Mastermind answering questions about it!"

"Then you'll know the one where Phoebe and Joey agree to be each other's back-up if anything happens to their main relationships. That's what you can be Dennis; my backup."

She went into the bathroom. Dennis played with some blond hairs on his fleshy chest. James was difficult to work with and an arrogant bastard who'd made him feel inadequate. Well not any more, now that he'd had Loretta. Dennis smirked, dropping into a sound hungover sleep.

He was drooling and snoring loudly when she emerged from the shower to dress in the soiled creased clothes from yesterday. Taking a diet coke for her raging thirst she let herself out of the Wilmslow town-house, four and a half miles from Manchester Airport where Dennis's airline was based. Her apparent composure lasted until she emerged from the stuffy building into late-morning sunshine, glad to retract the Jag's roof and get some wind in her hair. She ran spread fingers through it and sobbed; a decade of fidelity shattered and her future at risk for a meaningless fling. Dennis hadn't been a very good lay and a couple of times during the evening she'd been embarrassed by his self-centred pomposity but he was also charming, attentive and very witty. They'd had a lovely time together; taxi into town, Champagne tea at the Midland hotel, a great movie, dinner at an Italian in the gay quarter of Manchester where Dennis seemed to know everybody, then dancing in a club with yet more Champagne. It was no wonder she'd ended up shagging him, even without the Speed tablet. Those were all things James disliked doing. She hated her spontaneous drunken decision to let Dennis fuck her though it had seemed a good idea at the time, because lately James hadn't been much fun. Now she felt wretched and terrified. It would be a mess if he found out! She sometimes thought James might have a self-destructive urge; maybe she had caught it from him. Why did she feel so frightened? Fear of losing James or just fear of change?

She dashed hot tears away, dropping the J-shift a gear, floored the accelerator and pulled abruptly into the fast lane. The XK8 snarled and shot up over Barton Bridge, with the familiar Aerodrome visible just beyond and a hundred feet below. She took a swig of coke that burned on the tongue. She heard a "plink" as a text message arrived on the iPhone which she'd forgotten to put into the hands-free holder. She glanced aside looking for it. For too long: a blaring horn sounded followed by a sudden heart-stopping shriek.

-xxx-
Monday: Malta

James had gone out early to run off a hangover generated by their noisy celebration at the 'Black Gold' restaurant in Sliema the previous evening. Glancing in a jewellery store he saw a stunning matched set of earrings and a pendant in the shape of gold ingots, but half each bar was of obsidian to represent oil. He could just imagine them set off against Loretta's dark hair and dangling between her exquisitely shaped breasts. It got him all excited so he went in and bought them. Sometimes making love to the same woman seemed a bit mundane but he realised he was lucky to have such a hottie as his partner. His flight to Manchester wasn't 'till seventeen hundred hours so he joined Rod, Denzil and the others by the rooftop pool at the Diplomat Hotel and ordered a beer. He sent Loretta a cheerful text and relaxed. True to form Denzil had pulled a very pretty blonde woman in her early fifties the previous night but now he was working on the defence contractor, though she wasn't having any of it. Colinda Lasserre was one of the most stunning women James had ever seen and she was aware of it in a pleasant way. Her spectacular bronzed body was barely concealed in a brief bikini that had given all the men semis. She was urbane and witty, effortlessly deflecting Denzil's funny but coarse advances, and on several occasions James thought he caught her eyeing his own body. He sucked his tight belly in a little more and rolled into the pool for a swim to hide his burgeoning erection. He breast-stroked down the pool languidly and heard a phone ring.

"It's yours James" called Colinda.

"Do us a favour and see who it is."

She glanced over and down at the vibrating phone.

"Says 'number withheld;' What shall I do?"

"Be a good girl and answer it."

-xxx-
Lancashire

Loretta's eyes flicked to the mirror; there was a police motorcycle right on her tail, siren screaming, and blue light flashing. The speedo showed eighty-five and she began to back off slowly, indicating to move onto the hard shoulder. Her heart was hammering even faster; with six points on her licence already she could be banned, or have all their insurance ramped way-up. Either way James would be coldly furious. And she'd had a lot to drink last night! And taken drugs! She pulled onto the hard shoulder, stuffing the iPhone out of sight and nudging her handbag on top. The traffic cop parked behind, took off his gauntlets and strolled over. In the mirror he looked old for a motorcycle patrolman, overweight and a bit officious. He clocked her personalized number plate, BUSTY, without smiling.

"What did I do?" asked Loretta, smiling weakly but leaving sunglasses on to cover red eyes.

"You swerved very dangerously at high speed madam."

"A pair of shoes at the Trafford centre was casting a spell on me; I speeded up to get out of range."

"You also appeared to be looking down at something within the vehicle and not concentrating fully on the road; would you mind moving your handbag?"

Heart sinking, Loretta complied. The iPhone was invisible in the crack between backrest and seat.

"May I see your licence?"

"I only have the plastic one, not the counterpart."

She handed it over and he examined it.

"I see you have a hands-free phone facility but no handset connected; any idea where the phone is?"

Loretta flicked her eyes towards the seat and handbag, feeling ridiculously guilty, like a child caught doing something stupid by a teacher.

"Probably in my bag, I must have forgotten to slot it in."

"There is an open can of coke in the console. Drinking and eating affect attention; using a handheld device is a dangerous offence. You've held a class 1 licence for several years. As a professional driver you should know better than to take your eyes off the road or become distracted, and that it is hazardous both to yourself and others to change lanes suddenly and exceed the speed limit."

"Go lecture someone else sonny, I'm old enough to be your blooming mother!" Loretta thought, and then quickly quelled it because he was right.

"Yes I should." Unfeigned contrition; she hadn't known what was going on for long enough to cause a serious accident.

"Okay. You are obviously feeling embarrassed by the manner in which you were recently controlling, or rather, not controlling, your vehicle, so I shall just require a breath sample."

A nauseating wave of fright flooded over her.

The breathalyser proved negative by a small margin. The Motorcycle policeman looked disappointed and tapped Loretta's licence thoughtfully on his thumb, drawing out the suspense, then abruptly handed it back.

"Bustamante eh; unusual name round here. Are you a permanent resident in this country?"

She struggled to keep her rage under control, having a good idea what he thought she might be; a gypsy refugee from Rumania claiming benefits illegally, or a prostitute.

"British citizen of Italian descent. My father flew Hurricanes in the western desert against Rommel."

He flushed.

"And hence the exotic licence plate right?"

"Yes. It was a present from my partner, a bit of fun. A double-entendre."

He glanced involuntarily at her full breasts and then dragged his eyes away. Hers were full of naked scorn and he flushed even more deeply, beginning to fill in a form.

"Well whatever ridiculous amount of money he paid, it is illegal; the 5 has been altered to resemble an S. I am therefore issuing you a notice to have it corrected. Any MOT garage can carry out the work and if the notice is returned completed within seven days there will be no penalty. However I am also giving you a Notice of intended Prosecution for driving without due care and attention and for that there is likely to be a considerable penalty. This is a nice car; try and live long enough to enjoy it, I get tired of scraping human remains off these motorways. They are very unforgiving."

He handed her the first notice and proceeded to write on some other kind of official documentation. Loretta's heart dropped like a stone. She wanted to try and plead her case but couldn't bring herself to do it; she'd never grovelled and wasn't going to demean herself in front of this wanker, it would only give him some perverted pleasure. James would go ape-shit if she got more points or lost her licence though. She was an integral part of the European trucking team which relied on dual-manning, and they would need to keep operating that business to keep the revenue going while the Airfield operation got up to speed.

When he was gone she felt even more bummed out and paranoid. What a joyless shit! She retrieved the phone with trembling hands and checked the text from James. He was in Malta. The sun was shining and the job pleasant; wished she was there.

"Me too Hacking, me too" she muttered, dialling his number on impulse, suddenly wanting badly to hear his voice.

-xxx-
Holland: Monday

"We are similar men in many ways Lembede" said Othman Tahamata in Amsterdam.

"We are both exiles, you from Zimbabwe and me from South Molucca; yet we have risen above persecution and discrimination to become rich and powerful. Indeed my very name Othman means 'Wealthy Man.'"

They were in Tahamata's chauffeur-driven black BMW on the way to Schiphol Airport where Lembede was booked first-class on KLM to Johannesburg. He grunted in agreement and added "and also that we do not allow the scruples of little men to deflect us from our purpose."

The Moluccan, like many of his countrymen was of Dutch nationality, a direct result of merchants from the Netherlands trading with and colonising the Bandanese Spice Islands during the sixteenth century, when cloves, mace and nutmeg were worth their weight in gold. During the resultant Indonesian National Revolution of the 1950's, Holland's rulers had been forced to disband their indigenous KNIL Army which proved a very complicated political problem and in 1951 the Dutch government tried to solve it by transporting the men and their families to the Netherlands, classed as 'temporary residents.' Othman was born there soon after, but by 1968 more than eighty percent of the Moluccans, displaced for their own safety, had still been denied official Dutch citizenship. A movement arose to formalize their status and improve access to employment, education and social welfare. Little changed so militant action quickly followed. Young Othman had been deeply involved, participating in terrorist attacks within the Netherlands on Ambonese, Indonesian and Dutch targets which gave the Moluccan 'boys of action' great prestige. Othman then used his tough reputation to branch out into crime in Amsterdam and Rotterdam, clawing his way to the top in everything from drugs and prostitution to counterfeit money and arms. As his wealth multiplied he'd gradually sought to legitimize himself, buying a reputable diamond merchandising business and getting involved in politics. That enterprise also provided a chance to profit hugely from the trade in illicit 'conflict' or 'blood' diamonds from throughout Africa which were used to fund wars, causing untold misery.

It irritated Lembede that the smug Moluccan treated him as an equal however, because he was the ex-President of Zimbabwe and not a mere criminal. He had reluctantly told the man his real identity for two reasons; vanity, because the little Asian somehow made him feel he had to prove something, and for credibility because criminals at Tahamata's level in the International pecking order didn't deal with just anyone. Funds laundered through him were crucial though, to recapture power in Zimbabwe and like Tahamata, he didn't care what he had to do, or what happened to anyone who got in the way. They had just struck a deal that saw fruition of Lembede's plan to move diamonds from Zimbabwe's blacklisted Chiadzwa diamond field to his newly purchased mine in Botswana, from where they could appear on the world market through Tahamata in Amsterdam as squeaky clean Botswanan stones.

At the airport they parted with a handshake near a special VIP gate, as Lembede's bodyguards alighted from a beefed up Range Rover behind the BMW. The small party was whisked through immigration and customs formalities, boarding the first-class cabin of the London-bound KLM aircraft well before any other passengers. From Heathrow they would board the overnight British Airways Airbus A380 to Johannesburg.

-xxx-
Malta

Colinda pressed the green answer button on James's cell-phone.
"Hello? Who is it please?"
Denzil laughed, leaning forward towards the phone, and spoke loudly.
"Never mind who it is, get your lips back round his cock girl, that's what you're being paid for; he's about to come!"
Despite herself Colinda laughed but hit the red button hastily with her thumb. She wagged the phone at him.
"That wasn't funny Denzil, you are incorrigible! What if it had been James's wife and she heard?"

"He and Loretta aren't married and she'd know I was only joking."
"Who was it?" called James from further down the pool.
Colinda shrugged and the men all held their breath, hoping her breasts would escape from the tiny halter top.
"I'm sorry James; the caller rang off before I could answer."
-xxx-
Manchester

Loretta looked at her phone in disbelief, opened the car door and vomited onto the tarmac, then started up and hurtled away in a scream of rubber, swerving abruptly onto the motorway. Car horns blared in protest but she floored it and left them standing, round the M60 and up the M61, driving blindly and wildly, crying steadily and wiping her blurry vision. She believed what she'd just heard; James's past was littered with sexual affairs, as was hers, but she thought they'd both settled down, content at last to be together. They were as bad as each other; her drunken sexual adventure with Dennis Mallard seemed increasingly sordid. Even though James had obviously been at it himself in Malta, it was with a prostitute and didn't involve his affection, whereas she knew, and had even thought she fancied Mallard. God, what flaw was there in her, to make James consort with foreign prostitutes? If she didn't confess the guilt would drive her crazy, and it would be worse if James found out some other way. It would probably mean splitting up though and her very chest-cavity ached with sadness. Loretta couldn't think rationally.

She tried to remember the pre-drink discussions with Dennis about finance to take her mind off the misery. He would sell the Wilmslow town-house to raise his share of the working capital, and would live in his house in Parbold near Wigan. It meant a longer commute to work but he could live with that. She tried mentally to compute the value of her remaining shares, and thought about how to convince Brother George their new enterprise was a good risk. It would all be meaningless without James, and dead in the water. The Jaguar had eaten up the miles and she turned left off the M6 at junction 36 towards the Lake District, still driving at over a ton on the dual carriageway, and on impulse swung off again towards Barrow-in-Furness and Coniston.

Despite Dennis's compliments and apparent offer of marriage she felt cheap and dirty. Her mind was behaving erratically, thinking distorted by hangover, emotion, tiredness and the drug still apparently swirling round her bloodstream. Perhaps exercise would work the poisons out of her system and restore some self-respect; it had worked before. They both belonged to a mountaineering club and Loretta parked beside the CMC hut on the outskirts of Coniston, punched in the door-code and entered hurriedly. It was empty being mid-week and the solitude was welcome because all of a sudden her stomach rebelled again. She retched and retched noisily into one of the toilet bowls and when the heaves subsided felt weak but somewhat purged. Her gym bag was always left packed ready in the boot and she changed into shorts and put on her trainers. There was a banana in the glove-compartment and she grabbed that too then ran up the steep Walna Scar track on wobbly legs for several kilometres. The only sounds were of birds calling, sheep bleating and her ragged breathing. It reminded her of the sound she made when James made love to her and tears spurted anew. The residual hallucinatory effect of the drug suddenly conjured up Primrose Mpofu, now President of Zimbabwe, whom she'd hiked here with in the past, and who had always advocated optimism.

"So what if I'm a stupid bitch" she panted aloud as she ran, "born with a silver spoon in my mouth and drawers that drop too easily; I've at least done something of benefit to the world in my life, like ridding Zimbabwe of that barbarian Katsiru and getting Primrose into place." Loretta had been the black woman's main provider of moral and financial support during the bitter Zimbabwean power struggle after Primrose's husband Elias lost his life in a politically motivated killing.

A rambling couple heading downwards looked at her oddly but she ignored them and ran on, turning towards 'The Old Man of Coniston' on the Goats Water track, branching off the Walna Scar road. The Old Man loomed a couple of thousand feet above; sunlight played on the green and yellow of sward and bracken, and on the grey Lake District knolls and mountains. She was desperately thirsty and paused to drink, breathing heavily, at the flowing outfall of the quiet tarn waters, looking across at Dow Crag as the sun crept down its impressive cliffs, feeling drawn to them. She gulped water like a camel, forcing herself to drink more and yet more as her belly swelled uncomfortably. It was as if her body had taken over, knowing that only fluid would purge the filth from her system. She'd climbed 'Giants Crawl' with James before and it was hugely exposed but the holds were bomb-proof. She traced the route with her eyes across the vast steep slab and staggered on up towards a mountain rescue box. In twenty minutes she was catching her breath at a kitting-up stance below the route. She made the first few moves. Immediately she felt exposure and went back down, remembering a wry guidebook observation about 'Giant's Crawl.'

"Solo climbers often find themselves contemplating an overabundance of view and scuttle back down muttering about family responsibilities."

She laughed crazily; there was nothing responsible about her behaviour. She took another deep breath and set off again. Before long she was committed and her concentration became utter. Climbing quickly but in control she arrived at a broad ledge and stood shaking out forearm cramps, realizing that nervousness was making her hurry and grip holds unnecessarily tightly. She looked down at the dizzying abyss, at some tiny walkers on the distant path peering up and pointing. Gazing round the spectacular basin and up at the Old Man summit she experienced a sudden rush of vertigo and swayed outward to the very point of balance, then turned back to the rock-face.

"Oh God what am I doing here?"

-xxx-

Malta

James got out of the water and grabbed a towel.

"Where's Andreas?" he asked, rubbing his hair.

"Caught the first plane out of Malta this morning, and looks like Big G should have got out of Dodge City with us."

Denzil tossed over a newspaper brought to him by a waiter while James was swimming. James read the report of Muammar Gadaffi's death with mixed feelings. A major world sponsor of terrorism and tough on his own people, yet in many ways he had been a good leader, spending hugely on the education of Libyan citizens, sponsoring imaginative projects like the "Man-made River" scheme and helping to liberate Zimbabwe. The reported manner of his death made James feel rather ill. He dropped the paper and took his lager from the waiter.

"Want to hear something funny?" asked Denzil.

James and Rodriguez nodded expectantly. Lance looked sardonically amused.

"Big G paid the three million bucks into my bank account in Luxemburg; that's the good news."

"And? What's the funny part?"

"The European Banking Commission froze the transaction retrospectively and indefinitely, pending an investigation into all Gadaffi Regime finances; could take years before I see a penny, if ever. I just got off the phone with the bank manager."

Denzil was shaking his head and cackling.

"Jesus, all that fucking effort and expense for bloody nothing!" said Rodriguez in outrage.

"Not exactly" said James. "We probably saved fourteen souls from a hideous death."

"Yes, and I am now the proud owner of a twin Otter lying fucked on a runway in Ras Mohdir. Luckily Christopher saw the funny side and has agreed to wait a few days while I sort out his money."

Rod snorted.

"Marvellous; how are you going to pay him? And more importantly, me?"

"Ah. Well Christopher agreed to accept shares in a new Company, the board of which you two are also invited to join as shareholders and directors."

James was beginning to shake his head and chuckle, guessing what was coming.

"What kind of Company?"

"What you suggested; an airline, or more accurately, a seaplane-line."

Rod was gaping.

"And I'll be a shareholder?"

"Yes. Of Emerald Goose Airline; a seaplane service which will link Liverpool Bay with Dublin Bay, connecting Celtic Tiger Entrepreneurs from Ireland with Shell-suited citizens of Merseyside, the European city of culture. There will be other services following to London Bridge, Glasgow, Edinburgh and the moon."

James snorted in amusement at his rhetoric.

"Stuffed Goose would probably be a more appropriate name!"

Their laughter grew steadily louder until other sun-bathing guests were looking over and smiling. Then with one mind James and Rodriguez stood, picked up Denzil's sun-lounger with him on it and tossed it into the deep end.

He surfaced, still holding his beer glass with some in.

"Anything you believe in strongly enough must surely come to pass!"

At Luka airport Lance MacDonald and James got chatting over beers. They had been in a lot of military theatres at the same time but never met. James thought he was one of the most untrustworthy men he'd ever come across, with cold, pale reptilian eyes that reminded him of a watchful crocodile's.

"I like you James, and we have a possible contract coming up in Iraq that could net you a lot of dough to help in your new venture, and help us out at the same time."

"How do you know about that?" asked James sharply, thinking he meant Ringtail Airfield in Burscough.

"I was at the pool remember and jokingly asked Denzil if he wanted any more shareholders in that crazy seaplane idea of his."

"Well I'm always ready to earn a buck Lance, what's the score?"

"CLS are bidding on an Iraq-based transport contract soon, fairly small-scale to start off but with great growth potential. I'm looking for someone experienced to come on board."

"Sounds distinctly interesting; can you tell me anymore?"

"Not right now but let's exchange contact details and I'll be in touch soon."

In the departure lounge Colinda Lasserre took the seat beside James at the bar. She was from New Orleans, a spectacular Amazon of a woman with a lithe, muscled body and a cruel beautiful face.

"We haven't had much chance to talk James and I'm curious to find out more about you."

"The interest is mutual Colinda; I was very impressed by your coolness under pressure yesterday."

It turned out that she had attended the University of Louisiana at Lafayette and played football for the 'Cajun Ladies' team, part of the 'Ragin' Cajuns' squad. Her Dad ran a trucking Company and she'd driven trucks with him for a few years before joining the Marine Corps and getting a commission. James gave her his own potted history and before long they too had exchanged details.

-xxx-
Johannesburg: Monday

Exhaustion, alcohol and fantastic sex made Jemima sleep wonderfully; she woke just after dawn feeling hugely refreshed but was immediately plagued by doubts. God, she'd done it on their first date! Would that be the last time she saw him, now he'd had everything? She'd asked Sandro to go in the spare room so she could get a decent rest. Now what? Would he come up and want to make love again? And there was her relationship with Francois which wasn't yet resolved. Well actually it was, she just hadn't had the courage or decency to make it formal. Her musing was interrupted by Sandro knocking gently and bringing in a tray with tea, toast, marmalade and two boiled eggs complete with soldiers. He was shaved, dressed and showed few signs of the previous night's excesses, though his clothes weren't quite as immaculate as usual. He put the tray on the bed and they talked while she ate.

"Do you always get up so early?"

"Usually. I like to be one jump ahead."

"Got a lot to do today?"

"Always have; listen Jemima, I want to tell you something now because I smaak you big-style. I have a criminal record, pulled a few heists, but it's all like yesterday man, did it more for kicks than anything else. I copped a few months of choky and I don't want you to hear it somewhere else and think I wasn't being straight with you."

She regarded him levelly.

"You're not a gangster are you?"

"Heh! The real gangsters are all in the government. No, I make most of my money from gambling and bootleg booze. They are rough trades but mostly legal, though I admit to sailing close to the wind on occasion, even now."

"Somehow that doesn't surprise me but thanks for your honesty. I like you too and it's better that we're candid with each other from the start; there are some things from my youth that I'm not proud of either!"

"So good. Then we can see each other again?"

"Yes but there are a couple of things we need to clear up. I didn't mention it because I was so wired last night but that stuff Lembede pulled on the flight back from Botswana was sick. I should have done something, maybe radioed ahead to the South African authorities, had them meet the plane and arrest him and his goons. Something anyway; if that Customs guy makes a complaint Bustamante Construction could be held responsible causing a really big naus, with Theo and I in the middle, filling in a million forms, making statements or even in jail."

He sat down on the edge of the bed, being careful not to disturb the tray.

"Eat those eggs before they get hard. Believe me, that guy Phuti-whatsit, he isn't going to report what happened. You saw his face when Lembede whispered in his ear, he was massive bang, girl!"

She cut into an egg and dipped a soldier in, talking with her mouth full.

"Why the hell wouldn't he complain? He's a Botswana government official on his home territory, and it was a humiliating assault!"

"You know what Jemima? This is Africa and I don't even wonder anymore, but wherever Lembede goes he inspires the same terror, and there is never any comeback. You'll see."

"Sounds like a fun business partner! An alliance based on fear."

Sandro chuckled, reached out a finger and wiped a drop of egg from the corner of her lip.

"Not in my case sexy girl, not in my case."

"Why not?"

"Because I know something about him."

"I don't understand; how did you two even got involved together."

"Long story: I'll tell you sometime but right now we both got things to do."

"Oh shit, look at the time! Here, take this tray, I'm going to jump in the shower."

As she sprang naked from the bed he put down the tray and grabbed her for an intimate grope and a slobbery kiss.

"Nice pyjamas!"

"Glad you like them!" She drew back and looked him in the eye. "Thanks for the breakfast Sandro. And for last night, it felt special."

"It was." He smacked her bottom lightly and pushed her towards the bathroom.

"Maak gou, there's a good girl."

Water started splashing.

"I need to be at Oliver Tambo Airport sharpish" she called through the open door. I'll reposition the Beechjet to Lanseria, that way I'll get my car back without driving from one side of Jo'burg to the other and I can go straight to work."

"Ja, you said last night. I can drop you if you like."

"That would be perfect, thank you."

Above the splashing water she heard the phone ring and then stop. Getting out she dried herself and dressed quickly in a clean flying overall. The doorbell rang and when she got downstairs Theo was standing in the hall with Sandro, looking uncomfortable.

"Theo! What are you doing here?"

"Just checking you got home all right. I tried your cell and land-line on the way over but they just rang out. Thought I'd take you to Lanseria to collect your car and avoid being late for work. We could maybe get a spot of breakfast."

She touched his arm.

"Theo, that was really nice but I plan to move the Beech to Lanseria, pick my car up and go straight to the job. Sandro's running me to Oliver Tambo International, it's on his way."

He smiled wryly with a rather winsome expression in his eyes, and also a lot of unasked questions.

"I see you've got everything under control, as usual. Well some other time then, I was hoping to have a bit of a debrief….." Theo backed towards the door, an oddly bereft, almost disappointed expression on his face.

"We'll talk tomorrow. Goodbye."

To her dismay, as she was locking up the townhouse Francois Steenkamp's car pulled up and he got out carrying a bunch of roses.

"Jemima, hi. Listen, we've got to talk….."

She was flustered, running behind time.

"Yes I know we must Francois but I'm late for work. Can we do it another time?"

"Well when? How can we arrange it when you don't answer my calls?"

He suddenly did a double take at Sandro who was standing tossing his car-keys in one hand, obviously waiting. Francois's face darkened in anger and he grabbed her elbow, marching her several strides away.

"What the hell's that guy doing here?"

Her immediate reaction was defensive anger.

"What's it got to do with you? I damaged his car if you must know….."

"That's not what I meant but my God, are you seeing him?"

"Well sort of, since the accident….."

"Then you're even stupider than I thought! That guy is a criminal, known to Police, to my department! You can't get involved with him, I'm on the vice squad and he's on our radar all the time."

Jemima shook his hand off.

"I didn't actually know you thought I was stupid; funny how these little things will out hey?"

"I'm sorry, I didn't mean it that way" he called desperately as she stalked towards the Aston. "Jemima, I'm sorry; I'll call you and you have to answer! For your own good, please!"

"Jealous boyfriend?" asked Sandro as they drove past Francois who was sitting in his car, cell-phone to ear.

"Yes. We've been having our differences for a long while and it blew up last week. It's all over now bar the final shouting which I just couldn't face."

"It's never easy. That makes two in one day; popular girl."

"What do you mean?"

"Jealous boyfriends: what, you don't know that Theo carries a big torch for you too?"

"No! What? Why do you think that?"

"Plain to see, he wags his tail round you like a puppy, hangs on your every word, eats you up with his eyes."

"But he's like a brother to me….!"

"Nothing wrong with a little incest!"

She laughed.

"Don't be disgusting! I like being with you Sandro, not many people make me laugh."

"Hey, I'm still on a high; and you can make that three jealous boyfriends now, girl! Can I see you again tonight?"

She put her hand intimately on his thigh and stroked.

"Yes, the other two are on hold. For now."

-xxx-
English Lake District

Loretta took several deep breaths and climbed on. A nose-grinding crack followed that gave onto a good platform where she tried to still her trembling, then teetered left and peered into the jaws of Great gully, futilely hoping for an easier escape route, before looking upwards at the final steep fissure. She was hopelessly committed and there was no easy way out. The guide-book route description came back to her again. "You'll grip those holds in the final corner as if your life depended on them; which it does."

What had really brought her here; hope of a fatal accident to avoid the consequence of her actions? She had more guts than that. And pride. She didn't want to smash on the rocks below, or be ignominiously rescued from her crag-bound perch. Whatever had happened was just life and she would have to cope with it like always.

Breathing hard and wishing she had a rope on Loretta climbed up for a few more moves but half-heartedly and dropped back onto insecure out-of-balance holds. One sweaty hand slipped a bit and panic began to rise. Fatigue was making her clumsy. She grabbed for the hold. Missed! Her breath was coming in ragged sobs.

"Oh Jamesy, please help me!" she gasped, and it was if just saying his name calmed her nerves. She dragged in several deep lungfuls of air, visualized a sequence of moves and attacked the crux positively. The last pitch felt like a dance, springy muscles moving her powerfully wherever she wanted to go and it was over almost too fast. The rest was easy scrambling and gave way to a steep indistinct path leading to a grassy ridge overlooking Great gully, from some hundred feet below Dow Crag summit. The stillness and solitude was absolute; she could have been on the moon. With a strange sense of peace and exultation she sprawled on the grass, loosened her sweaty hair and lay with the hot sun on her body, chest heaving, feeling cleansed, aware that life is sweetest when one has come within reach of leaving it. Her breathing slowed and she dropped into a deep sleep.

-xxx-
Holland

On board a British Airways Airbus Lembede's entourage were settling down in first class for the long overnight haul to Johannesburg.

"I wouldn't trust that Asian boss," said Sharpness Malinga, referring to the Moluccan they had recently met. "He is very snake-like; is it wise to put one's heel so close to a serpents head?"

Lembede smiled humourlessly.

"With a heel close to the serpents head Malinga, one may stamp on it more easily."

Sharpness Malinga was the guerilla leader who had recruited Lembede almost forty years previously and had been his main "fixer" when he became President of Zimbabwe. The bodyguards all chuckled and drank their lemonade while Lembede sipped vintage champagne. On the forward bulkhead was a rack containing free newspapers. Silas snapped his fingers and pointed for one of the bodyguards to fetch him one, then leafed idly through it. It was the Lancashire Evening News; in the middle pages were gazette notices, and a word caught his eye as he flicked irritably past. He went back and read the short notice twice, heart beginning to thud. The advert was for a Company called HBT, Hacking Bustamante Transport, and was a notice announcing their intention to base heavy duty trucks and trailers at a site in Lancashire, gazetted by law in case anybody wanted to object. Finally he passed it to Malinga.

"Look who it is Sharpness: could it be them after all these years?" His Lieutenant read swiftly and whistled softly in surprise.

"Possibly boss. All hippos surface eventually huh?"

Lembede smiled thinly

"Yes, but these two are finally going to sink for good, if it is who we think." He tore the page out and placed it in his inside pocket. Malinga felt a twinge of unease; they were in a game for big stakes and he knew Lembede could be easily distracted by his obsession with old enemies, the Rhodesian Special Branch Operator James Hacking in particular, and the Bustamante woman had provided Primrose Mpofu the money and backbone to ask the Libyans for backing to overthrow Lembede and get him and Malinga indicted for war crimes.

The ex-President spent much of the long journey brooding on past times, and his current plans to overthrow the Zimbabwe government and reinstate himself as President. There was a sudden surreal moment when he saw, as through parting clouds, the many different paths he could have taken; there were always choices. He had been so busy for several years that he had infrequently thought about James Hacking, but now that he did so, fury churned anew in his guts. There was a need not just for revenge but to prove something; to Zimbabwe, to the world, but perhaps more than anything to his former school companion Hacking. And there was not one reasonable rational explanation for that compulsion. Through the clouds in his mind, he saw a sunny landscape far below, and himself as a teenager playing tennis and football; he hadn't done either for thirty years. Maureen Hove appeared and smiled at him too, and held out their son for inspection. A fog of rage and grief closed the cloud window and he summoned the steward to get a large whisky, imagining the revenge he would have on James Hacking and Loretta Bustamante.

-xxx-
English Lake District

The sound of her phone ringing eventually awoke Loretta and she looked at her watch groggily, astonished to see that almost two hours had passed. It stopped before she could answer but seconds later plinked to indicate the arrival of a text message. Though the sun was warm, she felt clammy from lying on the grass and pulled herself erect stiffly, doing some stretches before looking at it. She felt much better and the hyper-wired feeling caused by the Speed in her system had receded. The message was from James.

"Arriving Manchester terminal-one 2000 hours. Can't wait to see you."

Loretta paused for a few seconds, thinking carefully before replying. She felt more together both physically and mentally.

"Can't wait either, masses to discuss. See u at 8."

She was ravenous and wolfed the banana, realising there was still time to go over the Old Man and make it to the airport if she was quick. She scrambled up the remaining hundred feet and from the top of Dow crag set off down to the col and then upwards to Coniston's summit, jogging easily and feeling wonderfully alive, knowing what had to be done now that everything was back in perspective and the effects of drink and drugs purged. At the hut she showered and dressed in the mid-thigh-length white skirt she'd worn to take James to the airport and that showed off her brown legs to perfection, slipped the new gold thongs from Trafford Centre boutique on sexy feet and admired them, and finally added a pale yellow silk blouse she'd bought along with some matching earrings. She signed out of the hut register and paid the day-rate, then locked up carefully and drove off.

James cleared customs and emerged into the arrivals hall. Loretta was standing back with a strange look on her face. He waved the bottle of Champagne from airport-shopping cheerfully and moved forward, dodging other waiting groups. As he drew near she brandished another bottle of Champagne.

"Snap! Great minds think alike" she said and embraced him, lips moving against his ear to whisper "I can't wait to get you into bed so we're booked into an executive suite at the Crown Plaza two minutes away, hope you've been eating oysters!"

"And I can't wait to give you this!"

She opened the plush box right there and gasped.

"Oh, they're just me!"

"I thought so too, rare, precious and reliable in times of crisis."

"God I don't like to think what they must have cost!"

"Then don't. Get me to that hotel for a cold drink and some fun."

She paid at the machine for the short-stay car-park and led him to the Jag. When they were seated inside she turned to face him.

"Listen James I have something to confess. I've done something really stupid."

"What is it, shoes again?"

"This is serious!"

"Then I need a drink before hearing it. Go on, drive!"

"God you are so bossy!"

"Only when I'm thirsty; and horny."

"Which is pretty much all the time!"

James was like a whirlwind, still on a high from success. After a hurried check-in he swept her into the lift and up to their room, kissing and fondling her on the way.

Would a man be this horny if he'd been consorting with prostitutes in Malta she wondered as he popped and poured champagne and then dragged her to the wet-room shower where she had her first orgasm, slippery with soap. He loved to watch her, the sway of plump breast and jiggle of pert bottom, and to run his hands all over her like a buyer evaluating an expensive mare. On the luxurious bed he tugged her mane to the point of pain, squeezed her feet and ran his tongue into every enticing fold and crack. She took over, got on top and rode him, got on her knees and took him from behind, lay on her back and pushed his head between her legs, both panting and perspiring as the fever rose. She tugged his powerful thigh intimately over her torso and with wide jaws took him deep as his hot mouth engulfed her folds, sucking them in with tongue and lips pulsating on her clitoris. The tip of his right thumb rubbed the G spot then pressed downwards towards the back, as a wet finger slipped into her bottom. Feeling her tension soar he pinched gently. Loretta screamed and came as his tongue lapped on, extending the rush endlessly. He ejaculated spontaneously and she had to gulp frantically to avoid gagging. When they eventually untangled he kissed her silky swollen lips tenderly, then wiped his mouth.

"Wow. That stuff is rich and salty."

"You're telling me! Get us something to drink or I might be sick which wouldn't be very romantic."

They gulped from beer bottles he found in the mini-bar, smiling at each other and gasping.

"You don't often lose control like that, usually you finish in my pussy."

"I could actually feel your orgasm; it tipped me over the edge; that and something you did with your teeth."

"I nearly drowned when you came, could hardly breathe."
"Like those freaks that choke themselves with an orange?"
"Way more fun than an orange."
He gathered her against his chest.
"Well don't drown in the line of duty! So what have you got to confess?"
Loretta's lips moved on the skin of his chest.
"Now isn't a good time" she murmured.
"Worse than shoes? Credit card fraud?"
She slapped him lightly.
"No.... I got pulled by the traffic police yesterday, for driving without due care and attention."
"Not good. What happened?
"I was doing ninety over the Barton bridge, drinking a coke and trying to read your text at the time too. Stupid really. The policeman was a real tosser, gave me a producer for my 'BUSTY' number-plate too, but couldn't stop ogling my tits. Bet he wanked off all over his police car."
James laughed loudly.
"Yes! You're beginning to talk like a truck-driver. Call our lawyers! Anything else?"
Silence.
"Anything else?"
"Well...... today before meeting you I soloed Giants Crawl....."
"Bloody hell I'm hooked up with an adrenaline junky! Are you nuts?"
"You're not cross?"
"Not cross, no. I would have been ashamed if you fell off but I am impressed; don't think I would do it, not sober anyway. It's a ballsy achievement. Why?"
She flushed and squirmed, with un-recallable words on the tip of her tongue.
"I.......sometimes I just feel stupid and useless; doing something hard makes it better."
He hugged her close and squeezed.
"Been there. Girls need to talk things through and you can tell me anything. I'm a good listener, for a bloke."
Loretta could think of one thing he wouldn't want to listen to. She lay awake as his breathing slowed and he dropped off. At seven am the following day James was still gently snoring and Loretta was ravenous. For some reason swallowing semen always made her

hungry so she ordered coffee and a croissant to keep her going until they had breakfast together, speaking softly so as not to wake him. She wanted more sex too. The order arrived with a complimentary newspaper and shortly afterwards James was awoken by chilled water from the ice buckets being tipped over his head. He shot upright, roaring, looking round for a weapon, only to find a slender finger waving in front of his blurry eyes.

"James Hacking, I will slash your testicles off with a rusty razor-blade and feed them to you one ball at a time, if you ever, ever, deceive me about something like this again!"

James blinked.

"Too early for testicles; how about coffee and doughnuts?"

"Hah!"

A broadsheet newspaper slapped him in the chest. Front-page centre was a photograph of him in the Otter, sitting sideways-on in the pilot's seat, legs dangling in the sun as he smiled down tiredly down at a group of Arabs standing on a pier in Malta. A young boy was sitting right on the edge of the seat beside him, facing forward, hands on the control yolk and delight on his face. Several young Arab women in elegant western dress and headscarves were gazing up with expressions akin to adoration and an elderly man in a traditional robe was bent slightly forward with his hand on his chest, plainly in thanks. Another showed an explosion, viewed from an aircraft with James's profile left of centre.

The print stated that Captain James Hacking, a British pilot operating from Malta, had made a daring rescue of Libyan Regime relatives in a seaplane during a fierce fire-fight between Gadaffi loyalists and rebels. He looked quizzically at her.

"What's up? Like I said, it was a charter job."

James's mind was racing. Neither Denzil nor Rod would have been so unprofessional. Christopher? Unlikely, which left fucking Andreas; he must have snapped the pictures surreptitiously on a camera phone. Greedy bastard!

"What's up is I forbade you to take these lethal contracts anymore, and you agreed! We may be stretching ourselves a bit financially but money isn't worth getting killed for!"

"I didn't do it for money; I did it because someone I cared about needed my help."

After breakfast and more sex Loretta gunned the Jag northwards towards home.

"Why didn't you just tell me the truth?"
"Ah. The truth: a delicate commodity."
"Don't be smart, just answer the question."
"Well it is delicate. Do you always tell me the truth?"
Loretta quickly covered her eyes with the sun-glasses poised on her forehead and began to blush but James didn't notice, he was watching the road and his foot was pressing on an imaginary brake. She finally noticed the truck pulling out and shot into the fast lane.
"Fuck, arguing with you is like having a hot enema!"
James smiled.
"Thank you. The answer obviously is no. And do you sometimes lie to protect me or spare my feelings?"
"Yes I suppose so."
"Well I didn't lie, just omitted certain pertinent facts. That was because I knew you would kick off like this."
"Well how can you do stupid dangerous things like that when you know how much I love you? Dammit!"
James lowered his own sunglasses and peered at her pointedly. She flicked a glance at him and compressed her lips as he continued.
"Giant's Crawl ring any bells? Anyway, a situation arose and I had to deal with it, while causing the least distress possible to you."
She banged the walnut steering wheel.
"But your loyalty is to me!"
"Yes, and to others. Look, if I had mentioned the facts, you would have been worried sick, and I would have performed less well because I would have been worried about you being worried."
She ground her teeth.
"What the fuck does that mean? It'll take me a week to figure out!"
"Listen, you know very well that Denzil flew my father out of Rhodesia when he escaped from prison. If he'd been caught they'd have banged him up for years along with my Dad. So when Denzil called about his difficulty, I repaid the compliment."
"Wait until I see that fucking Denzil! I'll have his kidneys for breakfast for putting you in danger!"
James laughed loudly.
"Now you're on the right track!"
She swung angry eyes towards him, then laughed at him laughing, swerving wildly.
"Jesus Loretta, that truck-driver nearly shit himself!"

She was laughing so hard she could hardly see, so she put her foot down in case she hit anything, reaching for his hand.

"I fucking love you!"

"I can tolerate you too; for short spells anyway."

"That was the last time James, no more, or you can bloody-well find some other poor woman to worry about you!"

When they arrived home there were seven messages from reporters on the answer-phone, asking for comments by James on the news report. He erased them all as Loretta looked on.

"Why not give interviews and make some money out of your infamy?"

"Because there is great joy to be had in obscurity; if I don't comment the story will soon die and some things are better kept as secret as possible."

She nodded soberly in agreement.

☐

CHAPTER FIVE
PART TWO
UK: Friday one month later
Storm Clouds for James and Loretta

James jumped a deep drainage ditch beside the airfield then turned left onto a recently tarmacked driveway which ran through green sheep-cropped paddocks up to the clubhouse. He had been for a run through surrounding farms and stopped to admire their new Airfield sign. He, Loretta, Dennis, Haley and Arthur had worked relentlessly since Malta to get the aerodrome ready again as a flying venue, and despite the raft of permits required and anti-flying lobbies that objected, had finally managed, securing government and council grants in the process for bringing commerce and jobs to West Lancashire. Money had been advanced against the sale of both James's Farmhouse and Dennis's Bachelor pad and just when everything was settling down, Dennis dropped a bombshell. The Bachelor pad wasn't actually his to hock. His ex-wife was on the deeds and the lending bank had withheld two hundred thousand pounds of their loan until the legalities were settled. It put their new Company in a desperate cash-flow position in order to stay afloat and poisoned relationships because Dennis refused to take a bridging loan on his house in Parbold to make up the difference. James was an honest cash-on-the-barrelhead man and didn't believe in the greedy cheque-is-in-the-post mentality that withheld payment as long as possible; now he was having to carefully juggle who got what and when, which annoyed him extremely. He'd been all for ditching Dennis but it was almost impossible without bringing the whole project down round their ears. Luckily while they'd been occupied with their recriminations and manoeuvring, Art and Haley had done the continental driving without complaint or major mishap. She was a miracle with modern technology. She had a 4G connected IPAD and phone and managed the whole trucking operation from the cab of a truck, even when she and Art were in mainland Europe. James suspected that Art did most of the driving on Haley's tacho but he approved of artistic rule interpretation and civil disobedience.

So Ringtail Aviation was reborn and staggering along with each of the three principles having one ordinary share. Dennis was Chief Instructor because he liked titles. The hardest part for James had been borrowing the money; for most of his life he'd managed to avoid doing so. Despite development grants and using their other assets as collateral they had needed to borrow a frightening amount at above market interest rates, and listen to a depressing amount of nonsense from sanctimonious bankers. Dennis's deceit hadn't helped but somehow James's dogged determination had kept the project going. There were already substantial building improvements, runway refurbishments and general landscaping underway. In just six weeks Loretta's dream was up and running, if a bit raw, and they were pleased with their achievements, though James's relationship with Dennis remained strained.

The Airfield had once been Naval Air Station H.M.S Ringtail, a Royal Navy air-training facility built during WW2. There was a monument in the grounds and many pictures and artefacts of memorabilia in the old control tower buildings, the lower floors of which had been renovated as a club-house. There had originally been four runways as was usual for Naval Air Stations and contractors had resurfaced the longest, the nine-hundred meter East/West orientated runway 27/09 which corresponded to the predominant prevailing winds. The other landing areas, hard-standings, taxiways and many redundant hangers were available for further improvement and development.

The enjoyment of surveying their new Empire was suddenly interrupted by an unwelcome sight. James's eyes hardened in annoyed disbelief and he shouted "Oi!" Beside the smart sign that proclaimed "Welcome to Burscough's Ringtail Aerodrome" a walker had paused and his fat Rottweiler squatted with quivering legs, defecating on the grass while the owner struggled to control another.

"All right mate?" asked the man who was large, big-bellied and had a shaved head. He was stubbled, had one earring, several gold chains and wore a leather jacket, blue jeans and steel-toed boots.

"No actually, and I'm not your mate. Pick that up" replied James, pointing at the steaming dung which gave off the sickening stench of meat-fed dog.

"You what? Who the hell are you?"

"I'm the airfield owner and I have no objection to people walking dogs on my land if they clean up after them. Now pick it up."

"Who the hell do you think you're talking to?"

Behind him a vehicle turned into the drive, broad tyres swishing in the puddles. James glanced aside to see Loretta pull up alongside in her green Jaguar XK8, lowering the electric window. He raised a hand in greeting and twitched a forced smile.

"As far as I'm concerned, that dog shitting there is no different to you shitting there. It is disgusting, unsightly and a health risk. Why the hell should I pick up your dog's filth on my land?"

"Well they've got to shit somewhere! They're big animals and there isn't much space on the estate."

"Well how about in your garden on your own grass? Why does a big fellow like you need them anyway? Do you suffer from anxiety or masculine inadequacy?"

"You're asking for a slap mate!"

"Certainly am. Would you like to give me one?"

"James, don't, it isn't worth it!" called Loretta.

"Watch the dogs, I'm warning you!" shouted the owner, wrestling with the leads as James pressed forward.

"Why not drop their leads and give me that slap eh?"

"James!" shouted Loretta, getting out of the Jaguar.

"You're bloody crazy, keep away from me!"

The big man's face was ashen at the expression in James' eyes.

"I'm telling you, pick it up or I'll rub your face in it.""All right, all right!"

The Rottweilers were snarling and twisting their leads round his legs, making him wrench savagely to control them. With difficulty he got the leads in one hand and extracted a large dirty handkerchief, bending towards the shit. The smell got in his throat and he gagged.

"You're a fucking nutter you know that?"

"I just want people to show some civility, clean up after themselves and their animals, that kind of thing; I've got nothing against you and I quite like dogs but dog-owners who don't pick up are selfish pricks."

The man scooped up the shit sullenly, managing to get some on his hand.

"Jesus, you fucking bastard, look what you've made me do!"

"Well it's your pet and your shit. You deserve each other. Have a nice day."

Swearing monotonously the man was dragged away by the snorting slavering animals.

"Get some bags to pick up after them; big ones!" called James. "Then you won't get it on your hands. And don't hang the bags in trees for the shit fairy to collect either!"

"Very diplomatic James; Want a lift? It's starting to rain again."

He kissed her cheek, opened the passenger door and got in.

"I'm sick of people like that. The state has emasculated citizens and the police service alike. There is no consideration and no discipline. Children defy their parents, their teachers, even the police. Why would anyone go to the trouble of picking up an animal's shit and then hang it in a tree? Who do they think is going to collect it? No-one is prepared to make a stand about anything."

"Well you just did."

"Yeah but it won't stop him. He'll just let his dog shit on some old ladies' lawn instead. The moron probably thinks I'm in the wrong because I won't let his dog crap on my grass. We need teams of anti-dogshit police, big guys so the scallies can't intimidate them, and surveillance cameras to record the crime, and get DNA if necessary. I'll volunteer!"

"And flog them too I suppose?"

"Absolutely. It's good cheap justice, easy to administer, extremely painful and very humiliating; a more effective deterrent than prison."

"Just try not to piss the whole world off in your crusade; we have to live here too."

"Me piss the locals off? Jesus, I am the soul of consideration compared to most of them!"

James eyed the rain which was now hammering down, bouncing off the surface of the leased airplanes parked in front of the clubhouse.

"Bad day for flying, we won't get many customers in this deluge. You go on over, I'll just check on Haley in the office."

"I'll light a fire. We can have a cosy afternoon."

"Good idea, I won't be long."

He went across to the clubhouse which already had a friendly pub where members could meet, and a good cafe with an outside beer-garden for viewing. Well-kept flower gardens which were Loretta's new passion bordered the apron.

"How's it looking Haley?"

His nineteen year old daughter was contemplating the wet windswept runways stoically. She was plump and pretty, well groomed and expensively dressed.

"Horrid, Dad. Depression stalled out to the west with successive fronts coming in; winds strong and all over the place. I've cancelled all lessons for now."

"Bloody British climate."

"Yes, but it discourages foreigners like us from immigrating. Chill a bit for once and spend some time with Loretta."

He laughed and she stretched up to kiss him.

"Yugh! Sweaty boy!" She rubbed her lips in mock distaste and he poked a finger teasingly into her spare tyre.

"You should do a bit more sweating yourself; get some cardio-vascular, burn off that pork."

"Dad! I get lots of exercise riding Flopsy, mucking out, carrying horse-food and buckets."

"Actually, Flopsy gets the exercise, you just get saddle-sores on your bum."

"Dad, leave me alone! You can take our excess cash over to the main safe, I've made up the till floats and emptied the vending and games machines." She went into the office and handing him two heavy bags. James walked quickly through warm drizzle to the old Officers' Mess which had been converted into a large comfortable dwelling.

With fingers in so many pies he was perpetually busy and acutely aware that fortunes much bigger than his had been lost through lack of liquidity. A cash injection of some sort was urgently needed and available, but he knew Loretta would kick off big style if he told her. She was still touchy about his dodgy flight to rescue Denzil Harcourt from Libya and though it had become an off-limits subject it was very much an elephant in the room. Going into their new office he put the cash-bags in a wall-safe. A faded envelope inside caught his eye and he took it out. The Rhodesian post mark was more than thirty years old and he had never opened the letter. It had been forwarded to him by a friend, a lawyer called Anthony Jarvis, and was from a woman now dead called Dawn Visser whom James had loved then hated. He believed she had been responsible for his first wife's death. Anthony Jarvis had been killed by a huge bomb in the closing stages of the Rhodesian conflict; detonated by insurgents or "Communist Terrorists" as they were known back in non-pc days, in the supermarket adjoining his Salisbury chambers. The blast effectively destroyed both buildings and all his client records. James sniffed the envelope suspiciously out of habit, checking for evil leaking out, then tossed it back into the safe. Dawn Visser had been the wife of his best friend Gert. A printed email from Lance MacDonald at Conflict Logistic Solutions was on top of the in-basket and caught his eye. He cursed himself for being careless and tucked it into a pocket quickly, not wanting Loretta to see it before he had primed her for the news it contained.

-xxx-

He heard one of their trucks racing up the driveway at a ridiculous speed and crossed to look out of the window. It was being driven by potential son-in-law Arthur Slingsby. In full show-off mode Art gave a long blast on the air-horns, passed the car-park and swerved onto a hard-standing, heading for the disused war-time hanger where the trucks and trailers were parked-up at night. It was on sloping ground near the canal embankment. Art jumped down, opened sliding hanger doors and reversed the gleaming forty-four ton rig inside, transmission howling in protest at the speed. There was a loud clang and James massaged the bridge of his nose in a long suffering fashion. The phone rang and he picked it up.

"Yeah?"

"Dad, it's Haley" said his daughter in a persuasive tone.

"OK. What are you after?"

"Well Art just got in…"

"Yeah, the whole world heard. I've asked him not to hoot because it annoys the locals. And he's hit something in the barn too; I'm going to roast the bugger when I see him."

"Come on Dad, he's just naturally exuberant, he wants you to be proud of him, he worships you!"

"He's naturally a kak-handed idiot. So why are you phoning?"

"Well he's meant to drop that trailer here and pick one up from Heinz in Wigan for Grangemouth in Scotland tomorrow afternoon. I haven't seen him all week and you're not down for flying so could you please do it instead? We really need some quality time together; we're back down the road to Spain on Sunday.""OK, so long as whatever you've got planned doesn't involve getting pregnant. Arthur is a boy whose genes need to die out as soon as possible."

He smiled at his daughter's ecstatic thanks and rang off, a sudden sombre memory making him frown. Haley could sometimes be a bit winsome, perhaps because she had never had siblings; her mother Eve, his second wife, had disappeared in a light aircraft over the Mediterranean while travelling from Djerba Island in Tunisia to Malta through a storm, while he was on flying contract in Libya.

"Whose genes need to die out?" called Loretta from upstairs.

"Arthur's, he's a slapdash menace and Haley is as bad."

"Nonsense, they're great kids. You wouldn't be without them would you?"

"Suppose not but I wouldn't want any more either, it's too hard on the nerves."

"What did they want?"

"Time off, so I'm going up to Scotland instead of Arthur tomorrow. Why not come along? We can stop at Willy's place on the way back, park-up, have a good meal, some laughs and a few drinks."

"Okay, I'll pack us an overnight bag and some rations." She sounded really pleased.

"Good, I'll be back in a minute."

James went out to the transport hanger. If his money-making plan was to work he'd need a semi-permanent driver to cover the shifts he normally drove himself.

"What did you break this time Arthur, you bloody buffoon?"

"Just a tail-light James. Sorry."

"Lucky! Fix it; how about I make you a partner and then you'll be wasting your own money all the time instead of mine?"

"Sorry James."

"You bloody will be. Do you know any good Class 1 drivers locally?"

"Yeah, there's a very experienced bloke who was in the Army with me but he doesn't like you much."

"Really, why's that then?"

"I saw him as I was driving in. Complained about you not letting his dogs shit on our grass; said you had killers' eyes."

"Oh, him."

"He's a good bloke really, just having a hard time; his wife ran off leaving him with a young kid and those dogs, been struggling to get work."

"Where's he live?"

Art told him.

"Name?"

"Dave Swinnerton."

"OK. I'll give him your job shall I?"

"No! You're joking right?"

"Maybe."

Stepping back into the warm house from the raw rainy day made him shiver and he checked that the fire was still burning well.

"Loretta? Where are you?"

"Still up here waiting" she called faintly, causing excitement of a different kind and he jogged upstairs. She was naked on the large bed, waggling a bottle of Champagne and two flutes.

"Friday treat! I've been in the bath so I'm all fragrant and relaxed."
"And looking good enough to eat!"
He fired the cork into the ceiling, poured, and handed her a glass.
"Not the only cork that's going to pop; yours is next Loretta!"
He toasted her, and then ran his icy tongue from her belly button downwards.

Afterwards they rested, holding hands and panting as the love-sweats cooled and the fluids dried in tight patches on their skin. They dozed briefly then woke, drank more wine and talked. James idly caressed her firm curves, and she tickled his neck.

"I bet you feel better after that. You've looked tense and worried lately."

He nodded.

"Eased the springs a treat; I'm just jaded from long hours and worrying about finances; why the hell did we ever get into the transport game? It's a hard, brutal dirty business and I mean dirty in every sense of the word. I try to give the drivers decent wages and conditions but our bloody customers expect us to wait ninety days for payment. We're being squeezed from all sides, including fucking Dennis."

"Don't go off again about that, he's said he'll sort something out. The airfield revenue should pick up soon too. I've been inundated with enquiries by clubs and groups keen to move here. The grants we got are helping with cash-flow. We could sell the transport side and concentrate on aviation."

"Yes, but right now the trucking provides our bread and butter. Despite Dennis and the bloody government and the late-paying supermarkets, it makes steady money, but the next instalment on the aircraft leases is due and I don't know where the money will come from. Without planes there is no flying school. What we really need is a big cash injection."

Loretta pushed herself up on one elbow, looking suspicious.

"Any ideas, apart from suicidally dangerous rescue missions? You're not going to rob a bank next are you?"

"Nice thought but no. We could sell your Jaguar; save a fortune on petrol."

"Over my dead body! Maybe I can get some more money out of the family trust.

"George already said no, which he likes to do and anyway, I don't really want your family's money; it's still borrowing after all, on top of all the other borrowing."

"Yes but I wouldn't be paying bank interest. You just don't like taking anything from anyone! Jesus! 'James; the cat that walks alone!' If we need cash so badly, have you got any other ideas?"

A wry smile crossed James's face as he thought of the email in his pocket. He would have to show it to her some time but it would be cruel when she was in such a good mood.

"Yes, one or two actually; I'd rather earn the money somehow than borrow it. Anyway let's not spoil today talking about business. Shall we have dinner out, or in by the fire?"

"In. I don't want to go anywhere on a lousy wet night. I might not have finished with you yet either, so don't go anywhere."

Loretta went off to the bathroom and James lay in the rumpled bed thinking idle thoughts; about business, about Libya, the recent email, Colinda, and the old unopened letter in their safe. He slipped into a drowsy reverie about the past, trying to guess despite himself what news the letter might contain.

He began thinking about the period in 1980 just after his young wife and unborn child had been murdered in a landmine explosion, as a result of a boosted anti-tank mine laid by Spencer Katsiru. James and Denzil had left white Rhodesia shortly afterwards just as it transitioned to black Zimbabwe, to avoid the bitterness of seeing their enemies march into the country triumphantly, and had joined the South African Defence Forces Recce unit 'Koevoet,' fighting SWAPO in South West Africa and Angola. James had left his homeland reluctantly, unable to stomach defeat and the flamboyant return in 1980 of Robert Mugabe's victorious troops, but he was quickly pissed off by the monotonous hot bush of Northern Namibia and he was sick of carnage. It was pointless to him because he couldn't feel involved the way he had in Rhodesia, his birthplace.

He was growing pissed off too with his long-time older friend Denzil Harcourt's gung-ho enjoyment of the hazards, his dangerous recklessness and the continual slaying. It seemed that the smell of rotting human flesh had been in his nostrils forever. Denzil's favourite toy was a seventy-five mm recoilless rifle mounted on a Landrover. That very day he'd almost got them killed by pursuing fleeing SWAPO terrorists right into their own lines in Southern Angola. The first they'd known of the enormous camp was when Denzil drove the Landrover smack into the terrorists' trench system, sending them all flying out of the vehicle. Only the close proximity of a South African Defence Force "Casspir" Armoured Personnel Carrier bristling with cannon and machine-guns had saved their butts and they'd had to run to it through a storm of small-arms fire while Denzil roared with laughter, as if it was the funniest thing ever to crash into a heavily defended enemy trench. With American CIA backing, the South African Defence Forces were driving from Namibia into southern Angola once more, supporting UNITA against the Soviet/Cuban backed MPLA, and there had been increasing skirmishes with Cuban-led forces as a result.

Back at base James, for privacy, had sat on in the Cupola of the Casspir after the soldiers debussed, behind the co-mounted 20mm cannon and heavy MAG machine-gun and sipped a luke-warm Hansa beer as he flicked idly through a 'Scope' magazine full of girls in bikinis. In contrast there was not a solitary feminine thing about any of the brutal looking weapons and vehicles that surrounded him; they were all hard, drab, heavy and functional. He began to think of people doing normal things, his mother and father in the Cape, Peter in Argentina on the flowing pampas, Sheila and Patrick having kids on the Vumba farm in Zimbabwe. They would be riding horses, going to cinemas, fishing or walking in the hills. Suddenly a great surge of longing to be alone in remote mountains had swept over James, to be away from heat and flies and the smells of dust and diesel and paraffin. A tanned very-young soldier doing radio-op duty dressed only in green shorts and flip-flops had stooped out from under a flysheet rigged as an Afdek against the side of a truck. In the meagre shade were large maps above folding tables covered in radio and telephone equipment. James recognised him as the parabat machine-gunner on the Casspir that had rescued them.

"Ja James" he called. "There's a phone-skakel for you jong, sounds like some chick ek se!" James climbed down wondering if it could be his sister Sheila and at first the familiar voice didn't register at all.

"Who is it again please?" he asked in puzzlement.

"Dawn! Dawn Visser James, Gert's wife. It's taken me days to get through on the phone."

James's face had hardened.

"What the fuck do you want, you bitch?" he grated.

"Don't be like that.... please! Gert's dead James, a tractor rolled on him."

James closed his eyes and could think of nothing to say. The line sang and peeped emptily.

"I'm sorry, he was a great guy" he said eventually, remembering things about his friend.

"Is that all you can say? Look James, you have to give us a chance, I need you and Jemima needs a father. We're right for each other James, you know we are, we always were. I'm sorry Gert and Amanda are both gone but it's not my fault and we're both free now. You have to come back to me James, I'm desperate."

James looked at the receiver in distaste.

"Pull yourself together you horrible cow. Stop thinking about yourself for once and put your daughter first, she's going to need a lot of love from you with Gert gone. And as for Us, anything I felt for you died the night my wife did. And she died because you couldn't keep your spiteful fucking gob closed! I'd rather eat dogshit than live with you. Don't call me again, ever."

She sensed he was going to hang up and shouted "Wait James, I didn't just tell Amanda we'd been lovers, there was something else important too. I told her..."

"I don't want to fucking know about it, now or ever!" he shouted into the handset and crashed it down on the base, breathing hard. The radio op was looking embarrassed, pretending he was deaf. James took a shuddering breath.

"Thanks hey man. Listen, do me a favour, if she phones again, tell her I'm not here. And thanks for saving our gats. What's your name?"

"MAG Marais, the 7.62 music man."

And James never had heard from Dawn again, though she'd intended him to, from beyond the grave if necessary.

Following her humiliating, hope-defeating call to James, Dawn Visser had remembered a friend of his who was a lawyer and looked up the firm's address in Salisbury, which had already been renamed 'Harare', just as Rhodesia had been renamed 'Zimbabwe.' She drove into Umtali, bought some items in a stationary store and then went to the smart modern post office building near the cinemas. She mounted the steps and went to one of the writing desks in the hall, eyeing the long queues of patiently waiting black people resignedly. There were hardly any other white people in the building, they hadn't the patience for the snail-like service which had always been sluggish even under the colonial regime and was now even more lethargic.

"Dear Mr. Jarvis" she wrote. "I have known James Hacking through many years and whenever I heard him speak of you it was always with the highest regard for your professionalism and integrity. I also know that he regarded you as a very close friend. Knowing that James trusted you means that I can trust you too. I am a widow and have a young daughter Jemima. There exists some information that Jemima is at present too young to understand but will one day want to know, and I am concerned that should anything happen to me, this vital knowledge will be lost to her. I have nobody close who I can trust and am therefore asking you the considerable favour of guarding in your safe-keeping the enclosed letter addressed to Jemima, until her sixteenth birthday, and I would ask that in the event I am not able to tell her of the contents myself you will do your utmost to see that she receives this letter then. (Jemima was born on the seventh of August 1976.)

I also enclose a letter for James Hacking whose whereabouts I am unable to ascertain. Please do your best to forward it to him as soon as possible. Against the event that you will have to make disbursements I enclose 100 dollars on account. I know you will not let me down. Yours faithfully, Dawn Visser."

She enclosed her letter to James Hacking in one envelope, the letter to Jemima in another and then sealed all three letters and the money in a third, larger, tougher one. She waited interminably in line to get to the counter and finally despatched it to Anthony Jarvis by recorded delivery at his Salisbury chambers. Outwardly little had changed in Umtali since Independence but she drove through a road-block at Christmas Pass manned by smart black para-militaries all wearing very dark sunglasses; it made them look like dangerous wasps. They were not overtly disrespectful but their dispassionate sinister gaze made her skin crawl.

When Dawn returned to Gert's parents' farm near Old Umtali Mission, Jemima was sitting in the shade of a tree on a blanket with her African nanny. Her Grandmother sat on a canvas camp chair nearby, knitting. Dawn walked down the red-polished steps of the sprawling rundown farmhouse. Jemima shrieked "Mummy!" rushing towards her mother, full of life and tremendously strong but she tripped just before she got to Dawn and fell over. Jumping quickly up her cheeky face creased in a heart-melting smile. Small exquisite lips parted in a rich almost ribald chuckle that was pure James.

"Silly me!" she said.

Dawn hugged her until the child squirmed like a puppy to get free.
"Why are you crying Mummy? Have you hurt yourself?" she asked in interest.

"No, but I have to go away for a while darling. Ouma and Oupa will look after you. Here, I've got a present for you."

She undid the clasp at her neck and removed the thick gold chain. Jemima looked at the Saint Christopher medallion.

"Who's he Mummy?" she asked wrinkling her nose.

"Saint Christopher. He looks after people, especially when they go on a journey. Somebody I love very much gave it to me long ago. Look, it's engraved with our initials on the back. His are JH; He loves you too but he just doesn't know it yet. He will one day though."

"Do you mean my Daddy?"

The placid barefooted nanny strolled towards them as Dawn stood up and went back towards the house with long strides, almost running, skirt flying.

"Where are you going Mummy? Are you going to see Daddy? Can I come, Mummy? Can I come?" shouted Jemima starting after her.

The nanny stooped and swept her up.

"Hush baby, Mummy soon be back. Show me your beautiful chain. What a lucky girl you are!"

She started walking back towards the blanket in the shade but Jemima was looking over her shoulder and sobbing. Some minutes later a loud gunshot caused an explosion of panicked crows from the trees at the back of the house. Jemima Visser had become an orphan, just as her mother had been. Dawn Visser left no note at the scene but her final thought was "He'll be sorry now."

Before he died in a terrorist bomb-blast at the building containing his offices, Anthony Jarvis forwarded Dawn's letter to James, but the one to Jemima was destroyed along with all his other records. And decades later James had still not felt able to read Dawn's letter.

-xxx-

As they departed Burscough the next day in a bob-tailed Scania tractor-unit to pick up the ASDA Grangemouth trailer in Wigan, James turned off on impulse and parked beside the canal in Victoria Street.

"Won't be long Lorr."

He went into the garden of an attractive end-terraced cottage and knocked on the wooden porch entrance. Dogs began to bark hysterically and a male voice shouted in frustration before Dave

Swinnerton came to the door and jerked it open. Surprise and fear blossomed on his face as he took an involuntary step back, moving to close it again hurriedly.

"What the fuck do you want now? I'll have the police on you...." he stuttered.

"Relax; it's not about the dogs. Art says you can drive. Are you working at the moment?"

"Agency work sometimes but I have to commute a long way to get it. All costs money. And time."

The messy front room was small and smelt of dead embers from a fireplace near the stairs. An exposed wooden staircase led upstairs and there was a door to a kitchen diner. Swinnerton wiped a hand over his face looking embarrassed.

"Wife buggered off and left me with my little daughter and those two bastard dogs. Mum helps with Amy but she won't have the animals. I'm at my wits end with them."

"Haley runs transport admin so get your licence up to her. We have regular shifts to cover and I'd rather use locals than agency. It's part-time but could become permanent."

"OK, I'll give it a try."

When James was at the front gate Swinnerton called.

"Don't suppose you want a couple of guard dogs?"

James turned, about to refuse but paused. If he was going to be away trying to make money elsewhere, maybe it wasn't such a bad idea to have some security on the premises for Loretta and Haley.

"I'll let you know next week."

There was a group of young boys looking enviously at the customised Scania.

"Give us a blast on your horn mister!"

James laughed.

"Can't son; I'd break all the windows in the street. You can climb up and see inside the cab though. Just take those grubby shoes off."

James gave each a quick look and when they finally pulled away the excited kids ran along the grass opposite the Waterfront pub pretending to be truck drivers. James gave them a very tiny snort on the silver horns and pulled away into the high street.

"That was the dog-shit bloke back there wasn't it? What have you been up to now?"

"Offered him part-time work; Art and Haley both know him and say he grafts hard."

At Heinz in Wigan the manifest documents had to be collected from the Transport Office and the Security man in the gatehouse advised that the loaded trailer was parked in bay 84 of the herringbone park in the middle of the yard.

"Right Lorr, you couple-up while I get the paperwork."

"Why don't I get the paperwork?"

He slapped his upper arm with forked fingers to simulate military stripes.

"Because I am the boss and I need to see the Transport manager!"

She stuck her tongue out but climbed across behind the steering-wheel and backed under the semi-trailer, using airbags to raise the fifth wheel, taking the weight off the trailer landing gear legs and performing a 'split-couple' to avoid getting dirty on the deck behind the cab. Connecting the five air and electrical lines she struggled to get the red hose on, cursing under her breath because the air-pressure kept pushing against her. She felt a nail tear inside her glove. Climbing back into the Scania she reversed gently the rest of the way under and the pin engaged with the fifth wheel giving two barely detectable clicks. Shifting into forward she tugged twice to make sure the attachment was secure then put the retaining pin in and wound the landing gear up. It was old and stiff requiring lots of effort so she was sweating during the rest of the checks. In fifteen minutes they were ready to go. Once over the weighbridge she set the tachometer recorder mode for 'Driver Two' from 'work' to 'drive' and they were off through the streets of Wigan. Heading north up the M6 motorway it was one of those rare good days to be driving in the UK. Traffic was light and late shafts of sun were peeking spectacularly through some dissipating storm clouds, making the cloudy day less gloomy. Throttle set on cruise control, the Scania ghosted effortlessly up through the Lake District and the Scottish border hills, giant quietly-rumbling engine hardly stretched by the load, thrusting the heated leather seats gently against their backs in an exhilarating sense of power, as if they were riding on an elephant. Sitting so high-up gave great visibility and views beyond the motorway barriers of rural Britain at its best.

It grew dark and Loretta asked James to take over. She had century radio tuned and a female DJ with a sexy voice was playing back-to-back seventies disco hits with ridiculous lyrics, heavy on cheerful beat. James accelerated to maximum and set the cruise control, turning on the low blue foot-well lights making a cosy cabin of the walk-through cab. She took off her trousers and boots then stood up, barefoot, dressed comfortably in black stretch tights and a stripy tee-shirt and began to look in all the compartments and cupboards of the sleeper cab.

"You're as nosy as a pussy cat, this is Art and Haley's living space most of the time; have a little respect!"

"It's ours too, when we do the Europe run. And it is a woman's prerogative to be nosy; in fact it's very much part of our purpose on earth."

"I didn't know women had a purpose on earth; well, perhaps one maybe."

"Yes, and don't you forget it or you won't be getting any. Let's see what they've got in our fridge."

She opened the door and whistled.

"Jackpot! Eight cans of Stella and a few cokes."

She grabbed an ice-cold Stella Artois and popped the ring-pull, licking the foam that surged from the opening lasciviously, eyeing James mischievously.

"Hey, it's rude to drink alone, pass one over here."

"You can't drink, you're driving!"

"How is me drinking from a can of beer while driving different to you drinking a can of coke in the Jag?"

"Well. It just is!"

"It isn't. So long as I'm not over the legal blood/alcohol limit it is exactly the same. We both might be breaking some other law, like "without due care and attention" though. You can get done these days just for eating an apple apparently. Bloody nonsense."

"Smartass! I'd like to see you explaining all that to a Magistrate."

"I wouldn't, but if it happens my lawyer will do the explaining, I'll just sit there looking innocent and contrite. Come on, hand one over!"

She passed the opened can at eye level so he could keep his watchful gaze on the road ahead.

"You are a very evil man."

He grinned youthfully.

"Rules are for the guidance of the wise not slavish following by the thick masses."

He swigged and belched.

"So you keep saying, like a broken record!"

She sat down in the comfy seat, shaking her head in disbelief.

"And by the way, even if you are a nosy cat, you're the best pussy I've ever had!"

She banged her beer-can against his, humming with the music and tapping her shapely thigh, then rolled her head to look out of the window at the darkness. She felt really happy and relaxed which was just the way James wanted her.

-xxx-
Scotland, Saturday

The fork-lift truck drivers at ASDA's main distribution centre in Grangemouth on the Firth of Forth were keen to finish their shift for the night so James backed straight onto an unloading bay in the vast bustling yard, swished open the taut-liner's curtains and they whisked the 26-ton palletised load off in under ten minutes. When he went to collect the consignment notes, two ugly female clerks in a dirty office behind a small thick window studiously ignored him, though he knocked politely after a few minutes. As time ticked by a feeling of impotent rage began to build inside him so he went for a leak in the noisome driver's toilet and got foul coffee from a battered machine by one wall. When he returned they had disappeared altogether but he could see the notes on a shelf just inside the window slit, but out of reach. One of the middle-aged fork-lift drivers appeared from the warehouse on his way home.

"It's shift-change now so they're on a break. Did the blurry witches not give you the paperwork? It's no right, wait here a minute Drive."

He appeared in the office a few minutes later, checked the paperwork for signatures and returned.

"There you go pal, signed stamped and everythin'. They ken fine that time is money to hauliers but they get some kick out of treating drivers like shite. It's nae bloody wonder the bitches have to hide behind armoured glass is it? Mind how ye go."

With his faith in human nature partially restored James hurried back out to the truck.

"Jobs a good 'un Lorr. Let's get off to Willy's; I'm ready for a proper drink now."

The Scotsman ran a justifiably popular pub and restaurant called "The Claymore" not far off the M74 near Gretna Green, about two hours south of Glasgow. He also owned the adjacent caravan park and a secure truck-stop with good ablutions and showers.

"Too right partner, I'm going to call and tell him we're coming, I could eat a dead skunk" said Loretta.

James had just had the one can of beer on the way up but Loretta had had several, evidenced by a certain flamboyance of manner and speech. He hoped she wasn't going to get completely blotto; oiled with just the right amount of alcohol she was amusing, but a bit too much made her unpredictable. He decided to get some food into her as soon as they got to Willy's.

Loretta found the number and dialled it.

"Wully! It's Loretta you old reprobate. James and I are on our way, be about two hours. We need a couple of your biggest steaks!"

She waved her arms wide to show how big and splashed beer from her can on James. The Scotsman's loud but pleasant Edinburgh accent carried easily from the hands-free on the dash.

"Loretta! My favourite girl, where have ye been? I'll tell Howling Gail to get some steaks ready the noo, how will ye want them done?"

"Rare like usual Wully and big; in fact just cut off the horns and wipe the arse."

"Och you Sassenachs are getting awful soft, having the arses wiped. Anybody would think you're gentry."

"We damn well are! I'm going to need a big gin and tonic too."

"You got it. Call again when you're fifteen minutes away."

"Ten four Wully Whiskers, roger, dodger over and out."

She punched the phone off-button.

"To Willey's, James and don't spare the 580 horses. On second thoughts stop at once, my bladder is bursting!"

She had to run into some bushes behind a bus-stop to go, but after several years of trucking she was used to such inconveniences and returned past the waiting travellers with aplomb. Just over two hours later in the middle of an enjoyable meal she threw her fork down on the table and glared at the email James had given her.

"Fucking Iraq?" she shouted at the top of her strident voice.

"What is it with you mad bastards? What is your fascination with extreme violence? Ever since that whole sorry mess in the middle-east was instigated by the idiot Bush I could sense that you wanted to get involved!"

Willey's Restaurant was full and noisy but all of a sudden you could hear a pin drop. James tried to make himself small and inconspicuous.

"Lorr, shush, you'll give yourself a coronary; nothing's definite and time spent on reconnaissance is never wasted."

"You bastard! Typical scenario, soften the little woman up with booze and a nice dinner, then Whammo! So what is this safe, high-paying job in Iraq?"

"Transport, delivering aviation fuel for the Americans. Not much different from what we did today."

"Oh yeah right! Bloody marvellous! You told me yourself that private firms do as much work in Iraq, even the fighting, as the American Army, that many of their forces are ex-South African or Rhodesian and that quite a few get killed within a few months."

Her voice was cold and contemptuous.

"Yeah but I wouldn't be fighting. We need money and this is a way to get lots of it, quickly and legitimately. And it's safe. We'd be embedded, protected by the American Forces."

With her hot-blooded Italian ancestry, a Loretta paddy was a sight to behold but magnificent as she looked in her rage, James thought it wise not to remark upon it. She glared, gathering herself for another tirade.

"Look" he said hastily "as a professional soldier I can't deny that I find the conflict interesting but that's not why I'm going…."

"You're not fucking going! Forget about it, we don't need money that bad, only a really sad bastard would need money that bad! I told you after that Libya bullshit with Denzil bloody Harcourt, he's another suicidal idiot just like you!"

Loretta had a refined, clipped accent with a South African twang that carried beautifully to all parts of the restaurant and she seldom swore, a measure of her extreme agitation.

"You're sick James, a fucking war junkie!"

Willey looked up from behind the bar and strode over, easing his bulk apologetically between the tables.

"Everything all right folks?" he asked worriedly.

"No it's fucking not! James is being a shit Wully, he wants to leave me and go to Iraq."

Willy rolled his eyes at James.

"Does he now? I'm delighted to hear it; I've been after having ye to meself fer years but could ye curse a wee bit less loudly?"

She grabbed his big hand.

"Sorry Wully Whiskers. You're a treasure but that bastard there has spoiled everything. Can we just have the bill?"

Loretta stalked way ahead of James through the floodlit gardens round the Claymore Restaurant and savagely punched the code buttons on the gate into the lorry park. She kept up the frigid silence as they prepared for bed in the two bunks of the sleeper cab, climbing up onto the top one and turning her back. The bare soles of her feet looked incredibly sexy and vulnerable and James felt like a shit. She began to snore. He gently pulled up the covers, kissed her neck and turned out the lights, mind whirring. That was the trouble with greed, he reflected. Once a big enough carrot has been dangled it is almost impossible to ignore. And the Iraq job was a very big carrot, though he admitted part of his excitement was the thought of being in a combat zone again. Perhaps Lorr was right, perhaps he was sick.

-xxx-

CHAPTER SIX
Scotland, Sunday.

On Sunday morning James was woken by the clangour of a tractor unit in the lorry-park dropping one trailer and coupling another to its 5th wheel. He climbed out of the Scania cab to wash and shave in the truck-stop ablutions, then bought bacon butties and coffee for the journey. Loretta was still snoring gently when he pulled the big articulated vehicle onto the motorway. Setting the cruise control, he listened to the radio as he scoffed a bacon sandwich and drank coffee.

After a few miles she swung her smooth elegant legs out of the bunk. She was tousle-headed and wearing just a tee-shirt so James caught a glimpsed of her sexy Brazilian-trimmed minge, just a 'landing strip' of jet black hair above the voluptuous lips. He grew instantly hard and wished they weren't arguing so he could pull over and make love to her.

"Morning darling" he said brightly.

"Mmmm" she said and lowered herself like a gymnast onto the passenger seat, breasts moving enticingly under the thin T-shirt. Reaching for a moistened wipe from the box on the dash she dabbed her face with it, chewing a mouth-freshening mint.

She looked at James with cloudy spaniel eyes.

"I'm very sad, and very cross with you."

"What can I say Lorr?"

"Say you won't go to that awful place."

"This is all just tentative."

"Tell me about it then."

He fished the email out of his trouser pocket, handing it to her silently. It was badly creased because she had crumpled it and thrown it to the restaurant floor in her anger. She unfolded it.

"Conflict Logistics Solutions" she read aloud. "What's that?"

"Subsidiary of a big American company, competes with Halliburton and the like; big player in the oilfields particularly where things are complicated by political dissention and war. I came across them when I worked in Libya."

"Oh. So what, when, how much? And most importantly, knowing you, how dangerous?"

Loretta's voice was curiously dead and lifeless, far more uncomfortable for James than her outburst the previous night. The silence, ominous and threatening like the eye in a hurricane, drew out uncomfortably.

"Like I said last night, transport in Iraq, delivering bulk fuel for the Americans. It's commuter schedule, month on month off so the separations wouldn't be that long. No different than we've been used to in the past on overseas flying contracts."

"Very different than we've been used to; it's Iraq, probably still the most dangerous place in the world right now."

"Things have got a lot safer. We'd be embedded, protected by the American Forces." Unless they pull combat troops out on 31st October as they announced, he thought but didn't say.

"But you'll still be in an active war zone with roadside bombs, and suicide bombings and worst of all kidnappings. I watch the news you know, I'd go out of my mind worrying about you."

"Look Lorr, both the trucking and flying businesses are leveraged to the hilt, this is shit or bust for me; I'm getting on, over fifty already. The only way I've ever earned money is by taking chances; I haven't had a nice steady corporate career with healthcare, and a pension to look forward to at the end of it. Everything I've got is now tied up in speculative ventures and any of them could go pear-shaped through lack of cash-flow, compliments of Dennis. You two got me into this and I don't want to end up old and broke."

She exploded.

"And what about the future I bloody want? It certainly isn't to be trotting after you into ever more ambitious venture-deals that have us working like slaves. I'm tired, I want to relax a bit, maybe go skiing occasionally, have a holiday in the sun with you. I'm not rich by any means but the family Trust Fund is a safety net and there's enough for both of us when we retire."

"Jesus, what hypocrisy; it was you that talked me into the Burscough thing!"

"I wanted you to get out of trucking and back into flying, with some self-respect!"

"Ah ha, now I see; us being greasy haulage contractors actually embarrasses you, despite the kicks you get from playing the tough, chic female truck-driver at dinner parties."

"I don't just play at it; I'm quite good at it!"

"Either way you have to admit we're over-extended and as far as I'm concerned this is a safe, quick way to make enough bucks to get back on the rails."

"Well you can bullshit yourself all you like about the reasons but you can't bullshit me!"

-xxx-

James had been on his hands-free phone and managed to pick up a backload from Penrith to a trans-shipment warehouse at Skelmersdale in Lancashire, not far from Burscough.

"No money in running empty hey partner?" he said, leaning across to slap Loretta's sleek thigh.

She looked at him steadily, no smile.

"Don't smarm me Hacking. This isn't some tiff that'll go away with a make-up tumble in the hay. I am seriously unhappy and very worried that our relationship, let alone my peace of mind, means so little to you, How can you keep doing this to someone you love? I'm terrified and you haven't even gone yet!"

He sighed in exasperation.

"You're beginning to piss me off, nothing's been decided and we're fighting about something that might never happen. I'm just flying down to London to make a pitch at CLS's offices in Canary Wharf."

"Pitch for what exactly? I still don't fully understand exactly what's involved."

James thought she was beginning to crack.

"Lance, one of the Field Directors, wants someone who can recruit, outfit, transport and babysit a number of Class one drivers, preferably with military experience, to Kuwait to pick up some new articulated fuel-tankers in Kuwait City, deliver them to Baghdad and put them in service."

"So it's not just you who'll be going?"

"Not if I get the contract. They want me to take a dozen drivers out to Iraq for an initial six month period, six at a time on month-on-month off schedule. I can use our existing equipment to do the inductions and assess if they can really drive and I'll soon know if they are suitable for a military environment."

"Who is going to run things here while you're away?"

"You are, ably assisted by Dennis, Haley and Art. Look, safety will be top of the list on my agenda. Why don't you come, it might calm a few of your worries? We could stay over in London, see a show, do some shopping."

He knew it was possible the requirement for twelve Class-one drivers was due to attrition but he wasn't going to mention that.

The very faintest smile appeared on Loretta's lips.

"My goodness, you're transparent! Another classic male sop; shut the little woman up with the hint of some shopping!"

"Well has it worked?"

"No. If you go to that meeting in London we're finished."

She clamped her lips shut and gazed out of the side-window, eyes frosty and determined.

In the poisonous silence that followed James pondered the possibility of just sending the other drivers but knew from earlier discussions that Lance was as much interested in his military leadership experience as his driving and transport expertise, Denzil had talked him up a treat while they were waiting to be rescued in Libya. Without him on the ground as a controlling influence they wouldn't be interested.

-xxx-
Lancashire

The weather at Burscough flying school was clear and bright. James and Dennis had several student lessons each and the circuit was busy with visiting aircraft taking advantage of the good weather and low landing fees for practice touch and goes, free altogether if they bought fuel. Most pilots stayed and had a meal or snack so the cafe was busy too. There were a few curious non-flying visitors from the local area, come to plane-spot and ask questions.

James checked flight procedures and fees in and out of London City Airport. They were prohibitive so he settled for Biggin Hill, an ex-Battle of Britain fighter base eleven miles south-west of London and handy for the City. Towards sunset he fuelled the Turbo Arrow ready for the morning and put her away at the front of the hanger, then checked the airfield information in Pooleys flight-guide for Biggin hill, got charts and notams, then quickly made out his flight plan ready for filing with Liverpool John Lennon airport ATC. Dennis Mallard came into the flight-planning room to debrief a student. Though big blond and fleshy with receding fair hair, he was smartly uniformed and carried the air of a swashbuckling aviator. James thought he might be gay but Loretta always defended Dennis vehemently and insisted he wasn't. The student left and James discussed Special Visual Flight Rule procedures over London with the Chief Pilot. His route had to take into account the "Land Clear" rule under which any aircraft must avoid endangering life or property in the event of engine failure and Dennis often flew over the capital city. They checked the weather on one of several computers in the room. James noted that the wind was easterly while temperature and dew point were only a degree apart which often meant mist and haze near Liverpool. Loretta walked past and seeing them together entered the room with her arms folded over her breasts, a combative glint in her eye.

"Are you still planning to go ahead James?"

He shrugged.

"Well yes."

"Despite what I said?"

"Yes; I explained why."

"And so did I."

There was an awkward silence and Dennis cleared his throat uneasily.

"I'm going to eat at 'The Ship' on my way home. Do you two feel like joining me?"

"No thanks, I've a lot still to do" said James.

"I'll come Dennis. Meet you out front in a couple of minutes."

She stalked out and the Chief Instructor raised an eyebrow at James, who thought he looked a bit ill at ease and shifty.

"Don't ask" said James. "This is all your fault for getting us involved and then shystering about the contribution you were meant to make."

"Well there's nothing I could have done about that!"

"There was and there is, like take a bridging loan on the house in Parbold, we've hocked everything to keep this scheme afloat."

"I've risked enough already and I'm not jeopardising the roof over my head too, end of."

"Fine. Well someone's got to raise some more money and I may have the means, but it's causing major difficulties between us."

"Yeah, sorry about that."

"You could at least try and sound sincere. You might very well be too, if this whole applecart goes tits up for want of a few bob!"

Dennis sniffed and walked out.

Loretta still wasn't back at nine pm when James finished in the office and put the television on to catch some news. It covered renewed carnage and fighting all over Iraq, then switched to a male BBC correspondent in Zimbabwe. James sat up straighter because he recognised the view behind the reporter; it showed the road and rail bridges over the Odzi river.

"The biggest Diamond rush in a century began here in Zimbabwe, seven years ago" said the reporter. "In 2006, the Chiadzwa fields in Marange were discovered."

James turned the volume up.

"Up to 10,000 illegal artisanal miners are working small plots at Marange. These adults and children are desperately poor, many unemployed as a result of the previous Mugabe and Katsiru regimes during which disastrous land reform plans saw white farmers expelled and their huge black workforces made homeless. Isabel Mpofu won elections in 2003 and conditions in Zimbabwe have improved but progress is slow and whereas these deprived people initially sold their diamonds to the government, Militia groups have taken over a sizeable percentage of the workings and the miners are being treated as slave labour in squalid conditions. The potential for vast wealth may become the catalyst that tips Zimbabwe back into civil war. The Militias have reformed under former guerrilla leaders in Manicaland to control and exploit the fields and recent skirmishes between them and government troops threaten to paralyze the whole province. Zimbabwe is a participant in the "Kimberley Process" that regulates the worldwide trade in diamonds but the "World Diamond Council" has called for a clampdown on the smuggling of 'Blood' diamonds from Zimbabwe. The CIA meanwhile keeps a close eye on Marange because of suspicions that diamonds are being sold to Lebanese traders acting for Al Qaeda. Such Terrorist Groups rely on gems to move money because they are compact, and do not set off metal detectors."

A photograph appeared on the TV screen of a very deep hole, with elderly black women wielding shovels in and near it, barefooted and without any basic safety equipment. The report ended; James muted the set and sat thinking about his troubled former country for a minute.

Poor bloody Zimbabweans. At least they'd had the sense to keep Primrose Mpofu in power. His own struggles seemed minor by comparison. Looking at his watch he tried ringing Loretta's number but it went straight to answer-phone. A pint of Pendle Witch was enticing and it was a clear night so he walked down to the pub along the canal.

CHAPTER SEVEN
Zimbabwe

Simon Ndhlovu had been cultivating his new informer for six weeks and was still no nearer finding out who was sponsoring the re-arming of the Manicaland Militias. He decided it was time to start tightening the screws and arranged a personal contact. When the informer failed to show up at their primary RV on time, Simon, who had a battered nondescript white Peugeot from the CID car-pool, moved to the backup RV, approaching cautiously. He drove straight past the beerhall at Odzi scrutinizing everything carefully and parked a mile down the road, keeping an eye on his watch. At two minutes to schedule he started up again and went back, turning the car into the bumpy dirt car-park abutting the bus terminus and beerhall, parking in a shadowed area away from the buses and near a clump of trees. He climbed out and pretended to be opening his fly as he headed into the trees as if going to relieve himself, but in reality checking to make sure no-one was lurking there. It was clear and he emerged back into the open and leant against the wing of the car, taking a cigarette from a packet in his top pocket and lighting it, though he didn't smoke.

The immigration officer from Grand Reef who had stamped Katsiru's documents was dressed very scruffily and had a tray of cheap snacks slung round his neck, like a vendor. When Simon lit up the officer turned away from a bus boarding-queue where he was trying to sell the food and wandered through the car park, pausing at groups of men drinking from beer-bottles and playing dice games under the weak glow from lamp-standards. They barracked him but he sold a few packets of peanuts and arrived opposite Simon, gesturing at his wares; the CIO Chief Super shook his head in dismissal. The peanut salesman pointed at the cigarette packet in Simon's shirt pocket, requesting a smoke. Simon scowled but took the now-empty packet out and thumbed open the lid, offering it.

Other eyes were watching.

"What do you think?" asked the militia corporal of his sergeant, who had been tasked by Malinga with following the immigration officer. They were crouched on their haunches twenty yards from Simon's car, watching dice being thrown on a clear space scraped in the dust by gamblers.

"He's not dressed like that because he needs a second job, that's for sure, and the big guy looks too much like CIO not to be one. Why take chances, we'll kill them both."

As the informer lifted his hand, pretending to take a cigarette from Simon's packet, two deafening bangs rang through the car-park, followed by six or seven more. The tightly folded note in his fist fluttered down as he staggered forward and blood gouted from his mouth. Tranquility turned to chaos; men dived for cover, others ran shouting, dogs began to bark, women screamed, chickens squawked. Both militiamen had fired at the informer, killing him but giving Simon a chance. He jumped about three feet in the air from fright, then dragged the big police automatic from his shoulder rig, firing fast in the general direction of the gunmen who were the only ones left visible in the car-park. He put five quick rounds in their general direction, some cracking past their ears, others kicking up dust and they ran for cover. Simon hurled himself into the car, having left the driver's window down. Hearing his starter churn they stopped running, turned and raised their guns again. Gravel spurted as Simon tore forward. One spinning rear tyre spat the small folded note backwards, shredded and soiled. It was caught by a breeze and carried back into the trees, finally settling into the leaf-mould as if it had always been there. The Chief Super aimed his automatic through the open window, steadied, squeezed and watched one of the assailants punched backwards and flat. The windscreen shattered from a return round; he punched a hole with the heavy gun, jerked the steering wheel, trying to crush the second gunman as he ran again. At the last second before impact the man threw himself aside. Simon screeched out of the car-park and into the darkness, fumbling for the radio microphone.

"Contact!" he shouted, panting. When his backup arrived they combed the car-park for more than an hour without recovering any information. The best informant Simon had managed to cultivate among the militias at Grand Reef was dead, while both General Katsiru's presence in Zimbabwe and his alias of Silas Lembede remained secure. Simon was no further forward and on returning to Harare he placed a call to Brigadier Thandiwe in Johannesburg, outlining his suspicions and fears to the South African.

"Did you ever hear any whispers of ex-Zimbabwean president Spencer Katsiru in relation to organized crime in Southern Africa, after he avoided trial by escaping custody?" he asked.

"Can't say I did, never heard much about him at all after that. Maybe he called it quits and went to live in Cuba or South America with all his ill-gained millions. I hate it when such people benefit from their corruption."The Brigadier walked Simon through some of his own recent progress and promised to be alert for any information pertaining to organized crime in Zimbabwe and particularly with connections to armed militias. On impulse the Zimbabwean called another of his contacts. There was no exchange of names, their voices were sufficient identification.

"Can you give me your latest on our Eastern border situation with Mozambique?"

"Yes there are now four Sukhoi Su-25 ground strike aircraft and two Ilyushin Il-76 heavy transport aircraft at Chimoio, as well as ten tanks, four multi-barrel rocket launchers and enough infantry equipment and supplies to equip several Companies. They are dispersed under camouflage netting."

Simon rubbed his face worriedly.

"I can't think of a legitimate reason for them being there."

"No, it's a bit intimidating. Normally your government would have been notified as a courtesy of any exercise taking place so close to the border. Something else you should be aware of; there is a type 63 107mm twelve-barreled rocket launcher dug in under camouflage near Mutare heights. With an eight-kilometer range it dominates the entire City of Mutare including the airport. If it isn't yours you need to be nervous."

"I am. Thanks shamwari, please yell immediately if you get any further information. I think things are getting to the point where we need to do something."

"Looks that way; I'll keep you posted on anything I get."

Simon sat back, thinking worriedly and his phone rang immediately. It was Fanny Chabata inviting him for a sundowner, saying she had some news.

"Since we spoke I did some hard thinking about that Devil and I recalled two things from those days. As you know, when the British ceasefire-monitoring force were here in 1980, I used to take goods from our store to the guerilla Assembly Point nearby and sell to them. One of the fighters told me of a terrible battle in Mozambique, and that the Devil had had a woman in the camp, a nurse called Maureen, who was killed in the fighting. He also said that Katsiru had a son with this woman, only a baby at the time. The day following the fighting was dreadful; guerillas from other camps arrived to help care for the wounded and bury the dead. He remembers Katsiru taking his woman to the burial pit, and all day long he was hunting, hunting, hunting for his son, but they never found the infant."

Fanny took a sip of her Coke and sat back, putting the glass down.

"Interesting; I certainly never heard that before and I'm not sure if it helps much. What was the second thing?"

"Well as it happens, I also knew a nurse, one of my school friends from Makoni. When I recalled the first story, I also remembered her telling me that after a big battle in Mozambique, Rhodesian security forces brought to her hospital in Sakubva Township a very small child whose mother had been killed in the hostilities. The Rhodesians had brought the infant back because of the mother being dead and because it too was injured."

Simon sat forward. "So it might have been Katsiru's son? But surely, all those years afterwards, when he was in power, he would have made enquiries in hospitals himself!" He swilled beer through his teeth ruminatively.

"I don't think so! The action happened in Mozambique, and the child went missing in Mozambique; why would he enquire at hospitals in Zimbabwe? If he looked further at all, it would probably have been in Mozambique."

Simon whistled.

"Did your friend say what happened to this infant?"

"The Rhodesian soldiers had named him Tamuwana meaning 'we have found him' which can also mean 'we have found the Lord'. It was a good name in the circumstances and the hospital priest christened him so; when the baby's wounds were healed he was given to an orphanage. Here is the name, I have written it down."

"Well done Fanny. I will have to think about its significance and in the meantime, keep remembering!"

"Oh I shall! I don't wish to bring any joy to that Devil by helping him find his son and equally I would not wish the boy to find out what a creature his father was, so use the information wisely!" Simon leaned forward and patted her knee.

"I will my friend, I will."

-xxx-
Lancashire

"The Ship" was a pub on the Leeds/Liverpool canal dating back to the building of the inland waterways. Street lamps illuminated shiny pleasure barges and colourful hanging baskets outside. James walked into the pub and found Dennis, Loretta and Haley sitting beside the fire having coffee after their dinner. Loretta was also drinking a brandy. They didn't need anything so James went to the bar and ordered a pint.

"Oi, Hacking, I've got a bone to pick with you!"

James turned. A tall burley figure in dark slacks and a grey-checked jacket was shouldering rudely through the press. Cyril Mawdsley was in his seventies with a farmers complexion and the red patches and broken veins of a steady drinker.

"You've taken the ruddy meat from our table, thieving that bloody Cold Storage contract from under us noses! I mean, I know times are hard but there's no call to go about robbing other folks livelihoods! My lads are going to be on dole because of it!"

The conversation level had dropped and many ears were pricked.

"Good evening Mr Mawdsley. Personally I don't choose to conduct my private affairs in public."

A drunk-looking middle-aged man appeared at Cyril's shoulder and pointed belligerently.

"You'll bloody answer to us now Hacking where everyone can hear what a snake you are, creeping to our customers behind uz back."

James picked up his pint and walked directly towards them.

"No creeping involved. The Cold Storage Commission approached me, not the other way round. The reasons cited by them for dissatisfaction with their last haulier were gross inefficiency and consistent overcharging. I have no idea which company they referred to. Was it yours?"

"That's bloody defamation; I'll have my lawyer on you!"

Loretta was gripping Haley's hand tightly and biting her lip, tensed as if ready to rise from the seats they had found near the fire. Haley returned the pressure and held her down.

James inclined his head.

"Please yourself Mawdsley, but ask him to contact me during normal business hours, like a gentleman. Now I would ask you to stand aside, unless you wish to continue this outside?"

He walked forward and the press of drinkers moved. Mawdsley and his son were forced to give ground too. The son staggered and fell back, grabbed a chair for support and pulled it to the floor with him.

"By the heck Kevin get up, you're a bloody embarrassment. Stop making a show of us!" spluttered Cyril.

James stepped round the man writhing on the grubby carpet and paused to take a long draught of ale.

"We'll fucking sort you out for this Hacking" swore Kevin as his father helped him up.

"If that constitutes a threat, our lawyers may well be conversing. I hope they can keep their balance better than you."

The bar-room erupted in laughter and the Mawdsleys stamped out, Kevin pausing in the door to point threateningly at James and swear some more.

"Mind your language, and keep out of my pub if you can't behave, Kevin Mawdesley, or you're barred!" shouted the publican, lifting the bar-flap and coming round.

"Well that's effectively spoiled a rather pleasant evening" said Loretta in a tight voice. Given the state of their relationship James was unsure whether she meant his arrival or the fracas. He sat down with them anyway.

"Not necessarily, they say there's no such thing as bad publicity."

Haley hugged her Dad's arm. "The Mawdsleys just made themselves look like pillocks."

"Aye, they did. Your business is proving good for the whole area" agreed the pub Manager. "The towels are on but you're most welcome to stay for another drink."

"Thanks, I'd like one more" said James.

"Not for us" said Loretta. "Haley, Dennis and I are going to the late movie in Southport."

"I'll stay with Dad and give him a lift home."

James was home before Loretta and went straight to bed, tossing and turning for a long time before falling into an exhausted dream-ridden sleep. He awoke at six-thirty still feeling tired to find the bed next to him un-slept in. He went down to the kitchen for a cup of tea and found Loretta already there, fully dressed. She looked up from the sink and regarded him stonily.

"Morning" he said and switched the kettle on.

"Morning" she responded shortly.

"I was worried; tried to phone you several times."

"I was angry; the phone was off."

"Good film?"

"Fine thank you."

"So where did you sleep?"

"Spare room, the other en-suite. I shall be moving in there permanently until I get something else sorted out."

"Loretta, there's no need for this. I love you."

"Then you have ample opportunity to prove it. I've made my position clear; if you go to that meeting we're finished."

James felt a surge of irritation. His jaw jutted and he prepared his tea in silence then went back upstairs, pausing to push open the door of the spare bedroom she'd mentioned. The bed was immaculately made and there was a towel and toothbrush on the quilt. He regarded the room speculatively for a few more seconds, then carried on to their shared master bedroom where he tidied up and opened the curtains, to be confronted by dense fog. He cursed, checked some weather reports and one hour later lifted the Arrow off runway 09 despite the conditions being below legal minima. He entered a spiral climb overhead the runway and at fifteen hundred feet broke out of the inversion into bright sunshine, bound for London. Cloud stretched below in all directions as he contacted Manchester approach and requested clearance into the IFR-only airways; the view was simply magical.

-xxx-
London

James had an uneventful flight to Biggin Hill Airport, south of London. He parked and refuelled the Arrow, then had coffee at the Surrey and Kent Flying Club where he took the opportunity to talk with the Executive Officer about a reciprocal-rights deal between the two aero-clubs which would benefit members, offering reduced landing fees and fuel prices. A taxi then conveyed him into London's financial district.

Conflict Logistic Solutions' offices reeked of money with deep carpets, wood panelling and expensive pictures on the walls. A smart young woman relieved him of his driving licence, electronic tacho card, Certificate of Professional Competency, Transport Operator's licence and Company accounts, after which James was shown to a boardroom and left on his own with a tray of coffee and biscuits for half an hour. He grew restive and annoyed, just about to ask what the hell was going on when the door opened and five hard-faced men in expensive suits arrived and sat down across the long table. A patrician silver haired man made introductions cursorily, banged a stack of papers into neatness and laid them down; James' tender was on top.

"Right Mr Hacking, our Executive on the ground Lance MacDonald briefed you and you know what the contract entails. Your documentation and reputation stack up. We're prepared to offer three hundred thousand sterling for the initial six month contract, renewal dependent on performance."

James looked at him in silence for several seconds before speaking.

"Didn't you go to school?"

"Say what?"

"I said didn't you go to school? If you had, the figure on my tender would be easily readable."

He leant forward and tapped the paper.

"That number, as any five-year old could tell you, is a 6, not a 3."

"Who the hell do you think you're talking to?"

"I didn't quite catch your name during the perfunctory courtesies but my bid is six-hundred thousand, not three, non-negotiable. Either way you'll be getting an invoice for my time and travel."

In the late afternoon he walked out of the CLS building in a slight daze and once round the corner stopped abruptly and leant against a wall.

"Phew," he muttered, "I'm glad that's over! Talk about hostile interrogation; actually going to Iraq can't possibly be any worse than that!"

He had tuned his negotiation perfectly, angling for half a million sterling for a six month contract to supply twelve drivers, sensing beneath the antagonistically supercilious inquisition that there was a hint of desperation in their bargaining, for Iraq was still not the current work-destination of choice. Even with salaries of three hundred thousand pounds and airfares to pay he still stood to make a very handsome wedge. The Americans were due to pull out of Iraq by the end of October 2011, with the final few elements crossing the border by December, or at latest January 2012. However James knew that situations on the ground often influenced political intentions and there was every possibility that the deadline would be overrun. The initial contract balance was payable up-front and there was a clause allowing for extension. Even after a withdrawal there could be anything up to twenty thousand Americans remaining behind on Embassy duties and "training missions" to be supplied with fuel, PX and other rations so the outlook for the business was good. His figures indicated that the venture, even after all expenses and corporation tax, would net in the region of 100K sterling for the first six months. He took the advance payment cheque from his top pocket and kissed it.

"Time to get this beauty into the bank and have a drink Hacking!"

He bought a pint before settling into a quiet alcove of the pub. In his briefcase were the CV's he'd shortlisted from the dozens of replies to his speculative job advert in "Expats International" so he began making telephone calls and sending emails on his 3G-connected laptop to say the contract was firming up, trying to sift those genuinely interested from time-wasters. An hour later three had been eliminated as no longer available or unsuitable, while eight had been booked for interviews and an induction test in Burscough.

The twelfth, Colinda Lasserre, was already known to him and had a rented flat in nearby Wapping. She agreed to an immediate meeting. It was fruitful and she was a shoo-in for the job with extensive military and heavy goods driving experience. When James booked out of the Tower Bridge hotel next day he had a respectable hangover from their prolonged interview over dinner, and his first firm appointment for the Iraq contract. He also had a problem because the immediate sexual vibe which had been apparent between them in Malta had intensified. Over the past decade there had been opportunities for sex with women other than Loretta but he had always resisted them. The deceit of multiple relationships had always spoiled such affairs for him and in recent years masturbation and imagination had proved a reliable antidote to the almost irresistible urges which preyed on him at such times. So far with Colinda neither had worked and he couldn't get her out of his mind. Nor was he sure he wanted to. Having her along was making Iraq seem distinctly more attractive.

-xxx-

Burscough Airfield, Lancashire

"Burscough radio this is Golf India X-ray."

Haley recognised her Dad's voice and smiled.

"Golf India X-ray, pass your message."

"India X-ray is inbound ten miles south-east of the field currently transiting the low-level corridor; request airfield information."

Haley replied with runway in use, barometric pressure, wind speed and direction, further advising that there was no known traffic.

"Roger Burscough. I'll be joining overhead at two thousand feet and descending dead-side for runway 27."

Haley clicked the mike twice in acknowledgment and went outside with the hand-held radio to watch. A few minutes later she heard a powerful buzz to the north and another pilot joined the frequency. It was a retired Airforce Tornado pilot returning from doing aerobatics in Dennis's Extra.

"India X-ray this is Alpha Kilo, joining crosswind from the North."

"Got you visual Alpha Kilo, I'll be number two, Quentin."

"Very appropriate James, see you on the ground."

The wind was from due south, windsock standing out solid, indicating a strong crosswind of fifteen knots. The glistening Red Turbo Arrow appeared as a dot in the distance, grew rapidly larger and was soon standing on one wing in a steep turn directly over the signals area outside the club-house.

"India X-ray is overhead the field."

"Roger. Alpha Kilo downwind midfield."

"Got you; joining direct down-wind for 27."

James grinned exuberantly, cut the power and dived steeply to the south in a non-standard manoeuvre, joining late downwind at 1000 feet, setting the prop and flaps as he steep-turned onto base leg behind the Extra.

"Ratatattat Alpha Kilo, joining you for a formation landing! I'll take the grass" he said and saw the Extra's wings wobble slightly as Quentin glanced in his mirror.

"Be my guest."

James rolled level, raised the nose to scrub off speed and lowered the undercarriage. He turned smoothly onto final alongside Quentin, using left aileron into the wind and opposite rudder, both pilots side-slipping towards the threshold and greasing down right on the numbers without using power again, kicking straight and keeping left aileron in to stop wind getting under their wings.

"Perfect!" thought Haley proudly as the two brightly coloured aircraft taxied over, parked and shutdown. Some visitors having lunch in the beer-garden had stood up to watch and several clapped and cheered. The Arrow's door popped open and the Extra's canopy slid back.

"Nice flying James," called Quentin. "I looked in the mirror and saw you at sixty degrees of bank, lining me up like the Red Baron."

"Not too shoddy yourself Quen, that was fun, we should do some more formation stuff soon."

Dennis was taking a new student through the A-check procedure on a Cessna and hurried over, bristling indignantly. He climbed onto the Arrow's wing.

"You know I don't allow that sort of cowboy flying James, it sets a bad example to other pilots."

"Don't blow a gasket Dennis, the crowd seemed to enjoy it and there's no such thing as bad publicity."

"You know very well it's against regulations to fly in formation without prior agreement too!"

"We were in agreement; James called and said he was joining me."

"You're as bad as he is Quentin. Well I'm Chief Pilot and I won't have it!"

"You'll have to continue this bollocking later Dennis, I'm dying for the loo!" Quentin dropped to the ground and scuttled comically for the clubhouse.

"Lighten up Dennis, we were just having a little fun."

"You have far too much fun James, gadding off on your own ridiculous schemes whenever you feel like it. We're all meant to be pulling together on this project."

"We are, I was only trying to raise some cash because certain parties who promised funds haven't come up with them….."

"Another example of your 'never-land' world; if it's not bloody Libya, it's Iraq, where you'll apparently be away for a month at a time according to Loretta."

"Don't apply double standards; it doesn't seem to matter when you disappear for two weeks a month on long-haul. That's why we have part-time instructors like Quentin who are happy to take up the slack."

"Don't change the subject; I'm the Chief Pilot and I expect my rules to be obeyed!"

"You changed the subject Dennis. Do me a favour, try not to be such a pompous old woman and I'll try to stick to the rules you love so much."

"Hello Dad" called Haley, moving round the front of the wing.

Dennis glanced at her.

"See that you bloody do!"

He glared before stepping down and striding huffily away.

"Management disagreement father?"

"Sort of. Dennis is a woose and rules…."

"I know! Are for the guidance of the wise…."

"Just so." He began passing his stuff out to her.

"He is a bit of a stickler for the book, especially standard joins Dad; I've heard some visiting pilots taking the piss about him."

"Annoyingly, he's right. I should probably set a better example....Hurry up and make way Haley, this plane may have five hours endurance but these days my bladder only seems to have two!"

They stepped off the wing.

"How was London?"

"Go and put the kettle on and I'll tell you over a brew. Everything been ok here?"

"Yes fine. Art was home last night, left again this morning at five am."

"What did he break?"

"Nothing! I'll see you inside!"

James hurried to the lavatory and then over a cup of tea told Haley about the Iraq contract; she squealed and hugged him, then frowned.

"That's fantastic! I hope it's not going to be dangerous though Dad. I know you always play everything down."

"You know what Haley? The only way to make financial headway in this world is to take calculated risks."

"Is it causing aggro between you and Loretta? She's been really off since Sunday night."

"She doesn't like calculated risks anymore, so hence I am top of her shit-list. Think I'm in for a rocky ride Haley."

"Oh Dad, is making money worth risking your relationship for?"

He smiled sardonically.

"You know what John Wayne said about that and I agree with him."

"About what men have got to do? Yeah, I damn well do know, Arthur keeps telling me!"

James topped up the Arrow's tanks and filled in the tech-log before going home. There were suitcases of varying sizes scattered all over the hall and Loretta was in the office busily ripping open mail when he let himself into the house. They looked at each other for many seconds.

"What the hell's going on?"

"You completely disregarded my wishes and went ahead with a dangerous unnecessary project that I won't tolerate, so we're separating. I assume the negotiations were successful?

"Yes. Six month written contract and a sizeable advance."

"Okay. Then our personal relationship is over but the business one still exists. I intend to make alternative accommodation arrangements in due course but in the meantime I've moved my things into the spare room. We can be civilised about this I hope?"

"Undoubtedly" replied James drily.

"Fine. Well the situation has prompted me to have a good clear-out."

She picked up the old Rhodesian-postmarked letter from a pile of envelopes on her desk.

"So what are you going to do about this venerable article? Why don't you either read it or chuck it?"

He sat down across the desk uneasily.

"I don't know. I guess I'm scared to do either."

"Don't be so bloody wet! How can it possibly affect you after all these years?"

"You don't know the witch who wrote it, anything is possible!"

"Well I'm deciding for you; what's it to be? Read? Bin?"

As he hesitated she grinned maliciously and tossed it into the waste-paper basket.

"Of for Christ's sake, give it here then!"

James lunged and retrieved the envelope, then studied it intently as if trying to see what it contained. Abruptly he inserted his thumbnail under the flap and ripped. The contents took him back more than twenty-five years.

-xxx-

Dave Swinnerton had brought his class-1 licence, digital tachometer driver's card and social security details to Haley, as well as some employer references. She phoned the Government 'Driver and Vehicle Licensing Authority' to verify it all and to confirm there were no points on his licence while he filled in job-application forms.

"Well that's fine Dave, clean bill of health from the DVLA. Dad will want to do a short induction with you, show you the way he likes things done, then that should be it, you can start doing some driving" she said, ending her call to the government office. The phone rang again almost immediately.

-xxx-

James finished reading the letter and sat in stunned silence. Eventually, moving slowly like a man in a dream, he dialled the clubhouse extension.

"Haley? I have some unexpected news, please come over."

"What's that Dad?"

"You have a sister. "

"What did you say?" asked Loretta in disbelief as he replaced the receiver.

James passed the letter over and she read it in silence, finishing as Haley rushed into the house slamming the front door behind her.

"Am I hearing right?"

"According to this letter and I believe it to be genuine. Show it to her Loretta."

Haley read it and squealed.

"That's so exciting, when can I meet her? How did all this happen?"

"I'll tell you; sadly like so many things in my life it doesn't reflect particularly well on me. When I was a cocky youngster I was very involved in the Rhodesian war and along the way married a young and beautiful woman called Amanda. One night which has shamed me ever since, I was unfaithful to her with a former lover. My wife Amanda never found out and eventually became pregnant. Years later at a party on a farm in the bush she met the former lover who said something that upset her so much that she rushed out, jumped in an unprotected vehicle and drove over a landmine meant for me which killed her and our unborn child."

Haley looked at him with big shiny eyes and Loretta covered her face with a hand.

"Anyway, I always assumed that Dawn had just told Amanda we were lovers. In truth, according to this letter, she told her that I was the father of her own child, a girl called Jemima."

Haley walked over and draped her arm over his shoulder, squeezing.

"What are you going to do about it Dad?"

"I shall have to find and tell Jemima."

"Any idea how?"

"Yes. I was thinking about a quick trip to Johannesburg to recruit for the Iraq contract anyway, there are two guys I particularly want but they seem hard to get hold of; thought I might make a flying visit to my Mum and Dad in the Cape too. I seem to remember Dougie McIntyre became guardian to a girl called Jemima Visser. He and his wife are dead now but Loretta's brother George might remember. If that's a blank I'll get a Private Investigator on it before I come home."

"Well I have to get back to the club-house but keep me informed, I'm very excited about having a sister! I've got Dave Swinnerton there by the way. Do you want to do his driving test and induction?"

"Yes, might as well since he's here. I'll be over in a minute"

James and Loretta kept steady eye contact for some time before she spoke.

"Ironic, after saying recently that you wouldn't like any more children. Guilt must be riding rampant."

He shrugged.

"Guilt is a very useless emotion."

She flinched internally. Dennis had been trying to get her into bed again, with intimations of marriage as usual, which was something James had never done. Her fury with him was not to do with that though, but with his unbending single-minded attitude that he was always right. And had she misread the business in Malta that intimated he was catting around like he used to? She'd been so wired on booze and drugs she couldn't make a sensible judgement call but she did know she still loved him in a way she'd never love Dennis, The other man seemed to offer a more secure, relatively stable, if boring, companionship. The remorse she felt about the casual affair with the Chief Pilot gnawed at her like a painful tooth but she kept silent; when in doubt do nothing. Even that was one of James' adages! He spoke again in measured tones.

"The person who laid that landmine was Spencer Katsiru; he left a note at the scene."

"That bloody man; I am so glad that Zimbabwe and Primrose are rid of him."

They sat in silence for several minutes. Finally Loretta stirred in her chair.

"Would you like me to find you a flight to SA?"

"Yes, I'll go on the first available reasonably priced one. Thanks."

"Normally I would come with you and visit family, but with the way things are between us, and the manic business situation that exists, I shall stay. We will probably be taking separate holidays in future anyway, might as well get used to it."

"I would be very happy to have you with me, but you are right about the business."

"There's still time to draw back from the brink James."

"On my side there isn't. The contract is signed, with heavy withdrawal penalties. The ball is in your court Loretta, and I know which way I'd prefer it to bounce."

-xxx-

James took Dave Swinnerton for a brief road-test and induction which included coupling and uncoupling a semi-trailer and some reversing. The younger man seemed to have a grudge against the world but was methodical and obviously experienced so James pronounced himself happy and moved on to an airfield orientation.

"We often drop trailers or tip loads at some of the other businesses dotted round the airfield Dave, especially the other haulage outfits; that's North-West Farm foods over there; those old hangers back onto Wally Hunt's Farms, so the veg, leeks, mushrooms, salad and so on come straight off the land, get packaged and shipped straight out fresh. Then there's Merseyside Beverages, which as you would expect deal mainly in pop and alcoholic drinks. There's a big scrapyard beyond that; deals in vehicle spare-parts and recycling old electrical appliances like washing machines. Further to the right there's a Civil Engineering outfit, they have a lot of heavy low-loaders coming in with plant and machinery, drilling rigs, big dozers and the like. Behind that is the cold storage meat plant."

"I didn't realise the airfield was such a busy place. Aren't you worried about vehicles getting onto the runway when aircraft are using it?"

"Always, but there's a system in place to prevent that; some of the businesses have access roads from outside the airfield. Those that don't, mainly the ones abutting the Leeds/Liverpool canal, use the perimeter road that runs all the way round. You can't really go wrong because all the live runways and taxiways are gated off. There's a map of the Airfield layout in the cab of all our vehicles. If you're ever in doubt, ask. Listen, those dogs of yours; you still want to get shut of them?

"Too right! why? Do you want 'em?"

"Want is not strictly accurate but I'm going to be away quite a lot in the coming few months. Loretta can look after herself but it wouldn't do any harm to have them around as a deterrent to villains."

"I'll bring them and their kennels up in the next couple of days. Where will they be kept?"

"Probably in the gardens round the house, it's fenced off to stop assorted vermin getting at Loretta's flowers."

"Okay, they're yours, and good riddance!"

CHAPTER EIGHT

Loretta's brother George met James at Oliver Tambo International Airport in Johannesburg. Once close, they had not met for nearly ten years. He was still handsome but more florid, heavy in face and build, his blond hair thinning. He'd been consistently unfaithful to his wife when he was a young father and James wondered if age had made him any less of a satyr. His handshake remained strong and as they walked to his outsized Mercedes in the car-park he moved with the same ground-eating stride that James remembered from when they had hunted in the veld together.

The streets near his palatial home in the suburb of Sandton were flanked by jacaranda trees in full blossom and everything seemed peaceful but many of the avenues were partitioned off with heavy concrete girders to make chicanes, some manned by armed uniformed security guards.

"Jo'burg is like the Wild West these days James, got a lot worse since you and Loretta took the gap. A tenth of our South African business these days is tied up with security; we bought up several strong Companies that are booming, since crime seems to be our only growth industry. Bloody disgrace really. How are you faring over there in UK? I read the financials of course but things look tough everywhere."

"They are. The Airfield isn't doing much more than washing its face yet, but has huge potential because of the location and the fact that the bigger airports all want to squeeze General Aviation tiddlers out. The trucking side makes a decent profit though it isn't an easy industry to be in either. The big boys like Eddie Stobart with two thousand trucks undercut us all on price but we've managed to find some niche markets that we service really efficiently so we keep getting the business. Doesn't help that we have to wait up to ninety days for our money though, makes cash-flow very difficult at present."

"My boy Theo is moving aggressively into motor-parts including the second hand market. Our roads are carnage, must have the highest incident of accidents in the world and the demand for cheap parts is correspondingly enormous. He sold our mine and farm on the Limpopo to finance it which didn't please the old man much. Loretta mentioned some scheme of yours doing transport in Iraq?"

He raised a quizzical eyebrow at James, glancing at him sideways.

"Yes, our latest trucking venture is in Kuwait and Baghdad believe it or not. I negotiated a six-month contract worth half a million sterling on Monday with Conflict Logistics Solutions to supply a dozen agency drivers with military backgrounds to move fuel for them."

George grinned.

"You always did like to live life on the edge James; bet Loretta was livid and the job in Iraq sounds quite dicey too!"

They both laughed.

"She'll come round when I prove it works and I suppose her worry is understandable; she'd rather we tried to get some money from you but I like to do things my own way and the Iraq venture has tremendous potential if it initially goes well. Did she tell you about Stuffed Goose Airlines?"

George laughed. "At great length!"

"Last I heard from Denzil our bid for an aerodrome licence to operate from Liverpool was progressing well."

"What are you and Denzil like hey? Bloody mad! Where the hell does he get his money?"

James grinned.

"I don't really know. He is naturally acquisitive and willing to take huge risks to turn a buck. He calls it "Fun;" he's a great wheeler-dealer. I suspect after I bailed out of Namibia and Angola that he made contacts with all sorts of "Business" people there, in italics; and probably in the Congo too. He also met lots of CIA operators and he's a natural spook himself."

George grunted.

"I prefer a quiet life and sleeping in my own bed at night. Money's tight here too James, and the exchange rate isn't great; if push came to shove I would try and help though. Will you be going out to Iraq yourself?"

"For the first trip certainly, to set it all up. That's partly why I'm here. Couple of my buddies from Koevoet and Three-Two Battalion during the SWA and Angola Campaigns might be interested. They started up a transport company together but went bust. Eugene Potgieter and Louis Van Zyl. Bet they'd jump at the chance of an adventure in Iraq for good bucks."

They arrived at the big gates to George's property. He pointed up at the cameras and floodlights, then pipped the horn gently.

"If the guards aren't asleep, they know we're here already. One advantage of owning security companies is that you can use them to guard yourself! Most domestic hijack-type crimes occur at moments like this. They can drive up behind and box you, or just jump out of some bushes or a drainage ditch and smash in the windows. These are bullet proof, by the way!"

The gates swung open hydraulically and George gunned the big car through, waving to the guards in a small office that had been built just inside. The house was at the top of a two-hundred meter tarmac drive.

"Madeleine's out doing good works or something James, she'll be back for dinner. Do you want a shower or a beer first?"

"Beer, every time."

"Correct answer!"

James followed him into a vast kitchen where a small elderly Black woman was chopping vegetables.

"You remember Boss James Ethel?" he said, opening a walk-in sized American-style fridge and extracting two Castle lagers from the legions ranked within.

She smiled and curtsied slightly.

"Yes Sir. Welcome back to Johannesburg."

"Thank you Ethel. Mr Sibanda still keeping well?"

She and her husband came from Zimbabwe and had been with George and his family for more than thirty years.

Ethel laughed.

"Yes Sir, he still does the gardens. We don't let him inside; he's like one of the dogs!"

They all laughed at that, Ethel hiding her mouth shyly, delighted with the success of her joke. Out on the veranda overlooking a pool and tennis courts the sun was going down in a riot of colour. Birds were still flitting and calling and it was pleasantly warm, giving James a sudden rush of nostalgia for all things African. There was a lot to discuss and many people to ask about from their common past which went back to senior school but first he needed to ask the foremost question on his mind.

"Do you remember Dougie McIntyre becoming guardian to a young woman called Jemima?"

"I do. After Dougie and his wife died she carried on running their crop-spraying business and flying freelance on the side. She flies for us on occasion, was up in Botswana at the Limpopo farm with Theo in the Beechjet just last Saturday. James felt the hairs on his neck prickle; it was almost like history being repeated because he had also flown Bustamante aircraft up to the Botswana farm. He, George and

Loretta had rescued Elias and Primrose Mpofu from there when they were about to be assassinated by Spencer Katsiru.

"How is she doing these days?"

"Flourishing as far as I know. Theo mentioned a few money worries with the business but who hasn't got those?"

"I was going to look her up while I'm here actually. Have you got her address or phone number?"

"Yes, she still lives at Number One Eagle Court, those expensive Town-Houses by the entrance to Bryanston Country Club. I'll dig her phone number out for you. Between us and the gatepost I think young Theo carries a bit of a torch for her, along with half the young men in the city. You're in the Blue room by the way, whenever you're ready to freshen up."

After a second beer James went up to shower and phoned Loretta to let her know he'd arrived safely. Though still very cool she pestered him for news of her family and it turned into a lengthy call. He could hear cars arriving, voices and footsteps on stairs. His bedroom was very large, exquisitely decorated and the bathroom matched. A scalding shower followed by one minute of cold eased out the kinks of his long flight and refreshed he descended the wide ornamental staircase to find Georges' parents with him in the sitting room having drinks. Kisses and handshakes followed.

"How is that maverick daughter of mine? Do you two still get out climbing?" asked Emilio who in his early seventies was still spry.

"She's very well. We had an epic on Civetta in the Dolomites last autumn that you would have been sorry to miss. Sunny start, sudden snow storm, scary eight-hundred foot abseil retreat."

"The Civetta is a real mountaineer's mountain. I met Walter Bonatti there once at the Vazzoler Refuge you know. I am sorry that he is dead."

"Yes. He was a one-off. But at least he was vindicated over the K2 nonsense before he died."

"Stop them quick or we shall hear nothing all evening but mountains!" ordered his wife. "I am very sorry my daughter couldn't join us James, she said only one of you could leave the business?"

"I'm sorry too; yes, things are pretty crazy, lots of change, new ventures; it wouldn't be fair to leave it all to someone as young as Haley."

"We're having dinner in the small dining room James" said Madeleine. "There's just us, I didn't want to overwhelm you with guests while you were still jet-lagged. We'll probably have a braaivleis over the weekend so you can catch up with all your old gang."

Ethel waited on them efficiently and they had brandy and coffee when she left for the night.

"We manage with far fewer servants than we did in the old days James" said Emilio Bustamante puffing contentedly on a cigar.

"Where we can get away with it we use Motswanas and Zimbabweans, they're much more cheerful than the bolshy South Africans. These days they all know their rights and it's very difficult to get rid of them if they're no good."

"Stupid really" agreed George. "If the Black Unions weren't so aggressive, far more people would be willing to provide employment."

Emilio leant forward.

"The situation in South Africa though outwardly stable is very volatile James and tribalism as ever lurks just under the surface; the two main power blocks are Xhosas and Zulus, but Indians make up twenty percent and are very stroppy too. I'm still annoyed with young Theo for selling the Limpopo farm. Botswana is a safe haven in the chaotic sea of Africa and could have provided a pleasant nearby bolt-hole if the shit hits the fan here. Or should I say when!"

"You should say excuse me, and wash your mouth out with soap for swearing at the table" ordered his wife.

"Well I'm right dammit! Thanks to me our family has survived and prospered on this Dark Continent for fifty years so I resent my advice being ignored!"

James sniffed the Cognac appreciatively. "Why did Theo sell the farm? I seem to remember there was a workable goldmine on it too."

George nodded.

"There is, that was Theo's argument. The seam has been pinching out and is nearly unprofitable despite the soaring price of gold. He felt we should get shut at a decent price and use the money in emerging markets."

"So who bought it and why?"

"Some black businessman called Lembede and Theo doesn't care much about his reasons. He was just pleased with himself for screwing top dollar out of a guy who sounds a nasty piece of work."

He went on to tell James Theo's whole account of the day spent up in Selibe Pikwe with Jemima on the property inspection pending the deal.

"It all seems quite weird George, almost reminiscent of the day we whisked Elias Mpofu out from under President Katsiru's nose when he was trying to kill him. Will you all excuse me? I'm starting to feel pretty tired after the flight."

James was up early next day feeling refreshed and joined his host and hostess for breakfast on the veranda, waited on by Ethel who served fruit, cereal and poached haddock with eggs. On his way to work in the city, George dropped him at the car-hire firm in Sandton where Eugene Potgieter was now working for minimum wage, thanks to "pale-male" syndrome. James saw him tapping at a computer keyboard in the empty reception and went through the door.

"I want a car quickly, how bloody long must I wait you slaapgat?"

The big man froze as if stabbed in the back, then jumped up and turned, balling his fists.

"Potty!"

"James! You had me going there jong I was going to bloody donner you. How goes it? I thought you were in UK now?"

"I am, just here for a few days and I have a proposition for you and Louis."

"Then I'll go get him; he's a security guard just next door at the bank. You can make us some coffee while I call him."

When he came back he put the "closed" sign on the door and James outlined the Iraq job to them.

"Thanks man, count me in" said Louis immediately, stubbing out his third smoke in twenty minutes.

"Me too James; fuck, thank God something finally turned up that is interesting and pays good money. Life is blooming bleak here at the moment."

"I want to visit Denzil Harcourt too, see if he'd be interested. He bought a game ranch up in the Eastern Transvaal, somewhere near Castle Rock or Bushbuck Ridge. I met him in Malta earlier in the year and he gave me several numbers but no-one answers any of them. Emails have been bouncing too."

Potty laughed.

"Times have changed James, it isn't 'the Eastern Transvaal anymore' but 'Mpumalanga' which means 'where the sun rises', and the town you knew as Nelspruit is now Mbombela. Communications are chaos in this country anyway outside the big centers. I heard Denzil sometimes hangs out at a bar on the Castle Rock Caravan Park, apparently a friend of his owns it."

"Well if I can't get hold of him I'll head up there. You can rent me a car now Potty, make some money out of me for your commission."

"Jesus, my commission wouldn't even buy a white mouse or a tooth! I've got some top of the range Ford Mustangs; you can have one for the price of a Fiat Uno."

"Your boss probably won't be very pleased about that."

"Who's he going to complain to? I won't be here much longer. Besides, you're my boss now. Let's get together for a braai, or at least have a drink."

"We will. I'm just going to duck in that phone-shop across the street and buy a local 'pay as you go' cell, be back for the car just now."

Half an hour later James gunned a fiery red Mustang out of the garage, waved to Potty and spun the tyres, heading for Bryanston. A couple of miles short he pulled over and dialled the number George had given him the previous evening. He tried repeatedly but it was always engaged so he headed for Jemima's townhouse. There was only one entrance to the cluster of attractive dwellings which had a high wall all the way around, topped with razor-coils and backed onto the Bryanston country-club golf course. The entrance had CCTV cameras mounted and so did most of the houses. High gates which were obviously operated by remote control bore a sign saying that they were closed each night at ten pm. There was no intercom that he could see as he drove through and got out of the Mustang in front of Jemima's house. He looked around at the peaceful scene, enjoying the warm sunshine on his shoulders and rang the door-bell. Nothing happened so he tried her cell-phone again, pacing as it rang.

-xxx-

Jemima landed the Ag-cat at midday and grabbed a cold coke from the cool-box under the awning. Things were not going well. As he'd threatened, Klaasens at the Bank had cut off all personal and company credit and she was too busy to go looking for alternative finance. The thought of having to eat humble pie and beg if she couldn't persuade his superiors to reinstate her accounts was physically nauseating. She slumped in a lawn-chair feeling heat on her face through the thin sunshade, trying to relax, but worry gnawed at her, making it impossible. She even thought about asking Sandro if his venture capital company did short term loans, but realised getting involved with Lembede would be madness.

For distraction she went through missed calls and messages, replying to some and deleting others. Finally she was left with just one unknown number and called it. James was heading for Lanseria Airport to make a visit out of nostalgic curiosity. His new handset rang so he pulled onto the gravel road-shoulder and answered. An enchanting feminine voice sounded in his ear.

"Hi. I have a missed call from you."

"Hello. Is that Jemima?"

"Depends who wants to know. Are we acquainted?"

"Yes, James Hacking here but you probably won't have heard of me. I knew your parents Dawn and Gert, and Dougie McIntyre as well."

"I think I've heard the Bustamantes talk about you. You're a pilot right? Used to fly their aircraft freelance sometimes, same as me?"

"Yes George Bustamante's sister Loretta and I have been together for many years and I was wondering if we could meet up somewhere. I opened a letter recently that contained some information about your parents that I would rather discuss in person than over the phone."

Her heart skipped a beat and she hesitated. Was this more shit coming her way? James read her mind.

"Jemima, I would add that it is potentially good news rather than bad."

"Sure, well that's encouraging. Where are you now?"

"Near Lanseria. I was going to take a look at the Airport for old-time's sake then go for a walk in the Magaliesberg hills by Utopia. Loretta and I used to go there often."

"The Cock and Bull pub is in the Magaliesberg and we're spraying not too far away. I could meet you for a drink about half five?"

"That would be perfect. If I'm not in the bar try the beer-garden."

"Right then. See you later."

Her cell rang again immediately. She sighed in exasperation and looked at the screen. It was Sandro Marais. She smiled in delight and answered.

"Thought you'd forgotten about me!"

"Negative Jemima. Like I said, you have three boys carrying a torch for you now. Mine's the biggest though."

"Well you're my favourite at the moment too."

"So how about dinner?"

"That will make every night since our first date. I'd love to but I'm meeting someone else at the Cock and Bull in the Magaliesberg after work."

"So invite me too. I'm nearby, working at Sun City, trying to make a few bucks."

"Gambling again you mean; it isn't work unless you sweat doing it! You do know that betting is addictive and corrosive to the soul?"

"I've got a humungous corrosion-proof soul. It's my liver I'm worried about."

She laughed.

"Sure come on over but not until seven or so. Meanwhile some of us have real work to do! See you later."

She had forgotten the perpetual excitement that came with a new love affair, the inability to concentrate, the feeling of bubbling gaiety. She couldn't quite get a handle on Sandro but he was definitely under her skin. He was the most spontaneous, unpredictable yet confident man she had ever met. Nothing about him was ordinary from his lean hard scarred body to his inconsistent accent, one minute troopie street-coarse, the next almost refined with an unusually good vocabulary. Somehow he made her feel really alive and optimistic despite financial problems. Perhaps it was because they both came from broken homes.

-xxx-

James nursed the low-slung Mustang up a rough bush road to the cottages at Utopia and stopped outside an A-frame structure belonging to the Bustamante family. He changed into shorts, put a pair of veldschoen borrowed from George on his feet and shouldering a small rucksack set off towards the cleft of the Tonquani gorge which slashed the Magaliesberg ahead. He followed a steep path into the gorge, looking up at red rock-walls where he and Loretta had once climbed and came eventually to a clear green pool with a cliff behind it. They had dived in naked and made urgent love on the hot rocks. The memory also reminded him of Colinda and his desire to see her naked, make her come, fuck her furiously. The mating urge could be a curse that destroyed relationships and impeded coherent thought. He branched left out of the gorge and climbed to a high plateau with good views, covered in weird rock formations. He climbed one, drank a coke, ate a sandwich and thought about what life without Loretta would be like. James prided himself on being a man who never backed down, but maybe there came a time for everything.

He was at the Cock and Bull ten minutes early and took a Castle lager into the nearly deserted beer-garden, choosing a table in the sun and sliding onto the bench. He sat there trying to be calm but his heart was pounding. He had barely taken two swigs when a raven-haired young woman approached clad in flying overalls with the top rolled down and secured by the arms round her waist. She strode forward smiling and thrust her arm out, fingers spread wide.

"Hello, you must be James right? There's no one else here!"

He stood in greeting and his heart turned over, because as he gazed into her cobalt eyes he saw his own father staring back at him. He took her hand and shook it once, then kept holding it numbly, gazing at her. Jemima returned the stare, a small quizzical frown making a slight wrinkle between her eyebrows. For several heartbeats they stood like that and then she flexed her hand gently.

"May I have it back?"

James laughed self-consciously and released it.

"Sure. Sorry. What would you like to drink?" A waiter had appeared and she asked for a pint glass of shandy.

"I'm parched, I hope it comes quickly."

They sat down on opposite benches facing each other.

"So you knew my folks? I never did really because they both died before I was four years old."

James remained silent, looking at her and she shifted uncomfortably.

"You said on the phone you had some news about my parents?"

"In a manner of speaking."

Jemima continued to look at him in a puzzled way.

"Well, do you or don't you?"

"Yes. To be blunt, there is reason to believe I'm your natural father."

She went very still, eyes locked on his. The blood drained from her tanned cheeks leaving them pale.

"That is blunt. Oh my God, this is so weird but looking at you is like seeing myself in a mirror."

He nodded.

"I know, as you came towards me there was a particular expression in your eyes that reminded me absolutely of my father. Genes are amazing things."

"You mentioned opening a letter; have you known about this for long?"

The waiter placed a tall glass of shandy at her elbow and she flashed him a smile as James paid and asked for two more drinks. She drank a third of it down in a long swallow and wiped her mouth.

"That we are probably related, only a few days, but I have had the letter for about thirty years, I just never opened it."

"Good thing I like a mystery. Why was that?"

"I'm glad you're taking all this so calmly, it must be something of a shock."

"And that is something of an understatement; there's a lot going on under the surface here. Any chance I could see the letter?"

"Of course, I was getting to that. Here."

Jemima took the envelope with a raggedly opened flap and extracted the single sheet of paper. It was obviously old and of rather coarse quality. She noted the hand-written farm address at top right and the date in 1980. She smoothed it and began to read.

"Dear James,

I don't know why you won't even speak to me. As an act of desperation I am sending this letter to your lawyer Anthony Jarvis to forward. You are the only man I have ever truly loved. After you were expelled from Peterhouse I forced myself to spurn you for your own good, society as it was then would never have tolerated our relationship and it might well have ruined your life; letting you go was an agony for me that took years to get over. Our daughter Jemima was conceived the next time we met, on the night train to Umtali. Unfortunately by the time I knew I was pregnant with your child you had married Amanda, so I married Gert to give Jemima a father. He was a very good man, probably better than I deserved, but I grew to hate him because he wasn't you. It all came to a head that night of the party at our cottage in the bush; I wanted you desperately but your bloody principles wouldn't bend, so in a drunken rage I told Amanda that you were Jemima's father and she believed me. It caused her to flee the party and drive to her death.

What can a friendless person riven by guilt do but crave oblivion?

I know that in this life I have caused you much pain, but I have also given you Jemima. Please cherish her for she is our daughter, on my part at least, borne in love. Perhaps we shall meet in a better life.

Dawn."

Jemima held the letter between her fingers and looked up at James, to find him regarding her with a steady gaze.

"Some story! Pretty conclusive too I would say, if I wasn't so cynical and world-weary, constantly expecting to be scammed. How do I know any of this is true, or even that you are who you say?"

"You are right to be cautious but it's all verifiable through mutual friends, records and so on. If you are interested in picking up our relationship I would be happy to take a DNA test. People in our situation didn't used to have access to such proof."

"No. So assuming a test is positive and I am your daughter, which to tell the truth I hardly doubt, what kind of man is my father? Is he a good guy?"

"He tries to be. I do know that I already love you and bitterly regret the lost years when we might have been together."

Jemima's head dropped and her shoulders trembled. Tears dripped down her cheeks as her hand crept across the table to touch James's.

"I have felt somehow alone my whole life and turned a tough hard face to the world."

She shrugged.

"Other people loved me while I was growing up but I always longed for my own family, a mother and father, brothers and sisters. If you aren't being honest about this, if you have some ulterior motive, I swear I will kill you."

She looked up to see his eyes also glistening with tears and his fingers squeezed hers tightly.

"I promise to be your Father if you will only let me, and I will cherish and try to look after you always."

Jemima sobbed anew, dashing angrily at her tears with the back of a hand.

The returning waiter swerved discreetly away, put down the tray with drinks and pretended to clean a table, watching them out of the corner of his eye. James passed his clean handkerchief to Jemima and taking a paper napkin from the table-stand blew his nose thunderously, then signalled the man over. He placed the drinks delicately beside them and stepped back, bowing slightly.

"I am sorry boss."

James and Jemima laughed tearfully.

"Don't be my friend we are crying with joy, not sorrow. Will you have a drink with us to celebrate our good fortune?"

The man beamed.

"Yes Sir, I will trust a Castle!"

Jemima pulled her hand free and dried her face with paper napkins.

"That short letter reads like a whole movie script. So why wouldn't you even speak to her?"

"I'll try and make it brief. Your mother was an orphan brought up in Bulawayo and she craved security all her life. We met when I was about eighteen, in my final year at a remote boarding school in the bush. Dawn was several years older than me, the wife of a schoolmaster. We had an affair and when he found out, he beat us both savagely. Actually he tried to kill us but luckily the axe he used was very blunt. I managed to knock him out while he was concentrating on your Mum"

He looked away across the quiet garden, remembering and took a sip of beer.

"George had always beaten her. Anyway, I was expelled but she managed to see me while I was in isolation in the Sanatorium, pending departure. I loved her terribly and had some money in the post-office; she had a car, we could have left and got jobs, rented somewhere, lived together. I could have looked after her but she wouldn't have it, was frightened it would ruin my career, stop me going to Uni. She was also terrified what my parents and Rhodesian society as a whole would think because she had seduced a schoolboy, but she was really only a child herself."

He sighed. Jemima was watching him raptly.

"Go on."

"She went back to George who continued to make her life hell, until finally she divorced him and joined the Rhodesian Army. She was a Sergeant in the PTI corps by the time I next met her, a changed woman, very pretty and fit, hugely confident outwardly. She was seeing a married man in the Air-force, an officer, and I was in a long-term relationship with a girl my own age called Amanda. I met Dawn by chance on a night-train. War-fever was rampant and it was a very romantic journey; we got drunk together and ended up making love. Perhaps it should have told us something but it didn't. In the morning she went off with her Blue-job officer and shortly afterwards I married Amanda."

"Only you had got my Mum pregnant. With me."

James nodded.

"The Blue-job died in a helicopter accident, inspecting troops one Christmas. I was in the bush on operations. Your mum knew Amanda and went to our cottage; they spent Christmas together, which is how she met my best friend Gert Visser and married him, to give you a father. And he was a father, an outstanding father to you, while he was alive; he loved you to bits. Absolutely doted on you."

Jemima took his hand again.

"I'm not sure I like my mother; do you think she went to your cottage to try and get you back?"

"I've often wondered and it wouldn't have worked but a pregnant female of any species is going to fight pretty hard for her offspring. Any rule-book goes out the window. I tried to lean to the charitable view that your Mum fell in love with Gert but there's no doubt she was just using him; he was a pretty vulnerable bloke himself. It was her visceral craving for security and the need to be loved."

Jemima squeezed his hand.

"I know about that; I realise my Ouma and Oupa loved me, and so did Dougie who taught me to fly and became my guardian when they died but it isn't the same as parental love. I've always felt a bit alone in the world, like my Mum must have done."

"Well there are many different loves; the type a man feels for a woman, the shepherd his flock, a soldier his comrade. I probably still loved your mother deep down until she began to despise and belittle Gert, who was my best friend and deserved better. Eventually I couldn't go near them because of it, when I should have been most supportive of Gert."

He scratched at a knot in the wood of the table.

"So anyway, your christening was held in the garden of a cottage Gert did-up, on his father's farm, on a hill. Made a nice job of it and it was a house-warming party too. Rhodesia was pretty much on its last legs, fighting on empty, even South Africa was turning against us. The war-fever was manic and it was a hooley of gigantic proportions. Your mother…."

James stared away into the distance, sighing.

"Go on Dad, I know all this happened a long time ago and I'm an adult."

"You called me Dad."

"Yes, it just slipped out somehow. You don't mind do you?"

"Mind? My God no, I just feel humble, and honoured, and maybe a little angry that is has taken so long."

"You were saying; the party?"

"Oh yes. At the party your Mother was all over me in far too obvious a way. Amanda was heavily pregnant by this time with our first child and the last thing I wanted was for her to get upset. I ended up playing dodgems all night trying to avoid your Mum, and she knew it. She eventually cornered me, basically offered herself to me and

I...God males are stupid things....I was very turned on by it, but repulsed at the same time."

Jemima's eyes were big.

"You didn't!"

"No, I didn't. But you know, God loves his little pranks, because if I had, maybe things would have turned out better. I refused her advances and tore her off a strip; she went crazy with rage, rushed into the cottage where Amanda was looking after you for your Mum. I always thought Dawn just told Amanda we had been lovers, but obviously she told her I was your father which I didn't know myself at the time. My wife rushed out and jumped into our Beach-buggy. By this stage of the war, nothing but nothing moved at night because of landmines, and our buggy was unprotected. She drove over a biscuit-tin, a TMH46 anti-tank mine boosted with high-explosive. She died in hospital, along with our child."

They sat in silence for a long time, listening to the birds chatter. A Grey Lourie flapped clumsily from tree to tree in curious dipping flight, screeching "Go-Way!" at them.

Jemima cupped her chin in her hand and watched it.

"I understand now why you wouldn't speak to her."

"The last time I heard from her I was in southern Angola with the South African Army. She called to tell me your Dad had died in the tractor accident, wanted us to get back together. I think she tried again to tell me about you but I cut her off, wouldn't listen, called her a selfish cow. Must have been not long after that she wrote this letter, care of my friend and attorney Anthony Jarvis, to make sure I would know and look after you if anything happened to her."

"What did happen to her?"

"A firearms accident; I don't know the details" lied James. Word had got back to him of Dawn's suicide and his reaction had only been disgust. He knew that Jemima must never find out.

"That's what I was always told but it seems a bit odd; she was in the Army, must have been pretty good with weapons?"

"Weapons kill, and not always the right people. Everybody and his dog had been called up by then and there were some pretty incompetent people running around with guns. My guess would be an AD of some kind."

"AD?"

"Accidental discharge. When I got the letter from Dawn through Anthony I nearly ripped it up unopened but couldn't bring myself to do that: however I couldn't bear to open it either. The damn thing's been carted about in my personal effects ever since. Last week Loretta was having a clear out and made me decide. I nearly let her throw it in the bin, in which case we would never have known about each other."

"On such slender threads hang all our fates. I'm very glad you didn't"

"So am I. Loretta can't wait to meet you. Neither can your half-sister Haley."

"Haley? I have a sister? Oh my God, tell me about her!"

"I will and I have a letter from her for you, but right now I would like to know some more about you, what you've been doing all these years, what you do now."

They talked animatedly for nearly an hour, sharing a plate of slaap chips with tomato sauce and a couple more drinks. Naturally James was very interested in her flying career and she in his so the conversation followed no pattern, jumped forward and back in time and often they found themselves laughing together for they were both good story-tellers, sharing a wry sense of humour.

"To tell the truth James, it doesn't feel as if there is enough time in the world to catch up on everything; I feel a kind of exhilaration but still tinged with wariness that all this is too good to be true. You look like everything I would want my Dad to be; handsome, tough, trustworthy, reliable but are you for real?"

"I like it better when you call me Dad, and a DNA test will reassure you about our blood connection. As to the other qualities, I can only try to convince you by my future actions. Building any relationship takes time but on many occasions in my life it has been hugely comforting just to know that someone, somewhere gives a damn about me, and I hope to become such a person to you."

"Well you've made a good beginning; I already feel like I'm starting to know you. This can't have been an easy pitch to make!"

"Hardest of my life but most rewarding."

"How long are you here for?"

"I'm not quite sure but several days at least; I won a transport contract to supply heavy goods drivers to the Americans in Iraq and we have to be in place in less than a month so I can't linger too long."

"You're going to Iraq? I should have thought being imprisoned in Libya and the traumatic escape attempt would have put you off Muslim dictatorships for ever!"

"It's a democracy now, at least on paper, and where there's muck and bullets there's brass."

She shivered slightly.

"Doesn't sound good, there's more to life than money."

He smiled.

"Not if you haven't got any; things in a conflict zone often look worse from the outside than they are on the ground because of media hype. James Hacking adage number three coming up; the only way to find anything out is to do it."

Jemima smiled.

"Okay. Got much planned for the rest of your time here?"

"Not really; I've recruited a couple of old Army friends to drive in Iraq and I'm trying to contact another up in the Eastern Transvaal. Other than that I just plan to try and enjoy Africa a bit. I miss it sometimes."

"We're flat-out busy so I can't get much time off work until the weekend. Why don't you come out and see our operation tomorrow?"

"I'd love to."

"Ever flown a crop-duster?"

"Not yet; done some aerobatics in Extras and Tiger-Moths though."

"That will stand you in good stead; here, I'll draw a map on this napkin to the farm we're spraying. Just arrive when it suits you."

The sudden guttural roar of a powerful engine grew quickly louder on the still evening air as a fast-moving vehicle rocketed up the access road. Jemima smiled.

"Sounds like Sandro, I arranged to meet him here too. Wish I hadn't now, we have so much to catch up on."

"Sandro?"

"A guy I started seeing quite recently. Nice but a bit Tiggerish sometimes; You know, "bouncy bouncy fun fun fun!"

"I was going to ask if you're in a relationship. George didn't refer to one last night when he gave me your address."

"Nothing to tie me down yet, I'm too busy. I do like him a lot though. There he is."

She stood up and waved. When Sandro came over they touched each other's waists and kissed chastely on the cheek.

"James, this is Sandro Marais. Sandro, this is my Dad."

They shook hands and Sandro took off his shades.

"Really hey? You look well James considering Jemima told me her Dad is dead!"

They all laughed,

"I have a feeling I've met you somewhere before Sandro."

"Yeah, me too but I can't remember where. When did you come back from the dead?"

James looked at his watch.

"I'll let Jemima tell you about that. Dunno about you two but I'm feeling scroll." He was slipping back easily into southern African patois. "Can we eat here? I'll buy the dinner and she can explain."

"Well the graze here is ace. What do you say Jemima, shall we let your resurrected old man buy us some sadza?"

"Yes I'm famished actually and I can detect mouth-watering smells from the kitchen."

Over coffee after an excellent meal Jemima told the story of Lembede's property inspection to Botswana and the publicity-shy black tycoon's violent behaviour. Sandro, though he had been on the Botswana trip, made few comments and James looked at him searchingly.

"How much do you really know about him Sandro?"

The younger man folded his napkin carefully.

"Well Lembede is one crazy oke. The fact is that big business in this country is ruthless and so is big crime. Often the edges get blurred and the two overlap. Like Russia; where did all these mega-rich Oligarch Chinas suddenly come from? There was a big change, a vacuum and some merciless manne climbed out of the woodwork and ended up on top. Same in this country."

"How did you get involved with him?"

"It was like this. I came back to Hillbrow from Angola with quite a lot of dosh and I was bored so I took up cage-fighting, real brutal stuff but my MMA gave me an edge…"

"What's MMA?"

"Mixed Martial Arts. I already had a rep in Hillbrow and never lost a fight which is like cash in the bank round there. I began doing repossession work and security, then got into pawn-broking, gambling and bootleg booze. It was a goldmine, these okes round here will gamble on anything, whether a hookoo wants to cross the road even. The business grew and before I knew it I ran a whole organisation, whole districts, whole towns round Jo'burg. We were doing stuff that was technically illegal like alcohol and gambling without permits but nothing dirty like drugs or forced prostitution. Lembede appeared from nowhere and tried to muscle in. Things got pretty hairy so I broke into his mansion and discovered a secret he is desperate to conceal, so we have this understanding, because he knows I know. And if I go missing a lot of other people will find out too."

"What was the secret?"

He grinned. "Can't say or I'd have to kill you. But seriously, at the same time I arranged various conduits into his organization so that he can barely take a crap without me knowing. There were various parts of our businesses that complemented each other, so we cooperate now, when it suits me. Easier than fighting all the time."

"Why even involve yourself with such a person?"

Sandro shrugged.

"Money. Once I'd neutralized him there were some obvious advantages to cooperation. There are some markets here that only want to deal with whites and some with just blacks or coloureds."

"Sounds like a rough way to make a living."

"I guess so by most standards but corruption is a way of life here man, you don't get anywhere without an edge."

"Doesn't the continual violence bother you?"

"There is surprisingly little in my operation, that's what having a rep can do for you. The vice squad is a bit irritating but I regard any payoffs to them as a cost of doing business. I can't deny Lembede does some nasty stuff, like what happened when he pistol-whipped the Botswana customs guy but when we're working on something together I try to limit his excesses."

Jemima was watching him with a slightly troubled look.

"Why don't you just get out altogether, or operate on your own?"

"Partly because I like having my enemies where I can see what they're doing and because I'm making shekels Jem. Everyone's got to make a living, your Dad knows that, he's off to Iraq where they regularly blow hundreds of people to bits, all just to make a few bucks; someone's gonna do it, right James?"

The older man shifted uneasily on his chair.

"I suppose so but it feel like I'm on the side of the good guys there, Saddam's over-throwers, for the good of the people and democracy. Lembede sounds like a psychotic criminal which is a little different. If he got convicted for something you could be in deep shit too."

Sandro laughed. "It won't happen, I'm way smarter than he is."

Jemima and James smiled at his confident ebullience.

"Why are you guys buying that farm in Botswana?"

"The farm is productive with a good water-supply and infrastructure. The gold-mine is performing marginally but the dumps can be reprocessed with new techniques and the crazy man is convinced that as world economies fail the gold price may double again as investors seek safe havens. Lastly, wherever gold is found there are often other wealth-creating minerals in proximity. Looks like win-win to me. Develop it or flip the property for a big return."

Something was still nagging at James.

"What does he look like, this Lembede guy?"

Sandro shrugged and looked at Jemima.

"Quite handsome for a black, about five eleven or six foot, cold eyes, flat nose…."

Jemima exclaimed.

"I forgot all about it but when we were on the ground in Selibe I took a picture of a huge Kudu bull at the edge of the runway; I bet the whole party is in it, including Theo and Lembede."

She picked up the handset off the table and her thumb raced over buttons.

"Thought so. Theo's in the foreground but you can see Lembede, Sandro and the others behind. It's not very good because I was facing the sun."

James took the offered phone and squinted.

"Can't make much out, might be better with my glasses. They're in the car; I only use them for driving at night."

He offered it back.

"Mind if I have a look?"

Sandro took it, peered and grunted.

"Good photo, the Kudu stands out quite well, looking right at the camera. The rest is pretty indistinct."

He gave the phone back to Jemima and stood up.

"Now s'cuse us, I got to point Percy."

Sandro headed off to the lavatories as Jemima and James exchanged a long glance and smiled.

"Tigger indeed" said James.

"Do you like him?"

"I think so but it's like being near a whirlwind. I'm sure we've met before; I consider myself a good instinctive judge of character and feel ninety percent certain he's a legit square guy but there is an edge of doubt. Who am I to judge anyway? You've known him longer than me."

"Not by much and I already trust your judgement. He seemed a rough diamond when I first met him but he's been really gentle and considerate to me. He did admit that he has a criminal record for doing a couple of heists, but he gave the information off his own bat, I didn't find out."

"Hmmm."

"Yes."

Sandro returned as James was paying the bill.

"Dunno about you guys but I've decided to crash here, I'm too tired and drunk to drive to Joeys right now."

Jemima stood up.

"I might do that too, save time getting to work in the morning. Give me a few minutes Sandro, I'll see my Dad off."

They chatted a while longer in the car-park.

"Can I have another look at that photograph? I'll just get my glasses; I can zoom it a bit too."

While he was rummaging through his rucksack in the Mustang he heard Jemima swear in annoyance.

"The bloody thing's gone! Or I can't find it anyway, maybe it's moved itself to some other stupid directory."

James stood up slowly with his spectacles on.

"The specs suit you well, very distinguished!"

He smiled.

"I hate them; aging male vanity. Look, it's a bit odd that the photograph has vanished since Sandro looked at it."

Jemima looked thoughtful.

"That's true; and he deleted all the photos from Theo's camera. Cheeky bugger if he deleted something from my phone without asking!"

"We don't know that he did but it might be he doesn't like being in photographs either; understandably, given his profession. I still have a nagging suspicion that I'm missing something important though."

The next four days were among the most enjoyable of James's life as he got to know his daughter. He flew with her, water-skied with her and walked in the mountains with her. They never tired of talking and she felt able to confide anything to him, including the parlous state of ZU-KAT's finances. Over-ruling her loud protestations that it wasn't why she'd told him James insisted on making the company a two-hundred thousand rand loan to help liquidity until monies-owing caught up.

"After all, I've just experienced exactly the same thing in UK and since the Lord has sent me a windfall in the advance Iraq payment, I want to share it with you; helping daughters is what fathers like to do!"
Jemima was delighted because it would get Klaasens at the Bank off her back at least temporarily. The following day James, after failing yet again to contact Denzil by phone or email, rose before dawn and drove the Mustang two hundred and fifty miles to Mpumalanga Province with the top down. The weather was warm and the trip nostalgic, through beautiful African countryside; he had driven these roads many times, on holidays to Swaziland and the Kruger game-park. The N4 Highway took him to Nelspruit on the Crocodile River and the large town reminded him of Umtali, his birthplace in Rhodesia. Although it was officially renamed 'Mbombela' most signs still carried the original name. Surrounded by peaks of the Drakensburg Mountains, the high-plateau air was fresh and his travel brochure told him that local Industries included the canning of citrus fruit, paper production, furniture manufacture and timber mills. It added that fertile soils and a subtropical climate provided perfect conditions for the growing of many other fruits, mainly mango, avocado, banana and macadamia nuts. James cruised through busy streets and followed the R37 towards Sabie, a small country-town forty miles further north. Once there he found the Caravan Park at Castle Rock easily enough. There were a few families sitting in the sunny beer garden and perhaps fifteen more adults inside sitting at or near the counter: all scrutinised him openly when he stepped inside. They looked mostly like farmers or outdoor folk and seemed to know each other for a jovial banter was taking place between various small groups. There was a tough-looking bearded white barman in his sixties whom James took to be the property-owner because he mocked and cajoled his customers cheerily as he served them. Ordering steak and chips with salad at the bar, James purchased a beer too.
"Here on holiday?"
"I'm trying to trace a friend of mine; Denzil Harcourt."
The busy pub became instantly silent and many pairs of eyes swivelled towards him. The waitress dropped her pad.
"What's your business with Denzil?"
James smiled.
"Well I imagine that is between him and me. This is all a bit cloak and dagger isn't it?"

"Round here we look out for each other when strangers ask questions, because not everybody who claims to be a friend actually is."

"Understandable I suppose. Well I'm James Hacking and I grew up on the farm next to Denzil's. We were in the same military unit together, in Rhodesia and later Namibia."

"I'll see if I can contact him. Enjoy your meal, it's our own beef."

James took the food to a table and the barman came over ten minutes later.

"Someone will be along soon. Want another drink?"

Within the hour a battered Landrover pulled up and a big middle-aged man with leathery skin and bushy whiskers alighted.

"Name's Kobus; you ready to go? Your car will be safe here."

"Okay. Call me James."

He picked up his small rucksack and climbed in.

"Are we going far?"

"Not really. Denzil's Game Farm is about fifteen miles north-east."

"Has he got a woman there?"

Kobus laughed and looked across at James.

"Of course; I see you know him well! Sometimes there is more than one!"

He offered cigarettes which James declined and smoked continuously for the rest of the trip. Conversation was difficult over the wind-noise, constant rattles and accompanying whine of the tyres. It was a very picturesque hilly journey and once they turned north at Hazyview towards Bushbuck Ridge there were tantalizing glimpses down the abrupt two-thousand foot Eastern Escarpment to endless miles of dry bushveld. Turning off onto a track they arrived at a large friendly-looking stone house with superb views and out came Denzil with his familiar rolling gait and infectious laugh. Though he was nearly seventy he could have passed for mid-fifties and had lost none of his energy. He wrung James's hand with a powerful mitt.

"How are Loretta and Haley?"

"Everybody's fine. I'll explain the main reason why I came."

On his phone was a photo of Jemima standing by her crop-duster; James showed it to Denzil and explained their relationship.

"That Dawn was one crazy unbalanced mare but you've made a beautiful girl between you. What do you intend to do, now that you've found her?"

James shrugged. "Just be a father I suppose, whatever that entails. She knows her own mind. You'll have to meet her soon."

He looked around.

"This is a fabulous place. What a view!"

"It certainly is; reminds us all of the eastern Highlands in Rhodesia. On a clear day I can see right across into Mozambique, just like you could from my Forestry Plantation in Penhalonga. Come on, let's go for a tour."

"You're a hard man to get hold of Denzil; aren't all the precautions a bit elaborate?"

"Not really, some of the things we've done in the past didn't make us very popular and the South African 'Anti-Mercenary' legislation is pretty harsh. I don't intend to get slotted on my home-ground, far less banged up to appease the ANC's 'dogs of war' paranoia. There are a lot of us 'green men' living round here and there is still money to be made in Africa for those prepared to take a risk. Not to mention high-octane fun to be had."

"Yes, I remember your idea of fun Denzil and there's still a bit of shrapnel in my arse to remind me! I tried several times to contact you by civilised channels."

"I've got a whizz-kid with communications and the internet working for me but even he can't help when things get screwed up on the Post Office landlines."

James was impressed with the scale of the operation. Denzil had initially bought the farm for its timber and started a sawmill, but seeing the potential for tourism and game-farming he'd branched into that too. They wound all the way down the escarpment through several game-fences, laughing and shouting above the clattering vehicle as it got hotter. Denzil showed him some big antelope herds and one Rhino but it was already late in the day for game-viewing and they returned along another precipitous track to a grass runway on the plateau with a cluster of smart modern buildings at one end. A large matt-black aircraft with twin engines was parked by a metal hanger.

"Is that an Aviocar Denzil?"

"Yes, a 212-400, latest spec. We've a couple of other nice birds in the hanger too. Ever flown one?"

"No but it has a terrific reputation. Do you operate it yourself?"

"Yes. I usually fly it solo but there are a couple of other commercial pilots locally able to stand in as Captain or come along as First

Officer. We can move passengers, animals, cargo, you name it; fantastic toy and I can write it down as a business asset."

"Not still doing dodgy operations are you Den?"

The older man winked.

"Certainly not, I'm a Captain in the SANDF Airforce actually, 101 Squadron Light Transport Reserve. There are nine Reserve Squadrons of private aircraft and 101 are based at Hoedspruit about sixty clicks north. Each squadron is unique because the members have particular knowledge of the area of responsibility in which they operate and help the police in crime-prevention operations, border patrols and other police work. The smaller, slower planes are generally used for reconnaissance, while higher performance aircraft like this one undertake VIP transport roles and humanitarian missions, like the floods in Mozambique in 2000. It's good, keeps me in touch with some of the top honchos in the SANDF. They get useful assets at cheaper rates and we all get subsidised flying hours.""Would an adventure in Iraq interest you? I have a contract to supply heavy goods vehicle drivers for petrol tankers; you might enjoy the opportunity to have a look at that particular theatre since mayhem has long been one of your main interests."

"I've never been keen on Arabs James; the Afrikaans don't call them 'sand kaffirs' for nothing; devious and untrustworthy! A lot of blokes we served with are already in Europe working for private companies like Blackwater. I expect you'll find lots of recruits closer to home than this."

"Quantity isn't the problem, quality is, which is why I'm over here. The pay is good, month on/month off contract and there's still a hell of a conflict going on whatever the newspapers say; Potty and Louis are in."

"Have to pass James, can't say too much but I'm helping out some old buddies. Want to do circuits in the Aviocar? I'm an instructor so I can sign off your difference training. Always good to have another type on your licence."

"That would be cool, I'll pay you for the fuel."

"Not after what you did for me in Libya. Be my guest."

As they walked over to the twin turboprop James did a "Mark" on his wrist-watch GPS; time spent on reconnaissance was never wasted and whenever he was at a new airfield he added it to his database. Afterwards they toured the workshops with Denzil showing off his many ideas and projects. There were some powerful super-silenced scrambler bikes that he said were used by game scouts in order not to spook the animals, but James could imagine a few other uses they might be put to.

"We'll have a braai tonight, and sink some chibulies James. Have you seen your Mum and Dad down in the Cape this trip?"

"I'm going to rent a crate in Joeys and fly down. The nearest town other than Knysna is George which has a decent airport if I can get over the mountains. I'll only have time to stay for one night though. I'll give them your regards. Our family won't forget what you did to get Dad out of Rhodesia when he was on the run Den."

"It was a pleasure; Ian is one of the straightest men I ever met and he would have done the same for me. I probably still owe him some favours. Tell them hello"

"Look Den, if anything happens to me in Iraq or if any of my family needs help when I'm not around, can I count on you?"

"Are you joking, our kid? Of course, we're family! I lived next door to your Mum and Dad for more years than I ever spent anywhere else and they were the best ones too. I watched you grow up."

James laughed.

"Yeah, strange that, I haven't watched you grow up yet!"

"I don't bloody intend to either mate. Listen, I have a secure sat-phone number you can give your family. Don't bandy it about to rank and file though; I only share it with really important people."

They shook hands, feeling something good between them.

"I'll get Kobus to take you back to Castle Rock tomorrow."

James returned to George Bustamante's in Johannesburg in time for dinner the following evening. Jemima joined them, stayed the night and took her Dad to the airport in the morning. She would have liked to fly down with him to meet her grandparents but couldn't take time off. James enjoyed the trip south in a Cessna 182 and found his folks well, both spry despite being in their early eighties. After picking him up at George Airport they had a picnic on the beach at Plettenburg bay and a swim before going on to their dairy farm. There was a small graveyard on a knoll of their property with headstones for their daughter Sheila, her black husband Patrick and their young children, murdered by ex-president General Spencer Katsiru. Most people thought it had been motivated by greed, to get their land but James was in no doubt it was revenge against him. They sat quietly together for fifteen minutes remembering the past, said a prayer and went down for dinner. James spent his last night in Johannesburg with

Jemima at her townhouse and they parted at Oliver Tambo International, exchanging last minute words in the drop-off area.

"Jem, I think you should consider moving your assets out of Africa while they are worth something and setting up near us. The rand is still strong at the moment but there is increasing talk about Land Reform of the type that helped bankrupt Zimbabwe and the signs are not encouraging for whites in South Africa."

"Maybe but I'm a sunshine girl Dad, upping sticks isn't so easy. I've never even been to England, hear the weather is awful and don't have a British passport."

"True but you'll be entitled to one once the DNA test establishes me as your father, and the UK makes a good stepping stone to the world. You have transferrable skills, some capital and the Americas are only five or six hours away from Manchester. Promise you'll think about it."

"Sure. I'll come and check you all out when your first trip to Iraq is over. Be careful! I couldn't bear to lose you now."

"Or me you. Listen, I've a friend up in the Eastern Transvaal who really understands how things work in Africa. Copy this number into your phone and if you can't get hold of me anytime, contact him. Put these numbers in your GPS too, they're the co-ordinates of his aerodrome."

-xxx-

Simon Ndhlovu was on a field trip to Mutare with the Vice-Marshall to inspect work on the eastern border cordon and check on developments with his local operatives. He still didn't know who the sponsor of the Militias at Grand Reef was and couldn't think why finding ex-president Katsiru's son would be of any practical use but acting on impulse he dialled the orphanage in Mutare and made an appointment. The middle-aged black woman in charge was helpful on seeing his credentials and showed him around. It was more like a boarding-school than an orphanage, with younger children yelling in a pleasant playground and older ones looking after them tolerantly, arranging games. She explained that the institution had been founded by a well-off white woman before independence and was maintained by a trust formed from her estate after she died.

"Ah yes, Tamuwana, I know him, he was one of my favourites when I first came here as a young woman; a quiet boy, always reading, and good at sports, especially tennis and running. He did well at school and went on to become a teacher himself. I have no children of my own and was like a mother to him; I even kept clippings of his hair, and I would put money under his pillow for the tooth-fairy and keep the teeth!" She covered her mouth shyly and laughed as Simon's hope grew.

"Do you know where he is now?"

"Yes he is a teacher at Dangamvura primary school nearby and I see him quite often; he runs the young-farmers club and brings gifts of vegetables which are very welcome in these hard times. He is a devout 'Postle' too."

Ndhlovu knew of the sect whose full title was 'the African Apostolic Church of John Maranke,' an evangelizing faith that worshipped without buildings and espoused teetotalism. He had heard only good of them and had seen them performing full-submersion baptisms at large gatherings; the men looked very biblical with their shaved heads and long beards.

He stopped pacing and turned to face her.

"Do you still have his teeth and hair?"

"Yes I'm sure I do. Why do you ask?"

"Because I must ask you to lend them to me on a matter that could be of national importance. I will of course give you a signed receipt and return them, and I would prefer it if he didn't know about this at the moment. If necessary I will get President Mpofu to telephone you and confirm my request."

Her brow creased.

"Oh my, that won't be necessary but he's not in trouble is he? Oh Dear...."

"I am sure he is not in any trouble but he may somehow be instrumental in preventing it."

"Well in that case of course. Come with me to my quarters."

"Can you wait a minute? I'll just fetch some things from my truck." He ran to his vehicle and returned with evidence bags, seals and forms. If this was to lead anywhere the evidence provenance would have to be watertight. Until recently all DNA samples had had to be sent to South Africa but a very modern private facility had recently opened in Harare and he was sure he could get priority testing done in the circumstances. He would need Spencer Katsiru's genetic material too and it was sure to have been collected when he was in custody awaiting trial before his escape. Without being sure why, Simon felt a surge of excitement.

-xxx-

CHAPTER NINE
Iraq

Ringtail Logistics had been operating in Iraq for six week and James was pleased with the way things were going. The first field changeover of his drivers had gone smoothly and the second six were in place and bedded down. Malcontents and misfits had fallen by the wayside leaving a group of professionals with good morale. The Americans were glad to have them and several, including Eugene Potgieter and Colinda Lasserre had agreed to forgo their field-break to earn more money. James had also stayed to oversee the first crew-change.

"I gotta feeling we're going to die today" predicted Potty as he shrugged into his Kevlar armour. It was a sort of ritual that amused him but sometimes grated on the other drivers.

"You, dammit! You! Don't include the rest of us in your stupid predictions! You've got a feeling you're going to die today" raged Scouse Hughes irritably, his bootlaces tight.

"At least if we do it'll be quick" grinned James, fitting the Kevlar breastplate into his flack-jacket and tapping it home snug. "No need for a funeral either; twenty-six tons of aviation jet-fuel will give you the mother of all cremations. Nothing whatever to send home to Mum."

"Well thanks very much mate; I needed that reassurance like a hole in the head. What makes all you bastards so morbidly cheerful about dying a sudden death anyway?"

"Fear of the alternative, a living death Hughesy, that's what" said James, slapping the kneeling scouser encouragingly on his back. "I always feel cheerful when I hear that someone's gone quick, without suffering; a short life but a happy one eh?"

"Oof!" said Hughes as James's friendly pat drove the air from his lungs. "I'll settle for a long life and a happy one if you don't mind."

Potty Potgieter laughed.

"I have some bad news for you then boy; you're in the wrong job. Come on, let's get it over with."

Once ready for the short walk to the transport section, James and his six contract drivers left the huge 52-person tent full of camp stretchers that the TFN staff called home at the Airport. It was near the perimeter wall at Baghdad International and on some nights they could watch incoming fire arcing overhead to land on targets nearer the centre. James often chose to sleep on the bunk in his truck to escape the snoring, farting and continual human movement as people went to the toilets or changed shift.

"Ca va James?" asked Colinda Lasserre, their only female and only American driver, putting her arm through his as they walked.

"Ca va merde like usual" he replied, smiling and she guffawed, dark hair flying.

"Always so cheerful, you Brits! And what is wrong with your little friend Hughes today? Did he hurt his pinky finger when he drove into the truck in front?"

She grinned sardonically at the smaller man who'd hurried to join them. On some routes the dust got so bad that drivers at the rear of the convoy almost drove blind and accidents were not uncommon. Hughes had hit a broken-down truck which hadn't pulled over enough, totalling both units, and been lucky to escape so lightly. He held up his right hand on which two fingers were splinted together with Elastoplast.

"This is a genuine war wound and any lesser man would be using it as an excuse to avoid duty. Listen Colinda, the other Yanks have been telling me of an ancient remedy for serious injuries like this; you have to put your fingers between the naked legs of a Cajun Princess and rub until she floods them with healing maiden's water....."

She swatted his head.

"Rude boy! Je vais frotter ta langue avec une brique!"

"Ow! What does that mean James? Did she say yes?"

"I said I will scrub your tongue with a brick Hughes. And there is no such thing as a Cajun princess."

Adjusting her body armour, Colinda leant across to James's ear and whispered "But for you I could easily become one!"

He laughed uneasily, feeling a familiar stirring in his underwear.

The tankers stood waiting in protective berms inside the compound. The team had picked them up brand-new two months earlier, five hundred horsepower Mercedes six by four tractor units to pull the huge tanker-trailers. Colinda leant close to James' ear again and whispered in a sexy French/American accent, cutting her flashing eyes lasciviously at his groin.

"No kidding James; I volunteer to flood you with maiden's water anytime."

Her perfume and breath made him fully erect and he chuckled.

"You're spoiling my concentration Miss Lasserre. Don't run over any dead dogs today!"

He put his hand on her neck, kneading gently and she hunched her shoulders and arched her back like a stroked cat. Placing improvised explosive devices in dead animals near the road was a common tactic of the insurgents and the previous day they had been held up for hours while a bomb squad examined an IED in a dead mongrel before detonating it. The carcase had hurtled hundreds of feet through the air, to the delight of the young American soldiers. The American Captain in charge of the military escort dismounted from his light tank and ambled over, pushing up shades to show eyes glinting with sardonic humour.

"Raring to go huh folks? That's what I like to see. Well, nothing's changed since last night so it's still Route Tampa today. You may think the high mucky-mucks just tossed a coin but there was a big suicide bomb in Northern Baghdad early on and Route Jackson's snarled up good."

He ran quickly over the previous evening's tactics and route briefing, then refolded his map. "Right, give 'em a quick once-over then let's get to it."

James did a quick walk-around of the truck and trailer rig then climbed up into the high cab hefting his bag. The diesel started with a subdued growl and he immediately tapped the aircon button down to minimum temp, sweat running down his face; the rising whine of the fan wafted out waves of welcome cool air as he automatically checked fuel level and air pressures on the vehicle computer. The convoy moved out, Colinda's tanker amongst the first few to move. At the rear, following Potty and Hughes, James dipped the clutch, released the dead-man handbrake in a rush of air and nudged the auto-shift lever forward with his left hand. The truck ground forwards ponderously, the semi-automatic transmission clunking electronically as he shifted up through the gears.

Much of the fuel for the American forces in Iraq was driven in convoy from Kuwait to Baghdad where it was pumped into huge storage bladders for onward shipment to the Northern Logistics Support Areas. James was second last in the convoy of twenty-three aviation fuel tankers hauling spirit from Baghdad Airport to Camp Anaconda, also known as Balad Airforce Base, near the village of Balad, sixty eight miles north of Baghdad. 'Route Tampa' took an unpaved road across the desert to the west of 'Route Jackson' which used the busy Highway 1 to Sammara, Balad and the north. James preferred Tampa because it was more open, less hectic and because there were less man-made structures to hide IEDs and ambushing forces behind. It was also swept for landmines regularly.

The well-planned ambush of the convoy was initiated by a roadside bomb, planted at the edge of a village where a narrow defile led through a rock outcrop. The massive IED was designed to split the convoy and it trashed an armoured Humvee. Dead and injured American soldiers were hanging from the wreckage or crawling dazedly from the ruins. Hughes, in swerving to avoid the wrecked Humvee drove straight into a massive crater left by the bomb. The huge truck and trailer bucked and reared through the hole, all the wheels leaving the ground. The front axle collapsed and the Mercedes slid to a halt, the jack-knifed tanker shearing the fifth wheel pin and rolling onto its side. James swerved and braked, bouncing off the road onto the desert hard-shoulder, avoiding the crater and pulling up next to Hughes' stricken tractor unit. He clicked a switch to unlock the passenger door and hit the electric window.

"Scouse, get your arse in here pronto!" he yelled as tracer streaked towards the chaotic convoy and the loud flat DUM! of repeated strikes by rocket-propelled grenades rent the air. Smoke and flames roiled. The Liverpudlian vaulted from his cab and streaked across the hard sand, hurling himself up into the cab. Drive wheels spun as James jumped the clutch, weaving his way forwards at full throttle, intent on driving through the ambush, avoiding damaged vehicles and others returning fire. Ahead he could see one tanker disappearing into the defile with a tracked armoured personnel carrier following, firing furiously from its heavy machine gun. On the parapet of the village mosque a figure stood up, steadied an RPG 7 rocket launcher and fired. Flame, shrapnel and black smoke flew from the strike on the APC track, causing it to slew and halt in the killing ground, blocking the gorge. The rear door opened tentatively and then slammed shut as a hail of fire from the mosque struck it. The rocket man had been joined at the parapet by upwards of a dozen heavily armed men. There were also other dissidents on the higher ground at the entrance to the defile, pouring fire into the convoy behind them and James knew they were effectively trapped. He reached for the radio microphone.

"All units this is Delta 3 tanker. I'm going to park this mother under their mosque for you. If you can detonate it some of your troubles will be over. Copied anyone?"

"Copied fives and good thinking, good buddy!" replied a voice that James recognized as belonging to the Marine major in charge of the convoy.

"Just make sure you get out in good time!"

"What the hell are you on about?" asked Scouse Hughes, crouched in the passenger well.

"Get ready to abandon ship; we're going to crash this tanker into the mosque. There are some Yanks pinned down behind their APC just ahead, about a hundred yards from the Mosque. We'll jump there so they can cover us. The cruise control is set for max speed, I'll punch the button when we debus and she'll accelerate all the way in."

"I don't like this, can we get a second opinion, like mine maybe?"

"Negative, get your door open, it's time to go!"

They hit the ground and rolled in the dirt. Hughes was aware of the trailer wheels heading towards him and leopard-crawled frantically over to the APC, joined by James who sprinted in with tracer kicking up dirt behind his heels. The rising roar of the receding truck engine was followed twenty seconds later by a resounding crash. Looking upwards beyond the hull of the APC James saw the very pinnacle of the Mosque sway and then topple. Seconds later there was an almighty detonation as the aviation fuel exploded. The heavy APC rocked on its suspension; despite the hard sunshine there was a flash painful to the eyes, followed by a hot and roaring wind. James pulled Hughes in closer to the APC as bricks, tiles, timber and unspecified other shrapnel rained down from the sky, along with lumps of partially burnt meat.

"Guess those guys will be getting their virgins anytime now" shouted Scouse.

"I've heard there's a waiting list, not mentioned in the small-print. Anything up to eternity at present" James yelled back and the yanks jarheads laughed manically.

The welcome clatter of Apache helicopter gunships and the scream of A9 tank-busters putting in strikes could be heard over the battlefield and in less than an hour the follow-up operation was underway. James and Scouse Hughes were airlifted and dropped at camp Anaconda. The pilot touched his helmet and departed. News of the ambush had been relayed and a small crowd had gathered at the helipad for first-hand news. American soldiers and fellow convoy drivers shook their hands and slapped their backs.

"Any news of Potty?" James asked.

"Took a couple AK 47 hits but not too serious; he'll be OK. Got casevacced to the Field Hospital" said a communications Warrant Officer.

"Guess that means they hit him in the head" said Hughes in a shaky attempt at humour. They spent the night at Anaconda and returned to Baghdad airbase the following day. James was invited to travel in Colinda's truck since his own had ceased to exist, which made Hughes accuse him of pulling rank. She had the cab decorated with an unmistakably feminine touch that gave it a homely, tranquil ambiance.

"That was some cool action you took yesterday, you are no ordinary guy Hacking" she said admiringly.

"Thanks; I would hardly call you an ordinary woman either Colinda; aren't many self-employed female American truck-drivers in Iraq these days! And a real stunner at that!"

She frowned in mock-anger.

"What is 'stunner?' It is good yes? It better damn-well had be....!"

"I know, or you'll scrub me with a brick! Yes it's good; means 'Sensational,' or in your case: sexy, like a panther."

"Sensational like a panther, and sexy; yes that is very good, you are off the crook James."

"The hook."

"The hook?"

"By hook or by crook! I'm off the bloody thing!"

"What the hell are you talking about? Do you speak English?"

They passed the trip pleasantly discussing their past lives. Colinda had served two tours in Iraq as a 'MCTO' or Marine combat transportation officer which was one of the reasons she had a Heavy Goods Licence, then settled in London when her commission expired as a base to travel from. She had met James during his recruiting campaign and decided to join him for excitement and to make some money. Both were very aware of their mutual physical attraction; it was an almost tangible electricity in the air and though James intended to resist doing anything about it, the feeling of excitement made them laugh together often. Back at Baghdad Airport the convoy parked up and a voice like thunder roared across the sand making some of the drivers visibly flinch.

"Where's that goddam Limey who blew up my truck?"

Colonel Luis Sanchez burst into their midst like a short wide tank, dressed in crisp fatigues.

"Where is the bastard, where's this Hacking guy?" he demanded furiously, head darting about like an angry rhino looking for something to stomp.

"Guilty Colonel" said James stepping forward.

Sanchez put his hands on his hips and jutted his head forward belligerently.

"You huh? Well let me tell you Mr Hacking that I want to be the first grunt to buy you a drink. That was some smart thinking. Come on over to my office, I want to hear all about it! I'm going to see that you get a medal for this!"

"I'd rather have a pay rise, sir."

"Don't push your luck Mr Hacking, medals I got shit-loads of, money not!"

When James got back to the driver's quarters Hughes, who was reclining on his pit clad only in a towel, pointedly lifted his nose and averted his profile, sniffing.

"Back from Olympia huh? Gracing us mere mortals with your presence again now the Gods have kicked you out?"

"Fuck off Scouse" replied James without heat, dropping a big bundle of mail on the bed.

"Make yourself useful and sort these letters out while I get a shower, I called by the mailroom on the way back."

"Anything for me?" asked James, returning still damp in towel and flip-flops.

"Two."

Hughes held up a pair of identical narrow cream envelopes. James took them and sniffed, then frowned and sniffed again. He recognized Haley and Loretta's writing.

"What the hell are you doing?"

"Sniffing for evil. Letters are powerful medicine, like unexploded bombs. They bear information that can change lives. Sometimes they bring joy but other times you can almost see the evil leaking out of them."

Hughes glanced with trepidation at his own small bundle of letters.

"Well that's effectively killed any anticipatory enjoyment I was having. What's the verdict on that one?"

"Not good" said James, sitting on his bed and ripping open the envelope from Loretta. He read quickly with his face expressionless and stuffed the pages back into the envelope.

"Not as bad as it might have been" he said, managing to give a wry smile and keep his voice normal but inside he was crying. He dressed hurriedly and went outside to read the letter again. He was standing by the heli-pad with crossed arms, a set grim face and distant gaze when Hughes sought him out.

"Was it bad news mate?"

"You could say that. You know we have a flying school? Well Loretta's running off with the Chief instructor who has offered to marry her, and probably the business since they have more shares than me now."

Hughes whistled through his teeth in sympathy.

"Nasty one, she should have waited until you got back at least. Did you know it was coming?"

James sighed.

"Perhaps it's been on the cards for a good while; she was desperate for me not to come out here but I ignored her, thinking she'd come round. I obviously let her get lonely and frightened once too often. Still, it's always a shock to get 'Dear Johnned', particularly when the third party is someone like Dennis Mallard that you'd least suspect. What's even stranger is that Loretta is a loving, physical girl and the chief instructor she's taken up with, Dennis….well I could almost swear he's never had or wanted a woman in his life, whereas Loretta and I were always drawn to each other by a strong mutual lust which smoothed the turbulence beneath."

"Are you going to argue the toss, try and keep her?"

"It's probably too late."

"I hope it turns out the way you want. Come on, it's been a long two days. I'll buy you a beer."

James dropped a big hand on the smaller man's neck and squeezed.

"Yeah. Thank God for beer eh? Got a couple of things to do; meet you there in about fifteen minutes."

Colinda was already in the commissary tent, freshly showered, dressed in clean combat overalls and reading a paperback when Hughes arrived. He bought three beers and began to chat her up. She put down her book and amused herself by teasing him. She listened quietly, nodding when he told her about James' letter though.

"He is right about letters being powerful instruments; seems both Cajuns and Africans understand evil and black-magic."

She suddenly pounced towards Scouse.

"So watch it Hughes or I turn you into a frog and eat your fat little legs!"

Hughes leapt backwards on the bench, startled and nearly fell off. He fought to recover his balance and dignity.

"Well if we're going to get into eating one another Colinda I know where I want to start on you!"

She laughed and punched him on the arm, making him wince in genuine pain.

James joined them and sat down for a couple of tins of strictly rationed beer and some food, after which he excused himself and went out into the dusk. Colinda followed him and put her arm through his.

"Hughes told me about your 'Dear John'…I'm sorry."

"Hughes has got a big mouth."

"He meant well; he is sad for you, we both are. Come on, I have whisky in the truck."

A black-out privacy curtain was pulled round inside the big windscreen, making a cosy room of the cab. There was a huge cloth mural attached to it facing inward, a view of the sea and a sunny beach. There was subdued lighting and Barry White was playing softly on the stereo. The whisky was Kentucky straight bourbon; Wild Turkey "101" and fifty-percent proof. It went down like liquid gold. They listened in companionable silence for some time, James with his eyes closed. She stood to fetch the auto-changer remote-control from the bunk and on impulse put her arms round his shoulders and drew his head to her breast. After several minutes she crouched and touched her full lips gently, enquiringly on his. They listened to the music for several minutes more, breathing gently into each other's mouths, before his tongue traced the outline of her lips and probed gently inside. James could feel the strong alcohol distorting his sense of perspective.

"I'm not sure this is a good idea Colinda" he murmured.

"I understand. In your mind you are still attached; but your woman, she will have slept with this Dennis?"

"In all probability, though it's hard to imagine."

"Then sauce of her goose can be sauce for our gander."

"Put like that it seems very logical."

She began to undress him and then herself.

"Can't be any harm in a little cuddle" thought James, knowing he was lying to himself. They left the soft lights on and moved to the bunk where they were reflected in the big mirror she used for hair and makeup.

"We are like two beautiful animals playing on the beach huh James?" she murmured as they explored each other. A glint of gold between her legs caught his eye and when he moved to part them she opened willingly, displaying two gold rings which pierced her clitoris hood, one vertically and one horizontally so they were interlinked. He knelt beside her to look closer and his hot breath made her stir and his tongue made her groan. He was surprised somehow that when she came it was quietly, a series of racking low moans as her hips pumped spasmodically, hard thighs tensed and juddering. It was very sexy and his rigid penis jerked in tense sympathy. He kept his mouth on her and began again when she had relaxed from the first orgasm. Her groping hands found his straining erection and his excited secretions coated her hand. His thumb slid into her and his busy tongue gave her three more climaxes in quick succession.

"Enough!" she gasped at last "Fuck me James, I am more than ready!"

He chuckled and moved up between her legs, face slick with the thick juices of her gushing. She was hot and slippery but too tight to enter with just one thrust so she adjusted herself and swallowed him inch by inch. Once in they began to fuck vigorously, panting and staring into each other's eyes but suddenly Loretta intruded into his mind. Colinda felt the straining rigidity subside as he detumesced.

"James? What is wrong?"

She pushed herself up on her elbows and tried to see into his face. He frowned.

"I'm sorry Colinda, it isn't you! Loretta suddenly came into my mind and, well you can see the effect. I'm embarrassed."

"Don't worry James, I understand. Don't be distressed. Here, lie down beside me and tell me about it."

"Loretta and I have been together years and she has been like a mother to my daughter Haley. However as usual I have probably been too busy trying to make money and taken her for granted. It's a pattern of my life."

"But you know, maybe you are too hard on yourself. In my experience a woman does not just transfer from one man to another so easily, or so conveniently. Maybe something was going on already?"

"Yeah, I must admit that occurred to me too." He turned towards her.

"You are an enchanting woman Colinda and I'm sorry for my, ah, weakness at … ah, well, the culmination."

She squeezed his shoulder, and then he felt her hands and lips on him again.

"Let your Cajun Princess take over and work her magic" she whispered and this time when he mounted her his ride went all the way. Just before they slept she whispered contentedly "I still have my place in London if you need somewhere on R&R James."

-xxx-

CHAPTER TEN

Lembede sent for Sharpness Malinga unexpectedly and handed him the creased newspaper page he'd torn from the Lancashire Evening News.

"Remember this? Get yourself a plane ticket to England Colonel, it is time to take care of unfinished business with Hacking, he has gone unpunished long enough. Comrade Jongwe still controls my Liverpool interests does he not? It is near Lancashire. Instruct him by telephone to do an immediate recce on this airfield of Hacking's to confirm it is the right man, and tell him to use a white local for the initial enquiry to keep it discreet. I want you there to oversee things and work up a plan. If the identification is positive, I will join you."

Just twenty-four hours later Malinga went north from London by train, second class and picked up the hire-car Lembede had grudgingly authorised him to hire, paying extra from his own pocket to get a Mercedes saloon. Arriving in mid-afternoon he booked into an expensive hotel and went out to see the waterfront sights. He liked Liverpool. There were several clubs and restaurants with African themes where Zimbabweans flocked and the local women were comely and willing. The following day natural caution made him mount observation at Lembede's Garston dock premises before approaching. When Morris Jongwe pulled out from the barrier of the freight yard and set off eastwards Malinga followed him to Manchester Airport and watched the ex-political commissar collecting his wife and two daughters who had just flown in from a shopping trip to New York.

Jongwe was loading them and a plethora of expensive-looking boxes into a big black BMW X5 in the car park when he saw a man that caused his heart to sink; whenever Sharpness Malinga appeared it was because Lembede wanted something and usually it meant effort and trouble for Jongwe. Colonel Malinga had become a Major in ZANLA during the war against the whites, and high in Zimbabwe's secret police under both Mugabe and Katsiru. He was completely ruthless and had escaped from prison along with former President Katsiru when they were all awaiting trial after Primrose Mpofu's revolution. They had saved Jongwe too, and got his family out of Zimbabwe to Britain with enough money to get started in a new life, in case he talked to avoid prosecution.

The business Jongwe had opened in Liverpool for Lembede involved buying up used machinery and apparel to ship to Africa. It had flourished allowing the family to live very comfortably and more importantly for Jongwe, without dread. It had also proved a useful cover for the political activities he was called upon to supervise occasionally such as the beating or worse of Zimbabwean dissidents based in the UK, at the behest of the then President. He was unknown to Police and paid his taxes religiously which meant he could sleep soundly at night. It looked as if that was about to change again. Malinga jerked his head peremptorily and with a sinking heart Jongwe joined him, shaking hands and trying to appear delighted.

"So Jongwe, you are pleased to see me after all this time?"

"Of course, of course, Colonel, it is always good to see comrades from the struggle."

"It doesn't look like you are struggling too much now Jongwe. Nice car. Nice wife. Nice daughters. Nice life."

"Times are hard but they could be worse, yes."

He fidgeted as Malinga regarded him mockingly.

"You will be pleased to know that President Katsiru has a favour to ask of you."

"Certainly, certainly, I shall do my best to assist as always. How is Lembede, er, I mean President Katsiru these days?"

"Like a lion deprived of its prey; powerful, dangerous and unpredictable. He yearns to return to Zimbabwe and has a growing army in the east, ex-veterans of the Chimurenga struggle who are clamouring for him to lead them against the government forces. Now he has a way to get the Chiadzwa diamonds to world markets for the necessary finance, so it is only a matter of time before the new war of liberation starts."

"Remarkable; I always understood that loss of the testicles made men docile, hence the practice of making slaves eunuchs, but it has only made the President more ferocious."

Despite himself Malinga glanced round uneasily.

"I wouldn't talk about that too loudly Jongwe, it is the kind of personal secret that any man would kill to protect, let alone Lembede, which is really why I'm here. Read this."

He passed over the crumpled newspaper cutting. Jongwe perused it then regarded him quizzically.

"James Hacking eh? The man Lembede blames for the loss of his manhood? My God he caused us a lot of trouble during the war; and afterward helped Mpofu's wife get to power when we scribbled her husband! What of him?"

"The President's hatred never dimmed but the trail went cold. Now we suspect Hacking has settled in a village called Burscough not far from here; has some trucks and runs an airfield. We need you to confirm it is the right guy but discreetly. If it is him, ascertain as much about his operations as possible so that the boss can finish the business. Don't alert Hacking; remember he has a sixth sense for danger!"

Jongwe nodded.

"I understand; use a white man who won't stand out. There is a guy with a Driver Supply Agency that I use for my trucking interests; ex-cop, a ruffian called Rick McGann who also does private investigative and repossession work, and frequently brags about his underworld connections."

"Sounds just the man for this job."

"I'll make sure he does it immediately. I think I saw something in the Liverpool Echo about a man called Hacking trying to start a seaplane service from Pier Head to Dublin Bay as well."

Malinga put his powerful arm round Jongwe and gave him a mocking hug.

"I bet you miss all this intrigue; things will be great for you eh Rooster when the President is in charge of Zimbabwe again and orders you home? You'll have a chance to escape this dismal northern climate and the tedious ant-heaps of London, Manchester, Liverpool and New York; to return triumphant to your hut in Africa!"

Jongwe shuddered.

"Just between us Malinga, I wish the fucking President would drop dead! It is tiresome being like a dog on a leash, always at his beck and call and I like it here now."

Malinga laughed loudly and waved to the women in the car.

"You know, sometimes I even feel like that myself old friend; we take the risks, he takes the money and the credit. Give my regards to your beautiful girls. I will call you later."

-xxx-

On Friday Lembede received a visitor to his opulent house on the Rand, a period mansion that had belonged to a gold-rush magnate at the turn of the century. It had spectacular gardens and tight security. The corpulent black man was helped from the rear seat of a limousine by his chauffer and negotiated the few steps up with difficulty. He sat down puffing on the porch before proceeding to the dining room where they took lunch together. Lembede treated his Excellency the

Minister for Prisons with easy familiarity; they had done business together for many years.

"Is our plan progressing my friend? The gold mine in Botswana is ready to begin processing extra bullion at any time."

"Yes" replied the Minister indistinctly, beginning to fork food greedily into his mouth. "Acting on your intelligence overheard from the pilot, I studied the freight operation from Welkom to Johannesburg. The white guards in charge at the security firm are poorly paid and desperate for money, as you are aware from doing business with them before. You know Cornelius Kleinhans is reliable and he will do it himself. They will hijack the bullion aircraft after loading and divert it to Lenasia disused airfield where my armed operatives will meet it, having been released from prison as usual. They will unload the cargo and transport it to a place of safety. Smaller amounts can then be delivered to Thune mine, whose output production will gradually increase under your improved management."

"Perfect. I will lead the first retrieval operation at Lenasia myself. Security must be paramount with no trail back to me you or the prison hierarchy and absolutely no departures from standard procedure. What date do you envisage?"

"The next shipment is scheduled for the day after tomorrow but it is up to you. The white guards we have bribed are on duty every Sunday this month. They plan to take their money and vanish after the operation."

"They will certainly vanish" grunted Lembede. "I can't manage it this weekend but keep me apprised of all developments."

Sandro was sitting in a large room fitted out as an electronic workshop and filled with powerful Hewlett Packard computer servers and communications equipment. It was housed on the upper floor of his house in Kylami and overlooked downtown Johannesburg in the distance, which due to unusual light effects appeared to float above the earth like an enchanted city. Sandro's interest in electronics had begun in Namibia after reading Popular Science Magazines and he had subsequently studied avidly by correspondence courses, eventually getting Cisco's top Network Engineering 'CCIE' qualification and a Microsoft 'Certified Solutions Expert' ticket.

He listened throughout Lembede's conversation with the Minister for Prisons, and when it had concluded, listened again to a recording of their discussion. He would have to think hard about this new enterprise of Lembede's. He didn't want to get involved in such hard-core gangsterism but what should he do? Warn his business partner off? Tell the authorities? That was definitely out; corruption was so rife they would probably implicate him as a patsy. Most importantly of all he would have to make sure Jemima wasn't the pilot to get hijacked. Sandro had been with scores of women in his life and thought himself impervious to permanent attachment but he was finally head-over-heels in love and happy about it.

A buzzer sounded as a perimeter sensor activated and he glanced at a security monitor showing his main gate. She was bang on time for once and he opened the gate, smiling, then ran out to meet her on the drive with a tight embrace and a kiss.

"I've missed you! Welcome to the weekend Sweetheart, bet you could use a cold drink and a swim."

"I've missed you too. Let's not waste any time."

"'Kay! Last one in is a cissie then...."

They stripped hurriedly, laughing, ran and jumped naked into the pool. With her legs round his waist they cuddled, kissed and talked in the cool water, drinking beer out of bottles Sandro had placed in a cooler on the edge. The sun set as they played erotically in the water like teenagers, wet skin to wet skin.

"Hey sexy, you're not planning to do any work on Sunday are you?"

"Not that I know of. Why?"

"I wouldn't mind paying you for some more lessons."

She humped her loins against his erection.

"Lessons in what? This?"

"Hell yes, that's top of my list, I can't learn enough about you! Then maybe tomorrow we could do a training cross-country flight for my PPL, perhaps fly up to that farm in Botswana for a picnic. I've been meaning to have a closer look-round. Your Dad set me thinking, maybe my business partner is up to something."

"I'm game for that; meanwhile here beginith today's lesson."

She pulled up on her arms and lowered, touching his tip with her wet heat. He gasped and thrust automatically into her.

-xxx-

Jongwe didn't hang about getting the surveillance under way. Dave Swinnerton was on his way from Scotland to London in James's Scania and being short of driving hours on his tachograph decided to overnight at Burscough. He parked-up at the airfield and walked towards the village carrying his overnight bag, turning left out of the gate. A man leading a Jack-Russell terrier was crossing a ditch from the adjacent farmer's field. They nodded at each other and strode towards the village at the same pace on opposite sides of the road.

"Was it you that passed me just now in a flashy red Scania?" called the other man who was in his late forties, short with powerful shoulders, a fag smouldering between his lips.

"Probably, I've just finished for the day. Are you a driver?"

"Aye, for me sins. Used to enjoy it but the money's no good now; used to earn more thirty year ago when I first started. What's your bunch like to work for?"

"Bastards, same as all of them. Who do you drive for?"

"Agency. Self-employed so I've worked for most of these round 'ere."

They chatted about trucks and driving for the five minutes it took to get to the Riverside pub beside the canal in the middle of Burscough where Dave stopped.

"Well I'm going in here for a pint; do you fancy one?"

His companion appeared to hesitate and looked at his watch.

"Aye I do actually. Go on then. Name's Gerry by the way."

"Dave Swinnerton. Come on, my mouth's like the Gobi desert!"

He paid and they took their drinks to an alcove where they could stand and look out at the canal boats, and traffic crossing the bridge. He was thirsty after a long day and his Stella hardly touched sides.

"Blimey, looks like you needed that! I'll get you another."

"No rush."

"This Pedigree is good stuff, I won't be far behind you" said the stocky man, draining his own glass in two large swallows and going to the bar. He returned with the drinks and two bags of peanuts. He knew a great deal about the transport industry and they had lots to talk about. Pint followed pint in rapid succession and on an empty stomach Dave was soon getting tipsy.

"So where's he from then, this Hacking geezer you work for? He must have some money to be running tackle like you were driving."

"Zimbabwe but he came here when it turned bad; you know Mugabe and all that."

"Oh yes? One of those farmers what was chucked off their land?"

"Yeah, I think his family had a farm one time. He fought against the blacks in the Rhodesian war anyway. He was a Commercial Pilot in South Africa too, that's how come he re-opened Burscough Airfield for flying."

The other man raised an eyebrow.

"Oh, one of those Special Forces types was he? I was in the paras a few years myself and the Rhodesians were meant to be dead hard."

"He never talks about it but his daughter reckons he used to be in the Selous Scouts and did all kinds of cloak and dagger stuff."

"Is your boss around at the moment or away driving?"

"Are you thinking of applying for a job? We've nothing local but I do know he's recruiting ex-forces drivers for a job in Iraq. He's out there now, due back anytime I hear. I'd go myself, the money is big, but I can't leave my daughter."

"Give us his mobile number then, I might be interested if the missus would let me go."

Dave did so and McGann copied in into his own.

"What do you carry mostly round here? Is there much work?"

"All sorts. Supermarkets which are bloody hard work, moving pallets with a pump-truck and cages on a tail-lift. Then there's containers which is easy, and they pick up quite a lot of seasonal continental work, salad and veg from Spain. I like those long foreign trips but haven't done any with these. Sometimes they get really high-value loads, you know electronics stuff, phones, computers, whisky and vodka, they're worth a bomb and every villain knows it. There's a placard in the cab that says 'follow me to the next services'. If someone dodgy tries it on, even in a Highway Patrol car, you're supposed to show it to them, stop somewhere safe and phone the police. Every now and again they haul single malt from a distillery way up in the North of Scotland all the way to Cities in Europe, via Dover and each load's worth up to half a million quid."

His companion whistled.

"Really? As much as that? I enjoyed Continental work when I was young but I prefer being home at night in my own bed these days. Look pal, it's been great but I'm already half pissed, can't take my ale like you and my missus is going to kill me for being late. See you around. Take care."

Dave was pleased to be recognised as someone who could take his drink.

"Yeah, I'll look out for you. Drop in sometime. I live in that end terrace across the canal." He indicated with his glass.

"Yeah, I might just do that."

-xxx-

James flew back into the UK from Kuwait City with Colinda, who couldn't get a flight direct to London for several days so accompanied him to Manchester from where there was a shuttle south almost every hour. He felt strangely disconnected from everything that was familiar. Life with Loretta in recent years had felt normal and anchored though their recent personal and business life had been volatile. Now he felt adrift and uneasy, not sure what to expect or even what he wanted anymore. The Dear John letter had really taken him by surprise. His opinion had been she was using Dennis as a vague threat to try and keep him in line somehow.

They were waiting for him together at the airport as he and Colinda emerged from Customs & Immigration. Dennis was looking nervous and Loretta stunning in a grey business suit with a flattering skirt cut just above the knee. She looked beautiful, business-like and determined. He stopped just in front of them.

"Didn't expect to meet you two so soon."

Loretta looked at him and then quizzically at Colinda who had stopped at his shoulder.

"We chose to meet you here for a purpose James because it's in public. I won't tolerate any aggression from you towards Dennis."

She suddenly looked at Colinda again, and then at James.

"Excuse me; are you two together or something?"

"This is Colinda Lasserre; she joined our team in Iraq."

The two women eyed each other and nodded.

"I'll see you in a moment James, I need the washroom" said Colinda and strode away tactfully.

Loretta watched her long naked legs for a moment, gathering her thoughts, then stared at James and nodded knowingly.

"As I was saying, this situation is more the result of your behaviour than his. I still respect you but I don't love you anymore; worry bled it out of me."

James didn't altogether believe that.

"I'm not gunning for Dennis and my affection for you remains, as does my respect; it took guts for you both to come here. The larger situation isn't going to be easy though. What do you want to do about the business? Buy me out?"

"We discussed that but we can't afford to. You'll keep your share of course and perhaps when the business matures it can be managed."

"So what's the plan? Do you want Haley and I to move out? Has she still got a job and does she want it?"

"Of course. I explained the difficulties between us and she was understandably upset but practical about the situation. Nothing's changed since you left except that I've moved out to Dennis's house in Parbold and she's moved into the main house on the airfield. The flying and transport arms are mutually dependent and need your input. I suggest we carry on as before."

"Okay, let's give it a try. I must say I preferred our last meeting in this Airport."

Loretta blushed deeply and looked suddenly flustered and unsure. James looked at Dennis.

"Give us a minute will you?"

The other man moved towards a food outlet.

"Off in the endless search for fried-egg sandwiches to feed the inner man."

She bristled.

"I don't know quite what to make of that comment James. Your companion is very striking. Is there something you aren't telling me?"

"She's very efficient at her job. A retired US Marine Transport Combat Officer with Iraq experience who joined us to make some money. You know what I mean about our last meeting here."

"It was certainly much pleasanter than this. Were you screwing our new employee before the Iraq contract?"

"I thought we were going to keep it nice Loretta. How long were you receiving the good-news from Dennis before the officially notarised declaration I received in Iraq?"

"So you don't deny having a relationship with her?"

"Fifth Amendment; let's just say I was resisting manfully until your little bombshell hit me in Iraq."

"It can't have been that much of a surprise. I told you well before you left that our life together was over due to your selfish insistence on doing exactly what you wanted!"

"It was a complete and very unpleasant surprise."

Colinda re-joined them and Dennis reappeared too, ogling her rump. Loretta frowned in annoyance.

"Anyway, Haley's waiting for you in the short-stay pickup area outside. See you at the airfield tomorrow."

She nodded shortly, turned away and walked into the crowd.

"My shuttle flight's been called James. You need some space to deal with all of this. Give me a call when the fireworks have died down."

James kissed Colinda gratefully and watched her walk towards an escalator to departures.

Haley was standing by her car and gave him a huge hug before they set off.

"Great tan Dad! You look like Lawrence of Arabia; how was it out there?"

They spent the first fifteen minutes catching up and James glossed over his close call in Iraq. Finally his daughter looked across at him with a worried frown.

"Listen Dad, I'm really angry with Loretta and Dennis for the way they did this, and I feel guilty too because I could probably have warned you in time to do something about it. She has been acting pretty crazy for quite a while now."

James sighed.

"Well I brought it on myself and regret putting you in a difficult position. I remember you asking if my Iraq project was worth risking my relationship with Loretta over, which should have been ample warning. What's to blame is my pig-headedness. Loretta is a good person Haley and she brought you up to believe her values."

"My values don't include adultery!"

"We're not married Haley."

"No, I know but the principle is the same."

"That's part of the problem, maybe marriage would have made her feel more valued though I don't personally believe a piece of paper makes a couple any more likely to stick together."

"But to do it like that, send you a letter in a conflict zone; it must have been shattering, heart-breaking, and I hate to think of you being hurt. How can she possibly prefer that wimp Dennis to you?"

"It wasn't too pleasant I admit but it did give us both distance to face the reality of our natures. I have always had a tendency to pull away from total commitment Haley, which is what most women want from their men. I can't help it any more than she can help her craving for stability. Us white Africans were born into instability; it is almost as if we provoke disaster because it feels controllable if we initiate it ourselves."

"Wow. Heavy stuff Pater! And are you heart-broken?"

He smiled.

"A little perhaps; it's the end of something big in our lives after all, but also a beginning of whatever comes next. I'm relieved our business partners apparently didn't intend to run off with the bank immediately. We've both still got jobs to do and a roof over our heads. How's Arthur? Broken anything nice recently?"

"Dad! Now I know you haven't changed and I'm glad. I love you the way you are."

She clasped his hand and dabbed a kiss on his ear.

"I love you too. Watch the damn road!"

Loretta had plainly set out to demonstrate what he was missing and it had certainly worked at a Neanderthal sexual level. If she had dragged him to a hotel for sex again he wouldn't have resisted but he felt no overpowering rage or jealousy. Without a catalyst they might well have jogged on into a comfortable old-age together and if he had backed down over the Iraq project it would probably have panned out that way. But it hadn't and since leaving him had been Loretta's choice he might as well try and enjoy the excitement of his nascent relationship with Colinda free of guilt. He would be wise to keep it under wraps as long as possible however; though Loretta had instigated their separation, 'woman scorned' syndrome could still make his life very difficult.

-xxx-

Jongwe and Malinga were in the filthy first-floor office of Jongwe's Transport Company, 'ANC Import/Export' near Garston docks in Liverpool, listening to "Scouse" Rick McGann's debriefing on what he had found out about James Hacking from Swinnerton. Jongwe sat on an ancient grease-stained swivel chair behind a desk made out of a door. McGann reclined next to Malinga on a stained lumpy sofa that looked as if it had been found on a rubbish-pile, which it had. There was scrap everywhere in the big chaotic room; tea-boxes of dirty redundant truck parts, tubs of grease with the lids off, oil-drums, stacks of old magazines and newspapers, inspection lamps, legal box-files piled haphazardly and several old typewriters. They were all smoking and smog hung low over their heads. Jongwe and Malinga noted the mobile number they were given for Hacking, then looked at a picture of him in running attire which McGann had taken on his phone, copied to his computer and printed. Jongwe tapped it thoughtfully on the littered desk.

"Well this is almost definitely the man our principal is interested in, so you have earned your money Rick. I'll let you know if your services are required for anything else."

McGann grunted.

"Okay, but I'll take payment now for what I've already done. Just in case you forget."

Jongwe gave him a sour look but paid up in cash from a bulky roll of banknotes. Malinga immediately sent Lembede a brief text message; "Positive on the Hippos. What are your orders?"

-xxx-

CHAPTER ELEVEN

Jemima and Sandro spent Saturday afternoon water-skiing and the evening beside his braai pit under the stars. On Sunday morning he went out early to get fresh croissants and Prego-rolls for breakfast. Her phone rang and she looked at the screen. It was Piet Schuman and she nearly rejected it.

"Morning Sexy-legs, hou gand it? Listen, our regular weekend pilot has dropped us in the shit. Can you do the Welkom gold run in the Twin Otter for us today? I'll pay top dollar."

Jemima havered. She liked time-off on Saturday and Sunday but with the state her finances were in despite James's help, every rand was useful.

"I'm sorry Piet, I already have plans."

"Ag please Jemima, don't make me beg hey? We could lose the contract!"

"I'm sorry Piet, really...."

"Don't be sorry, be helpful! Haven't I always looked after you?"

"Yes I suppose so. Look, can I take someone with me?"

"The insurance doesn't allow passengers, even other pilots need security clearance for the job, you know that! Gimme a break here sexy."

OK Christ! Allright Piet but you're ruining my weekend!"

"I'll make it up to you. Leave now if you can, we're already behind time! Thanks girl, we always call the best first."

"Transparent male chauvinist. The bullshit just trips from your tongue. Bugger off."

She hung up on a rich chuckle and immediately dialled Sandro but his phone was engaged so she left a message.

"Look lover, I hate to spoil our day out in Botswana but Piet Schuman is in a real fix and needs a pilot today so I'm going to Welkom. Should be back mid-afternoon so we could still do some local flying. Call me when you get a chance."

Sandro was already on his phone, sitting in the Aston outside the delicatessen listening intently because one of his servers had paged him. A voice-recorder activated by a listening device in Lembede's mansion had picked up one of several new words he had programmed it to scan for, and the server was relaying the conversation to his IPhone.

He saw Jemima's incoming call flash up on the phone screen, then a minute later heard the peep as she left a voice-message; she probably wanted something else from the Dellie. He returned his attention to the recording.

"Can you mobilise your team and the Security guards at short notice?" Lembede asked the Director of prisons.

"Certainly, it will just take a couple of calls. When do you have in mind?"

"Today."

"Today! No reason why not I suppose. What's the sudden rush?"

"Something has come up requiring my urgent attention overseas. Today may be the only spare day I have all month. Say I will meet them at an RV on the way to Lenasia disused aerodrome and we will get the job done. I have some massive expenditure coming up and the sooner that bullion starts moving through Thune mine the better."

Sandro disconnected and sat considering his position. If Silas wanted to hijack gold shipments it was one thing, but laundering stolen gold through a mine they jointly owned implicated him too. Something would have to be done. He went to voicemail and picked up Jemima's message which turned his mild concern to horror and he called her immediately.

"You mustn't do that job for Schuman Jemima."

"What? Why?"

"Because we already have plans, just tell him you won't do it, I'm sure he can find someone else."

"There is no-one else available, that's why he called me."

He was floundering.

"Well at least take me along!"

"That's not possible either, for insurance and security reasons."

"But we had an agreement! It's just work, tell Schuman to stick it!"

There was a silence.

"Sorry Sandro, but I'm a professional and I don't mess my clients about like that, this is a small industry. You should understand. I have to go now."

Sandro cursed on putting down the phone. Jemima was deep under his skin and wheels had been set in motion that put her in serious danger. What the hell should he do?

It took forty minutes to get to Oliver Tambo International Airport. Jemima drove round to the freight area where she was well known, picked up the aircraft keys and began inspecting the twin Otter used for the Welkom run. The day was unseasonably hot and humid. Jemima found she was sweating and took off her jacket just as her cell rang. It was Piet Schuman.

"Listen Jem, another slight hiccup, your co-pilot isn't going to show so just go ahead on your own OK?"

"No it's not bloody OK Piet! Sure, the Otter can be operated single pilot provided there are 9 passengers or less but it's not Standard Ops Procedure. Besides, there's the security aspect, this is a bullion run."

"Okay, Okay, don't bite my head off, sexy one. Listen the guys have done that flight single-pilot quite often and I'll up your rate 1.5 times."

"Double it and I'll go."

"Done" said Piet quickly and her eyes narrowed suspiciously.

"You didn't have this planned all along did you Schuman? You're a slim son of a bitch…."

"Perish the thought my China. Smooth skies hey?"

Forty-five minutes later she was cleared for a standard Grasmere departure from Oliver Tambo International and the Otter lifted off the runway, making a left-hand turnout to the south. The flight to Welkom was bumpy and turbulent but the autopilot took care of the flying. Jemima relaxed and enjoyed the views, checking the instruments and filling in the flight log periodically. The trip and landing were uneventful, and as usual the Tower directed her to a remote hard-standing away from prying eyes for the shipment transfer.

Security firm employees in two vans and a little car were waiting there with the bullion. The white Warrant Officer in charge was a hard-faced, rough-looking Afrikaner with woolly grey hair and snaggly teeth but he was friendly and introduced himself as Cornelius. His men began loading with the smoothness of long practice. The hugely heavy ingots were in small individual boxes with a rope handle at each side and could barely be lifted individually. The straining security men hefted them up into the fuselage complaining constantly, and placed them in a single row along the shallow channel between the passenger seats which Jemima had exposed by taking up the carpet, and she kept a close eye on them for the weight and balance calculations.

Cornelius wasn't the usual boss though and she regarded him thoughtfully.

"What's up? Don't you trust us Meisie?" he asked, eyes twinkling.

"Not bloody likely. You skellums would have an ingot each down your trousers if I blinked."

"Can you blame us, the lives we lead? We're not rich like some folks."

Jemima shook her head and smiled.

"I know the feeling."

A narrow chain was threaded through each rope handle from rear to front, then secured round the leg of a forward aisle passenger seat to prevent forward/aft movement of the bullion and she was ready to go.

She signed for the heavy cargo and handed back the clipboard.

"Thanks jong" said the Afrikaner. "If you put your foot on the gas you can be home in time for the Rugby. Kick-off's at four pm."

"I'm a girl Oom!"

"Ja, I can see that; doesn't mean you can't enjoy the game of Kings though! Anyway, regulations say I've got to wait 'till you shut your doors and start engines but I'll let the blacks go."

He dismissed the black security guards who drove off in the two vans. Jemima did a quick walk-around ground check. When she got back the two white security men were pointing Uzi sub machine guns at her. The Warrant Officer was carrying what looked like a small rucksack.

"Don't do anything foolish" he said. "Have you got any fire-arms?"

Jemima nodded. She raised the cuff of her elegantly cut uniform trouser-leg.

"A thirty-eight revolver, here, in my ankle holster."

"Get it out, finger and thumb only; put it on the tarmac."

She did so. He picked it up it, thumbed open the chamber to check loads and raised his eyebrows.

"Nice weapon. Okay, now climb up, get into your seat and put the belt on, ready for a normal departure. My colleague will watch from the ground here until you taxi out, and I'll be in the cabin behind you all the time. Try anything in the air and I'll drill you. Let's go."

In the cabin he covered her as the door was secured and she took her place. He sat behind on a passenger seat where he could see into the flight deck. For some reason Jemima didn't feel particularly threatened and went through the checks and start-up normally.

"Okay my friend, where are we going?" she called over her shoulder.

"Do everything standard for an Oliver Tambo International departure and don't try to alert the Tower or anything clever like that. I've escorted this flight before and I know the procedure. Don't try to squawk an emergency code either, I'll be watching the transponder."

Her heart sank. She had been hoping to put 7500 up on the transponder to signify she was being hijacked. It would have been visible in the Tower and military jets would probably have been scrambled. Now she was frightened, because when a violent criminal allows their face to be seen it could mean they would kill any witnesses.

"Also Meisie, I'm not a pilot but I have thousands of freefall descents in my logbook. If you try anything dodgy I will still drill you and exit the plane safely, I have a canopy with me. Understand?"

"Yes. What next?"

"The plan is simple. Practice a normal approach and descent for Smuts. Sixty nautical miles out report engine trouble and request diversion to the nearest field, which is Westonaria, but land at Lenasia disused airfield instead, the runway has been checked and it's still serviceable for this weight of aircraft. Vehicles will be waiting. The unload will take fifteen minutes. Just do everything like I say and you won't get hurt."

"Don't you care that I've seen you?"

"Not a damn, they're going to know soon enough who took their gold. Hell, I want them to, because I'll be long gone to Mexico or somewhere. I worked hard all my life and I've got nothing. Now it's payback time. This is what I'm owed, my retirement fund, before the blacks get hold of it all and buy big black cars to drive into trees with."

The departure went smoothly and at two thousand feet Welkom approach approved her request for a frequency change so Jemima dialled in 118.4 on the radio to get Oliver Tambo International's ATIS. The fast metallic voice of the Automated Traffic Information Service barked in her ear and she frowned as she listened to the weather, which had worsened dramatically since her departure a few hours earlier. Rain, lightning storms and squalls were sweeping the Rand. Visibility was down to three kilometres with winds high and variable. The reports for Grand Central were no better. Jemima mentally got her arse into gear and began preparing for a possible instrument approach. It was a technique she'd used thousands of times before but without a co-pilot and in bad weather it was always a tense affair, with a very high workload in the cockpit. In flying parlance she would have to Aviate, Navigate and Communicate simultaneously, and on instruments to make it more complicated yet, tasks that were much easier with a co-pilot to share the load. The recent traumatic engine-out approach in the Beechjet was large in her mind.

"Hey, China, listen to this" called Jemima and put the ATIS on the overhead speaker as it began to repeat. He came forward, listened in silence and scanned the horizon. The storm clouds of the cold front moving over Johannesburg appeared ahead as a black wall. High thin stratus was already overhead Westonaria as the front rolled south, and as icing on the cake there was no ILS at Westonaria or Lenasia disused anyway, thought Jemima

"Be OK. Still VFR weather where we're going. Be better in fact, no need to fake engine failure, just say you'll sit the storm out down there. Almost time to divert anyway. Do it."

Jemima called the diversion and the approach controller approved her plan, notifying her of very poor visibility, severe wind-shear and violently gusting crosswinds at Oliver Tambo International. Her mind churned for a way out of the predicament, hating the growing gnawing fear that she would be killed to preserve identities. She could think of no way bar crashing the plane to save herself, and that probably wouldn't work. If she survived, he probably would too, and shoot her. The sky and earth had a leaden scary hue. The Otter flew steadily along on the new course and she began to let down as green smudges representing towering cumulonimbus began to appear on the weather radar. Jemima knew that away from the actual showers and cloud masses, visibility could be quite good but that in their proximity there were likely to be violent horizontal and vertical winds causing severe turbulence and possible hail, freezing rain and icing. She prepared herself for a bouncy ride and got as many cockpit tasks out of the way as she could. Luckily she had over-flown Lenasia disused airfield many times and she could see it from a long way out. The main 6000 foot runway orientation was the same as Smuts at 03/21, with a shorter cross runway that was no good to her. The wind was mainly from the north so she steered to line up for a straight in approach on runway 03.

Without warning all hell broke loose. The plane seemed to stagger in the air as violent winds hit it. For several minutes malignant forces seemed to be trying to shake it apart. Jemima's seat appeared to kick her in the backside as the Otter flew into a one-hundred knot downdraft. Bits of dust and gravel flew off the floor and stung her in the face and eyes and her charts went flying. Increasing power to maximum to try and arrest the descent put the plane in a nose-high attitude. Dimly in the pandemonium she heard a metallic snap, then screeching and rumbling sounds from the main cabin behind as the thin restraining chain threaded through the bullion boxes snapped under load. In the wildly pitching plane the heavy containers slid rearwards into a pile, drastically altering the centre of gravity. As the nose pitched ever higher and vital airspeed fell away she pulled the power right back and pushed forward desperately on the yoke to try and get the nose down. The stall warning began to honk in outrage and Jemima knew she was going to die.

"What the fuck's going on?" screamed the Hijacker but she ignored him. The yoke was forward at full travel but the mass of the bullion aft was like a big weight on the long arm of a see-saw, holding the nose high. The plane reached stall speed, all lift from the wings disappeared and the left wing dropped as it began to roll onto its back in the first stage of a death plunge. In desperation Jemima hit opposite rudder to stop the wing dropping. Waveringly they levelled but the ship was almost dead in the air, the vertical speed indicator jammed against the down stop. Jemima put her feet on the yoke pushing as hard as she could and cranked the trim fully forward. The nose dropped perceptibly and abruptly the downdraft turned into an updraft. There was a thud as if they'd hit the bottom of a lift shaft. The airframe and wings flexed and groaned. Jemima was tossed about like a rag-doll, the side of her head smashing against the left fuselage but the new wind direction changed the angle of attack and unstalled the wing. The Otter was flying again but in dire straits.

With heavy bullion to the rear and yoke fully forward, the horizontal stabilizer still had no further authority to pitch the nose down. The plane mushed along close to the stall, controls sluggish. The updraft was dissipating and, fighting the pain in her head, Jemima concentrated on instruments. She'd lost six thousand feet, from eight down to two thousand AGL. With power off, the VSI showed a gentle descent rate of two hundred feet per minute. Gingerly increasing power to stop the descent caused the nose to pitch up and flying speed to creep down. She needed power to climb but using it could stall the plane again. To all intents the engines were useless. Jemima doubted they could pull the bullion boxes forward, even if she could afford to leave the controls.

"Oi, you! Can you see into the cabin? Can you get those crates forward again on your own?"

He looked.

"No fucking chance, I'd have to pull them uphill."

"Then get your arse up here beside me, we need all the weight forward we can get to survive this. Bring anything heavy and moveable you can see too."

-xxx-

The Aston Martin got Sandro to Lenasia in record time, hoping he would arrive before Lembede and his thugs. He left the car in a suburb of very ostentatious houses built by rich Indian businessmen. It was a predominantly Asian area of the city and the Aston would stand out less among all the Mercedes and BMW's than it would near the disused airfield. He had altered his appearance and clothes by simple but subtle changes so he looked like a well-to-do sub-continental Indian. Carrying a small suitcase he rapidly walked the half mile to the disused airfield perimeter fence, in an area where it passed close to a copse of trees, cut the wire and slipped through. With relief he found the apron between an old control-tower and fire-hall deserted. He climbed rapidly onto the fire-hall roof by a tubular inspection ladder, checked arcs of fire and then undid the suitcase to check his automatic rifle over. There was a door into an air-conditioning room where he could hide if anybody checked the roof out.

-xxx-

The Warrant-Officer had moved a few fire-extinguishers and other items forward then strapped in next to her.

"Move your seat all the way forward too."

He did so and succinctly she explained their aerodynamic difficulties and told him he might need to push forward on the yoke with her but not to touch anything else.

"Of course, you could always put on your parachute and get the hell out instead" she remarked with a humourless grin.

"Negative Meisie, I don't know enough about flying to tell if you're bullshitting; you might be exaggerating and fly off with our gold after I jumped."

She laughed mirthlessly.

"You better believe we are in deep shit! A bookmaker wouldn't give a rand to a pinch of ratshit we'll get down in one piece."

"From what I've seen you are damn good at this. Looks to me like we can still make it. Ask Smuts for a freecall frequency-change to Westonaria, but don't make it. That way Smuts will forget about you and won't pass your details to the other airport."

"You little kerels have really done your homework, haven't you?"

"Better believe it Meisie; this is shit or bust for most of us. Death or a comfortable retirement, don't much care which, either, to be honest. The world has gone to the dogs."

Jemima experienced a feeling of complete unreality as her eyes focused on the field. She made a very careful turn towards it to avoid losing lift and once lined up experience told her that they might make it if she could stretch the glide somehow. The runway was moving higher up in the windshield indicating an undershoot unless something changed but adding power would make the nose pitch up and slow the aircraft still further. Jemima weighed alternatives, a glimmer of a plan forming. She had to maintain flying speed; to stall at any time now would cause the plane to stop flying and crash to the ground. Lowering ten degrees of flap would cause slight drag but would also pitch the nose further down, as well as improve lift and lower the stall-speed. She realised the chances of walking away from the coming landing were slim but she wasn't frightened. Her professional capabilities were being tested to the limit and she was determined to make the best landing she could. She selected the ten degrees of flap with bated breath, pushing against the yoke to stop any initial pitch up. The Fokker seemed to gather lift under its wings and feel more buoyant. The props were already fully fine and she nudged the power up. The runway stopped sliding away and steadied.

-xxx-

Sandro focused his binoculars on an approaching aircraft. It appeared to be flying very slowly, in an unusual attitude. Hearing the murmur of vehicle engines and the slam of doors, he retired to the air-con room; the door opened inwards and he closed it, then lay down, feet braced against it to keep it shut and lower his profile if anyone was so determined to get in that they fired at it. The rifle was across his chest facing the door, ready. His professionalism paid off because a sinister figure dressed all in black and wearing a hood sprang from the ladder to the roof and made a thorough inspection, rattling the door hard and pushing against it. Obviously satisfied it was locked he moved on; Sandro heard his feet move away and sprang quietly up, putting his eye to the sloping ventilation slots in the door. He was in time to see the criminal swing back onto the ladder and go down. He went out onto the roof again, keeping back from the parapet, and focused his glasses on the Fokker.

-xxx-

The Twin Otter floated on, stretching the glide further than Jemima could ever have hoped, the runway staying centred in the windshield as if she was flying a totally controlled powered approach. Her right hand as always was ready on the throttles, feet and left hand making slight corrections to rudder and aileron, yoke pushed hard forward, no further authority available. The headwind in her favour changed abruptly to a quartering tailwind close to the ground, effectively chopping twenty knots from the Otter's' airspeed. At fifteen feet above the ground and a hundred feet from the runway the wings stalled and the left dropped suddenly. With nothing to lose Jemima kicked right rudder to counteract it and rammed the throttles fully open. The engines howled in protest and the nose began to lift. Power cushioned their arrival in the few seconds before impact and thanks to her quick response on the rudder the aircraft banged onto the runway wings-level, nose-wheel coming down hard but hopefully not enough to damage it; the DHC-6's were among the toughest planes in the world. They rolled rapidly to a halt and Jemima sat back panting and sweating.

"Jesus, my China, it wasn't pretty but that was probably the best landing I ever made in my life."

A sudden wind squall shook the plane and spots of rain pattered on the windscreen. He smiled thinly.

"Ja, you are a brave competent young woman and I am sorry you got involved in this. Now taxi over to where those minivans are."

They both flinched as a blinding flash of lightning was followed immediately by a resounding bang of thunder right overhead. A group of black-clad men in balaclavas were standing beside two vehicles. Heart in mouth, she taxied to the vehicles where a figure gave her standard parking signals and the sign to cut engines. The Warrant-Officer sent Jemima out of the aircraft first, tossing her .38 onto the co-pilot's seat before he followed and stood covering her. They watched eight sinister figures, all with machine pistols slung on their backs, transferring the gold efficiently, observed by two others who appeared to be in charge. On completion all the hijackers climbed into the vehicles except for these two men, one of whom barked an instruction with horribly ominous implications.

"Okay, do it now: both of them."

Jemima could tell he was black by his intonation and the voice seemed familiar; her heart was hammering with panic and she felt sick, wanting to run for her life but unable to make herself do so, as if she were in a bad dream. The second man raised a heavy hand-gun from his side and swung it towards her and Warrant-Officer Cornelius, who had obviously been alert for some sort of double-cross.

"Fuck you Lembede" he shouted and ducked to one side, raising his Uzi muzzle and squeezing off several rounds that went wide because Jemima was in his way. He was shot and dropped like a stone. The killer, big handgun held in a professional way with one hand under the butt, pumped off two more rounds, one to head, one to body, then swung it her way.

"Quickly you fool, leave no survivors or witnesses!"

The executioner nodded a split second before his own head exploded in a welter of gore, some of which splashed on Jemima, making her stagger back. The man who'd given the order reacted fast, ducking, drawing his own handgun and crouching down against the vehicle for cover. Glittering merciless eyes gleamed malevolently at her from the holes in his balaclava. They belonged beyond any shadow of doubt to Silas Lembede, whom she'd last seen glaring at her with the same malignancy on the apron at Oliver Tambo following the flight to Botswana. She stared, horrified, into the round hole of his gun-muzzle as it came to bear. Suddenly rounds kicked up tarmac close in front of Lembede. Sandro couldn't get a clear shot but chunks of flying blacktop startled Silas so his shot went wide and he scuttled crablike further round the van out of sight as Jemima dropped to the ground and rolled sideways towards the bodies, trying to use them as cover. There was confused panicky shouting and doors slammed as both loaded vans engaged gear and charged away with tyres screaming as another prolonged burst of fire went overhead. The heavens opened and cold hard rain pelted down reducing visibility instantly. She lay rooted to the spot for several more seconds, looking with shock at the bodies on the tarmac and the dark-coloured blood being diluted by the downpour. She had no idea who had killed the second man and she jumped up, backing fearfully towards the plane, then climbed hurriedly aboard, fired up and got out of there, the Otter leaping blithely into the air without its heavy cargo. Only when she was airborne did realisation of the investigation she was going to face start sinking in. With a shaking hand she clicked to the Oliver Tambo International frequency, put 7500 on the transponder for "Hijack" and waited. Instantly a voice came back.

"Zulu Sierra-Bravo Kilo Bravo, confirm you are squawking 7500."

"Affirmative" choked Jemima and then broke into uncontrollable racking sobs. When the sound of vehicle engines had faded and the aircraft was airborne Sandro removed the magazine from his rifle and collected up his used cartridges, mentally cursing himself for missing Lembede, but if he had continued shooting and immobilised the vans there was a good chance both he and Jemima would have been killed by the superior fire-power of the criminals.

-xxx-

Immediately on landing Jemima tried to ring Sandro but the call went to voicemail. She tried Theo's number next but her old Nokia suddenly peeped and shut down. It was becoming increasingly unreliable and she dropped it into her flight-bag with a curse, making a mental note to buy a new battery. The NIS people were already at Oliver Tambo airport and when she shut down, guards were posted round the aircraft. The Bureau of State Security had become the National Intelligence Service, but the shady secretive organisation had lost none of its power to induce fear. In an empty airport function room she was searched and relieved of all her possessions, including her phone, revolver and flight bag. Then she was allowed to drive her own car to the former BOSS offices in downtown Johannesburg, but with two taciturn black operatives riding along, one male and one female. She was directed to park in an underground car park and technicians began to examine the car in a special bay as soon as they all got out. In a dimly-lit basement interrogation room smelling of stale urine she was robustly interrogated by shouting, desk-banging, chair-crashing men and women in plainclothes. It was a hostile but not physically violent interview though the threat of it was overt, spittle from their shouting jaws spattering her face on many occasions. After perhaps two hours the Rottweiler brigade were joined by a more authoritative softly-spoken older man who took her through the story yet again. Feeling exhausted filthy and violated she wished desperately that James Hacking was in South Africa and able to bolster her with his solid confidence. She wished that someone, anyone, knew where she was and began to demand to be allowed to ring her family, not knowing any lawyers who were likely to do her any good. There was an ancient dust-covered telephone sitting on the desk and eventually the older man who was evidently in charge acquiesced, shoving it towards her. Taken somewhat by surprise she lifted the receiver and thought for a moment before reluctantly dialling the only personal phone-number her tired mind could reliably remember. Francoise Steenkamp answered promptly. He found her an hour later in a dismal airless interrogation room in the basement level several floors below street-level, looking exhausted with a tearstained face. He took her in his arms. She sagged against him briefly, but then freed herself, conscious of the cynical eyes of the spook that had been left to mind her who was leaning against the wall, picking his teeth. Wearily she went back through her story again with Francois. As she completed it the distinguished middle-aged black man who had questioned her came back and the spook hurriedly stood up straight.

"Good afternoon Brigadier Thandiwe," he said respectfully, straightening his jacket nervously. The Senior Officer nodded at him.

"Sergeant Nyala, go and get yourself something from the canteen and I will see you presently."

"This is all bullshit man" said Francois furiously. "She didn't have anything to do with this heist, obviously. I've known her for years, she is my fiancée."

"Regrettably, nothing is obvious; to some people it would be entirely conceivable that this young woman was a willing accomplice who flew the gold to a pre-arranged place and then pretended to have been forced to do so. And who might you be, are you her representative?"

"I gave my details in order to be admitted. I am Captain Steenkamp, Jemima's fiancé and I'm also an officer of the South African Police Force, Criminal Investigation Department. Who are you?"

"Brigadier Thandiwe, Deputy Director of the National Intelligence Service. May I see your warrant card?"

Steenkamp displayed his id card and Thandiwe bowed a little forward from the waist to see better. He nodded thoughtfully and invited them both to sit down, placing an electronic device of some sort on the desk and sitting himself.

"Is that a recorder of some description?" asked Steenkamp.

"No, almost the opposite: it is a noise generator that will serve to obscure our conversation. What I am about to say is highly confidential and I am taking a chance in saying it."

He tapped a pen butt-down on the desk, clearly thinking, then sighed.

"The criminal gang that probably performed this robbery is so powerful it can influence even Government Ministers. It is able to corrupt the integrity of the most honest citizens, by threat, actual violence or bribery. Gang members serving sentences are released from prison specifically to carry out violent crimes and are "rented" the firearms to do so. Afterwards they can return to their cells with perfect alibis."

Francois grunted.

"I spend half my life building cases that get dropped because witnesses suddenly turn up dead or missing but my fiancée is innocent and has just been the victim of a terrible ordeal."

"I might be willing to believe that, but lawyers from the Prosecution Service could claim that she was an inside accomplice."

"I'll tell you who I do suspect. Jemima has been flying the gold-run from Welkom for years and never had a problem, but recently she met a guy called Marais and bingo, she gets hijacked."

"That's rubbish Francois! Sandro didn't even know I was doing it today. Neither did I, until Piet Schuman talked me into it."

Steenkamp folded his arms, looking stubborn and sullen.

"Well Marais has a record, even if he hasn't been convicted of anything for several years."

"What you mean is you'd love him to be guilty. Well he isn't, but his business partner most certainly is. Silas Lembede was at Lenasia disused airfield and he deliberately tried to kill me. If the unknown party who intervened hadn't done so, Lembede would have succeeded. And I think he overheard me talking on the phone to Piet Schuman about flying gold on a previous occasion, now that I think about it."

She stopped talking abruptly, remembering that Sandro had overheard too. It triggered a moment of niggling doubt. Thandiwe leaned forward.

"You're absolutely sure it was Silas Lembede?"

"Positive. He has eyes like a cross between a rabid dog and a snake, I would know them anywhere. In fact I think one is a very good prosthetic ocular."

The Deputy Director looked interested and made a rapid note.

"Lembede is not unknown to me and I have made discreet enquiries. He is politically connected and apparently very wealthy but his background has so far proved impossible to verify, as has the source of his affluence. He is secretive, seldom socialises and is almost never photographed. He holds no official government portfolio yet appears to have the ear of many in the ruling elite. His activities could have implications beyond the mere criminal if he is able to influence and control elected politicians."

Francois stirred impatiently on the uncomfortable chair.

"Well if my fiancé can identify Lembede as having been at the scene, why not arrest him?"

"He is already out of the country, having departed on a British Airways flight a few hours after the incident."

"But you will arrest him when he returns?"

"Perhaps not immediately, since the only evidence we have at present is Miss Visser's testimony and mistakes can be made."

"I'm not mistaken, and I assume I'm no longer a suspect?"

"Did anyone say you were a suspect?"

"I assumed it from my earlier rather harsh interrogation. Am I?"

"Not at this time, and I apologise for the excessive zeal of my excitable junior colleagues. Would you like me to arrange protective custody, until I know more?"

"Absolutely not!" Jemima shivered. "This place gives me the creeps and I can look after myself; those guys got the jump on me once but it won't happen again, I've been on self-defence courses for women."

Thandiwe nodded, looking resigned.

"Then you are free to go but don't discuss this case with the press; if they try to get in touch say the matter is under investigation. Lastly don't forget that according to your statement, the man you think is Lembede intended no survivors or witnesses so he probably regards you as unfinished business. The Black Mambas have a long reach in this part of the country."

Jemima looked puzzled.

"The Black Mambas?"

"It's what the gang in question, which governs the lives of most black people in Gauteng and the Northern provinces, calls itself. As well as robbery, extortion and protection rackets their Chief controls everything, food, liquor, licences of all types, fuel. The membership pass themselves off as 'Robin Hood' types of outlaw, robbing and giving to the poor but it is a cynical pretence. Indirectly this one criminal organisation causes massive inflation, widespread misery and significant damage to the free economy. And like the Mafia they police their territory with absolute brutality."

Francoise Steenkamp was already standing up.

"And you think Lembede might be the Chief?"

"Exactly: So be vigilant, Miss Visser's life may depend on it."

He produced a business card, thought better of it and tucked it away again, then tore a corner from a sheet of paper on the desk and wrote on it, handing it to her.

"That's my personal cell-phone number, put it in your phone address-book then get rid of the paper. If at any time you feel threatened, I can offer you protective custody, though how safe even that will be in these dark times is impossible to say. Good day."

Jemima glanced down at the paper and nodded.

"Okay. Thanks."

She retrieved her car from the car-park and Francois followed her home.

While she was driving Theo called and she took it on her hands-free.

"Hi Jemima, I have a few missed call from you? Everything all right?"

"Well not exactly, some shit hit the fan in a big way and you can probably expect a call from the Police, or BOSS or some bloody mob, I've been with them all afternoon."

"What the hell was it all about? That ruckus Lembede caused on the aircraft in Botswana?"

"No, worse than that but it may be connected." She told him what had happened and he replied with a barrage of questions until she was ready to scream.

"Theo listen, this is one of those days that have already gone on too long for me! Just tell Brigadier Thandiwe exactly what happened in Botswana so our stories match and we'll talk again soon."

"Yeah, sorry. Maybe I better come over in case those thugs do try something."

"No need, Francois is following me home, he'll probably want to stay; I'll be fine, I just need to sleep."

Her phone showed another incoming caller.

"Gotta go Theo, bye."

Piet Schuman had spent the day water-skiing and he'd had a few beers.

"Jemima my China, how did it go? All OK?"

"No it bloody didn't! Jesus I wish I'd never listened to you and taken the job. Haven't you heard what happened? The grapevine can't be working like it used to!"

"Yussus Jemima slow down, you nearly gave my ear grievous bodily harm! So tell me then but go easy on the volume ja?"

He received the story in a tirade, seldom interrupting and finally she ran out of steam.

"Hey, I'm sorry this happened to you Jemima, maybe if there'd been two pilots they wouldn't have tried it. I better get onto those goons at NIS and try to release the aircraft, or scare up another one from somewhere. Shit, I was looking forward to a chilled Sunday night at a braai!"

"You can expect some questioning too Piet, those spooks suspect everyone and their methods aren't very nice."

"Yeah, thanks for the warning."

"I'll get my invoice to you tomorrow."

"What? I thought you did it just for the fun….!"

"Go to hell Schuman!"

Jemima rang off, smiling tiredly. She liked the Afrikaner's irrepressible approach to life. There was a deep ache inside her to summon Sandro Marais again and feel his strong arms around her but she realised it needed thinking through. If Lembede was responsible, could Sandro be involved too? It was a hateful idea but one she had to consider. As she expected, Francois insisted on staying the night to protect her. She was too tired to argue, just poured herself a massive whiskey and took it to bed, shutting the door firmly behind her and falling asleep exhausted. It was a troubled dream-ridden slumber in which she struggled for hours in the cockpits of ailing aircraft, watched by baleful eyes.

Silas Lembede was awake though and darkly brooding on the British Airways flight north to the United Kingdom. The heist though successful left dangerous loose-ends because a witness remained alive and there had been some kind of intelligence leak. Who had ambushed them at Lenasia? When Lembede arrived at Heathrow a chauffeur-driven Mercedes conveyed him in silence to his five-bedroomed house in Wilton Row, Belgravia, a short walk from the Serpentine in Hyde Park, and later the same day to Liverpool.

-xxx-

Rick McGann was at Jongwe's yard, smoking outside on the steps and looking out at big stacks of old fridges, washing machines, dryers and other electrical detritus. There were several battered semi-trailers, containers and trucks too, and some DAF tractor units his class-one Agency drivers used when they did driving jobs here. If he couldn't get a driver Rick drove them himself, keeping the whole eighteen pounds an hour he billed for their time, even though he only paid his men eight. Through the partially open door he could hear the Zimbabwean's voice.

"What? The General is coming here himself for my report? In two minutes? Okay. Okay!" He dialled another number hurriedly. "Gatehouse security? A blue car will arrive any minute. Admit it and direct the driver to my office."

He clattered past down the bare staircase.

"Stay there Rick, I'll be with you in a few minutes" he called over his shoulder and hurried into the small staff car-park below his office where he paced anxiously and lit another cigarette, drawing on it deeply so the tip flared brightly. A Mercedes arrived and Jongwe chucked his butt away before climbing into the front seat where he began speaking to two other black men. Rick could see him half-twisted round to include the person in the back seat, talking animatedly as the other men listened. Jongwe was showing the photograph of James Hacking to Lembede who snatched it and glared, then placed it in his inside coat pocket.

"And what of these high-value shipments your informant mentioned, Jongwe?"

"Apparently one of Hackings drivers called Dave dislikes him intensely, and remarked that hijacking stuff like electronics and whisky from his Company trucks would be extremely easy. His investigations also revealed that not all Hacking's neighbours are happy with West Lancashire Council allowing the airfield to reopen. There are complaints of too much noise, and danger to properties under the flight path as well as excessive industrial racket from trucks coming and going."

Lembede grunted.

"Plenty of suspects then, when something unpleasant happens to Hacking, but perhaps there is money to be made first. I will do some reconnaissance myself."

"McGann could take you. I'll tell him you're a relative from Zimbabwe who is going to work with me and we are interested in the business being generated by the new airfield, as an alternate import destination for our Zimbabwean flower business, because Liverpool John Lennon Airport is getting too expensive. There is a scrap-yard on the airfield perimeter that keeps old household machines for me and I have them picked up occasionally when a truck is nearby. I'll ask him to show you the route, and coach you a little on British trucks and driving."

"I suppose he might believe that. Okay, set it up."

Jongwe hesitated.

"May I advise you against doing anything rash? The police here and in Europe are a lot more efficient than in most African countries."

"Thank you! I can assure you any actions will be taken with my normal subtlety!"

His voice was cold.

"That's what I'm afraid of!" thought Jongwe.

-xxx-

"Chilly for the time of year isn't it?" said Rick McGann leading the way across Jongwe's yard to a battered six by four twin-steer DAF 4200 tractor unit. He checked the oil and water and made a walk-round inspection, chatting as he did so, then climbed up behind the wheel. Lembede hoisted himself more awkwardly into the seat on the passenger side while Malinga watched cynically from beside the gleaming Mercedes, glad there was only room for two in the cab.

"So what do I call you?"

Lembede was taken by surprise and replied without thinking.

"Silas. And you?"

"Rick."

The starter churned and the engine rattled and banged but failed to start. White smoke oozed from the exhaust in a thick cloud.

"Fuckin' shed!" swore McGann, trying again and this time the motor caught and burst into life, clattering like a dustbin full of tins being rolled down a hill. He turned on the space heater and blew into his hands, grinning at Lembede who was shivering.

"Soon warm up."

"I hope so. What are we doing today?"

"Picking up that semi-trailer over there and taking it empty to a place in Wigan first."

He pointed to a rusty high-sided box-van trailer parked on an incline against the high fence.

"We drop it and pick one up containing scrap household machines, go round a few other yards in the area collecting more of the same stuff, then bring the trailer back here. Jongwe's wage-slaves from the Eastern-bloc then pack the shite into containers ready for shipment to the third world. You can see the cranes of Garston Dock container basin right there. Handy for him eh?"

Lembede's forehead wrinkled.

"I don't understand; Jongwe has slaves?"

"Almost! He employs local deadbeats who can't get anything else and Poles, Latvians and the like. Jongwe pays them peanuts by UK standards but it's still good money for the foreigners compared to what they get at home. The black man's burden hey?"

He laughed at his own joke and drove the unit over to the trailer, then backed partially under and lifted it with the airbag suspension so the legs were off the ground. He applied the hand-brake with a hiss of air and patted the lever.

"First trucking law, always apply hand brakes! Come on, I'll show you how to couple a trailer, you might as well learn something and I won't even charge you!"

"My family had a haulage business and I used to work with my father before he died but the trucks were mainly rigid and smaller than this."

"Are you going to be doing Jongwe's transport then?" McGann asked suspiciously, worried that he was going to lose business.

"He is a close relative and we plan to do some trade together but I only have an International licence at present. He suggested I come along with you to get a feel for this business. I don't mind learning anything new though."

"Okay. Well I'll talk you through it as I go along; it may come in useful down the line. Most driving schools teach jack-shit about coupling up and the real job."

Rick dismounted and demonstrated the trailer handbrake, checking it was set; a red knob that was pushed in to disengage, or pulled to set, then scrambled nimbly onto the unit deck between the cab and trailer, waving Lembede up beside him.

"This is the fifth wheel; see those jaws? They guide that pin on the trailer into the coupling which then grips and locks it. Understand?"

"Yes.""We're doing a split couple, because this trailer headboard comes too close to the cab to do it when it's coupled. So we connect the two airlines, two electric lines, and this Automatic Braking System line. Can be dangerous; if the trailer is on sloping ground like here without the handbrake on and you connect this red airline, the trailer will roll forward and crush you against the cab. If you've left the tractor handbrake off too, the whole combination will run away. So get ready to jump!"

Deftly he snapped the red hose on, pushing hard against the air-pressure and snapping the knurled collar. Lembede twitched, preparing to jump but Rick grabbed his arm, laughing, then held his empty hands up.

"No problem, see? Because I checked the trailer-brake was on, because I'm smart."

"So what would happen if the trailer brakes failed now? Or some idiot pushed that red knob on the trailer?"

"We'd be jam, instantly."

"Hmmm. I can see why it might be dangerous, easy to forget if you were in a hurry or something. What next?"

"The trailer legs are off the floor. Now I back under and engage the coupling. You stand on the ground and watch."

Rick reversed further under and the fifth-wheel engaged the towing-pin with a click followed by a loud clang that made Lembede flinch. He cursed himself, realising that fatigue, jetlag and poor sleep were making him jumpy. Rick engaged first gear and tugged twice against the trailer brakes to make sure the coupling was firmly connected and jumped down again.

"Sound. Now for the legs; that's the winding gear handle, give it a twirl, it'll warm you up!"

He demonstrated then left it to Lembede as Malinga looked on in disbelief. The former President cranked vigorously, raising the legs, then stowed the handle.

"Now the trailer brake."

Rick pointed and Lembede pushed it in gingerly. Compressed air rushed and the box-van creaked and moved almost imperceptibly.

"See? Now it's just the tractor handbrake holding the combination still. That's nearly it. There's a pneumonic checklist I use; Brakes, Legs, Air-hoses, Coupling, Clip, Number-plate. BLACKN."

He took the registration plate, clipped it to the back of the box-van and they set off.

"What are you doing driving trucks? I understand you used to be a policeman."

"I was but my pension isn't huge so I still have to grub for a living. I run an Agency with ten drivers working full-time and I earn five pounds an hour on each. I only drive when one of them doesn't turn in. I sorted a problem for Morris when I was in the police and we've helped each other out ever since."

They dropped the empty trailer in a bustling scrap-yard in Wigan and picked another up half-full of household appliances that had seen much better days.

"I can't believe Jongwe makes money out of this rubbish, even in Africa" said Lembede as they shut the rear doors of the trailer.

"They're not economic to repair here because everyone wants new but with a clean-up and simple repairs, a set of bearings say, these can work for many years more in third-world countries. The secret is, Morris actually gets paid to take them away for recycling, then sells them."

From Wigan Rick crossed the M6 motorway at junction 27 and stopped at a lay-by opposite a pub on top of Parbold hill.

"Nice view from here, might as well take a fifteen-minute tacho break; I'll treat you to an ice-cream from that van."

The weather was clear and sunny as they ate and admired the view of rolling hills speckled with small hamlets and farms. Beyond lay Southport to the west where the sea gleamed dully. A light aircraft flew low overhead descending gradually, visible long after the engine noise diminished by sunlight glinting off it.

"That is probably landing at Burscough Airfield where we're picking up some more knackered washing-machines. It was a Naval Airbase in the war and fell into disuse; only been opened again recently."

On the Airfield access lane Rick paused for oncoming traffic, a green Jaguar sports car, at a yellow sign saying "All HGV Traffic MUST Turn Right."

"Bit of allright, driving that Jag" commented McGann as it passed, noting Lembede's malevolent gaze follow the car; he had recognized Loretta and was remembering how her persistence had led to his downfall. McGann made the turn and ground in a low gear around the perimeter of the airfield where a light plane had just taken off. By the time they were near the scrap-yard entrance it was landing again so Rick pulled over and stopped.

"Jongwe asked me to make some enquiries about this place and its owner a while back. There's a Cessna doing circuits for practice" he said, producing a small set of binoculars and passing them across.

"Yes, my relative says Burscough village is a thriving agriculture and transport hub. Maybe the new airfield will be a good place to bring in light imports like flowers."

McGann grunted cynically and indicated relevant structures and geographical features including fences, canals and roads.

"Have you got flowers in Zimbabwe? I thought it was a desert; don't know much about Africa"

"Oh yes, along with many other easily transportable commodities. There is quite an extensive bloom-export trade to Europe already."

The Cessna returned, bounced several times on the next landing and took off again, wings wobbling. A man walked out of the club-house to watch and Lembede re-focused.

"Why did Jongwe refer to you as "the General?"

Lembede gave McGann a look that sent a shiver down his spine."Did Jongwe tell you who I am?"

"He didn't have to, everyone knows who you are."

"What? Who the hell knows?" hissed the big African with disconcerting eyes, glaring at Rick.

"Everyone; you're the bad black guy that James Bond chases in 'Casino Royale.' James Bond? Daniel Craig? He's from Liverpool too you know; well Chester anyway but we made him an honorary scouser. Dead hard, us scousers, you wouldn't want to mess with us."

Lembede continued glaring for several seconds then chuckled darkly.

"Half the time I don't understand what you're talking about but your ridiculous humour could get you killed one day; you respect nothing. It was a good James Bond film though, except of course that the white man won as usual; not very realistic."

He unconsciously touched his left eye-socket, remembering starkly the nightmare events after the original was destroyed during a night attack on the Hacking farm in Rhodesia. The insurgent group had been pursued relentlessly by security forces and at some point during the running battle his eye had been surgically removed in a botched operation at a mission clinic, a fact not revealed to him until he woke up in an American hospital in Libya. The Cessna landed, taxied to a fuel-stand and after several minutes the two occupants got out, a young woman and a man. Lembede's stomach felt hollow and the muscles fluttered as excitement coursed through him, mixed with a familiar feeling of dread which he would not acknowledge as such and dismissed as the effects of adrenalin. The old familiar hatred surged too. It was James Hacking and Lembede's hands were shaking slightly as he stared through the binos. Rick remained silent, picking his teeth, letting him look. Finally he spoke.

"That's James Hacking the owner. You know, as an avid film watcher, I would be inclined to say you guys were casing this joint."

"You have a vivid imagination; it could get you into trouble."

"I was just going to mention that if you have any particular... erm...redistribution enterprise in hand, I am not unskilled in that field and know many competent operators. I might be interested in being involved as a shareholder. Handling high-value consignments can be very lucrative, and easy if you know the right people. Which I do."

"I will bear that in mind but in the meantime it would be wise to curb your curiosity. If we want something we will ask you!"

"Okay; just saying."

"What other information do you have about this family?"

"Well I have Hacking's personal cell-phone number."

"Jongwe already told us. Who else lives here apart from Hacking's woman? Any other relatives?"

"One daughter called Haley."

"What about alarms, sentries and guard dogs, that sort of thing?"

"No dogs that I know about but quite high-tech security from what I could see."

-xxx-
Johannesburg: Monday

Feeling like death Jemima hauled herself out of bed at four am to be on the job at six, being as quiet as she could, but her movements woke Francois who came into the kitchen as she was making coffee.

"Jesus Jem-Squash, you look rough! What are you doing, you're not going to work after yesterday are you?"

She shrugged and sipped her coffee, free arm across her breasts in negative body-language.

"What else am I supposed to do? My job is the only normality I know and right now I need normal really badly!"

He took a step forward but she backed against the counter.

"Don't Francois, I appreciate what you did yesterday but right now the last thing on my mind is us!"

He slapped the counter so hard his hand stung, increasing his sudden frustrated rage.

"Jesus you are such a cold bitch! How many years have we been together? Then because of one lovers tiff, just one, you walk out and blank me ever since! Then you get in the shit and suddenly you're on the phone! Don't you think you at least owe me the decency to discuss things and tell me why?"

"I did tell you, lots of times but you wouldn't listen! We're different Francois, I don't want what you want and I can't do this right now, I've got enough on my plate. Please just accept that it's over and one day I'll try and explain it to you when things aren't so raw. I've got to go so please let yourself out when you're ready."

"No need, I'm out of here now, and you can take this bloody door-key and shove it!"

With trembling hands he tore it from his key-fob, threw it ringing on the tiles at her feet and stormed out. She heard him slamming doors as he collected his stuff and a final crash that made the house shake as he exited the front door. Jemima gave a mirthless chuckle that turned into a sob and went up to the bathroom to pull herself together. Once ready, she mentally went through an inventory in the hall to check she had all she needed, then checked the loads in her .38 and slipped it back into the ankle holster. On an impulse she ran upstairs to a front window and scrutinised the floodlit forecourt where her car was parked, probing the shadows for threats, then went back down, picked up her flight-bag, briefcase and carry-all and exited awkwardly, trying to lock the door without turning her back on the grey dawn, feeling ridiculously melodramatic. She made it to the operating base on time and found the whole crew present and correct for once which she took as a good omen, until her telephone rang showing "unknown caller." When she answered cautiously it turned out to be a female reporter from the Johannesburg Star who had received a tip from someone in the police about the bullion robbery. She offered Jemima a substantial sum for her exclusive story. Thinking quickly she used a line she'd heard in a cop drama.

"Sorry, can't comment at the moment, sub-judice." She was about to hang up but added an afterthought. "Listen, since you've got my number, text me yours; I'll check with the authorities and if it's legal for me to give interviews I'll get back to you."

She rang off and her phone beeped within seconds with the incoming text. She tapped the Nokia against her teeth thoughtfully. If that reporter was willing to pay then so would others be, and playing hard to get would only increase the going rate. Why shouldn't she make something out of an ordeal that had damn near killed her?"

The ZU-KAT team moved smoothly into action and as her hopper was being replenished after the first spraying sortie, Jack Dowding came over looking worried and stepped up onto her wing.

"There isn't much fuel Jemima, enough for today and maybe tomorrow. We need both Avgas and Avtur for the Turbine aircraft but when I phoned the fuel supplier they turned me down. Normally it's a formality, they just send a bowser out to refill our tanker and charge it against your company credit card. Today it didn't go through."

"Oh great!" thought Jemima, "probably fucking Klaasens again, the gay Afrikaans bank manager; as if I didn't have enough on my plate!"

She looked at Dowding calmly.

"OK Jack, leave it with me, I'll get it sorted when I take a break."

"Everything all right Jemima? Anything I can help with?"

She smiled wryly.

"I had a couple of adventures over the weekend that might amuse you. Tell you about it later."

Doing her job somehow helped Jemima to rationalise and prioritise her difficulties and she revelled in the simplicity and joy of the flying, throwing the powerful aircraft about and swooping like a swallow over the sea of crops in bright sunshine. On the next hopper refill she took her coffee flask over to the flysheet stretched from the ramshackle barn as an awning and sank into one of the deck-chairs beneath it. Sipping from a plastic cup of the fragrant brew she relaxed for a moment, enjoying the brightness of the day, the dew, the birds and the sparkling sunlight, then dialled Piet Schuman. His voice sounded hoarse.

"I've got a groot bubble-arse China so talk softly. What's up?"

"You even sound rough Piet; listen I need a favour, we're low on fuel and the bowser that was coming out to us has broken down. We're operating pretty close to you, can I send my fuel-truck and borrow a few thousand litres, enough for a couple of days 'till they get their shit right?"

"Ja I suppose I owe you sexy legs. Send it. Meanwhile I'm up to my pink bloodshot orbs in that gold hijack shit. Have they been back to you today?"

"Not yet."

"They will be, the suspicious bastards suspect everyone! They're threatening to search everywhere, even up my wife's…"

Jemima interrupted hastily.

"Okay, Okay, I get the picture. If anything new happens I'll bell you. The fuel truck will be there now."

"When will you pay me?"

"Take it out of my wages! Really Piet don't worry, we'll get square. I'm selling my story to the newspapers to bring in some cash."

"Now that will be a best-seller, if some of the stories I've heard are true!"

Jemima smiled.

"Not my life-story and nothing pornographic, just the one about the hijack for the moment. Totsiens."

Julius Jongintaba overheard as he lowered himself gingerly onto a well-used deck-chair with a drinks bottle and plastic sandwich box on his lap. He cleared his throat diffidently.

"Listen Jemima, I have some savings in the bank; you're welcome to a short-term loan for cash-flow. I know a lot of our customers like to sit on their money rather than pay when it's due."

He avoided her gaze shyly, grabbed a doorstep sandwich from the box and took a huge bite.

"That's a really generous offer Julius. Thanks, I'll let you know."

He shrugged.

"The money's available if you need it, and so am I."

She eyed his bulk thoughtfully.

"I wish I'd had you with me at the weekend when those bastards hijacked me!"

She told the story yet again and the young man's eyes bulged in outrage and disbelief.

-xxx-

Brigadier Thandiwe made a secure call to Chief Superintendent Ndhlovu in Harare.

"Simon? Thandiwe here. Did you ever hear of a person named Lembede?"

Ndhlovu racked his brains to no avail.

"I'm afraid not, why?"

"We have had a gold heist here that looks like it was the Mambas, with two deaths on their side. That name came up and on the off chance I just thought I would check with you. Things are coming to a head here on the corruption taskforce, I have a feeling something will break soon. I'll keep you informed."

"Please do, and I will start enquiries about Lembede here. Anything else you can tell me about him?"

"Well one potential witness who had a narrow escape thinks the person who might be Lembede had a false eye."

-xxx-

"So how was it boss, rubbing shoulders with the British working classes?" asked Malinga sarcastically as he drove the Mercedes through Aigburth, back towards Liverpool city centre.

"Fruitful; McGann provided a free ice-cream and I haven't had one for ten years. He is a cheeky bastard but very efficient. He got me close enough to identify Hacking and I had a damned good look at his environment too. You and I are going back there to finish what was started in the Chimurenga. We need dark waterproof clothing, balaclavas, decent boots, torches and baseball bats. Stop in the city centre."

In his suite at the Oriental Plaza Hotel near Liverpool One, Lembede poured himself a glass of Single Malt whiskey and looked out across the wide Mersey to New Brighton's twinkling lights on the Wirral peninsula. He gestured out at the dark water.

"You know, this port hosted the ships that transported more than half of all slaves from Africa to America."

Malinga helped himself to a beer from the mini-bar and joined him at the window.

"Really? How do you know?"

"History was one of my "A" level subjects at Peterhouse in a different life. The ships carried slaves to the Southern States and brought cotton back from America for the English cotton-mills. Both were huge industries. Maybe McGann's ancestors were sailors or merchants; time was, nearly everyone in this city was involved in slavery."

Malinga thought cynically of the press-ganged workers in the Chiadzwa diamond field but didn't say anything.

-xxx-

At midday Jemima landed the Ag-cat again and grabbed a cold coke from the cool-box under the awning. She closed her eyes and felt the sun's heat on her face through the thin awning. Exhausted she fell asleep and had a vivid unpleasant dream. The elderly Afrikaans Security Guard called Cornelius shouted "Fuck you Lembede" as he tried to bring up his Uzi and was ruthlessly shot, collapsing like a sack onto wet tarmac. She watched a gun-arm swing towards her and cold eyes behind a balaclava, then saw that face distort and collapse on itself as the contents of the head behind it were blown out in a welter of blood and gore. The second body struck the ground with a wet meaty splat and Jemima heard herself scream. Frantically she forced her eyes open, staring round in panic but there was only sunshine and peace, birds twittering and the drone of the crop-duster aero-engines, as distant and soothing as lawn-mowers on a Sunday morning. She stood up shakily, hyperventilating, and walked to and fro, running fingers through her hair. Her racing heartbeat gradually slowed as she breathed deeply, taking out her phone for something to do, to blot out the vivid images that still lingered in her subconscious. She wished again that James was in South Africa and remembered him asking to see the picture of Lembede on her phone, and it being missing after Sandro had a look.

She walked quickly to her car and fired up the laptop. In five minutes it was ready and a short search found the latest download of pictures from her phone. Sure enough the one of the Kudu and Lembede in the background was there. She zoomed it and nodded in satisfaction. Her Dad should be back from Iraq and perhaps it would mean something to him. She would email it and phone him tonight. She didn't want to ask for yet more money though; she wanted to be independently successful, particularly in his eyes but had been remiss as usual in chasing her debtors and needed cash to keep operating until she could sort out her banking arrangements.

She made a snap decision and called the first magazine reporter who had contacted her for information about the hijack. There had been several and from the bidding war she had a ball-park figure for what her story was worth. The case might be sub-judice but someone in the police had already talked to the press and she could describe her ordeal in broad terms without mentioning any names. They came to a swift deal and agreed a meeting.

As she went back to work her phone rang showing Sandro's number but she let it go to answerphone.

-xxx-

CHAPTER TWELVE

A cold front moving in with strong gusting winds and persistent rain had made James cancel his last flying lesson of the day. Haley asked if he could take a load to the docks in Bootle, giving him the trailer number. The clocks had just gone back ending British summer time and it was already growing dark as James walked down to the Transport hanger. The gates in the outer yard fence stood open and were seldom closed. A harsh security lamp under a video camera came on as he crossed the hard-standing towards the huge sliding door, illuminating sheeting rain and spattered puddles.

Lembede and Malinga, clad in dark waterproof clothing and boots, had crossed the runway and paused to investigate the hangers. Sharpness wasn't exactly clear what their mission was but on hearing footsteps approaching they moved into some bushes adjacent to trailers parked outside the building. When the light came on Lembede recognized James and his hands clenched tightly round the baseball bat.

James glanced at the wet trailers and identified one with the number given him by Haley. It was parked outside on sloping ground at the edge of the dispersal area, against the raised canal embankment; it was elderly and had no sliding services 'mavis-rail' like modern ones. He unlocked a man-gate into the main hanger, went through and rolled the main door open. Inside he climbed up into the Scania cab, filled in a card, put it in the tachograph and did his pre-trip walk-round. The space-heater for the cab began to hum and quickly warmed it up. He filled in his trip paperwork while waiting the obligatory fifteen minutes the Freight Transport Association considered necessary for inspection then fired the Scania up, turned on the headlights and backed it under the trailer. He could tell it was extremely heavy by the feel of the suspension as the truck guide-bars slid under the leading edge. The wheels spun and slipped slightly as the tractor muscled its way under the load. He applied the unit handbrake and put on the four-way flashers so he could check the indicators once the services were connected, then lifted the legs clear of the ground with the inflatable truck suspension and turned on the rear platform light. He slipped a head-torch on and walked back to check that the trailer-brake was applied. Cold rain was running off his high-visibility waterproof, and drips from the hood blew in his eyes. He was only about ten feet from Lembede, and Malinga could feel the former President quivering beside him like a palsied dog. He waited the instruction to attack. They both tensed in surprise as James spoke unexpectedly.

"Jesus I hate this fuckin' job sometimes!"

Astonishment caused them to pause as James walked back and climbed onto the slippery illuminated deck to couple the services.

"I don't know if this will work but I cannot miss the opportunity!" hissed Lembede in a low voice to Malinga. Ducking low he covered the distance to the trailer in three long strides and pushed the red button of the trailer handbrake in, to the 'off' position, then ducked back into the bushes, watching expectantly. The furthest connection away from James was the red supply airline, and was therefore the first to be coupled. He shoved it on and snapped the knurled knob to secure it, as always ready to whip it off again if there was any sign of the trailer moving, even though he had checked it was safe. Detecting no movement he turned his attention to the other lines and to keeping his clothes away from the filthy grease that was crusted on various surfaces of the old vehicle. On the sloping hard-standing, gravity gradually overcame the friction of the trailer tyres and imperceptibly it began to roll. James froze momentarily in disbelief as he felt it, a very slight tremble in the deck beneath his feet. The other services were connected and impeded him as he lunged for the red connection, hoping to snatch it off so that the trailer spring-brakes would dynamite on. The headboard moved closer to him as if in the slow-motion of a dream, but accelerating as his fingers slipped on the wet connection. Finally in desperation he flung himself across the rapidly closing gap towards the ground. The coupling slammed home and the headboard stopped inches from the rear of the cab.

His headlong dive was arrested and he shouted in pain as his left foot was trapped briefly. The steel-toed boot twisted and his weight pulled it free, collapsing head and shoulders first onto the wet concrete, rolling instinctively from years of parachuting experience. He let momentum carry him lithely onto his feet again. Hobbling awkwardly on the sore ankle he lunged back to check the trailer brake. It was off and the pain in his foot was subsiding.

"Where the hell are you Mawdesley you cowardly fucking wanker!" shouted James, listening hard. The wind rasped a branch against Lembede's waterproof jacket and James's acute hearing picked it up. He opened a storage locker, extracting a heavy six-foot length of metal ground-anchor. Fumbling the head-torch straight he charged at the bushes where the sound had come from, thrashing in rage at the undergrowth. The iron bar hit Malinga a numbing blow on the mid upper-arm and he cannoned into Lembede. Both dropped their baseball bats as they fell. James reversed the direction of his swing awkwardly and the iron whistled back above their heads, shredding leaves and twigs. The two Africans grabbed the bats and scrambled through brush with the ground-anchor snapping and shattering branches just behind them, finally jogging in darkness across the grass bordering the runway towards the perimeter fence, Malinga nursing his aching arm. Hopping on his bad foot James yelled threats and insults but finally gave up the pursuit. They reached the Mercedes five minutes later.

"You'll have to drive, my arm is still too painful to steer with. I'm lucky it isn't broken" said Malinga. "Though older he is still a very dangerous man."

Lembede was grinning wolfishly.

"Yes but I nearly got him! It would have been perfect, an obvious accident caused by incompetence!"

"From what he shouted, Hacking thought we were local enemies."

"It is good, he deserves to worry, and next time I will get him for sure."

-xxx-

Loretta was still in her office when James stormed in. She regarded his dishevelled appearance in astonishment; yellow waterproofs torn and filthy from rolling on the ground, hands grubby, grease on his boots and trousers. She could also sense his dangerous mood in an instant.

"You don't normally get so dirty; what's going on?"

"Some pricks just tried to kill me is what's going on!"

"Who? What happened?"

James replied, talking in clipped sentences.

"I don't suppose you could be mistaken about the brake?"

"No way; those two pricks in the bushes intended to kill or maim me by taking off that brake, and they were carrying baseball bats or something when they ran away."

He clicked his fingers.

"Can you bring up the video feed from that web-camera on the hanger? Might be something on it."

Loretta connected to the security PC with internet explorer, found the right camera and went back twenty minutes then forward. James appeared on the screen as a dark figure, thrown into relief when the light went on. The trailer was dimly visible right on the edge of the display, with the brake on the side away from the camera. Fast-forwarding in bursts they came eventually to footage of James climbing onto the cat-walk and forty seconds later diving off it as the headboard rushed forward, narrowly avoiding being crushed.

"Oh my God!"

"Nothing there! Go back a bit further."

Ten minutes before his arrival at the yard, two indistinct figures clad in dark clothing with hoods and balaclavas sidled round the hanger into the dim perimeter lights, and were picked out in more detail by the camera a moment later when the security light flared on. They didn't appear fazed and tried to open the Judas door before standing and pointing things out to each other. Then they looked up the road and retreated quickly across the hard-standing into some bushes behind the trailers.

"Bastards!" swore James, leaning forward, staring intently as Loretta re-ran the sequence.

"The smaller of those two could just about be Kevin Mawdesley I suppose, which is who I immediately suspect. The large one is about Dave Swinnerton's size but that doesn't make much sense!"

"Would even Kevin Mawdesley be stupid enough to try and hurt you after a public altercation and threats? This is serious James, what are we going to do about it? Call the police?"

He considered.

"No, be a waste of time, they won't find anything else. Mawdesley might think our argument was all forgotten but it bloody isn't. I'm going to go round there and confront him."

"That would be very stupid considering the mood you're in; assault him or his son and you will automatically be in the wrong" she called but he'd already gone and she heard his car start. He drove into the Mawdesley yard ten minutes later and screeching to a stop.

"Where the hell is your gaffer?" he snarled at a surprised fork-lift driver loading a trailer in the yard.

"They're all at a family funeral in Scarborough, left yesterday. Why? Can I help?"

James glanced at an empty double-garage beside the farmhouse.

"You're sure? All of them?"

"Yes, my niece is Kevin Mawdesley's girlfriend. She went with them and phoned me earlier; they're all there reet enough."

"Kevin too?"

"Aye; what's all the bother about?"

"Nothing; forget about it!"

Back at the airfield James speculated wildly, combing hooked fingers through his hair.

"Maybe it was just some opportunistic scumbags on a thieving recce who thought it might be amusing to squash me. Whoever it was knew how trucks and trailers work."

Loretta shivered.

"I didn't think Burscough was that kind of place. Are there really people so callous just walking around out there? In England?"

"I'm afraid so, plenty of frighteningly mindless thugs who wouldn't think twice about it. Organised crime is huge in Liverpool; the Kirby estate is one of the hotbeds and it's only a few miles away. There have been gun-battles between gangs in Walton and someone burned a drug-dealer alive in the boot of a car a few weeks ago. Was there any trouble while I was away in Iraq?"

"Not for us personally but the police helicopter was busy around here on a few nights."

"I was safer in Iraq."

"Didn't anyone try to get you in Baghdad?"

"Not personally, not like this. I better get that trailer down to the docks before Haley kills me."

-xxx-

Jemima met the female magazine reporter and a photographer on the farm as spraying wrapped up for the day. She read the publishing contract twice, glanced at the first of several cheques in a graduated payment scheme, then stuffed them in her pocket and began to relate the details of the hijack, leaving out any mention of Silas Lembede's name. Later she took the photographer for a flip in the Ag-Cat and posed for other pictures beside it.

"This is a great exclusive and I can guarantee it will be on our front page tomorrow, after which all the other papers will pick up on it" said the reporter. "With luck it will cause a public outcry and the police will have to come up with some solid answers about how they plan to tackle organized crime at last."

While preparing to drive home Jemima's old Nokia, of which she was still very fond, began to make a series of hi pitched peeps and when she looked at the screen it went dead. She frowned and turned it back on, getting the "battery low" alarm for a few seconds before it died again. The battery-life had once been excellent but it hardly seemed to hold a charge at all anymore. She cursed and called into Sandton on her way home to get a replacement battery. She got one but was also talked into buying a brand-new iPhone. The salesman escorted his attractive client to the door.

"Your Apple needs to be charged for 24 hours before use. Just call me if you want your old cell-phone number switched to the new handset. Call me if you need anything in fact."

Being in the mall anyway, she went into a supermarket and stocked up on food before driving home and plugging the new cell in by her bedside. When the ailing Nokia was charged again she copied all her contacts from phone to sim, moved the sim to the Apple phone and copied them over. She turned the iPhone off again and left it on charge.

-xxx-

The Director of South African Prisons nervously phoned Lembede on his GoldLock 4G-encrypted cell-phone, which used the same totally secure voice systems as the Israeli Defence Forces.

"Are you still in the UK Silas?"

"Yes. In Liverpool. Why?"

"Some complications with the Welkom Operation; it is still not clear who was responsible for killing the second of the two dead men. The Director of the National Intelligence Service is one of us as you know and the Deputy Director has been personally overseeing the investigation. Disturbingly his preliminary report says the pilot, a white female, alleges hearing you addressed by name, and giving orders for the shooting. She also claims to have recognised you."

Lembede was furious.

"I was surprised to see her there. She flew me to Botswana and might have recognised me despite the balaclava but I was sure I killed the bitch: I saw her fall to the ground near the other bodies. Was she injured? Is she in hospital?"

"No, completely unharmed. She was released pending further enquiries."

"Well deal with her and do it immediately!"

"More dead bodies would only draw greater attention to the investigation; there is no evidential threat to anyone, other than her statement."

"Exactly, and that mentions my involvement! It is vital to my whole scheme that I am able to operate transparently in South Africa; any exposure of this sort is unacceptable. I am coming back immediately. Make sure the Director supresses that report and I strongly recommend sticking to your normal procedure where witnesses are concerned!"

He terminated the call, muttering angrily under his breath.

"Trouble boss?" asked Malinga and Lembede explained with ill-concealed venom.

"Do you want me to take care of the problem when we get back? The woman pilot?"

"No, I need someone trustworthy here, in case anything else goes wrong at the European end. Bullion and diamonds will soon be moving through Thune mine. The stones will be transported onwards from Botswana to Holland by Diplomatic bag and thus to Tahamata. I'll brief you on what to do."

"OK but what do you want me to do about Hacking? He's obviously a bit of a handful."

"Nothing directly for the moment; now that I have found him he is not an immediate priority. Talk to Jongwe and McGann though, it would be profitable to take Hacking's trucks when they have high-value loads. Tahamata could easily handle the disposal of liquor and small expensive electronics. Making Hacking's life difficult might be more enjoyable than simply killing him but what I am really worried about is this development in South Africa; my plan to re-take Zimbabwe is very close to fruition and I don't like loose ends Malinga, I really don't!"

"Perhaps you're one yourself" thought his henchman, mind racing with sudden thoughts that caused both dread and excitement.

-xxx-
Lancashire

The phone-line from South Africa was very clear as James listened in consternation to Jemima's rendition of the hijack and subsequent events. He was sitting at his laptop and opened her email. The attached four-megapixel camera shot was grainy when enlarged but reasonable quality and James felt an immediate nostalgia for the hot dry climate so well depicted. He thought fleetingly that George would have loved the spectacular Kudu for a trophy and then zoomed on the figures individually. Coming to one of the black men he stopped, feeling the hairs on his neck rise. He played with the mouse roller to get the biggest image without distortion, then sat and stared with his chin on his hand and a sinking sensation in the pit of his stomach.

"I have the picture Jemima" he said at last, "And I am afraid it might be extremely bad news; that man second from right looks uncannily like Spencer Katsiru, the ruthless ex-Dictator of Zimbabwe and a fugitive from international justice, but he only had one eye and wore a patch…."

Jemima had the same photo open on her computer.

"That person is called Silas Lembede as far as I know and he has an almost undetectable artificial eye. The Investigating Officer Thandiwe seems to suspect him of being an organized-crime gang boss; said he might regard me as a threat, or 'unfinished business.' How worried should I be James?"

"Very I am afraid because a picture is beginning to emerge; Katsiru and Lembede are obviously one and the same. What better way to launder stolen gold bullion and possibly Zimbabwean blood diamonds than through an innocent little mine in neutral, innocuous Botswana?"

There was silence on the line for several seconds.

"Wow!" said Jemima in a low voice. "That would be big money and a seriously nasty scenario. I'm beginning to take Brigadier Thandiwe's warning seriously! Have you ever heard of the Black Mamba Dad?"

They were both becoming more used to their relationship and he smiled.

"Certainly have; most deadly snake in Africa; the longest ever recorded was in Zimbabwe at just under fifteen feet and it weighed twenty-six pounds; so fast and agile a group of people is usually required to kill it; strikes in all directions while a third of its body is 3–4 feet off the ground. Front-fanged, the most dangerous type and the venom is the most rapid-acting of any snake species. Neurotoxic; its bite is often called "the kiss of death" and can potentially kill a human within 20 minutes depending on the nature of the bite but death usually occurs after 30–60 minutes on average; causes suffocation resulting from paralysis of the respiratory muscles."

"I had no idea mambas were so dangerous, they sound like a nightmare!"

"They are; scratch any African and they will have a few snake stories! My dad drove over one at fifty miles an hour and it still managed to get up into the truck."

"Well I'm talking about a human who calls himself the Black Mamba, shadowy boss of a gang called the Mambas out here. Guess if you wanted to inspire fear it is a pretty deadly icon."

"Very, but can't say I've ever heard of the gang; nasty bunch I presume?"

"Dreadful. According to Brigadier Thandiwe they are in virtual control of about one third of South Africa's economy, insidious, brutal and spreading. Maybe this Lembede or Katsiru is the Black Mamba."

"That is frightening and exactly the kind of thing he might be involved in. I'm coming out as soon as I can get away, can't say too much on the phone but I'll forward my ETA: And Jemima? Be really careful 'till I get there, try to have someone dependable around at all times, preferably armed."

James deliberated hard when they hung up but there was no possible way Katsiru could know that Jemima was his daughter, though he was quite conceivably complicit with criminals who might want her silenced; it was exactly his style. He jumped up and paced agitatedly. Surely it couldn't have been Katsiru who had just tried to kill him by removing the trailer brake? That really was inconceivable. Or was it? Years ago he and Loretta had discussed running from the threat of Katsiru or going after him; James fervently wished he had chosen the latter because he was going to have to do something about it now.

-xxx-

Lembede was so anxious to get back to South Africa and supervise events there that he took the Manchester shuttle direct to Heathrow for a connecting flight. Having dropped him at Manchester airport, Malinga drove the Mercedes straight back to Jongwe's yard and found him upstairs in the grubby office. Jongwe made tea and grunted when Malinga told him of recent events and the ex-Presidents departure.

"Good riddance" he muttered.

Malinga grinned.

"That was the good news, now for the bad; our mission is to scribble Hacking, disguising it as a truck hijacking."

Jongwe spat hot tea onto his suit.

"For fuck's sake, the guy is a lunatic! This is England, not a banana republic; there are so many surveillance cameras it would be virtually impossible to get away with stealing a load like that! And as for murder, he can do his own dirty work!"

"Calm down, I'm just joking Jongwe, but you mirror my own sentiments exactly."

"What? Really?"

"Yes. Tell me, who is top man in Lembede's organization should he suffer an unfortunate demise?"

"Well…. you probably."

"Exactly, and I think it is about time for him to retire; permanently."

"That is never going to happen; he won't give up his obsession to be ruler of Zimbabwe until he is dead!"

"You misunderstand: I mean retire really permanently. Who would benefit most from that happening? Apart from me?"

"James Hacking; Katsiru has been intending to kill him for years and almost succeeded just the other day."

"Exactly, but Hacking won't know for sure it was Katsiru that tried to crush him, so maybe we should tell him; just wind him up and watch him go."

"That's brilliant! All of us stand to gain! Hacking does the dirty work, scribbles Katsiru and you take over his African and European operations; I get Katsiru off my back for good and keep control of his British business, it's all in my name. How will we inform Hacking?"

"I'll do it; anonymously of course and from a throwaway handset. Give me that number again, the one McGann got from Hacking's truck driver."

-xxx-

Lembede had no problem getting a first-class overnight ticket from London to Johannesburg and was driven straight to a meeting with the Director of Prisons and the Director of the National Intelligence Service, conducted clandestinely near an old mine dump. Both men were in the political hierarchy but also benefitting massively from their involvement in the Mambas. The Prison Director's fear was pungently apparent as soon as Silas entered the black limousine and sat facing the two Senior South African officials, face dark with anger.

"Right, what have you found out while I was gone? Who killed our guy at the airfield in Lenasia? Did somebody betray us? Is another gang trying to muscle in? What?"

The enormously fat DOP was sweating rancidly with fear; his normally unblinking greedy eyes flickered with agitation and his face was beaded with moisture. He spoke immediately, chins wobbling.

"We haven't been able to find out anything useful from the surviving operators Silas. You were there and their story is unanimous; they were all in the transport ready to depart when the two killings happened. You probably know more than anyone."

"Was it the Police then? Has some new undercover taskforce penetrated our operation?"

The urbane NIS boss replied.

"Unlikely Lembede, though the woman pilot was firearms trained and armed according to Thandiwe's report. Perhaps she was an undercover police officer."

"Bullshit, but I wish I'd nailed her. She dropped and someone else kept shooting so we had no choice but to retreat."

"Exactly; the bullion was retained and very little damage was actually done."

Lembede glowered thoughtfully.

"It must have been the Security Guards trying to get it all for themselves, nothing else makes sense. Only they had sufficient information. In any event there is ample reason to silence the woman in my view and I wish someone other than Brigadier Thandiwe were the investigating Officer. He worries me. Can't you control him, get him on board?"

"I have tried, without being too explicit, and he never bites. Either he doesn't understand or is so straight he doesn't want to understand. Look Silas, if you are so worried, the most credible way to sort this out is for me to order Thandiwe to charge her with the crime, which is serious so she will be remanded in custody indefinitely, pending trial. The remand prisons are terrible places as we all know. While there she can be made to sign a confession admitting involvement, saying that the white security guards initiated the shooting and they planned to abscond with all the gold."

The DOP could sense Lembede wavering and was quick to back his colleague up.

"It will be far more credible if she dies in an official institution; suicides and murder are very common in those remand prisons. It could happen without her naming the remainder of the gang or saying where the gold has ended up. Everybody will buy that, especially the public; it happens all the time in those over-crowded hell-holes!"

Lembede glowered.

"Fine, except that my name appears in Thandiwe's report and I'm not happy about that! I still lean towards taking her out."

"That will definitely make it look like she was killed to silence her, and would invite deeper investigation, especially if the newspapers start demanding an enquiry; my way is safer. Leave it to me Silas. When she disappears into the remand prison her testimony will disappear too, and your name from Thandiwe's report; I guarantee it."

The ex-President frowned.

"What about replacing Thandiwe with someone more sympathetic to our cause?"

"We have no-one in the Mambas high-ranking enough in NIS. Thandiwe is outspokenly anti-corruption and has the President's overt support. He also appears to trust me as his superior. In fact he was very forthcoming so I expect to be kept up to speed with every development. How can that be bad?"

Lembede nodded shortly and ducked out of the limousine. The Prison DOP was letting out a relieved sigh when he leant his head back in.

"OK. Do it your way then but make it quick. I won't tolerate complacency or failure. We stand or fall together."

He left, telephoning Sandro Marais by cell-phone on the way and suggesting they meet to review business at Lembede's home in a brusque manner that sounded more like an order. Once there he sat evaluating the situation until Sandro arrived, bristling, because as usual his black 'business partner' had spoken to him more like an underling than an equal but that was nothing new. It was a strange meeting. Lembede seemed preoccupied and unfocused.

"What's up Silas? As far as I know all our operations are running smoothly. Gambling is a little down and alcohol a little up. Normal stuff. Are you suffering from pre-menstrual stress or something?"

"Don't be insolent. And yes, I have some stress as always. What were you up to last Sunday when I flew to the UK?"

"Looking for my dog. You seem to be pussyfooting around some issue. What's really bothering you? Tell me and maybe I can help but I'm not psychic."

"That woman pilot who took us to Botswana? You are friendly with her?"

"Jemima? Sure, we've become quite good friends. She had a very nasty experience on Sunday actually; got hijacked flying gold from Welkom to Joeys. She was pretty angry about your behaviour at the airport in Selibe too. She was hell-bent on making a complaint about you but I talked her out of it. Is that what's on your mind?"

"Partly, she is too full of herself and intent on making trouble. She may become a problem; you should choose your friends more wisely."

"I don't have any friends, I just know people and some better than others. Eh Silas? It would be unfortunate if anything untoward happened to Miss Visser. Or to me. There are arrangements in place for that skeleton in your cupboard to come out under a variety of circumstances."

"There is no need for threats Marais, especially from a business associate but rest assured there are enough items in your own cupboard to which I have the key."

"Not a threat Silas. Look, I know you have activities going on outside our joint interests and I don't care about them, so long as they don't affect me. Or Miss Visser now that we've become friends."

"Very well but do me a favour. Try and convince Miss Visser to keep her mouth shut and nose out of my business."

"Sure. I'll try to put that across without being offensive. Wish me luck with it."

"Always Sandro; our luck is interlinked. Help yourself to a drink if you'd like, I'm travel weary and need a shower."

Silas moved towards the door unfastening expensive gold cufflinks, leaving his suit jacket draped over the arm of a couch.

"Thanks Silas but I'll get on my way and come back at breakfast time for an update when you've had time to rest. I'll be going past to meetings in town tomorrow anyway" called Sandro as Lembede's footsteps receded. He rapidly frisked the jacket and found a wallet in the left breast pocket. It contained high-denomination notes in several currencies and many credit cards. He slipped another card amongst them and replaced the billfold before laying the garment carefully back where it had been casually thrown.

-xxx-

Working quickly on the internet James managed to book an evening KLM seat from Amsterdam to Johannesburg and a mid-afternoon shuttle from Manchester to connect with it. Haley called from the Flying school.

"Someone foreign-sounding on the telephone for you Dad. Came up 'unknown caller' on the switch; transferring it now."

He knew straight away from the accent that it was a black Zimbabwean, but he couldn't remember hearing the voice previously.

"Did you enjoy your recent close call Mr Selous Scout?"

"Who the hell are you?"

"An old enemy but not your worst; President Katsiru is the one who tried to kill you; he calls himself Silas Lembede these days."

"I just found that out but why are you telling me this? How did he find me?"

"He found you by chance and acted on the spur of the moment when an opportunity presented itself. I am telling you this because I have an opportunity too."

"Oh yeah, what would that be?"

"Katsiru has been my leader for many years but his obsessions are ruining our business; he is more concerned with regaining power in Zimbabwe, with killing you, than making money. He is a loose cannon and it is perhaps time he was put out to grass."

"Permanently you mean, so you can take over."

"Precisely."

"Why not just do it yourself?"

"Because he has very powerful friends in our organisation who might not accept me under such circumstances, they might even kill me for it. However I am his natural successor and if he is neutralized by a known adversary from the past, well the mantle will fall naturally on my shoulders."

"Sounds like some sort of scam or trap to me."

"Our particular argument was politically motivated and over long ago Hacking, but yours with Katsiru will never go away permanently until he does, because it is very personal. You understand. I personally no longer have any axe to grind with you."

"Does Katsiru still seriously harbour intentions of a comeback to power in Zimbabwe?"

"Very much so. He has two obsessions; that, and killing you."

"Is he still in the UK?"

"No. A crisis called him back to South Africa but I can give you as much information as you need to do the job."

James tapped his fingers on the desk, mind racing.

"OK, whoever you are. Give me everything you've got."

"Get ready to copy then. But understand, you cannot approach the South African authorities over any of this because some elements are deeply implicated. You will have to handle it yourself."

Afterwards James sat digesting what he had learnt and then called Colinda in London.

"James. I miss you. Is it all still going OK up there?"

"Miss you too."

He filled her in on recent developments locally and in South Africa.

"Could I ask a favour Colinda? I need to get over to SA to protect my daughter Jemima and do something about this tip-off. Would you come up to Lancashire as security for Haley and Loretta while I'm gone?"

"That could prove interesting. Wouldn't I be more use coming with you?"

"Yes, but it's possible whoever had a go at me might try and target those close to me too. I'd feel happier doing what I have to in Africa knowing they were safe."

"Then of course I'll come. On my iPad I can see a Heathrow-Manchester shuttle that gets in at 1400 hours. Will that do?"

"Works perfectly. I'll get Haley to drop me in Manchester for my flight and you can ride back here with her. We'll have about an hour together."

"I wish it could be longer."

"So do I. And thanks."

"You can thank me properly when you get back; have to rush now to make that shuttle."

James explained Jemima's hijacking to Loretta and Haley, stressing his need to get to South Africa quickly, omitting his anonymous caller's information about Katsiru to avoid alarming them unnecessarily. Haley went to get ready to run him to Manchester.

"If you are getting some bodyguard up from London for us do I need to be worried James?" asked Loretta.

"Not worried but vigilant until I get back."

"Is this related to what happened to you?"

"Anything is possible and I don't intend to take any chances with your safety."

"For once try not to take any unnecessary risks. Let the authorities deal with it for all our sakes."

"I'll try but things aren't always that simple; look what happened to Elias Mpofu all those years ago."

A short while later Loretta watched with her arms folded as Haley climbed into the Jag and James put his rucksack in the boot.

"Take care. I don't want to lose you James!" she suddenly called.

He turned and looked at her, smiling in bemusement, then raised a hand in farewell. She had left him for fat harmless Dennis, so what the hell did that mean? Women! His mind turned back to timetables. The flight from Amsterdam would get into Johannesburg in the afternoon.

Haley was obviously a little in awe of Colinda when they met, and said so when the American woman went to the washroom.

"You didn't tell me the bodyguard was Amazon woman Dad!"

"That would have spoiled my fun, seeing your face when I introduced her. You'll like Colinda though."

"Possibly, but will Loretta? She might not take kindly to being bossed about by another woman."

"She won't be bossy, just ultra-efficient. They don't come better trained than Colinda; she was an Officer in the American Marine Corps. You'll be in safe hands and I will have peace of mind." She hugged him tightly.

"Be safe Dad, and give my love to Jemima. I can't wait to meet my Sis."

-xxx-

Thursday

A van pulled up outside Lembede's Johannesburg mansion and the driver pushed several newspapers through the letter-box. They thudded onto the floor inside the security lodge and were taken straight to Lembede at his breakfast table. It was half an hour before he noticed the banner-headline on one particular newspaper; 'South Africa is being hijacked!" With growing rage he read a lurid account of the Welkom gold robbery told from the female pilot's perspective, followed by a damning analysis of crime and corruption in high places. It ended with the information that the pilot was a key prosecution witness who had recognised some of the perpetrators and that arrests were imminently expected. The Editor called on the Government to act swiftly, beginning with a public enquiry.

"Malinga!" he bellowed before remembering that his right-hand man was still in the UK. His hands shook with fury as he found his cell-phone and called the Director of the National Intelligence Service, speaking as soon as he answered.

"Have you seen the damn newspapers today?"

"Yes but so what? It's never going to get to court; our people at the top are too powerful and the public too terrified of reprisals for anything to change."

Lembede was livid.

"Your complacency is unbelievable! I know you will hold your nerve but that fat swine the Director of Prisons is shitting himself, all it takes is one like him to bolt to the authorities and do an immunity deal for everything to fall apart. This is a bloody dangerous situation. Arrest and terminate that woman as a matter of urgency, do you understand me? That journalist will have to be silenced now too."

"Okay Silas perhaps you're right; don't get your knickers in a twist I'll take care of it."

"Don't tell me about my bloody knickers! Start acting like a professional and get on with it. Phone me within an hour to report she is in custody or I will do it myself, and make sure the job is done properly this time!"

Breathing heavily he slapped his phone down on expensive polished inlaid wood, shattering the table's exquisite veneer. Immediately he was beset by doubts, the same nagging fears that would be working on the DOP. Who could he trust? Marais was bound to realise he'd overheard the woman talking about the Welkom bullion shipments; she'd blatantly shut up as soon as she noticed him listening and Sandro had obviously known why. So had one of them given the authorities a heads up? Why would Sandro do that, except that he seemed to have an interest in the woman?

In weeks, perhaps even days it wouldn't matter because he would be back in power in Zimbabwe and untouchable, but until then he was as vulnerable to arrest as a common criminal. In a lightning decision he decided to eradicate her personally. The only person he could trust was himself and there was too much to lose if Jemima Visser lived. He needed an address and rifled through a stack of phone directories in his study to find one. There were nearly two pages of Vissers and he missed it first time, cursed and began again. His finger stabbed the tiny print and he underlined the name with a pen so he could more easily see it; Visser, Jemima. Number One, Eagle Court, Bryanston. He snapped the thick book shut and turned away, then had a thought and went back to the directory pile, selecting the yellow-pages. ZU-KAT Agricultural Aviation was among the last entries and he scribbled the address and several telephone numbers on a bit of paper. He would try Visser's house first as it was closest but realised he would probably have to call and find out where the company was currently operating in order to find her if she wasn't there. He strode quickly off to arm himself appropriately and organise transport, grabbing his jacket and shrugging into it.

"Get my car round to the front" he roared, heard chairs scraping and feet thudding in the kitchen as his bodyguards rushed to comply, all too familiar with that tone of voice. He caught sight of himself in a full-length mirror, dark-skinned face, immaculately ironed starched shirt and twenty thousand-rand blue pin-striped suit; he looked like an African President not an assassin and preened for a moment before crossing quickly to the front door and opening it. His entourage were walking quickly or jogging across the wide brick-paved forecourt.

"Wait!"

They stopped and his eyes darted about, noticing a battered Ford Fiesta used by the garden-boy to move his tools around Lembede's properties; there was a lawnmower crammed into the back.

"I will go in that, alone! Don't admit anyone while I'm gone!"

His goons looked at each other open-mouthed, then shrugged and walked on to the gate-house. Lembede was a prick to work for but he paid well. Back inside he changed into his scruffiest clothes, covering them with a corduroy jacket, and selected a Makarov 9mm automatic with a rare-edition suppressor from the hand-guns in his safe, and took two extra full magazines. It was an ugly, unwieldy weapon but one he was very familiar with from his days in the Rhodesian bush war; a faithful companion over many long years. There were several passports and on a hunch he put them in an inside pocket too. The instinct for danger that had kept him alive through all the long years of that war told him that things were beginning to change and he was above all a survivor. He also stuffed a substantial roll of cash in his pockets and in the kitchen noticed a Tom-Tom sat-nav charging on the worktop. The car-charger was with it and he grabbed both, then did a quick mental inventory. Money; Passports; Credit-cards; Keys; Telephone! He needed that charger too and went back for it. There was nothing else he might need in a crisis and he went onto the sweeping driveway and climbed into the small Ford. It was grubby inside and smelt of dried grass and dust. He sneezed and noticed a much older jacket, ripped and faded, on the back seat so he put it on instead of the corduroy and transferred all the pocket contents from one coat to the other. There was also a battered straw hat and he put that on too, then started the engine and drove towards the gates which began to open. He pulled over to put Bryanston Drive into the satnav, then set off again, trying to imagine every eventuality.

-xxx-

Brigadier Thandiwe was at his desk by seven am on Thursday and immediately received a call. After a brief acrimonious conversation he put down the secure telephone thoughtfully. In every big investigation there occurred at some point a catalyst that precipitated action based on all the planning and conjecture. Operation Redemption was now on the brink of that point. He had just received a direct order from the NIS Director to issue an arrest warrant for Jemima Visser and he could not afford to delay very long, yet he knew that in reality it could also be her death warrant. She would in all probability be remanded indefinitely pending trial to 'Sun City' the notorious Johannesburg prison and be effectively beyond help. He considered himself a good judge of character and had been impressed by the young woman, believing her to be a victim of circumstance; he could not in all conscience throw her to the wolves. He took out a clean handkerchief and patted his brow, on which an oily patina of fearful sweat had sprung as he contemplated various actions. He was a steadfast opponent of the corruption which was endemic in South African Government Institutions including Prisons, Police and Parliament and the leader of a task-force against it, yet he was also a family man with vulnerable relatives from his wife down to several grand-children.

One course was just to follow orders but he was well aware of a quote attributed to Burke, that all it takes for evil to flourish is for good men to do nothing. To this end he had been gathering evidence against high officials for years, piece by painful piece. Another course was to pervert the course of justice in a good cause by warning Miss Visser of her impending arrest but to do so without exposing himself was difficult and hazardous.

A third way would be to prematurely begin the huge anti-corruption clean-up he had been working towards for years but that might be even more dangerous to himself and those trusted colleagues who toiled with him, especially if it failed. His sharp brain had been juggling resources, consequences and evidence while he prevaricated and suddenly the pieces fell into place like the tumblers of a precision lock. He sat up straighter and reached for his secure telephone with resolve; perhaps now was the time to kick it all off. Sooner or later there had to be a beginning and there was no way to find out other than to do it. His office was swept daily by an Israeli-trained graduate Police Officer of the Technical Branch whom he trusted implicitly, not least because the boy was his nephew.

He dialled the personal cell-phone number of General Mervin Tumelo, Commanding Officer of the Military Police Agency. The MPA was the disciplinary body for all branches of the South African National Defence Force and was headquartered at Waterkloof Airstation, conveniently located between the cities of Pretoria and

Johannesburg. As the number rang Thandiwe's mind drifted back several years to the beginning of his task and his initial dismay. It was the Great Man himself who had, before his retirement, given him the job of heading up Operation Redemption and as the scale of the investigation and the power and ruthlessness of those involved became apparent Thandiwe had decided that the only way to successfully complete the mission was to use the resources of the military police rather than the civil authorities. They were far less exposed to the bribery and corruption endemic in the civil police, correctional and judicial systems where inducement and payoffs were common currency from the lowest officials to the highest.

Once the arrests began a National crisis would be precipitated. As well as detaining the suspects, anybody else involved in the Investigation including judges, lawyers and witnesses would have to be protected, as would their dependents, both for safety and to ensure their integrity. The magnitude and detail of the planning had been immense; all those involved in the scheme would have to be looked after indefinitely, free of outside influence such as threat or enticement. Transport between bases, prisons and courts would similarly be secure. The phone rang on and he was about to hang up when Tumelo's deep tones came on the line.

"Sorry about the delay Thandiwe but I was in a meeting; then I couldn't get this damn thing out of my pocket! What's happening my friend?"

"Operation Redemption is about to happen."

There was a brief pause.

"Are you serious? I never thought it would!" Mervin was a big heavy man, over six feet tall and strong but running to fat despite regular exercise. He was very black with a large forbidding face but his lumpish appearance belied a quick mind and sharp sense of humour honed by a lifetime in the armed forces.

"Deadly serious Mervin; realistically, what is the minimum notice you need to execute?"

"Bloody hell, bloody hell; let me just get this damn computer up, you've caught me on the hop Thandiwe. Can I call you back in fifteen minutes? I don't think there's anything to stop us……! How long can you give me if I need a bit of time?"

"Not more than an hour. I have received a direct instruction from one of our main suspects to make an arrest on suspicious grounds, of an important witness whose safety is at stake. One way or another I need to act swiftly."

"Leave it with me. Talk to you now."

Thandiwe sat back and breathed deeply, pulse racing as he envisaged the enormity of the exercise he was about to put into practice. The South African National Defence Forces had rehearsed their role many times in scenarios that were similar but disguised as Civil Defence operations against both outside and internal threats.

Security would be increased at all ports of entry and exit, and identity photographs circulated to pre-empt any rats that evaded the net and attempted to escape. Armed arrest squads would each be accompanied by a ranking Military Police Officer bearing a warrant already signed by the President. Once all the players, both hunters and hunted had been assembled on Military bases, legal proceedings would begin.

Movements of accused, witnesses and judicial personnel alike would be orchestrated under Military law. The President would announce a National State of Emergency, taking to himself any extra powers necessary to see that the guilty did not squirm from their responsibilities either through the delaying tactics of lawyers, or through direct violence directed at witnesses. It was intended that justice should be swiftly applied and the operation over within a month, after which an extraordinary general election would be held to signal a new beginning for South Africa, freed of the criminal financial leeches which had plagued the early years of Independence and slowed growth and progress. His secure cell-phone rang and he snatched it up.

"I can see no impediments to implementation my friend. All units fully manned and where they are supposed to be. Are you really ready? Shall I push the button?"

Thandiwe sighed.

"There is always a bit more to do but sooner or later one must shit or get off the pot. Push it Mervin and good luck to us all. We shall be talking often before we emerge from the far-end of this particular tunnel."

As soon as they were off the line he called Francois Steenkamp who answered promptly.

"Brigadier Thandiwe here, perhaps you remember me? The Welkom affair…"

"Of course; have you made any progress with the investigation?"

"Considerable. You know at the end of a harvest how all the rodents gather in the last bushels of corn before making a break for it? Well my Operation is at that stage. Unfortunately some are seeking to cover their guilt by eliminating witnesses, one of them being Miss Visser."

"Jesus Christ, you said that could happen, and that she might not even be safe in custody! What do you intend to do?"

"I have had you positively vetted and am seconding you as of now to my unit. Miss Visser knows and trusts you, so I would like you to act as her bodyguard until this is over."

"Had me vetted?" exploded Francois.

"Desist from the injured pride routine Steenkamp I don't have the time! Consider it a direct order and if you prevaricate I will have to put someone less reliable on it!"

"I'll do it, I'll do it. She's not being arrested?"

"An arrest warrant will be issued because I have been ordered to do so by a corrupt higher authority and for the time being I need to be seen to comply; all hell is going to break loose once the Mambas realise what is happening. So you must get to her first. You can provide cover as the Arresting Officer but take her somewhere safe and don't alarm her; she is a potentially valuable witness needing protection. Arm yourself and be prepared to use deadly force in the protection of the witness. Keep me informed but use your own judgement in securing her safety. Good Luck! I can give you half an hour to act before the warrant is executed."

-xxx-

CHAPTER THIRTEEN

On the Boeing 747 James drank a couple of beers and tried to relax but it was difficult with his emotions in turmoil. He was over fifty years old but felt little different to when he was twenty; he was thankfully free of any major medical problem such as beset many of his contemporaries; prostrate problems, cancers and failing organs. He could still mountaineer hard, fly with the best of them and work long shifts at arduous physical jobs but he was aware of a growing mental tiredness. The last thing he had expected at this age was to be still involved in a murderous personal vendetta with a boyhood enemy. There was a sense of fantasy attached to the whole scenario which he needed to shake off in order to deal with it properly.

Feelings of unreality and trepidation kept surging; he knew Katsiru posed a deadly threat to himself and his family, particularly Jemima though it seemed too incredible to be true. Yet according to the senior policeman investigating the gold hijack, the man would think nothing of killing to ensure her silence: what extraordinary coincidence had caused his own worst enemy to master-mind a heist that involved a daughter he didn't know he had until recently? He knew what he needed to do but after living so long in the normal world the thought of finding and hunting a man seemed bizarre.

His thoughts kept returning to Denzil Harcourt. They had been friends for much of his life and though in Rhodesia James had outranked him because he was a regular and Denzil a reservist, and in Namibia an Officer while Denzil was a non-com, there was something hugely dependable and comforting about the ex-Sergeant Major. Like Sergeant Simon Ndhlovu all those years ago, Denzil had warned him about leaving Katsiru alive; was it fair to involve him all these years later in what amounted to the planning of a murder? His friend was successful and settled; if James asked him for help and things went wrong he could spend what years remained in an African prison cell. Yet he was also the best hope of both finding and dealing with the ex-Dictator and in doing so to save Jemima.

His memory flicked to their departure from Rhodesia on the eve of independence, driving across the Limpopo River to join the South Africa Defence Forces. He and Denzil had cached some weapons, burying them just over the border. That would solve one problem that had been nagging at him. The other was how to find Katsiru, or

Lembede, or whatever the hell he called himself now. He had some addresses from his mystery caller but Sandro Marais could probably provide more accurate information, though he was also too much of an unknown quantity to be trusted very far. He fished in the capacious chest pockets of his Berghaus mountain coat for the packet containing documents. His South African firearms licence was among them but was it still valid? Much had changed since apartheid collapsed in 1994. George Bustamante should know, and he had handguns belonging to James and Loretta in his gun-safe. A vague plan, a sequence of necessary steps was falling into place as James ate his airline meal and tried to sleep, oblivious to the fact that outside influences were already rendering his nascent plans obsolete.

-xxx-

Francois Steenkamp looked at his watch in consternation. He had called Jemima's home and cell-phones repeatedly but only got her voicemail; he left a message each time. He went to her Sandton townhouse and rang the bell continuously for five minutes until a suspicious neighbour came out and threatened to call the police. Francois snarled at her and showed his badge.

"I am the bloody police! Have you seen the lady from this house today? It's important!"

"Ja, okay okay. She left about fifteen minutes ago in her car. I was in the garden and saw her go."

"Thanks!"

He reached for his phone and sent an urgent text.

"Jemima this is not personal! You must phone me immediately about the Welkom Hijack, and what Brigadier Thandiwe said about unfinished business. You are in danger!"

He paced agitatedly, wishing he had kept her house keys so he could get in out of sight of curious neighbours. Nothing happened and after five minutes he had a brainstorm and dialled her number from his police phone, in case she was deliberately not looking at messages from him. Sure enough she answered her Nokia right away. She hadn't had time to mess about with the new iPhone which was still charging by her bedside.

"Hello, who is this?"

"It's Francoise; don't hang up, you are in deep shit. I'll call you back on my phone. Answer this time, I am not messing about!"

"What's going on Francoise?" There was an edge of fear in her voice.

"I'll phone you back now on my own cell!"

Jemima clicked off the blue-tooth hands-free attached to her ear, then answered quickly when it buzzed again straight away.

"Listen, Thandiwe had to issue a warrant for your arrest but he doesn't want you in custody because they probably plan to kill you in jail. He appointed me to keep you safe until he straightens things out and gets these people in court. Where are you?"

"About fifteen minutes away on the R512 to Hartebeestport, we're spraying a farm near there. Who's 'They?' Oh shit, I can't just drop everything!"

"You will if you're dead. I'll meet you…no wait, wait. This might take a while, you need some stuff. Come back to your place, I'm there now. You can have five minutes to grab some things and then we're out of here."

"Where to? For how long?"

"Dunno, not long I hope. Move it! And be aware, watch for cars full of men, and don't get boxed at traffic lights and stuff, leave space so you can gap it if something kicks off. Maak gou!"

"Okay!"

Jemima's stomach swooped and a wave of terror washed over her as she braked abruptly onto the dirt hard-shoulder. Her heart-rate had jumped and the pulse was thudding in her ears. She executed a tyre-howling U-turn and stopped again facing the other way, slipping the .38 from her ankle-holster and checking the loads, then wedged it barrel-down in the crack between backrest and seat on the passenger side. She took several deep breaths. She was used to danger! With an effort she regained control.

"Be professional, just deal with it, as if it were an engine failure! Don't panic; slow down and be methodical!"

The fear was still there in the background but now she felt keyed up, alert, wired. And very angry; "Fuck them!" she shouted and jumped the clutch.

-xxx-

Thandiwe's superior, Director of the National Intelligence Service regarded the Director of Prisons with disdain. His opposite number in the correctional institution was fat, greedy, cowardly and worst of all he smelt; a kind of blubbery sweaty smell that was most offensive.

"Will Thandiwe do it?" asked the DOP in a quavering voice.

The other man depressed the cut-off button on his phone, severing the connection to Thandiwe and dialled another number, smiling thinly.

"I don't see why not but I'm a belt and braces man so I am about to hedge my bets and repeat the arrest order to some NIS Operatives I know who are definitely sympathetic to our cause; or in other words, implicated up to their necks."

He looked down at the newspaper on his desk and sneered.

"South Africa is being hijacked! Big deal! This reporter is another one who is going to get a visit soon!"

He spoke concisely into the phone and answered a couple of questions. Finally he nodded.

"That is correct. Apprehend Miss Visser at all costs; alive preferably but dead if necessary." He put down the receiver and smiled thinly at the DOP, wrinkling his nose and breathing through his mouth so as not to smell him.

"There you are Herman, you can relax now."

"I haven't relaxed for nearly twenty years! How did this bloody 'Black Mamba' person ever get so powerful that he can tell people like us what to do?"

The urbane NIS Commander threw back his head and laughed.

"Because we don't know who he is, do we? Probably not even Lembede does. But he knows about the skeletons in all our cupboards! Our little secrets and misdemeanours; or in your case Herman, bloody big ones! How many murders have been committed by the gangs let out of your prisons?"

-xxx-

Lembede beat an impatient tattoo on his knee as he drove, then looked at his watch. What time would the woman leave for work? The rush-hour into town was in full swing but he was going opposite the flow and making good progress. If she was not at home what could he do? He'd have to bring Marais in, he apparently knew all about her, where her spraying outfit was working. It would be far better if he did it now, at her home though; just another random mugging of a white woman in one of the most murderous towns in the world!

-xxx-

The NIS arrest team had the advantage of access to the vehicle number-plate recognition centre. It reported to their car by radio that an emerald-green Porsche Carrera registered to Jemima Visser had passed a camera on the junction of the R512 and N14 highway going

North fifteen minutes before, and then again going South five minutes later.

"If she's heading back home she'll probably come south to join the N1 Western bypass near Randburg, then follow it round to Sandton" said the arrest-team Sergeant to his driver. "Put the blue light on and cane it over there, we'll wait on the slip-road for her."

-xxx-

A hunch made Jemima turn east onto the Witkoppen road that paralleled the Western Bypass. There were road-works on it and the going was slow but she felt less conspicuous. Her stomach muscles were tense and she felt keyed-up, sharp as a razor, keeping a continuous all-round surveillance going. When the phone rang she actually jumped, tense buttock muscles jerking her in the seat.

"Where are you?"

"Witkoppen road heading for Fourways, then I'm coming down William Nicol and Bryanston Drive. Be about five, ten minutes."

"Okay. Don't hang about when you arrive, straight in and get your stuff. We'll go in my car, leave yours here; they will be looking for it soon if not already."

"Thanks a lot!"

"Just keep coming, it'll be fine."

-xxx-

Sandro pulled up at the gates of his colleague's mansion at 8am and an insolent-looking guard in plain-clothes appeared. He was a stroppy shit who fancied himself and figured he could diss the white man with impunity when his boss wasn't around. He was dressed in a cheap suit that bulged with a shoulder-holster and wore a tight garish tie that cut into his thick neck.

"Voetsek" he grinned, calling through the bars. "Boss isn't here and he said not to let anyone in."

Sandro put the Aston in 'park' and sauntered up to the gate.

"Ag please hey man, this is me. Lembede asked me to come by and pick up some stuff" he replied, getting right up close. The black bodyguard smirked derisively at Marais' subservient tone and also moved closer. Sandro's long arms darted through the bars, one powerful hand grabbing the tie and yanking. The guard pulled back, and against the resistance Sandro was able to smash his face repeatedly into the thick sharp-angled uprights, cuts appearing and blood flying. Sandro's other hand yanked a heavy automatic from the man's ostentatious holster, accessible as his jacket sagged open.

"How long ago did he leave you puss? Quick or I'll let your shit-for-brains out of that kak-ugly head!"

"Five minutes, only five minutes! Sorry boss!" spluttered the guard through pulped lips. Sandro knotted the tough tie tightly round the bars, pinning his face to the gate, then ejected the magazine and threw the heavy gun against his head in fury. It bounced off with a meaty 'clunk' opening another deep cut and the guard slumped semi-conscious, strangled noises coming from his throat.

"I hope that will improve your manners you fucking cheeky shit" snarled Sandro before jumping into the Aston and flooring it.

-xxx-

The radio crackled in the NIS vehicle.

"Your target just passed the recognition camera at Fourways heading South on William Nicol."

"Roger copied. Is there a camera at the N1 Highway junction with William Nicol?"

"Affirmative."

"Call us when she passes it asseblief."

The radio clicked twice in acknowledgment.

"Make off the blue light so we don't alert her and floor it Strydom! Try and beat her to the junction; you'll have to fly low!"

The driver was a petrol-head and needed no encouragement. He floored the accelerator of the supercharged Audi RS4 and the occupants' heads slammed against their headrests. Cars passed in a blur as it accelerated to sixty miles an hour in five seconds and shortly afterwards hit one hundred and fifty mph.

"Nyo kanyoko! Take it easy Strijdom you mad duus!" called a black Xhosa Detective-Constable from the back, grabbing for a hand-strap but the driver just neighed an insane laugh, swerving into the middle lane to undertake a Mercedes.

-xxx-

The Prime-Minister's cavalcade swept up to Broadcasting House in Pretoria and he stepped out, buttoning the jacket of his smart suit. The National Broadcasting Corporation staff prepared him and an anchor-man chatted with him over a cup of coffee before leading him into the studio and introducing him on air in sombre tones.

The Prime Minister reached into his pocket for a sheet of paper which he smoothed on the desk in front of him, then put on his spectacles and looked at the cameras.

"Fellow South Africans, today the Anti-Corruption Committee have ordered the beginning of an operation code-named "Redemption." Since Independence, our Nation has been plagued by powerful parasitic mafia-like organisations that have drained resources and diverted wealth that belongs to all into the pockets of an undeserving few. These organisations have also undermined the integrity of our Public Service Bodies to such an extent that nobody knows who to trust or who to turn to; they have stolen public funds dedicated to such projects as affordable house-building and education which should be leading to full employment, so thousands are without jobs, money to buy food or a place to live.

Because of this the President has courageously taken an unprecedented step by declaring a State of Emergency to finally curtail the appalling situation, and has announced Emergency Powers to deal with it. Meticulous evidence has been gathered against the most powerful and therefore most culpable of these criminals; they are to be given fair and transparent trials but if found guilty will be given very long custodial sentences so their malign influence shall be terminated; a system of amnesty has been compiled to run hand in hand with the prosecutions of the worst offenders. Those who have drifted or been forced into lesser offences will be able to come forward, admit to their involvement and give evidence.

The South African National Defence Force has been chosen to lead this operation and though you will be seeing a lot more of them in public I want to assure you that this is not a Military coup. Elected civilian authorities will remain firmly in control except those amongst them who have abused their position, and they will be removed and replaced by suitable deputies until such time as new elections can be held. Please cooperate and this regrettable necessity will soon be over, after which we can all enjoy a new dawn for our great Country.

-xxx-

Sandro was driving slickly, using the power and agility of the Aston to power northwards past slow-moving traffic, cursing the ordinary drivers with reactions like slugs who sat at traffic lights for five seconds before moving, drove in incorrect lanes and positioned themselves so badly at intersections that other cars couldn't get by. At one stage he drove onto the pavement outside a shopping mall and cruised along at thirty with parking meters swishing by his window and shoppers hopping and cursing. His phone was in the hands-free holder at eyelevel and he managed to punch in Jemima's number as he swerved in and out through the crush. It rang and rang, then went to answer-phone.

"Jemima where are you? Some shit is hitting the fan! Skakel me and be careful!" He punched off with a curse, glancing at his Rolex. She would probably already be at work but he decided to check her townhouse first.

-xxx-

Jemima glanced at the cell-phone ringing on the seat beside her. The screen showed the caller to be Sandro. She swithered, on the point of answering then decided against it. Right now time was precious and she didn't see how speaking to him would help, or even how far she could trust him. She let it go to answer-phone.

Driver Strijdom and the Sergeant noticed the tailback from Junction 95 off-ramp at the same time. The driver veered onto the hard shoulder and the Sergeant clicked on the siren, giving a couple of warning blips as they undertook stationary traffic, still doing over a hundred. As the ramp dipped down to the roundabout junction beneath the Highway Strijdom began to brake hard. There were cars backed up in the robot-controlled intersection which had yellow cross-hatching to prohibit entering the junction unless the exit was clear.

"Target just passed the camera South-bound on Bill Nicol" crackled the radio laconically and ahead Jemima's car rolled up to the cross-hatching where she paused, desperately willing the traffic ahead to move.

"Daars Sy!" yelled Strijdom just before an impatient car pulled onto the hard shoulder in front of him to try and creep a few spaces forward. He was forced to slam on the anchors.

"Stupid son of a bitch!" cursed the Sergeant and gave an outraged squawk on the siren. The Xhosa Detective wound down his rear window and hurled abuse at the civilian driver as Strijdom bounced through a shallow culvert to miss him. Jemima glanced right towards the sudden noise and her stomach swooped hollowly as if she'd flown into turbulence. A car full of men with a siren on: Not good!

Checking quickly left at a clear on-ramp she spun the steering wheel and floored the Porsche; it fish-tailed, tyres smoking, and roared up towards the Highway, her eyes glued to the mirror. The Audi roared straight across the intersection and followed her up the on-ramp. Blue lights began to blink on the grill and the howl of a siren screeched into her ears. There were several men in the car. Her phone had been on the seat beside her but when she glanced down it wasn't there, and the blue-tooth earpiece was only hands free on incoming calls. She spotted the handset on the floor and lunged downwards but the Porsche swerved left as she did so, forcing her to sit up and veer back right. Gravity slid the handset further away and it bounced against the far door before disappearing partly under the passenger seat. Jemima was in no doubt that the car behind was after her but she had no intention of stopping until she reached Francois, and the Porsche was a match for just about anything on the road. She dropped a gear and smoked it on joining the Freeway, howling right across the carriageway into the fast lane, filtering fluidly into the pattern and flashing an Alfa Romeo doing ninety out of her way.

-xxx-

Francois Steenkamp glanced impatiently at his watch, and paced anxiously in the sunshine. He was trying to give up smoking but there were some long butts in the ashtray of his car and he fished in the rank tray and smoothed one out, then lit the two inch stub with a plastic lighter from the glove compartment. Sucking heavily he looked at his phone in case, impossibly, it had rung and he'd not heard it. Nothing. His thoughts roiled; he still loved Jemima and the thought of something terrible happening to her made him feel physically sick and infuriatingly powerless. He punched her number again. Where the hell was she? She should be here by now! No answer. What the hell to do? He tried to focus on a plan but he didn't have much of one. Probably the best thing was just to get her to his place; it was a small-holding on a hill at Halfway House. Good for privacy and watching the approaches but he'd have to get rid of his maid who lived in a kia at the back; send her on a few days holiday maybe because everything was going to be on the news and if she recognised Jemima she might alert the Police. Where the hell was she dammit?

-xxx-

To begin with it looked like Jemima could outdistance the Audi as it lost ground slightly due to a heavier load of men but then a tour-bus pulled into the fast lane doing eighty miles an hour ahead of her. She was forced to brake down harshly from 130 mph, prevented from weaving left to undertake by other traffic. She cursed, flicked a glance in the mirror and saw the Audi racing up, blue grill-lights flashing and headlamps blazing. An arm came out of the rear window unmistakeably brandishing a hand-gun. She gritted her teeth and grabbed the butt of the .38, pulling the barrel gently from the seat cushions so as not to snag the stubby foresight. The way she saw it she had everything to lose and she was not about to let herself be arrested when she had done nothing wrong, especially after Thandiwe's warning, and she had no intention whatsoever of stopping until she reached Francois. He was a senior Police Officer and presumably could at least prevent them killing her.

The Freeway was curving right, banked slightly with a long drop on the left down to the parallel Witkoppen Road and Ritfontein-Ridge Nature Reserve. Her eyes flicked back up to the mirror and the Audi was nowhere to be seen; her head jerked about, searching. Where the hell could it have gone? A blur in peripheral vision caught her eye; it was on the hard-shoulder undertaking at an insane speed and would soon be able to get in front. Her mind was working like a super-computer and as though on a chess-board she saw a pattern open up amongst the vehicles in the three lanes ahead. Jemima gunned the Porsche, zig-zagging like a racing driver going through the field. Suddenly a car changed lanes unexpectedly and her only option was to swerve onto the hard shoulder to avoid it. She hurtled past a pantechnicon trundling along in the slow lane, only one hundred metres in front of the Audi and this time there were more weapons being waved about. She wound the tacho up still further until the engine was screaming, dust from the verge soaring into the sky.

Gammat Terblanche was cruising along the slow lane of the N1 in a huge 1987 Peterbilt B-train rig, pulling two long trailers coupled by fifth wheels. He was feeling mellow, smoking mild blow and listening to Nagtroepeor music from the Cape Town Carnival. He watched with mild interest as a Green Porsche driven by a mooi white meisie with terrified eyes appeared in his mirror, weaving in and out of lanes, obviously trying to get away from a thicket of plain-clothes cops in an Audi with blues on and the screecher going. If they were cops at all; these days it was hard to tell, they could just as easy be skellums trying to Ny her and steal her nice car. Gammat hated cops and robbers equally; they were both always shaking him down, giving him a hard time, the cops often fining him for petty infringements if he didn't submit to their omkopery. Why couldn't the fuckwits just get a proper job like him? There was always some small defect to find on a huge truck like this and whether he paid a fine or a bribe or protection money to gangsters, it always meant he was working for pretty much nothing that day.

His eyes narrowed as the Porsche was blocked in the fast lane and the Audi swerved across three lanes and began streaking up the hard shoulder like a rocket, one goon waving a gun from the rear driver's-side window. The Porsche began to zigzag again, picking up speed but got trapped and had to swerve onto the hard shoulder too, just in front of the Audi, passing Gammat on the left as if fired from a rifle.

"That chick got balls and she can sommer drive!" he breathed in admiration.

Slouched comfortably in an air-sprung seat, Gammat watched the Audi coming in his big nearside mirrors and with the dexterity of a top ping-pong player flicked the steering wheel left as it hurtled alongside. The truck's steel fender and hard tyre swatted the Police car aside with only a muted clang of metal and a few sparks.

The Audi, with trajectory drastically altered but velocity undiminished, smashed through the barrier and sailed into the air far ahead of Gammat. He threw back his head and laughed, then sang "Fly with the Eagles, kerels" and laughed some more at his own wit. He flashed the Porsche and made a two-fingered gesture towards the flying car. Jemima gasped, then punched her four-way flashers for two clicks in thanks and kept going. Now she was really in the shit though, if they somehow linked her with a fatal car accident involving Police Officers. Behind her from his high cab Gammat saw the doomed Audi's rear doors open and two bodies jump out.

"Won't do you any good boys!"

The car hit the ground far below and bounced back into the air, the other doors flying open as it somersaulted on at speed. Another body flew out and the next time it hit, the car caught fire, hurling flames like a Catherine wheel.

"Aina!" said Gammat and flicked the butt of his reefer out the window.

"Gan kak with the Devil maatjies!" he cackled. The beauty of it was, even if anyone had noticed, he couldn't possibly be prosecuted when the cops had been breaking the law by overtaking on the left! A few miles ahead three normal police patrol-cars raced up the next on-ramp and merged into the traffic, sirens howling and blues on. They braked and set up a rolling road-block, gradually edging down the speed.

-xxx-

Lembede listened to the Prime Minister's speech announcing Operation Redemption on Highveld Radio in disbelief. He'd tuned it trying to get traffic information and surely what he was hearing couldn't be right; his associates occupied positions of power so senior that they couldn't possibly be prosecuted. The Prime Minister's speech was followed by a Security Force spokesman who admonished the public to stay tuned and watch television when possible as names and photographs of wanted persons would shortly be screened repetitively until apprehended. Suspects should not be approached but reported on one of the announced numbers.

"Operation Redemption my arse, Witch-hunt more like" Lembede snarled aloud, glad that he had made the decision to arm himself and travel light. The GPS showed three miles to Bryanston.

-xxx-

Jemima saw many brake-lights coming on ahead and the vehicles getting denser, slowing appreciably. Her mind was computing routes and she took the next exit ramp down to Rivonia road, narrowly missing the rolling road-block which had now almost halted the East-bound Highway.

She pulled over, grabbed the cell-phone and called Francois.

"Where the hell are you?"

"Got chased on the Freeway and had to go too far east. I'm on Rivonia, be back there in about fifteen."

"Did you lose them?" he asked worriedly.

"I'll say. You won't believe it when I tell you. See you now!"

She was on very familiar ground and remained alert but started thinking too about what she needed from the house. Passport definitely, and she already had her new bank cards from a different bank, but they could mark her movements; cash then; there was several thousand rand in her small safe. Clothes, phone-charger, that was a must! But which phone? Both! What was that bloke's name that James had given her. Denzil something? The number was in her phone. If only her Dad had already arrived. Francois was right; they would have to take his car. She had a sudden good idea and decided to dump the Porsche on Bryanston golf-course behind her house and walk in. Ten minutes later she was there and could see the houses in her complex ahead. She slowed right down. There was a thick copse of trees beside the golf-course fairway near the road and waiting until there was no traffic coming she turned onto a narrow track for maintenance vehicles across the storm-drain, zipped across the grass and nosed the Porsche into the trees.

-xxx-

Sandro had Maneru Radio tuned, a local all-news equivalent of CCN, and excited reporters gabbled nineteen to the dozen about the State of Emergency, the Black Mamba and what it all meant.
"The massive Operation is already under way and many arrests of suspected Senior Black Mamba gang-bosses have already been made" said an announcer.

-xxx-

Francois Steenkamp looked at his watch yet again, in major discomfort from a full bladder but there was nowhere even remotely discrete to relieve himself on the big parking-area in front of several townhouses. He stiffened hopefully as an engine note sounded; a car came round the corner but it was only some ill-kempt black guy in a Ford jalopy with a lawnmower in the back; obviously a jobbing gardener.

The pressure in his bladder was excruciating and he walked rapidly towards a black iron gate leading to the communal gardens and swimming pool where there were toilets. He had to take a piss urgently and passed through the opening, almost running.

Lembede parked the little car where he could get to any of the front doors quickly and sat thinking about his next move.

-xxx-

Jemima walked quickly through the town-house entrance gate expecting to see Francois. She could see his car but he wasn't in it; where the hell was he? It was mid-morning and since most people were at work there was no-one about except a black gardener, fiddling with a mower on the ground behind a battered Fiesta. Lembede recognised her immediately. She went towards her front door, eyes scanning, as wary as a cat. She wondered again where Francoise was and kept facing outwards as she put her key in the lock. The gardener was semi-visible, his arm flying into sight repeatedly as he pulled the starter cord on his mower. It fired loudly, engine sputtering and he began to push it towards the front square of grass next to Jemima's house, head down, fiddling with the choke. She glanced round a final time and went in, taking out her phone to call Francois, pushing the door behind her to close it.

-xxx-

James had arrived in late afternoon and was queuing for Customs and Immigration at Oliver Tambo International. The process seemed even slower than usual and there was a greater presence of armed personnel in the large immigration hall than he remembered. Many were soldiers rather than police and they seemed highly alert. Behind each immigration official was an SANDF Officer, also scrutinising passport photographs and documents. There was a growing grumble of discontent amongst the tired passengers, mostly off long-haul flights, and growing speculation. James heard the word "coup" mentioned in a frightened voice by a nearby woman but her husband removed an earpiece, shaking his head and James could hear the tinny voice of a radio broadcaster from the FM radio on the man's cell-phone.

"Don't panic Mary it's not a military coup, just some police operation to tackle organised crime; I've got it on the news."

Containing frustrated impatience with difficulty, James got his own phone out. He'd better call Jemima first of all.

-xxx-

The front door slammed back open as Jemima was pushing it closed sending her reeling into the corridor and she went down in a sprawling heap as Lembede crashed through. She lost her grip on the phone and it bounced across the floor, hitting the wall and coming to rest in the shadows. The heavy impact caused it to switch off. The door banged against the corridor wall and bounced off, swinging partly shut behind Lembede as he struggled to clear the Makarov, awkward and ungainly with the silencer attached, from his pocket. Outside the lawn-mower engine roared at full throttle and blue oily smoke drifted in through the door.

Bladder relieved, Francois walked back through the iron gate, then noticed the door to Jemima's house swinging shut with only an inch or two to go. A blaring mower was parked outside. He lunged forward to reach the entrance before it closed, tripped on the brick verge and flew headfirst towards the opening, cracking his head against the wood and knocking the door open again. Lembede spun round in surprise and fired instinctively. Francoise gave a hoarse shout of agony as the bullet thudded home, throwing his body against the wall where it twitched spasmodically, feet thudding on the parquet floor. A dark, fast-spreading pool of blood began to spread out beneath him, creeping across the shiny wood. Jemima screamed and scrabbled towards Francois on her knees. Lembede saw the revolver in her ankle holster beneath the flight-suit and he trained the Makarov muzzle on her.

"Hold it! Draw your weapon with finger and thumb then slide it over."

Jemima had to comply and he scooped it up and placed it in his pocket.

"Now your cell-phone, pass it here!"

She grabbed it off the floor, tossing it at him and he caught it adeptly, left-handed.

"Who the hell is this idiot on the floor?"

"My fiancé, he needs attention."

"He doesn't, he'll be bled out long before anything can be done."

"You callous bastard!" shouted Jemima crawling closer to Francois. There was a small hole in his shirt which made a slurping sound. She moved his coat aside, tugged the garment loose at his waist and lifted it, exclaiming at the ugly little wound and his heaving chest. Francois's handgun was exposed and she grabbed for it.

"Forget it or I'll kill you right now; pass it over, and his telephone, and you might get to live a few minutes more."

She froze momentarily, trembling in reaction, then complied.

"Right bitch, what really happened on the Welkom hijack?"

"Don't call me a bitch! I knew you were a nasty bastard the minute I first set eyes on you at Lanseria; you're just a common criminal!"

"There is nothing common about me! I am the ex-President of Zimbabwe and soon will be again!"

Jemima sneered in scathing derision.

"Don't think so! My Dad recognised you from a photograph on my phone straight away and he's on his way here now. Even if you do something to me he'll tell the authorities who 'Lembede' really is and then it'll be off to the International Court where you'll be tried for genocide against your own people and exposed as a seedy gangster; I hope they hang you!"

Lembede was looking murderous.

"Who the hell is your damn father? What photograph?"

"The photograph I took of a Kudu in Botswana during your Thune Mine inspection, with you in the foreground. And my father is James Hacking."

Lembede looked as if he'd been hit by a bus and his mouth worked soundlessly for a few seconds, unable to keep up with the thoughts racing through his head; by what ridiculous coincidence had the daughter of his greatest enemy become involved in his life too? It was almost enough to make him believe in some malicious deity moving humanity like pawns for amusement.

"I told Marais to get rid of all those photographs when we were in Botswana!"

She almost mentioned her camera phone then thought better of it.

"Well my Dad has the photo, complete with a gps location and the date; that's going to screw your bullion and diamond laundering scam through Thune mine hey Silas?"

"Don't talk to me in that tone of voice you young Umfaazi!" hissed Lembede; he twitched the Makarov threateningly, gesturing with it towards the open lounge door.

"Get in there; where is your bloody Father now Umfaazi?"

"On his way out from England."

Lembede crossed to a television, picked up the remote control and found a news channel. He watched in glowering silence for some minutes, thinking hard. If Hacking was on his way to South Africa, either Malinga had failed, or would be following.....or had turned traitor and given the Rhodesian Lembede's secrets for his own ends. Perhaps everybody saw him as an old Lion too weak to defend his territory. According to the news broadcasts he'd heard, the Redemption Operation against organized crime and the Black Mambas in particular was gathering momentum. The authorities were naming dozens of high-profile suspects on television and showing id photos, warning the public not to approach them but help the Armed forces by reporting sightings. Jemima could see into the hall. She went back to Francois and as gently as possible began to tug the unconscious policeman into the lounge by his armpits, leaving a trail of blood on wood and carpet.

"Leave him!" ordered Lembede but she ignored that, rolling Steenkamp partly onto his front in the recovery position and gasping at the fist-sized exit in his back. She stood and went into the kitchen, grabbed cling-film, scissors from a draw, a bottle of Dettol and some tea-towels. The black man strode in, grabbed her elbow in a painful grip and dragged her back to the lounge. Wrenching free she knelt again, splashed Dettol liberally in the back wound and plugged it with tea-towels, then eased Steenkamp onto his back, putting cushions from the settee under his head and a throw over his lower body. Cutting Francois' shirt off she swabbed gently round the sucking wound with Dettol and then spread cling film on his chest, trying to remember the treatment on her first aid course for an open pneumothorax injury. On her knees she shuffled to a desk drawer, grabbed a roll of thick cello-tape and taped three sides of the cling-film down, to let air out but not in, then smoothed it down to stick to his chest. His agonised breathing seemed to ease slightly and she covered his top half too. It wasn't much but better than nothing. She stood and looked at her assailant.

"So are you the head Honcho then Silas?" mocked Jemima. "The legendary Black Mamba who pulls all the levers?"

Lembede sneered arrogantly.

"The Mambas are a purely commercial domestic operation driven by greed, in which I invested my capital and expertise for a phenomenal profit. The money will speed my return to power in Zimbabwe and give me a platform from which to unite the whole of Southern Africa in a political and commercial block that will eclipse even the rise of the BRIC economies! The Black Mamba controls a crime syndicate; I intend to control Zimbabwe and influence all of Southern Africa."

Jemima snorted.

"Don't think so! My father will soon expose you as a brutal delusional maniac, it's never going to happen!"

Lembede gave an ugly chuckle.

"Hacking won't get the chance because I am going to annihilate him first, and it will be you who brings him to me! We are old acquaintances you see, with unfinished business between us."

He tossed the TV remote onto a settee and pulled the GoldLock secure cell-phone from his scruffy jacket, selected a contact and pushed the call button, then spoke sparingly.

"It is Lembede; I need to be uplifted urgently but discreetly. Can you see my position from the phone's GPS function?"

He listened intently to the rustling voice in his ear as it answered.

"Affirmative Sir; the helicopter will put down across from your location, on the golf-course fairway at eighteen thirty hours. Darkness will offer less for prying eyes to see; use standard light identification signals to the pilot."

"Copied; there will be two packs. Make sure there is full fuel in case of emergencies."

"Roger that."

A loud knock sounded at the door, followed by the doorbell ringing and Lembede looked up, startled.

"Get up the stairs, immediately and be quiet" he hissed, following her.

-xxx-

CHAPTER FOURTEEN

Sandro arrived in front of Jemima's house and got out of his car warily; hers was not there. He went to the front door and stood indecisively, called her phones for the umpteenth time. He could faintly hear the landline ringing when he put his ear to the door despite the roar of an unattended lawnmower close behind. He stepped across in irritation and closed the throttle right down, so it sputtered into silence, looking round for the user. No-one came so he knocked and rang the bell, then listened again. After a few seconds he walked through the gate and round to Jemima's garden where he peered in through the glass patio doors, shielding his eyes because the bright sun made them reflect like a mirror; he looked carefully but couldn't see anyone inside. There were several possible reasons why she wasn't answering her phone and he needed to check with the ZU-KAT crop-spraying outfit before he began to panic. He tried Lembede's phone quickly but it rang out too so he jumped into the Aston and headed for Hartebeestport.

Standing well back from an upstairs bedroom window Lembede watched him go; he was able to see the woman across the landing, sitting on the bed in her own room where he'd roughly placed her. He had been tempted to let the white man in and kill him as a precaution because of what he knew but hadn't been quick enough. Jemima's heart was thudding rapidly as she grabbed the new iPhone from its charger and slipped it into a leg-pocket on her baggy flight suit just as Lembede appeared, opened her closet and rifled behind the clothes on hangers, looking for a gun-safe.

"Any other weapons?" he barked and she shook her head.

"Okay, downstairs again to the kitchen."

Once there he began to rummage and came up with a medium sized rucksack in the broom cupboard which he proceeded to fill with groceries from her recent shop. He took bread, cold meats, tins of fish and meat with ring-pull lids, packets of biltong, peanuts, and two plastic 1 litre bottles of diet coke. Afterwards they went back upstairs and he watched the news on television again while they waited for the helicopter.

-xxx-

The ZU-KAT team were not where Sandro had last visited them and he spent valuable time finding the farmer to ask if he knew where they had gone next. He did know and gave elaborate directions which Sandro foolishly tried to memorize instead of writing down. Half an hour later after several wrong turns he was at the edge of a soggy field where an aluminium irrigation pipe had become disconnected, turning the red dusty land into a quagmire. He was into it almost before he knew and when he tried to back out the Aston Martin's slick tyres spun and dug in. After five minutes of trying all his best bush-driving tricks to escape and covering the heavy car with mud he admitted defeat and began to run back to the farm, hoping to get towed out with a tractor.

-xxx-

Lembede had taped Jemima's hands behind her. Ten minutes before the helicopter was due he stood up and released them.

"You are going to drive my Ford across to the golf-course. If anything untoward happens, I will shoot you dead. Understand?"

She nodded her head sullenly. The helicopter arrived on time at dusk and Lembede illuminated the ground with the Fiesta's headlights. The machine's spotlight also shone down. It landed safely and they were signalled aboard.

Getting his car unstuck had taken Sandro hours and finding that Jemima hadn't been seen at work all day he was racing back to her house to check yet again and break into her house if necessary. He braked hard as he saw a hovering chopper landing cautiously on the golf-course and his headlights glinted on the paintwork of her Porsche parked halfway under some trees. He backed up, tyres howling and drove over the culvert, his lights further illuminating the LZ. There was a small Ford car parked with its lights on too. Shading his eyes he was just in time to see his business partner about to enter the aircraft cabin.

"Silas! Hold it, what's going on?" he yelled and ducked back as Lembede aimed a handgun towards him, without firing. A second later the helicopter was noisily lifting off. On board, Jemima's abductor pushed her into a rear seat and secured the seatbelt over her lap. There were two black ex-Zimbabwe military pilots in the cockpit of the aircraft which he had purchased in South Africa and based at the Botswana farm; for the last few days it had been on Standby at Lanseria. Lembede put on headphones and spoke to them in Shona which Jemima couldn't understand.

"File an in-flight plan with South African ATC for Mokopane but pass to the west. Let them think we have landed there and then proceed to Thune farm for fuel."

Jemima was wondering who had been in the car that suddenly appeared as they were leaving. All she had seen were headlights and a dim figure; it had been impossible to hear anything. Her mind was racing; who could she text or call if the opportunity arose? If Brigadier Thandiwe was straight and could somehow be informed that Lembede and Katsiru, ex-president of Zimbabwe, were one and the same, the policeman would probably mobilise all neighbouring countries' law enforcement bodies but it was a big if. Theo then, or the name James Hacking had given her. She cursed herself for not having done something as soon as her Dad made the connection. Badly frightened but also outraged, her mind churned with ideas, possibilities and fears.

On the ground Sandro tapped the South African registration letters of the helicopter into his phone notepad in case he forgot and tapped his teeth thoughtfully with it, then decisively dialled a number. He was hoping like hell Jemima was on the aircraft because if she wasn't the alternative was too awful to contemplate.

-xxx-

When James eventually cleared customs and immigration it was six pm at night. He'd tried several times to phone Jemima on the cell he had bought on his recent trip but her house and mobile just rang out. He quickly rented a car and phoned Loretta's brother George.

"James, thank God, we've been expecting you! You'd better get over to Jemima's house fast. Some guy named Sandro Marais just called Theo with a story about her being in trouble and possibly abducted in a helicopter; they're going to meet at her place. Theo's leaving now and I'm really glad there's someone to watch his back."

"Okay, I'll see him there. Listen George before he leaves, give him my .38 and Loretta's automatic from your gun-safe please, with spare ammunition and magazines. How are we going to get into the house?"

"Theo has a key, he used to look after the joint when she was away for long periods, to water the plants and stuff."

"OK I'm on my way. Tell Theo to wait outside if he's there before me, we need to be damn careful until we know what's going on!"

James saw Theo's 750i BMW parked on the townhouse carpark at a discreet distance from her front door, next to Sandro's Aston. Theo and Sandro got out and they converged, exchanging peremptory greetings. James detected an atmosphere between the two younger men straight away.

"Okay, where's Jemima and what's going on?" he asked Sandro grimly.

"I saw Lembede climbing into a helicopter on the golf-course, and her Porsche is parked there so I don't know for sure. Maybe she's hiding in her house, not answering the phone, or maybe he took her with him but she wouldn't have gone voluntarily. I had a quick look through a little Ford hatchback parked there without finding anything; we need to check the house next."

"This is his bloody fault" snapped Theo.

Sandro tensed.

"My skuld? If you hadn't sold the bloody mine they would never have met!"

"Leave it, both of you. Sandro, you go round to the garden while Theo and I go in the front. Just let me prepare my weapon in your car."

Theo let him in; they immediately noticed the stickiness of Steenkamp's blood under their feet and could smell it too.

"Oh shit, Jemima? Are you all right?" Theo shouted as James grabbed his arm.

"Hold it man, we need to be cautious" he hissed.

With drawn weapons they opened the lounge door and advanced cautiously. Raucous breathing sounded and James snapped on a light, spotting Francois at once.

"Let Sandro in through the French windows then examine that guy, I'm going to check the other ground-floor rooms and upstairs" said James with his heart in his mouth. Quickly but cautiously he did so, checking anywhere a person might hide or a body be hidden. There was nothing but his relief was tinged with continued fear for her whereabouts and well-being. He jogged downstairs, knelt and briefly examined Jemima's rudimentary first aid on the policeman.

"She's not in the house. Anybody know this bloke?"

"Yes, he's a policeman, he and Jemima used to be together. He helped her out after the hijacking" replied Theo.

"Better call an ambulance right away, but not the police. Sandro, what do you think is going on?"

"Well according to Theo, the investigating Officer of the Gold hijack, Brigadier Thandiwe, warned Jemima that Lembede might be involved and might want to eliminate her as a witness. If she's not here then I hope she's okay; would he have bothered abducting her instead?"

James took a deep breath.

"It's possible, because Lembede is actually ex-president Spencer Katsiru of Zimbabwe; if he knows I am Jemima's father, he would like nothing better than to kill me, he's already tried several times. Probably that is why he has her, as bait for me."

There was shock and disbelief on his companions faces.

"Don't ask why right now, it's a long story and we need to make a plan."

Sandro clicked his fingers.

"True. Listen, I put a GPS tracking device like a credit card in Lembede's wallet just recently and we need to know where the hell that prick is heading right now with Jemima. I'll fire up her computer and see if the transmitter is working."

He crossed to the PC, turned it on, hit a couple of function keys that allowed him to bypass the password and waited for windows to boot.

"How did you do that?" asked Theo.

"Miss-spent youth!" he rattled on the keyboard and swished the mouse, loading an app through internet explorer; a program similar to google-earth appeared on the screen with a pulsing arrow showing the current location of something on a large map, and a mouse-dropping trail behind it.

"Bingo" he breathed, zooming in and then standing back. "Look where the bastard is!" Theo and James leaned forward.

"Looks like Thune Farm at Selibe-Pikwe in Botswana!" said the younger man.

"You know what?" said James; "we need to get out of here before the Ambulance arrives because they may bring police and I don't want to get tied up in all that bullshit while Jemima is in danger." He stopped abruptly as a loud knock sounded on the door.

-xxx-

Julius Jongintaba had very strong feelings for his boss, almost amounting to hero-worship, so when at the end of the day Jack Dowding had still not been able to contact Jemima, he volunteered to go past her house and check; on knocking he was met at the front door by a large revolver pointing at his nose. When it was established who he was James waved him in; they had met at the ZU-KAT site and Sandro knew him too.

"Kind of you to offer help Julius. Right, fast planning; Theo, if necessary can we use your Beechjet?"

"Certainly; you still certified James?"

"Yes."

"What about you Julius?"

Jongintaba nodded.

"Affirmative, I'm rated on several business jets but I'm a bit rusty."

"Okay, so we can get there in Theo's jet but we haven't got much fire-power between us" remarked Sandro. "Question is, what will he do next, park there in Botswana awhile or continue north to his muckers in Zim?"

Theo smoothed his hair worriedly.

"Dunno. We can't just go howling around Africa waving pistols like vigilantes but can we afford to involve the police either? Brigadier Thandiwe gave Jemima an emergency number for his cell in case she felt threatened and offered her protective custody which she refused. I made her give me the number. I'm not sure he can be trusted though, there is this huge Operation against organized crime and corruption going on."

The sound of sirens became faintly audible and James nodded impatiently.

"We can discuss that in a minute. There might be police coming with the ambulance anyway and I don't want to get bogged down. Leave the door open on the snub so the medics can sort that poor guy out and let's hit the road. We'll take all the cars and meet at that pub nearby in Rivonia, the Fox."

-xxx-

The helicopter landed at Thune farm; Aviation fuel tanks containing Avtur and Avgas had been installed on the airfield and the pilots were instructed to refuel the chopper with turbine fuel, leaving Jemima, hands tied with tape, in the aircraft. Lembede had removed the cumbersome suppressor from his Makarov and paced outside with it partly concealed in his jacket pocket, obviously thinking furiously. Two vehicles driven by armed black-clad security men arrived from the farm buildings. He climbed into one 4x4 and could be seen talking; the apron was brightly lit by floodlights operated via proximity switches and if she tried to run for it she would be in plain sight and close range.

Jemima began to wriggle and managed to get her taped hands to the pocket of the flight-suit where she could feel her new IPhone. It was not zippered and she began to shove her bound thumbs underneath the lump, working it to the top of the pocket. Finally it toppled onto the carpeted floor. She grabbed it awkwardly and hit the "on" button, scrolled with both thumbs to an entry in the address book, then frantically typed a text message, gaze flickering from the screen to the outside. She saw Lembede coming over and hastily pressed "send". He was followed by two of the security guards and she fumbled desperately to turn the phone off and get it back in her pocket, not wanting to run the battery down and knowing that even switched off it could be triangulated and her position fixed. He slid the door back and looked at her contortions suspiciously, just as she got it put away.

"What is the matter with you Umfaazi?"

She writhed some more. "I need to go to the lavatory, urgently."

"Take her" he ordered two of the men and her hands were freed but she had to squat in the shadows just beyond the floodlights. It afforded some privacy but not much. She was shoved back into her seat by Lembede.

"You will stay in the aircraft and be given water and rations but you may not leave it except for bodily functions. These men will not hesitate to kill so don't even think about escaping."

"What's going to happen? How long am I going to be here?" she asked furiously but he ignored her, got into a truck and departed. Jemima's mind was working overtime but after a while she fell into an exhausted doze.

-xxx-

It was a warm evening so they sat outside at the Fox, well away from other customers. All ordered coffee or soft drinks and hamburgers, not knowing when they would eat next.

"I don't think we can involve the police" said James. "One of Katsiru's main men contacted me to sell him out, and he specifically warned me not trust the authorities because they are heavily corrupted by the Black Mamba gang. On the plus side there are some important people in Zimbabwe who owe me favours and might be able to help, and a friend here called Denzil Harcourt with connections in the Airforce. I'm going to call him before we do anything else."

"Bloody hell, so you know Denzil?" said Sandro.

James paused.

"Yes, do you?"

"Ja man, I did National Service as a young troopie in the Parabats and fought in SWA/Namibia."

"I've had a nagging feeling we'd met before; Machine Gun Marais, the 7.62 music man right? I was there too with Denzil. Christ you were young."

"Ja I lied about my age to get in. Later I earned some good bucks with Jonas Savimbi and UNITA in Angola, fighting the Cubans and MPLA; that's where I ran into Denzil again. He was close to the boss-man and the CIA; we even went to New York with Savimbi as bodyguards when he met with George Bush. You know, there was money just sloshing around that place, mainly diamonds; you had to be really stupid not to be able to start a little nest-egg. He and I did some really hairy ops together. He's kind of like the only Dad I ever had but don't for fuck's sake tell him I told you that! One of my specialities is surveillance and communications and I look after Denzil's comms. How do you know him?"

"I was with the crazy bugger in Rhodesia. So, let's talk about what to do next; tell us what else you know about Lembede and Jemima, Sandro."

"Ja okay; I already told you how our business involvement came about. So one day he blocks me, do I know anything about diamonds? Well I used to; Unita took maybe $4 billion US out of Angola in diamonds, to finance the War and line the top ou's pockets. Most of the mercenaries took at least some of their wages in stones too and I became a dealer as well, buying their stones and selling for a profit. So Lembede had this idea to get boycotted 'blood' diamonds from the Chiadzwa diamond field cheap and sanitize them through that farm in Botswana, and I gave him my contact in Amsterdam from the old days, horrible bastard called Tahamata. It was all going good then, because he's already in with the Black Mambas and their heists and has an idea to ship stolen gold through the mine too; hence the hijacking of Jemima's bullion aircraft, and why maybe he wants her out of the way. That's what I know; so what about this ex-Zimbabwe president number?"

"Well Lembede is ex-President Katsiru and probably he wanted that money to finance a comeback in Zimbabwe. Denzil and I made a bad mistake not scribbling him in 1980 when we had the chance, and if he knows I'm Jemima's father, he'll probably use her to get at me. Problem is, we don't know she's with him for sure."

"We've got nothing else to go on, we have to assume she is, and follow my electronic tag."

Theo and Julius were listening open-mouthed. The discussion was interrupted by a trill as Theo's phone received a text message and the others watched as he opened it.

"Shit, it's from Jemima" he said and read aloud;

"theo, francois shot by lembede my house he is hijacker aka ex-zim president katsiru we both need help my current location thune farm helicopter hostage pls phone my dad james hacking jem"

"At least its confirmation she's still alive" said James flatly and called Denzil. This time he answered immediately and with the phone in the middle of the table on speaker, a hurried 'O' Group was held. Finally Denzil summed things up.

"James, I know your primary concern is Jemima's safety but this affects Zimbabwe big-time too. I'm going to contact Simon Ndhlovu, he's as high as they get in Zim intelligence and between us I'm sure we can work something out. Sandro you bloody skellum, I need to talk to you about a few things too. I'll get back to you shortly."

He was as good as his word.

"Right, how do like this plan? We all fly in right now to Airforce base Makhado at Louis Trichardt, me and my guys in the Aviocar, your team in the Beechjet. It's only about ninety klicks from there to both Thune farm and the arms-cache James and I left years ago, if we should need it. My mate Major Tuckies Prinsloo commands 102 Reserve Squadron there, we'll make like it's a planned exercise. I'll have five of the silenced dirt bikes so Sandro could lead a recce or assault at the mine in under three hours, taking Theo for local knowledge and three others. Simon advises that the Zim Airforce has managed to re-equip two squadrons of Lynx 337 Skymasters with over-wing machine-guns, Gatlings, 37mm rocket launchers and Napalm. He and two of the Lynxes are heading for Masvingo Airport shortly. It is in a direct line between the Botswana farm and Grand Reef, which he thinks Katsiru is most likely to make for next if he departs the farm. The two Skymasters could potentially do an intercept and force his helicopter down."

James nodded. "Sounds like an excellent interim plan anyway."

-xxx-

Spencer Katsiru contacted his Commanders at Grand Reef. They had informers in the Zimbabwe National Army who believed that the Militia's best chance of mounting a coup was immediate; the regular army was rapidly growing in both head-count and morale. He decided to fly to Grand Reef via Chimoio in Mozambique to brief the North Koreans on his intentions. Flying too low to be detected by Zimbabwean radar, the most direct flight-path would take them thirty kilometres east of Masvingo City centre over Lake Mutinkwi, two excellent visual reference points even in darkness, and then directly over the high ground of the Chimanimani mountains to Chimoio.

After being served food in the farmhouse he retired to one of the bedrooms to rest for a few hours and lay thinking. The purge on organized crime in South Africa would probably peter-out as they usually did, and if necessary he could change his identity again and become someone else with power and influence there. By then he might anyway be Premier of Zimbabwe again, and visiting as a Head of State, not just a business investor. The white woman was a complication; on the one hand she presented him with an opportunity to even the score with James Hacking once and for all and move on. On the other she was a liability with the potential to have him arraigned as an accomplice on murder charges. Military action was the main priority, before the window created by President Mpofu's under-manning of the army closed again. Hackings daughter could kick her heels and her father could fret meanwhile. He was probably already in South Africa thought Katsiru, just before falling into a light doze.

-xxx-

At Airforce base Makhado Sandro had argued that the best they could hope for was a chance to snatch Jemima, and for that no more than two men was the best number, since they would be operating illegally in Botswana. He took Theo and at 0330 hours, stiff from the long ride on dirt bikes, they approached the Thune Mine airfield on foot to verify if the helicopter was still there. They bellied down and looked through the green-tinged night-scopes of their R4 folding-butt assault rifles, identifying two guards pacing idly back and forth, one smoking. Engines sounded and before long headlights could be seen approaching. Floodlights were suddenly switched on making the night-sights flare out and playing havoc with their night vision. Two pilots strode into the light, one climbing into the P1 seat and the other starting to do a quick pre-flight of the exterior while half a dozen security guards with automatic weapons deployed round the LZ facing outwards. Lembede appeared, a rifle slung over his shoulder and carrying a rucksack and briefcase. He slid back the main cabin door and as the turbine began to whine up and the rotor to turn, the watchers clearly heard Jemima's raised voice and she appeared crouched at the cabin door, wrists tied in front of her. Lembede pushed her roughly back inside.

"What the fuck are we going to do?" hissed Theo, sighting through the iron sights.

"Nothing; if we try to disable that chopper with gunfire there is a very good chance shrapnel will kill Jemima or that the whole thing will burn. If we initiate a fire-fight we might zap her by mistake or they might on purpose."

Theo dropped his eye to the open sights again, looking for a place to shoot at and disable the aircraft. "We can't do nothing, Christ knows where they'll take her next, this might be our only chance!"

Lembede and the second pilot boarded and closed up the doors.

Sandro gripped the other man's rifle-muzzle and pulled it aside, holding it with enough strength that Theo could not resist, surprising him.

"Our time wasn't wasted; we've established that Lembede and Jemima are aboard. Denzil will be able to track the helicopter when it moves, on that program I showed you. Simon Ndhlovu has huge resources available to mobilise if they head into Zimbabwe. I'm going to report now, then we'll bug out back to Louis Trichardt ready for another attempt when the odds are in our favour."

Theo thumped the earth with his fist in frustration as they began to wriggle backwards into the scrub. As the helicopter lifted off Sandro switched on their secure military radio and talked to Denzil and the team at Louis Trichardt. The time was 0500 hours.

"Roger Sandro, copied, your transmitter is still working and the targets initial heading is north-east into Zimbabwe. We are moving north now to Masvingo Airfield to RV with Simon Ndhlovu and the Skymasters, our groundspeed is roughly twice the helicopter's. Recover yourselves to here and see Major Tuckies, I'll keep him in the loop."

"Copied; good luck, out" said Sandro and told Theo the news.

Taxiing out at Makhado James noticed several pilots sitting in the cockpits of their Saab Gripen fighters at combat readiness and wondered why. Denzil departed first but James arrived at Masvingo Airport well ahead of him in the jet, and landed just after dawn on the main six-thousand foot tarmac runway 17/36. The tower directed him to shut down beside the two camouflaged Skymasters and a helicopter, which were parked at one threshold of the four-thousand foot grass airstrip 10/28 which crossed the main almost at right-angles. It was well away from prying eyes. Some glider-trailers and a few assembled gliders stood around a small building like a clubhouse nearby. James thought there must still be a few people in Zimbabwe with money for leisure pursuits. It was the first time he had seen Simon Ndhlovu for over nine years and he was offered a welcome cup of tea for breakfast from the billy on a small gas stove.

"I am sorry we have to meet again in such unpleasant circumstances James. We will do everything in our power to effect a safe recovery of your daughter. In the Eastern Highlands a large joint-service Offensive Operation is currently underway in Manicaland against Lembede's Militias. Grand Reef has been surrounded and our other Ground-attack Lynx's are overhead there as we speak. A sky-shout will announce that their commander, ex-President Katsiru has been detained, and order all the Militia present there to lay down their arms and surrender to the ground columns, or be annihilated. Primrose is offering free pardons to all who submit but she isn't going to pull punches; one of our Skymasters opened proceedings by blasting an enemy 'Stalin's Organ' multiple rocket-launcher to bits on Mutare Heights a few minutes ago."

"You've been busy, that could have wreaked havoc on the whole city, and the Mutare airfield." replied James with a tense smile, sipping the strong sweet tea. "All you have to do now is actually detain Katsiru without jeopardizing Jemima; tall order!"

"We had to strike quickly and hard. The Militia in Manicaland was a growing and serious threat and now it appears that just as we feared all those years ago when we discussed it in the Vumba, Katsiru has returned to haunt Zimbabwe. President Primrose has been talking to the Premiers of Mozambique and South Africa. SA has promised us some jets if we need them, and the North Korean Ambassador has been called in front of the Mozambique president."

"What about the plan to intercept Katsiru's helicopter?"

"Still on."

He indicated the four crewmen standing talking near the Lynxes.

"The guys are about ready to take off. As soon as Denzil is on the ground again he can tell us where his tracking device places the helicopter, we haven't picked anything up on radar yet, Katsiru is obviously flying low and clandestine. But don't worry, we have a number of ideas up our sleeve both to secure your daughter's safety and deal with Katsiru."

Twenty kilometres south of Masvingo airport at eight thousand feet AGL and west-abeam Lake Mutinkwi, Denzil Harcourt noticed a moving shadow far below, to starboard. The dark shape moved across the waters of the sizeable dam, silvered by fading moonlight. Curiosity piqued, he extinguished all lights and put the Aviocar into a steep descent to intercept the other aircraft which was heading northeast towards Mutare. It was a helicopter, also flying without lights and he confirmed it was the Registration Sandro had advised. He swept across the top of it and banked left towards Masvingo, climbing and thumbing his mike to call James and Simon Ndhlovu on the ground.

-xxx-

"Who or what the hell was that?" asked Katsiru as the helicopter bounced in sudden turbulence. A black twin-engined aircraft had overflown them close by and was climbing away again, not showing any nav lights. The pilot in charge shrugged.

"We're monitoring the Advisory frequency and they didn't call us. Didn't catch the registration either; probably smugglers or just some bored nosy-parker jerking us around for a cheap laugh."

"Out here in the middle of nowhere? I don't believe in coincidences like that! Steer more easterly towards Birchenough Bridge and the Mozambique border, I want to keep some options open. You can track that road, the A9."

A suspicion was starting to form and he turned towards Jemima. "Have you got a tracking device or something?"

"What? Don't be ridiculous, why would anyone have such a thing?"

She could see the burgeoning rage and paranoia on his face and shrank from it because she had been intermittently turning her IPhone on for fifteen minute stretches in the hope it could be triangulated, if indeed a search for her had been started. The cell was a possible instrument of salvation and without it she would feel utterly lost. Katsiru was trying to think if he himself might have been subject to a tracking device because of the investigation against him as part of Operation Redemption. He had changed from his scruffy gardener's clothes in Botswana and now wore jungle fatigues; virtually the only thing in common with his previous clothing was his wallet. He pulled it out and felt round all the edges for a metallic bulge or alien feel. Nothing. He opened it, flicked through currency notes and a couple of business cards, then pulled out his credit cards. Right in the middle was one he didn't recognize. It appeared to be a MasterCard but on close inspection obviously wasn't; the writing was not embossed and the card was noticeably thicker than normal plastic. Marais! Only Marais could have put it there, and only for some prying underhand purpose. With a growl of rage he drew a bulky Swiss army knife and began hacking at the card with a saw-edged blade. Inside the plastic was a paper-thin circuit board. He stood, hurled the sliding side-door back and tossed the tracking device into the lightening sky, then turned and grabbed Jemima's arm in a powerful grip, unsnapping her seatbelt and jerking her towards the opening.

"You can damn-well follow it, just in case you have a device also! I don't need you in person anymore, Hacking will come to me anyway, whether I have you or not!"

"No!"

Jemima snagged a seat headrest with her tethered hands and flailed her body frantically to escape the powerful hold on her. The co-pilot was watching over his shoulder, the whites of his eyes large and worried. Wind was howling into the cabin and Jemima had to yell desperately over the noise.

"Okay, okay, I'm sorry, I admit it! I have a cell phone but I haven't used it! Please don't do this!"

Katsiru shifted his balance to pull harder and she changed her resistance, lunging towards him. Taken by surprise he staggered backwards, swinging out into the rushing air.

-xxx-

Denzil landed at Masvingo on the shorter grass strip and taxied directly to the end alongside the Beechjet and a helicopter. The two Skymasters had departed shortly after his transmission about the low-flying helicopter. He shut-down and immediately rebooted his powerful quad-processor laptop, loading the tracking program, jabbing keys and muttering in frustration.

"Bastard, maybe I was too smart, overflying that chopper! The device is still chirping sporadically but it's stationary, not far from where I made the intercept. I think Katsiru found it and chucked it out."

"Oh shit!" said James, slapping the fuselage. "That was our only hope of remaining in contact; he could take Jemima to any hell-hole in Africa".

"Unless the Lynxes can find him and force him down" agreed Simon, glancing over their shoulders. He was carrying a modern radio with a long antenna and was listening to the action around Grand Reef on a Command Net.

The two bird-dog aircraft were flying northeast along either side of the helicopter's reported track ten miles apart, one at five thousand feet and one at eight, hoping the early sunrays would highlight their quarry. They were both T337B Turbo Super Skymasters, specifically chosen for the search because their twin Continental turbocharged fuel-injected engines boosted service-ceiling to 33,000 feet, cruise speed to 233 mph and range to 1,640 miles. They also had a far longer loiter-time if flown for endurance.

-xxx-

Spencer Katsiru was taken completely by surprise when Jemima used his own energy against him. Having shoved towards him, she stopped dead by bracing her hands against the fuselage frame. Katsiru's momentum carried him through the door and his grip ripped free of her. Absolute fear was written on his face but his left hand managed to grip tenuously to the door frame. With finger tendons shrieking he swung further out into the buffeting slipstream, right arm wind-milling for balance, eyes dropping to the earth and back to Jemima's implacable gaze. With lips drawn back from teeth in a snarl, she raised her tethered hands, preparing to punch his slipping fingers and send him tumbling to a violent death.

"Help me" he yelled but there was nothing the two pilots could do in the few seconds that remained before his grip weakened or Jemima struck.

"Oh my God!" shouted the co-pilot.

-xxx-

CHAPTER FIFTEEN

"It's like looking for a needle in a haystack up here" commented Hawk Leader in the first Skymaster. "Can you provide a more specific area for us to search?"

"Negative at this time, we're working on that" replied Simon. "Keep flying the last track the target was sighted on for the moment, direct Grand Reef, but be aware he may have adopted a more easterly heading to hug the Mozambique border with a view to evading intercept. Remember, the intention is a force-down adjacent to own troops."

-xxx-

The helicopter was flying at about five hundred feet AGL. Jemima looked out at the ground slipping by below and shuddered. She was physically incapable of sending another human into the void. Bracing her left shoulder against the sliding door which Katsiru had slid open so angrily, she stuck her joined hands into the slipstream, reaching for his freely flailing right hand. He hauled with his left shoulder and screamed as the fingers on that hand slipped under the extra load. With the strength of desperation he lunged for Jemima's outstretched hands, pivoting back inwards towards the door, but out of balance and with no remaining hand-hold. It was a trapeze-act.

-xxx-

"Target in sight!" said the Observer/co-pilot in Hawk-2 jubilantly. He had been using binoculars to peer east as suggested, towards the glinting silver span of Birchenough Bridge over the Sabi River twenty kilometers away, a landmark that naturally drew the eye. A shape flitted across the graticule like a dark spec and was gone, but over the pale earth and sparse lowveld vegetation he was able to capture it again and give steering instructions, though it bobbed about infuriatingly in the magnified field of view.

"Approximately three o clock lowdown; heading towards Mozambique; steer 010 degrees."

-xxx-

Katsiru's right hand went between Jemima's taped-together wrists, his fingers groping for some hold. Gravity and the slipstream began to pull him back out of the cabin. His feet and hips were inboard, his shoulders out, and he began to fall backwards.

"Shit!" shouted the Captain, glancing over his shoulder.

Jemima snapped her forearms closed on the wrist between hers and he made a fist. She heaved backwards with her shoulder against the door, using her weight to fall back into the cabin and pull Katsiru inwards too. She fell awkwardly, hitting her hip on a seat with numbing pain and the black man sprawled half on top of her, but staggered instantly to his feet again, snot streaming from his nose and tears from his good eye because of the slipstream gale. He pointed a finger at her.

"Don't think this changes anything!" he shouted, then nearly fell again as wake turbulence buffeted the rotary-wing.

-xxx-

The co-pilot of Hawk-Leader dialed the Emergency frequency, 121.5 on the non-active side of the NAV2 radio, clicked it to active, then selected "both" so they could hear Simon on the ground and the other Skymaster on NAV1 radio. Having made a close low pass across the helicopter that made it buffet in turbulence, the Skymaster hauled back around and dropped into station off the port side, slightly ahead and above the helicopter. Hawk-2 stayed higher yet and forward of the target to be clearly seen. Hawk-Leader co-pilot pressed his transmit switch, reading off the South African registration.

"South African helicopter Zulu Tango Quebec Sierra Whisky, this is Zimbabwe warplane Hawk-Leader. You are required to follow us to Mavingo Airport immediately."

His voice was clearly heard aboard the helicopter because the Captain was already monitoring 121.5, the Guard frequency, on his nav2 radio and both radios were selected. He looked apprehensively out at the Skymaster, noting the twin machine-guns rigged just above the cabin to fire over the front prop, and the rockets under the wings. Earlier he had flicked the switch to "speaker" so Katsiru could hear, having not replaced his headphones.

"Don't answer, just smile and wave!" he growled.

His mind was churning; to have intercepted him, the authorities had to have access to some critical information, either from Sandro Marais or as a result of questioning by Op Redemption personnel. It could equally have come from Brigadier Thandiwe. Any doubt was removed a second later as the intercepting aircraft rocked its wings in the International Interception procedure for "Follow me" and began a slow left turn. The radio squawked again too.

"Zulu Tango Quebec Sierra Whisky, we are aware that former President Katsiru and Jemima Hacking are aboard. I say again, you are to follow us to Masvingo Airport, and Miss Hacking must not be harmed. If you have radio transmission failure, flash all navigation lights to indicate compliance and follow me."

"Ignore them completely, they will not attack with the woman on board" instructed Katsiru, thinking hard. He could no longer proceed to Grand Reef without knowing the situation on the ground there. He made up his mind.

"Proceed direct to Chimoio" he instructed. From Mozambique he could contact his Commanders at Grand Reef and consult with the North Korean. If his forces were ready, he could make his move against Primrose Mpofu. If not and all was lost, he had a good chance of escaping on neutral territory. He had almost forgotten his plan for James Hacking but suddenly it intruded again. Strangely, it seemed almost pointless and he remembered that day long ago when he had detonated a grenade against a policeman's head to save his father from death. He also remembered the wild swing of emotions from believing that mere confession would save him, and the realisation that from murder there was no going back. That weird sensation of being able to put the clock back engulfed him briefly, enticingly, but he shook it off.

The Captain was looking at a map. "Heading direct Chimoio will take us over the high ground of the Chimanimani range Sir, with peaks up to eight and a half thousand feet, minimum safe altitude nearly ten thousand."

"So?"

"Well it's the rainy season and there appears to be weather building ahead, a storm over the hills with possible icing at those altitudes. It will also affect performance and with the recent evasive diversions we don't have all that much fuel. Not good conditions, especially if we have to go onto instruments in a mountainous area."

"Well what about if we go round the mountains to the east?"

"Then we definitely won't have enough fuel. A precautionary landing on the Mozambique plains would be a certainty and there's nothing much there except wild animals. It is virtually waterless and uninhabited for scores of miles in every direction."

Katsiru punched a seat in frustration.

"Then stop wasting my time, you have just answered your own question! I cannot land anywhere in Zimbabwe yet, so go direct to Chimoio; flying into weather might at least get rid of these damn pursuit planes. I will see what can be jettisoned to increase endurance!" The two pilots exchanged a worried glance. The ex-General clearly didn't fully understand the situation, and they were beginning to wonder if they should do something about that, to save their own lives.

Katsiru looked at Jemima.

"You said you have a cell-phone; give it to me!"

She complied, fearful eyes not leaving his face. He made a move to throw it out of the open door behind him, then realised it was fruitless since his whereabouts were blown, and that the handset might even come in useful. He tucked it in his shirt pocket and with an almost kindly expression motioned with one hand for the woman to come forward.

-xxx-

"Completely negative response and no indication of compliance" remarked Hawk-2 to ground. "What are your instructions now?"

"Say your fuel states, continue surveillance and stand-by" replied Simon, looking at the map they had spread out behind the Aviocar, then enquiringly at Denzil and James.

"Better get someone to request a Military Air Penetration from Mozambique for your Skymasters, in pursuit of an International fugitive, or we might lose them altogether" suggested James. Ndhlovu nodded soberly and moved away, talking into his radio. He was back shortly.

"Someone's on it, any other thoughts?"

James nodded.

"If they land anytime now, Katsiru could get away from the aircraft using Jemima as a shield, because the Skymasters can't land, or fire, and on the ground could be evaded by someone as bush-wise as Katsiru. I think you and I should take off in your helicopter right now Simon. If they do put down we'd probably only be an hour behind and the spoor would be fresh."

"I agree' said Denzil. "There are still things I can do from here, otherwise I would come with you. If necessary I can fly on to Chipinga or Mutare later and assist from there, or be uplifted by chopper to join you."

"I concur" said Simon, "only I need to remain on the Command Net with Primrose and the Vice-Marshall too for the present. Take my helicopter and a tracker, I'll stay with Denzil and come forward later, the Aviocar is STOL enough for Chipinga or Mutare, unlike the jet. I'll tell one of the surveillance planes to head to Mutare now to refuel, while the second monitors Katsiru. The other can do likewise when the first returns on station. This can't last forever, that chopper has limited fuel, even if there are long-range tanks on it."

"Come with me James, I'll get you kitted up for war" said Denzil soberly, as Ndhlovu went to brief his helicopter crew. Shortly afterwards James walked towards the Alouette 3 well-armed, with fighting webbing, rucksack holding supplies for four days and a radio. A person covered from head to knee in a sack-like garment was being helped like a blind-man from the chopper by a soldier, then guided towards Ndhlovu, who stilled the captive by grasping one forearm through the material. The soldier in camouflage saluted smartly and Simon waved a lazy salute back.

"We don't normally salute in the field" Simon admonished casually. "This guy is called Isaac James, the best tracker in Zimbabwe, according to Isaac!"

Big white teeth flashed in a round brown face as Isaac smiled. "I actually said, in the whole of bloody Africa Sir!"

He had a padded rifle carrying-case slung from his shoulder. James smiled at him.

"You're just what I need Isaac, glad to follow along; take it easy on an old man if we have to start running though."

He nodded towards the passive shrouded figure.

"Who's this guy?"

"You probably wouldn't believe me, but he's part of a plan President Primrose has up her sleeve."

Simon put out his hand.

"Good luck my friend. Maybe this time the bullshit ends once and for all."

James grinned.

"Yes, but for who?" They laughed sardonically and shook briefly.

James raised his rifle in salute to Denzil and climbed aboard the Alouette. The turbine began to whine.

-xxx-

Jemima shrank away from Katsiru's beckoning hand and he realised she still thought he would throw her out. He turned and slid the door shut, then motioned again.

"Just put your face to the window, it will help ensure this aircraft's safety."

She obeyed, tentatively, and saw the co-pilot of the Skymaster raise his thumb to her and nod encouragingly. The second fixed-wing was climbing in a northerly direction and diminishing in size quickly. Katsiru looked over the pilots' shoulders and through the windscreen. He could see the tiny settlements of Chipinga village to the South and Chimanimani village to the northeast. His stomach lurched a bit as he saw the forbidding black clouds that reared up over the mountains, seeming to reach higher into the sky as he watched, thunderheads building into big anvil-shapes. Although not a pilot himself he had flown hundreds of hours as a passenger and knew the Alouette was not equipped to fly into icing condition.

"Might be a bit bumpy but I think we can get between those cumulo-nimbus before they develop fully; better start climbing boys, we want to above minimum safe altitude when we get there."

"Roger boss" said the Captain and exchanged glances with the co-pilot again.

Hawk-Leader had moved a bit further off the helicopter's starboard side and the altimeter showed six thousand feet above sea level. He called Simon Ndhlovu. "The target is within fifteen kilometres of the Mozambique border and climbing towards weather over the mountains. If it flies in there I will lose contact and it could pop out again anywhere. Or not at all."

Simon grasped the implications immediately.

"Copied. Make a pass firing tracer and see if it turns them away."

Hawk-leader accelerated, circled and made an attack run at forty-five degrees towards the helicopter's nose. He fired several five-second bursts. From the helicopter, speeding tracers were plainly visible against the dark clouds ahead. The impression was that the rounds would inevitably close the distance and blow the chopper apart. The guns above the Cessna's cabin were spitting fire; Jemima flinched as the Skymaster howled overhead. The Captain nodded at the co-pilot and put the rotary wing into a sharp descending banking turn. Katsiru, unrestrained, rose into the air, flew across the cabin and landed hard. The co-pilot rapidly pulled two circuit breakers; red lights flashed instantly on an annunciator panel and a horn began to sound. Katsiru dragged himself up, holding a bruised rib.

"What the hell is going on?" he snarled.

The Captain was juggling controls and the other airman answered.

"Low fuel and rear-transmission chip detector warning lamp both on together."

"What the hell does that mean, we should have enough fuel!"

"Maybe; that violent manoeuvre might have caused the sender to register empty momentarily, I'll see if it goes out. The rear gear-box lamp is serious though! If the tail-rotor seizes we will have no control. It could have failed naturally, or maybe that warning-pass gunfire was a bit close and chipped a blade."

"No choice either way; I must land immediately" agreed the Captain. "I require silence too, this could be a delicate operation and I need a sterile cockpit. Please strap yourself in General."

He glanced at the co-pilot.

"Landing checklist please."

Katsiru remained standing a moment longer. He knew these mountains well from Outward bound visits both during and after the war, when Skeleton pass between Mozambique and Rhodesia had been a main infiltration route. He had recognized Mutekeswane base camp in the foothills just before the Skymaster attacked.

"Very well, but turn east and descend straight ahead. I want you to land as near the border as our altitude makes possible."

"Roger" said the Captain.

"There seems to be a likely meadow a couple of kilometers east of the Base camp, near a hut. I'll make for that."

Rain was beginning to streak the windscreen and mist tendrils were descending out of the lowering clouds. The mountains had disappeared from view in the murk.

-xxx-

"Target appears to be attempting a landing near some sort of hut three or four kilometres from the border" reported Hawk-Leader. "The boundary-line makes a right-angle dogleg nearby, so a fugitive could head in any direction from due north to due south and cross the eastern frontier within about five kilometres through a number of passes. Cloud is descending so I am shortly going to lose contact."

"Roger copied. Keep on station for as long as possible and try to maintain contact if the main target proceeds on foot."

"Wilco."

Simon Ndhlovu was looking thoughtful.

"Denzil, have we got the cell-phone number for the handset from which Miss Visser's text was sent? The one advising that she was Katsiru's prisoner in Botswana?"

"I think so. It was sent to Theo Bustamante and he gave it to us all at our initial O-group. Yes, here, I put it in my own mobile phone address book."

Simon pushed the radio transmit. "Hawk-Leader, let me know if the rotors stop turning or the passengers de-bus."

"Wilco, but viz deteriorating fast."

-xxx-

The chopper co-pilot unbuckled and squeezed into the rear compartment, donning a set of headphones that allowed him to move around. As the Captain transitioned into a hover near his chosen LZ the co-pilot opened the sliding hatch and lay down on the floor. Cold wet air entered the cabin. He could just see the hut about five hundred yards away through intermittent hill-fog. Under the helicopter was heathery turf and long grey boulders like sleeping reptiles. The ground looked spongy but firm and the co-pilot directed the Captain down, head swivelling, watching for any dangers. The Bell Longranger's skids sank about an inch and the rotors began to slow. Katsiru unbuckled and began to gather equipment, including the rucksack he had taken from Jemima's house. The turbine whined down to silence and Jemima shivered as she was helped down, looking at the swirling mist and inhospitable surroundings.

"What are your intentions General?" asked the Captain.

"Continue on foot to Mozambique and then to Grand Reef as planned. It is just going to take a lot longer. What are yours?"

"We'll take the covers off the rear gear-box and assess. If there are no iron filings and it seems like just a sensor fault we might risk flying somewhere when the weather clears."

The unmistakable snarl of the Lynx engines sounded from above the clouds, nearby. Katsiru shivered; it was a sound he had heard several times during the Rhodesian war but always evaded death. He grimaced.

"Well don't forget about your friend up there and think carefully where you go. Try to RV with me in Chimoio if things go well."

The Captain saluted and the younger officer followed suit.

"Good luck General."

"And to you."

The co-pilot leapt into the cabin, rummaged and jumped down again, holding out two jackets.

"They're pretty water-resistant and fully windproof. Better than nothing anyway."

"Thank you."

Jemima smiled at him and shrugged hurriedly into hers, feeling immediately relief from the damp rain-spotted wind. Katsiru pointed towards the barely visible mountaineering hut and gave her a slight shove. After two hundred yards a flurry of stinging rain fell then abruptly stopped. A cell-phone rang and Katsiru halted in surprise. He rummaged in pockets and pulled out Jemima's recently purchased IPhone. He looked at her and raised it to his face.

"Yes? Who is this?"

The caller answered in Shona.

"I assume you are Spencer Katsiru. This is Chief Superintendent Simon Ndhlovu of the Zimbabwe armed forces."

"I certainly remember you Ndhlovu. What do you want?" Spencer replied coldly in the same language.

"A compromise; we have today neutralized your Army at Grand Reef but President Mpofu in her wisdom is willing to offer you a free pardon and discharge, and the right to live as a free citizen again in Zimbabwe, even as a revered and acknowledged hero of the struggle."

Katsiru grunted cynically.

"Oh sure; in return for what?"

"Firstly that you will not again challenge the elected government except by lawful and peaceful means. And secondly that you will in future not seek to harm James Hacking, and will return unharmed his daughter Miss Jemima Visser in exchange for the life of your son."

Katsiru frowned.

"What nonsense is this? You know full-well that I have no children, and you know damned well why! That more than anything is why I will have my revenge on James Hacking!"

"Listen to me now. You do have a son, called Tamuwana, meaning "We have found him" and he is a Minister in the church of John Maranke. He is standing next to me now. These are the circumstances."

Simon then spoke for some minutes and Katsiru listened without interrupting, a swelling of joy and confused emotion making him feel breathless with hope but also filled with dread that it was some cruel trick.

"I will put Tamuwana on; speak now with your son."

"Father?" said a young melodious voice in his ear.

"Do you believe me to be so?"

"I believe the evidence; they have told me the story and compared my DNA to yours. I have read the report from the Professor at the new clinic and it has been notarised as true."

Katsiru's gaze flicked to Jemima but she was shivering and miserable, unable to understand a word.

"And what do you know of me?"

"That you were once a great man who lost his way. I urge you to return and be great again. Both the Lord and President Primrose wish this, and so do I. I want to meet my father at last!"

To Jemima's astonishment her captor began to cry deep racking sobs and she stirred uneasily, aware of the rifle over his shoulder. In Masvingo Simon retrieved the telephone gently from Tamuwana and strolled fifty yards away from the aircraft with Denzil alongside.

"Ndhlovu here again Katsiru. Jemima Visser must be released unharmed. If she is not, I guarantee that you will never see your son alive, because I will kill him myself and bury him where he will never be found. What is your answer?"

Spencer controlled his sobbing with an effort, gulping several times.

"Give President Mpofu's written pardon and the DNA report to James Hacking, together with some photographs of my alleged son. Tell him to bring them all to me on Mount Binga at midday tomorrow by the west-face approach, alone, and I will consider an exchange. If anything seems suspicious Miss Visser will pay the price. Remember, I will be able to see everything from there more clearly than you."

"Don't bet on it you cocky bastard!" muttered Denzil.

"Agreed" said Simon. "I suggest you turn off the cell-phone to conserve the battery, but I can be contacted at any time on the number you will see on it. If there is a signal, listen out every six hours, otherwise James Hacking will see you on Mount Binga tomorrow."

The connection was abruptly broken.

The two pilots by the helicopter had replaced the circuit breakers, dipped the fuel tanks and were debating what to do when a manic howl drifted repeatedly from the eerie mist, carried on the wind from several hundred yards away. The co-pilot shivered.

"What the hell is that?"

The Captain cocked his ear.

"It sounds like someone shouting "I have a son" over and over again. I don't like this place; let's get the hell out before that crazy bastard comes back! We'll contact that orbiting Lynx and go to Chipinga Airfield for fuel, it's only about fifty clicks. He can land there too and we'll explain that Katsiru went benzi and forced us to fly on at gunpoint."

-xxx-

Jemima watched in dismay as Spencer Katsiru stopped crying and went crazy, executing a wild African dance such as she had seen Zulu warriors and Witchdoctors perform, screaming the same phrase repeatedly in a language she did not know. The rucksack bounced crazily on his back as he brandished the Kalashnikov and mud flew from his stamping boots. Her eyes darted about, weighing up the chances of an escape into the mist. He noticed, calming down at once. Chest heaving he pointed east into the mist and rain and her heart sank.

"I, I thought we'd be spending the night in that hut at least...."

"No, that is exactly what my pursuers would suspect. I know a warm dry place about two hours from here. Go ahead, I will direct you from behind and observe our back-trail; the path is mainly good and easy to follow."

Two and a half hours later after a steep climb and descent they entered a large cave smelling delightfully of wood-smoke with evidence of long use as a shelter.

"Digby's dugout" announced Spencer dropping the pack and going immediately to a stack of firewood in one corner and beginning to light a fire. Jemima huddled close and extended her hands to the first licking flames.

"How did you know about this place?"

He paused and looked directly at her, as if remembering and suddenly he gave a short bark of laughter.

"I first came as a schoolboy on an outward-bound expedition. We were searched and those of us found with cigarettes or alcohol were beaten, right beside the road there! Your father was smarter than most and not all his tobacco was found; he shared the smokes out among the rest."

He began to make food and realised with a start that was becoming familiar, that he was most contented when carrying out simple tasks, such as driving a truck, or walking, or cooking. The fire was burning strongly and Katsiru had stuck several candles to the rock with their hot wax. Jemima hugged her knees and shuffled on her bottom closer to the heat.

"You sounded almost affectionate then; so you and my father weren't always enemies?"

Again he became still and looked at her with his disconcerting eyes.

"No, not always."

"I have not known my father long. Can you tell me about him?"

Katsiru stirred a mess of pasta-mix and passed it to her.

"How can you not have known your father?"

"My mother had an affair with him during which I was conceived but she never got a chance to tell him about me. Later in the Rhodesian war, she and my non-biological father were killed and any records were lost, so I was brought up first by my grandparents and then by strangers. It was only recently by chance that he learned of our relationship and traced me."

Katsiru stared into the fire and chewed mechanically, mind ranging back to events of so long ago that they now seemed unreal. Why had he blamed Hacking for the loss of his eye, when he had precipitated the course his life would take by a rash impulsive act? And all those years of hating, and fighting, culminating in another self-inflicted wound, caused, he now reluctantly admitted by an attempted act of treachery of which deep-down he was ashamed. He looked into his plastic dish.

"Today I too learned that a child of mine that was lost in the war is found and my heart was rejoicing; I have a son."

Jemima licked her spoon; the food had been fairly disgusting but welcome and filling. She leant forward.

"Then I rejoice for you too. Tell me about everything."

Katsiru sighed and put aside his dish and spoon.

"They were terrible days...."

-xxx-

CHAPTER SIXTEEN

Scout Isaac and James were dropped by the Alouette several kilometres short of the location that Hawk-Leader had provided as the LZ of Katsiru's chopper. Their own transport could not fly them right there without entering cloud in rising terrain so dropped them short. Fifteen minutes later they heard rotors and the fugitive helicopter roared slowly overhead, the Captain content to fly in the IMC because he was heading towards lower ground. Isaac looked at James questioningly; were the targets still on board, or had they departed? Hawk-Leader had departed for fuel but 2 had returned and was still loitering overhead. James figured he should press on.

At Masvingo Simon Ndhlovu looked at Denzil.

"Since we know the RV for Katsiru and James is the top of Mount Binga, what do you say we brief Isaac for a bit of long-range sniper support as backup?"

The other man nodded.

"Couldn't do any harm since he's got the hardware; let's take a look at the maps. It won't do much good if the weather stays like this though."

Ten minutes later Simon dialled a number and James's cell-phone shrilled. Isaac smiled but rebuked him.

"That 'screaming in the pocket' should be on silent or it could get us killed!"

James flushed with embarrassment, nodding.

"I will put it on vibrate only. There probably won't be a signal for much longer anyway."

He answered the phone and Simon Ndhlovu briefed him on Primrose's plan and the recent exchange with Spencer Katsiru.

"So he wants a meeting on Binga. Wait where you were dropped James, Hawk-Leader refuelled here at Masvingo and is returning inbound to you with the documents in a drop-canister, you should have them in about forty minutes. After that it is up to you but keep me informed of your intentions for as long as a phone or radio signal is available."

He asked to speak to Isaac and the Scout, after listening at length responding mainly just "aiho", hung up and handed the telephone back. James and Isaac backtracked and collected the canister. They spread a poncho and James examined the documents briefly without getting them wet. He stared curiously at the photographs which showed a close resemblance to the young Spencer Katsiru he remembered, despite the long untrimmed beard of a 'Postle". As he thoughtfully packed the canister again his phone vibrated, showing 'unknown caller' and he answered tersely with just his name.

"Hello James, it is Primrose Mpofu."

"Madam President, how are you?" he said in surprise.

"Fine James, it would be good to see you again but listen; I know what must be going through your head at this time and no matter how strong your instinct and temptation is to kill Katsiru you must resist it. He did that to Elias, my husband and your friend. We mustn't be like him. Somebody has to be the first to turn the other cheek. The clemency when publicized will set a precedent for all Africa."

James was silent for some time, wrestling with many emotions and Primrose remained silent, understanding. Finally he breathed out in a long sigh.

"Okay Primrose. I'm not sure you're right but I admire your courage. I'll try and play it your way."

"Thank you James; my trust and faith in you are implicit. Come and see me when it's all over."

An hour later having jogged much of the way they were at the eight-figure grid reference supplied by the Skymaster as Katsiru's drop-off point and cast about in the mist and rain, working a grid pattern between them. Isaac found helicopter skid-indentations and the tracks of two people heading away east.

"Do we follow sir?"

"I don't think so; there is a rest-hut shown about half a k away. It will soon be dark and the spoor won't last long in this rain. We'll clear the hut and if they aren't there, possie up for the night and see what the morning brings. It will take me less than three hours to Binga from here."

They recced the hut and cast outward for several hundred yards but found no recent tracks. The hut felt dank but they decided against a fire, ate cold rations quickly and bedded down. In the morning the rain had stopped but hill-fog lingered thick and swirling. They brewed sweet tea and breakfasted on dry rations. James had a knot of tension in his stomach but felt outwardly calm, focused on what he had to do, equipment prepared and ready. He looked at the map once more and they set off gaining height steadily. Two hours later, still in gloomy cloud, they reached a cairn where the path split. The right fork headed towards forbidding crags below the west face route which could just be seen through breaks in the swirling mists. The left headed to the north-shoulder col of Binga. James and Isaac parted there.

To the south, Spencer Katsiru took out a knife.

"Hold out your hands" he instructed, and cut the tape. Jemima massaged her sticky wrists; the binding had not been tight but there was still discomfort as the blood flowed more freely.

"What happens now?" she asked.

He handed her a compass.

"You are a pilot so you know how to navigate. Go north for one kilometer, counting your paces. You will find a cairn of rocks and a well-used path heading uphill to the west. Take it for about fifteen hundred feet vertical, to the col, where there is another very large square cairn about ten feet tall with steps up the side. Wait there for your father. If by mid-afternoon no-one has come, continue west, downhill and a good path will bring you out at the Bundi river plain where we came in."

She looked down at the compass, turning it slowly and watching the needle, then back up into his eyes.

"Don't kill my father; if you do the feud will continue."

He stared back into a pair of implacable cobalt orbs, luminescent with calm confidence, and shivered imperceptibly.

"It is not completely in my control."

As James climbed the steep switchback path through dripping crags, using his hands on occasions, a strong breeze sprang up, and at about seven-thousand five hundred feet the sun appeared through the clouds as a diffused silver disc. One hundred feet later the cloud dissipated into rags and was gone. Bright sunshine beat on the grey rock and green tussocky grass which clung to thin soil in places. Around him was a sea of white clouds, all other peaks obscured below by a temperature inversion.

He walked another one-hundred and fifty feet to the domed grey summit, feeling his customary lift of spirits at reaching any mountain top. It was deserted and he patted a rock, thinking his habitual prayer and remembering the people dear to him, particularly Jemima. His stomach swooped in trepidation, recalling his purpose. To the south, slightly lower, Turret Towers began to emerge from cloud like another island being created.

James scanned in all directions but he was completely alone. His watch showed 1230 hours. He made another three-sixty, gazing intently at the few possible sheltering rocks and areas of dead ground. He chewed some biltong and began to worry that something had gone wrong. Hot sun warmed the air in the valleys and the clouds below gradually thinned and all but disappeared, leaving perfect visibility in most directions. An hour had passed; how long should he wait before doing something? Another hour crawled by and yet again he began his methodical scan. This time movement caught his eye; a black man on his own was striding athletically up the eastern slopes. James drew his 9mm automatic and held it casually at his side, heart beginning to pound in his chest and before long he and Spencer Katsiru were five meters apart, staring at each other with curiosity.

"Where is my daughter Jemima?" asked James at length.

"I released her three hours ago, she should already have reached safety. If the clouds below and to the west clear a bit more you should be able to see her with binoculars. Now give me the documents."

"First you can do a little striptease. I haven't forgotten the last time we met. Take everything off."

"I give you my word I have no weapons."

"Not worth much I'm afraid. Do as I said."

"Looking for some sick kick out of seeing what you did?"

"Last time I offered a fair fight but you pulled a concealed weapon and shot your own balls off by mistake. How is that my fault? And talking of concealment, was that you who was skulking in the bushes at my place in the UK, trying to kill me with my own truck?"

Katsiru just looked at him and began to disrobe.

"I'll take that as a yes then. Where will my daughter be?"

"On that coll by the big square cairn."

James moved so he could see the area but keep his adversary covered and raised his mini-binoculars. Jemima was sitting on the cairn with her legs dangling. Relief flooded through him and he scanned the area carefully to see if any potential threats or guards were in her proximity. Reasonably sure there were none he motioned Katsiru back from his clothes with the handgun, then lifted each garment and boot before tossing them aside. There was nothing heavy, sharp or potentially harmful. His gaze flickered over the black man's body. He was still muscular and athletic looking with a long bulky penis but no visible testicles. James resisted the urge to stare in fascination.

"Turn round" he ordered, checking for knives or blades taped to skin.

"Satisfied?"

"Yes. You can put your underwear on."

James handed over the canister: Katsiru scanned both pages and then leafed through the photographs; tears pricked as he saw a face like his own but younger, gazing back at him with calm eyes. He remained staring down until the moisture faded. He looked at James.

"Will Ndhlovu and Mpofu honour their side of the bargain, about letting me and my son live?"

"I believe they will."

"What about you? I presume you still want to kill me?"

James looked at him.

"I should, because alive you will always be a threat to me but right now you look pretty harmless. Like seeing a bank manager without his trousers; all the mystique and power is gone. What are the chances of you settling down to a contented old age under Primrose's protection? And not causing any more shit?"

Katsiru looked into the distance, then squatted in the African style, considering his response carefully. James felt he was talking mainly to himself when he finally spoke

"Even ten days ago I would have said none but I have been experiencing a kind of slow-motion epiphany for the last year. Your daughter is a remarkable young woman and last night we had a long and frank discussion. I have been an arrogant man for most of my life and it has brought me little contentment. I have often felt inadequate too, sometimes masking cowardice with brutality, and frequently I have blamed others for my own shortcomings, including you. The craving for power and money were to prove something, mainly to myself, but repeatedly in recent months I have felt serenity in simple actions; like being here, naked, looking at mountains, or doing manual work. People have shunned my company because I was harsh and since you killed my woman at Junction Camp I have not known the comfort of genuine human tenderness. In retribution I placed a landmine which killed your first wife. We have been wounding each other for decades without gain and I have been striving for barren rewards. Now we both have children who value us greatly and know nothing of our past vanity and sins. So yes, if Primrose will let me, I would like to quietly enjoy the miracle of my restored son in our native land. If you kill me I will just be dead and I have no fear of the prospect but probably my son, if he lives, will be felt by you as a threat in my place because of your own actions. For the first time in half a century I feel at peace. Do what you will."

His reference to vanity, sins and arrogance made James acknowledge the truth about himself and it hurt. His valued personal integrity had too often been compromised, and expediency had frequently been allowed to triumph over empathy. He stood in silence for many minutes remembering some of those times, knowing Loretta would have agreed with Katsiru for once. He missed her suddenly with a great and hurtful intensity. He wondered how she and Colinda were getting on together. God life was complicated. He focused his binoculars affectionately on Jemima again. His older daughter would have to make choices between multiple suitors too, that much was obvious. For a supposedly benign emotion, love caused a staggering amount of hurt. He lowered the far-lookers and stared at Katsiru again.

"Well then, our business is concluded, or will be once Jemima is actually back under my immediate care. There are no nasty surprises down there I hope? No henchmen waiting to snatch her back?"

"No. As far as I am concerned it is over."

Spencer held up a smart-phone.

"I have kept Jemima's pocket-screamer. Go down; when you have seen that she is truly safe, tell Ndhlovu to set my son free and call me, by then I will be at a place with a signal."

James nodded at him, then turned to go. After a few paces Katsiru spoke again.

"You still owe me for a broken tennis racquet."

James turned. There was the sardonic suggestion of a smile on his old enemy's lips. He almost smiled back but managed to curb it.

"Ah yes, the 'Magic Racquet.' You weren't much good and it was a pile of crap, keep the phone instead."

James turned and started down again. Katsiru watched until the mountain swallowed him and he was alone, but didn't rush to get dressed, remaining comfortably seated on his haunches semi-naked like a savage, enjoying the sun on his skin and the sense of isolation on Binga. He thumbed hungrily through the photographs. In one Tamuwana looked like his dead mother, in another the expression was of Spencer's own father. Perhaps there would be grand-children and he could sit like this with his back against a hut, drinking beer and teasing them. He felt reluctant to leave the summit; somehow there was a feeling of safety so long as he was there. From an adjacent peak Scout Isaac watched them both through his sniper-scope and a radio whispered static quietly beside him.

-xxx-

In Masvingo Simon Ndhlovu and Denzil were scrutinizing a large display screen on top of a remote-control box, standing on the Aviocar ramp shaded by the tailplane. On the dry grass adjacent were packing-cases which had contained an aircraft similar to the gliders moored nearby, but smaller. Denzil toggled a switch and the camera on the drone zoomed in on two figures striding towards the outward-bound school.

'Well James and his daughter have met up and are safe."

He operated the controls and a few minutes later the monitor showed a lone man squatting semi-naked on the summit of a great mountain. His hands dangled between bony jutting knees and the resolution was sufficient to show a fan of photographs held loosely as he stared out at the horizon in contemplation.

Denzil's finger hovered over a 'fire' button as he looked at Simon Ndhlovu, who was thinking of Fanny and her admonition to "find that Devil."

And do what? Was it his place to break Primrose's word on amnesty, given as the President of a sovereign nation?

Denzil's impatient voice interrupted his thoughts.

"We had a chance like this once before at the end of the Rhodesian war and didn't take it Simon. Yes or no?"

Denzil's sleeve rode up and his companion of many years noticed a small tattoo on his stringy bicep that could have been a coiled rope. Or a black snake.

THE END
-xxx-

ABOUT THE AUTHOR

Gordon Orr's childhood was spent on a Rhodesian farm and he attended Peterhouse, a multi-racial private boarding-school in the bush near Marondera. He is a keen mountaineer and has climbed in Africa, Britain, Europe, Canada and the Himalayas. He served during the Rhodesian conflict in the B.S.A.P. and in Britain, Germany and Northern Ireland in the R.E.M.E. He is an active pilot and holds British and Canadian PPL's and Class 1 Licences. Gordon enjoys drinking beer (which in emergency he can make, having learned out of necessity while working in Libya.)
"A day spent without drinking beer is a day wasted."

If you enjoyed reading "Losing The Spoon" you might like the other two books in this Trilogy. They are:
Book 1, "Taking The Gap."
Book 2, "Grasping The Nettle."

Find internet links to vendors, author information, blogs and social media at http://www.gordonorr.net

GLOSSARY OF TERMS

For any terms found whose meaning is not clear from the context or which have inadvertently been left out, submission to a search engine will often provide clarification, including foreign language items.

a bitje jag. Do a bit of hunting
AGL. above Ground Level
Aiho. Yes
Aikona. No
Aina! Ow!
ATIS. Automated Traffic Information Service. Looped Airfield Info.
Bakkie. Pickup Truck
Barbel. Flatfish. Vundu is a very large Flatfish in Zambezi River 50/60 Kg
Bimbling. Walking, Hiking
Bliksum. roughly the same as bastard. Also to hit strike or punch
Bobbejaan. Baboon or monkey
Boeremusiek. Afrikaans Folk Music. Fiddles, Accordian, bass etc. Tea dance
Boers. Afrikaans farmers. Sometimes applied by Africans generically to Whites
Boet. brother
bright-light. Men beyond Military callup-age deployed to protect farms etc.
Casevacc. Casualty Evacuation
Chesa Manzi. Hot water
Chibuku. Brand of Commercial African Beer. Very thick.
Chimurenga. Revolution
Confyt Jam
Daars hy. There he/it is
Dassie. Small rock-rabbit like a marmot
Dominee. Dutch Reformed Priest
Donner. Beat Up
Dorp. Small sleepy town or village
Eenie indaba boss? What's the trouble boss?
Endegi. Airplane
FLOT. forward Line of Own Troops
Gaan kak in die mielies. Afrikaans: Go shit in the maize. Piss off

Gan kak with the Devil maatjies! Go and shit with the devil mates!
Gooi. Throw (Lead) Shoot (Afrikaans)
Groot. Big or massive (Afrikaans)
Hamba gashle. Go slowly, or Travel Well (Shona)
Hokoyo umfaan. Watch it boy!
IED. Improvised Explosive Device
IFR. Instrument Flight Rules
Impashle. Luggage, Equipment
Imshe. Go
Injinga. Bicycle
Jong. Young, youngster
kaffir-boetie. Negrophile. A White deemed too friendly to Blacks by peers.
hout-kop. Afrikaans for wooden-head. Derogatory term for Africans
kerel. a chap or fellow
klaar. clear
Koeksysters. Sweet sticky pastry in honey or syrup, in shape of plait
kom esau. Come Here
Kyk daar. Look there
Lekker. Good, Nice, tasty
Maak Gou. Hurry up!
Magtig. Exclamation
Maiwe Zangu. Exclamation
Majonnie. Policeman or Security Man
Makiwa. European or white (After a pale fig-like fruit)
Mampoer. Homemade Brandy (very powerful)
Maneru. Good evening
Mbeche. Expletive
Mealie. Green maize cob
Mevrou. Mrs
Mombies. Mombes. Cows
Mooi. Lovely, pretty, good
Muckers. Friends or Mates
Mujiba. Doves. Small boys used by guerrillas as spies
Muntu. man or people
Nyo Kanyoko! Your Mother's vagina! Xhosa
old toppie. dad
Oupa. Uncle
Ous; Okies. Men or group of people
Pangolin. Small anteater, with sharp claws

Pap and vors. Maize meal (Sadza) and Afrikaans sausage with gravy
Pawpaws. Large fleshy fruit which grows on pulpy grey trees
Pungwe. Forced-attendance Political meeting
Riempie. Rawhide thongs, chair seats
Rooinek. Red neck (Britisher)
Sabenza sterick. Hard work
Sadza. Maize meal porridge, staple food
Shala gashle. Stay well
Simbi. Any piece of metal: Crowbar, ploughshare or wire
Situpa. Pass required to be carried as ID by Africans only
Sjambok. Long hard Rhino hide whip
Skakle. Phone call
Skelems. Wide boys, scoundrels
Skinnering. Gossiping
Skokiaan. illicit home-brewed alcohol, moonshine
Skuld. Fault or Guilt
slim Jannies. Cunning people
smaaks you maningi sterick. Likes you a lot
soet-gats. Derogatory term for British. Salt-arse(hole)
Soutpiel. As above. Salt penis. (One leg in Africa, one in Europe)
Stoep. Veranda
Suikerbos. Sugar bush (famous Afrikaans song)
Tackies. Plimsolls (or car tyres.)
Terrs. Terrorists, CT's Communist terrorists
Tikkie-draai. Afrikaans folk dancing, sometimes at afternoon tea-dances.
Totsiens. Goodbye. See you
Tsotsi. Ne'er do well, thug
TTL. Tribal Trust Land
UD. Unauthorised (unintentional) discharges
Umfaazi. Woman. Can be derogatory depending on tone of voice
undiziwe chete. Know just nothing
Unita. Angolan War. Political and Military faction fighting FNLA & MPLA
Vakhomana. wild men
Vat jou goud en trek. Take your stuff and go (Piss off)
Veldschoen. Soft lace-up ankle-boot
Vetkoek. Very rich sticky confection cooked in fat
VFR. Visual Flight Rules
Viz. Visibility

Voetsek. Fuck Off
Voortrekkers. Afrikaans Pioneers
Vroukie. Little woman. Pet name
Vuka. Get Up
Wa'chia N'simbi. The gong has sounded
Waarloos bliksums. Useless bastards
Waffa Waffa. Selous Scouts training camp near Kamba
Wag a bitjie. Wait a bit. Also a type of hooked thorn
Wat maak jy easu? What are you doing here?
Wat makeer? What's the matter?
Wena. You
Wilco. Have understood and will comply/cooperate
ZAPU. Zimbabwe African Nationalist Party. Military wing **ZIPRA**
ZANU. Zimbabwe African Nationalist Union. Military wing **ZANLA**
PF. Patriotic Front. Combined **ZIPRA & ZIPRA**
Zim. Zimbabwe

Printed in Dunstable, United Kingdom